REVIEWS FOR REAPERS

Reapers is Bryan Davis's best work yet. With a refreshing new concept that takes you deep into a dystopian world, *Reapers* will keep you riveted through the last page. Phoenix, Singapore, and Shanghai create a strong new cast of characters who must navigate the underbelly of ghost-filled Chicago to discover the secrets behind the mysterious Gateway.

—Amanda L. Davis
(Author of The Cantral Chronicles)

Bryan Davis's *Reapers* is hands down the best science fiction/fantasy book I have read in decades! Not since I was first introduced to the genre's greats like Asimov, Heinlein, Anthony, and Tolkien have I been so engrossed in a story from page one to the cliff-hanging ending. This fresh take on a post-apocalyptic world is captivating and engaging with enough plot twists to keep even the most ardent sci-fi aficionados on their toes. Bravo, Bryan! This is your best novel to date. Now please, back to work! I need to know what happens next!

— Donna Daigle

With a thrilling and austere brush, Bryan Davis paints a world of dystopian beauty where nothing is quite what it seems. Hidden deep within this dark and fascinating world are many gems; gems of masterful storytelling, gems of character begging to be discovered, and gems of mind-bending science fiction. From cover to cover *Reapers* thrills the imagination. Every time I pick up a Bryan Davis book late in the evening, I rediscover the joys of turning the last page to the light of morning's dawn, and *Reapers* was no exception.

— Jeremy Fear

Reapers is by far one of the most intense books I have ever read. It literally left me gasping for breath by the end. Mr. Davis's dive into the first-person point of view serves to make the emotions of this pulse-pounding tale even more electrifying. Be ready to sacrifice some sleep, because once you pick this book up, you're sucked in—and there's no going back.

—Cassidy Clayton

Reapers is by far one of Mr. Davis's best works. It carries a darker, grittier tone than his previous novels yet still remains clean enough for the young-adult audience. The characters will endear and terrify you in this imaginative dystopian tale, and the pacing and mystery will keep you turning the pages. This is a definite must-add to your bookshelf.

—Victoria Tucker

Reapers had me staying up at late hours with the main characters. It was hard to stop reading!

— Natasha Sapienza

To Susie – Thank you for taking my hand. Our clasp will stay firm until the Great Reaper carries one of us beyond the Gateway, where we will be reunited—hand-in-hand forever.

Books by Bryan Davis

Tales of Starlight

Masters & Slayers
Third Starlighter
Exodus Rising

Dragons of Starlight

Starlighter
Warrior
Diviner
Liberator

Dragons in our Midst

Raising Dragons
The Candlestone
Circles of Seven
Tears of a Dragon

Oracles of Fire

Eye of the Oracle
Enoch's Ghost
Last of the Nephilim
The Bones of Makaidos

Children of the Bard

Song of the Ovulum
From the Mouth of Elijah
The Seventh Door
Omega Dragon

To learn more about Bryan's books, go to
www.daviscrossing.com

REAPERS

BOOK 1 OF THE REAPERS TRILOGY

BY BRYAN DAVIS

Published by Scrub Jay Journeys

P. O. Box 512

Middleton, TN 38052

www.scrubjayjourneys.com

email: info@scrubjayjourneys.com

ISBN: 978-0-9898122-1-4

Printed in the U.S.A.

Library of Congress Control Number: 2013923687

"The people who walked in darkness have seen a great light: they who dwell in the land of the shadow of death, upon them the light has shone." May those who walk in dark places find that blazing light and never walk in darkness again.

CHAPTER ONE

T HE DEATH ALARM sounded, that phantom punch in the gut I always dreaded. I touched the metallic gateway valve embedded in my chest at the top of my sternum—warm but not yet hot. The alarm was real. Someone in my territory would die tonight, and I had to find the poor soul. Death didn't care about the late hour. Reapers like me always stayed on call.

I rose from my moth-eaten reading chair, blew out the hanging lantern's flame, and stalked across my one-room apartment to the window, guided by light from outside. The internal alarm grew stronger. Prickly vibrations raced across my cloak from the baggy sleeves to the top of the hood, tickling the two-day stubble across my cheeks and chin. Time was growing short—probably less than an hour left.

I shoved open the window sash and leaned into the darkness of the urban alley. With electricity cut-off hour long past for residents, only streetlamps glowed from a neighborhood road to the left. A tall woman in a black trench coat stood at the corner holding an umbrella over her head and a suitcase at her side, as if she were waiting for a ride, maybe a taxi.

I leaned farther out to get a better look. It hadn't rained

in three days, and the skies were clear—a dry night in Chicago and too warm for a trench coat. No cabbie would pick up this woman even if he could see her.

A slight glow around her eyes confirmed her status. She was a ghost, probably level two, far too opaque to be newly dead and glowing too much to have wandered for more than a couple of weeks. If not for the death alarm, I could take the time to collect her. For now she would have to keep wandering. I had to use all my senses to figure out who was about to die.

Moist air wafted past my nose, carrying the odor of a nearby brewery—malt and hops. A horn blared far away, and a siren wailed farther still. Otherwise, all was quiet.

Across the alley, a dark silhouette sat on the railing of a fire-escape landing barely more than a leap away—Sing, short for Singapore, the female Reaper from the bordering district. Although I met her for the first time only two weeks ago, I could never mistake her petite, yet athletic form.

She stared at me from her second-floor perch. Her dangling legs kicked slowly into and out of the light, providing glimpses of her forest green pants and black running shoes—standard garb for a Reaper.

"Hello, Phoenix," she said in her low, silky voice.

I squinted, hoping to read her expression, but darkness veiled her face. I attempted a teasing tone. "What're you doing out here in the dark? Spying on me?"

"Wouldn't you like to know?" She added a friendly laugh. "If you don't like being watched, you should lower your shade."

"I'll keep that in mind."

"And what are you doing poking half your body out the window? Did you get an alarm?"

I nodded. "Early warning. Just thought I'd look for a messenger."

"My guess is Molly. Word on the street says she had a seizure a few hours ago. From fever, I heard."

"Molly." I hid a tight swallow. "She's only seven."

"All the better. You'll meet quota faster." Her cloak shimmered, evidence that she carried at least one soul in its fibers. "Who do you have on board now?"

"A middle-aged man, a young mother, and a teenager." I felt their photo sticks in my cloak pocket, their tickets to paradise. "Molly wouldn't quite put me over the top, but I could go to tonight's executions. I should be able to get enough there."

"Then will you take them to the Gateway in the morning?"

"Maybe." I bent to one side, again trying to catch a glimpse of her expression. "What's it to you?"

"I thought you might like to have… I don't know… an extra set of eyes to watch for bandits. I've never been to the Gateway, so…"

"Right. Your first cycle." I glanced along the trash-cluttered alleyway below. Still no messenger. With bandits abundant lately, a messenger likely wouldn't venture out until the last minute. "How many souls do you have?"

"Not enough." She leaned into the light, revealing the whites of her eyes, a stark contrast against her skin's lovely dark tone, a hue resembling coffee with a shot of cream, quite different from my cream-only complexion, though her hair color matched mine—darker brown than her skin.

"If I meet quota by morning," she said, "will you take me with you?"

"If you knew what the Gateway extraction feels like, you wouldn't be so anxious to go."

"A Reaper has to learn sometime, and I'd rather go with someone who knows the ropes."

"Fair enough." I wrinkled my brow. "Are you going to the executions to make quota? Do you have any idea how dangerous it is?"

"You go reap Molly. I can handle a little danger." She thrust herself off the rail and dropped, plunging through the brighter light. With her shimmering black cloak fanned out, she looked like a glowing raven sailing toward the pavement, though sepia curls lifting above her head spoiled the image.

She landed, bending her knees to absorb the impact, and ran toward the alley opening. The ghost at the corner stood nearby, but Sing paid no attention as she breezed past and slinked into the shadows—a sable cat, stealthy and sleek.

I leaned out again. Why didn't she try to collect the ghost? As a rookie, maybe she thought she wasn't experienced enough to handle such a difficult reaping.

A motorcycle rumbled to life in the direction Sing had run, and the sound slowly drifted away. That could mean trouble—a Death Enforcement Officer had probably spotted Sing and was now tailing her. These DEOs couldn't stand to let a death go by without harassing a Reaper and tracking every soul's progress through the Gateway.

I didn't have time to worry about Sing. She would have to handle her own troubles.

I slammed the window down and whispered, "Molly…

anyone but Molly." The dosage I gave her must have been too low. But how could I have known? No doctor had darkened any door in my territory in months. The going bribe was just too high.

Again guided by light from outside, I reached behind my radiator, pried a wall panel loose, and pulled out the white plastic box lodged within. I sat on my unmade bed and opened the box. Inside lay three pill bottles, two empty syringes, and four vials of various drugs. I snatched up a bottle and shook it. Two pills rattled inside, the last of the antibiotic I got in trade for a pair of leather work boots—payment for reaping a construction worker's soul last month.

I filled a syringe from one of the vials, slid a plastic sleeve over the needle, and laid it and the pill bottle carefully in my cloak's outer pocket. The powerful liquid antibiotic had expired long ago. For all I knew, it might now be toxic, so it would have to be the last resort. Maybe, just maybe, the pills would work, if I could get to Molly in time.

I stowed the medicine box back in its hiding place, grabbed my weapons belt from under the bed, and checked the attached equipment—camera, smoke capsules, flare pellets, twin daggers, spool line and throw weight, and a flashlight. Everything seemed intact, including the three keys to my door's deadbolts.

After strapping the belt on under the cloak and relighting the lantern, I walked to my dresser and picked up a pocket watch, a gift from Kwame, a black man who lived in a former cash-for-title business wedged between a liquor store and a strip joint.

I popped open the watch's brass-colored cover and read the analog face—ten fifteen—then closed it and looked at the partial engraving for the thousandth time—*From A.* The rest of the message had been worn down.

I pushed the watch into my pants pocket. If I hurried, I could make it to Molly's home by ten-thirty and still get to the midnight executions. One issue remained. I needed a bribe, something that would get a DEO off my back, just in case he decided to ask too many questions. Walking the streets with medical contraband in my pocket was never safe.

I yanked open the dresser's bottom drawer and rummaged through my collection of reaping payments—an electric razor, wool socks, two cans of Sterno, and... I picked up a portable police-band scanner, complete with ear buds. Perfect. Legal, but scarce.

After adding the scanner to the items in my pocket, I fastened the cloak at my chest and inserted the clasp's key into my sternum's gateway valve, giving it the usual turn to lock it in place. The metal in the clasp warmed to the valve's temperature, though still not hot. The energy cell within the clasp would need more of my blood soon, but the current supply was likely enough to collect a little girl.

"What's in the cloak pocket, Phoenix?"

As my cloak shimmered to life, I rolled my eyes. Crandyke. Always ready to jabber the moment the fibers energized. I didn't need to answer him. After all, he was dead, a disembodied passenger in my cloak, though a talkative one. "Just some pills, Crandyke. You're too dead to take them."

"Very funny." He let out an exaggerated laugh. "Hear me laughing at your wit?"

"Glad you're entertained." On the dresser's top, I slid a tri-fold picture frame closer and ran a finger along the photos of my father, mother, and Misty. I touched her image. *Misty*. The girl across the street. The girl I had known all my life before I had to leave for good.

I rubbed the pewter band on my ring finger, a gift from Misty when we were both thirteen, the day we confirmed our promise to each other—the day I left home for the last time.

Her voice, flavored as always with a lovely Scottish accent, filtered into my mind. "Twenty years is a long time," she had whispered as she rested her head on my shoulder. "No matter what, I'll be waiting for you. Just promise me you'll do everything you can to get out early. I hear there are shortcuts."

I pushed the frame back in place. Someday I would see her again… if she was still alive.

After blowing out the lantern again, I walked to the window and reopened it, letting in warm air. With the gossip network burning people's ears about Molly's condition, bandits could be lurking at the apartment building's main entrance. The window was a safer option.

I climbed out to my fire-escape platform, closed the sash behind me, and vaulted over the railing. The plunge felt oddly pleasurable, like leaping into death itself. Most people feared death. Reapers welcomed it. The end of life meant the end of pain, the end of suffering, the end of mystery. We longed for the revelation, to see where we had been taking souls all these years… to see if we had been conducting them to promise or perdition.

After copying Sing's landing on the alley's pavement, I whipped the flashlight from my belt and dashed toward the street. As I closed in on the ghost, I slowed and pointed the beam at her. The light passed through her body and shone on the sidewalk. Definitely a level two. Her eyes carried the typical aspect—confused about her where-abouts and circumstances, not yet accepting her status as a departed spirit. Non-Reapers might be able to see her by now, at least in sporadic glimpses.

"Can you help me?" she called, her voice frail. "I need to find my husband. He was supposed to pick me up here at nine."

My cloak vibrated again, pricklier than ever. I shook my head and hurried on. This ghost was too entrenched, too difficult to collect. I had to get to Molly in time.

I hustled into the park, a shortcut. Molly lived near the center of my forty-block territory, in the midst of what we called shantytown. I had asked to live in a more centralized apartment to allow for better ability to detect death alarms and for quicker access to the dying, but the powers-that-be said nothing suitable was available, meaning that they hadn't yet found a mid-district apartment worth stealing from its owner.

I aimed the flashlight at a dirt path and ducked low. At the speed I was running, no bandits would likely ambush me, at least not in numbers. I could always handle a lone assailant. Fortunately, this former kiddie playground wasn't nearly as dangerous as the more forested park that lay between here and the train station. I avoided that place at night.

"Why the hurry?" Crandyke's voice again filtered into my ears, muted and tinny, as if ear buds had been inserted at the wrong angle.

"I'm checking on a sick little girl named Molly. I don't have much time."

"Well, even if she's already dead, you'll have at least an

hour to collect her. They say the souls always stay around to watch their loved ones weep."

"Is that what you did?"

"No… I didn't have any loved ones."

"Figures." As I ran, I glanced in all directions, watching for the DEO. If he came anywhere close, I would hear his motorcycle. Considering my plans, I preferred to work without anyone looking over my shoulder. "I hope to heal Molly, not collect her."

"Ah! That explains the pills."

"Brilliant deduction."

"If she's close to death, pills won't help. Too slow."

I leaped over a toppled swing set without slowing my pace. No need to tell him about the antibiotic in the syringe. I didn't want to field more inane questions. "As if you know anything about medicine."

"Nothing about medicine, but I was a clerk at DEO headquarters, so I know the danger. I compliment you on your willingness to risk your neck to save a little girl, but you'd better watch your step. The Council's spies abound."

"I'm not looking for compliments." I reached the edge of the park near a streetlamp and stopped within sight of Molly's house. As I paused to catch my breath, I scanned the area for shifting shadows. "You just want me to get to the Gateway in one piece. You're thinking about saving your own eternal hide."

"How little you know about me and what I value. But I will admit that going to heaven would be a lot better than being stuck in your cloak, especially when you sweat. It gets uncomfortable."

I let myself smile in spite of the danger. Even though Crandyke was irritating at times, having him around was better than being alone. Fortunately, he couldn't tell anyone what I was up to, unless another Reaper happened by. "Don't con me, Crandyke. It's not that bad. I've been a Reaper long enough to know better."

"Is that so? How old are you? Sixteen? Seventeen?"

"One of those." Using the flashlight, I scanned Molly's home, a narrow, two-story row house with three crumbling concrete steps leading to a windowless front door. I aimed the beam at scraggly rosebushes near each side of the steps. No bandits lurked. "They took me at the usual age."

"Then you've been a Reaper three years, four at the most. And since you've never been inside your cloak, you can't possibly know how it feels when—"

"Quiet. I have to concentrate." I disconnected the clasp from my valve, silencing Crandyke. I returned the flashlight to the belt and pulled my hood over my head far enough to shade my eyes. I had to display the persona. To the dying and the bereaved, confidence in my abilities meant everything.

I patted my cloak pocket where the pill bottle and syringe lay. Communicating my hope to cure instead of collect would be tricky. As Crandyke said, the Council's spies could be anywhere, even in the midst of a close-knit family.

"Phoenix?"

I turned toward the voice. A man in Reaper garb approached on the sidewalk, his gait tenuous, cautious. His hood shadowed his eyes.

"Who are you?" I pushed back my cloak and grasped the hilt of a dagger on my belt. "Show your face."

He stopped out of reach and lowered his hood, revealing the pockmarked face of a man with dark, shaggy locks and a long scar from ear to chin. I barely recognized Mex. Looking much older than his thirty-three years, he had deteriorated a lot since his banishment. His cloak—ratty, stained, and bearing a roamer's triangular patch at the end of the right sleeve—shimmered up and down that side from shoulder to knee.

I gave him a casual nod. "What's up, Mex?"

"Glad you recognized me." His usual hint of a southern accent gave away his Texas roots, and his voice jittered as he glanced from side to side. "Listen, Phoenix. I'm in trouble. I need one more soul to meet quota. Just one. Age doesn't matter."

"Okay." I stretched out the word. "Just go to the executions and pick one up."

"It's not that easy." He took a step closer. "I'm on the probation list. Suspicion of trafficking souls."

"Just suspicion, huh?"

"Of course." He glanced both ways again but said nothing more.

I knew where he was leading, but making him ask would put me on higher ground. "Why are you telling me your sob story?"

"Well, I heard you're about to hit up Molly, so you'll have plenty, right? I mean, she's what? Six years old? She'll put you way over the top. You can transfer someone to me."

"My quota is higher than you think." I looked at my cloak, no longer shimmering. Mex must have seen me before I disconnected the clasp. "Look. Even if she did put me over the top, I don't have an adapter, and besides, I have to get going—"

"No worries." From his cloak pocket he withdrew a

four-foot-long opaque tube, slightly curled and about the diameter of a garden hose. "You can keep your distance. I'm not crazy about valve locking anyway."

"I wouldn't know, but I—"

"Right. Solitary confinement." Mex laughed. "I don't envy you district hounds. At least roamers can find a little companionship now and then. No worrying about feeling those nighttime alarms."

"Don't rub it in, Mex." My cheeks grew warm. "If you're trying to schmooze your way into getting a soul, you're doing a lousy job. And I don't have time—"

"You're right. You're right. Let's talk business." Mex nodded toward Molly's window. "And don't fret about Molly. The Fitzpatricks haven't blown out her candle. You have time."

I turned that way. A silver taper stood just inside the pane, its wick burning. If I were to rush now, Mex would suspect that I had more in mind than reaping. "Okay. What do you want?"

"A trade." Mex dug into a cloak pocket, withdrew a gold chain, and let it sway under his fingers. "This'll fetch a pretty price almost anywhere."

I cocked my head and eyed it skeptically. "Is that real gold?"

"Fourteen karat."

"Then why don't you barter at the shroud? There's always a bandit or two fencing souls."

"It's not that simple. The Resistance has been too active for the Gatekeeper's liking. There's a crackdown going on, especially at the shroud."

I half closed an eye. "What kind of crackdown?"

"Meds and souls. You can hardly trade anything shadowy anymore. Spies are everywhere."

"That's not my problem." I waved him off. "Gold is worthless to me. Around here, if you can't eat it, keep warm with it, or use it for fuel, it's useless."

"Yeah, yeah, I get that." Mex stuffed the chain into his pocket. "But the crackdown might be your problem soon. Weird stuff is going on. I saw an Owl marching three families with children onto a bus. I don't like the looks of it."

"Maybe it's an isolated incident." I doubted my own words. Whispers about emptying the corrections camps buzzed among my district dwellers, but their murmurings of mass exterminations didn't make sense. Every city regularly executed criminals in the crematoriums. Why would they kill the camp dwellers? "If you see anything else like that, let me know."

"If I last long enough." As Mex glanced around again, his face twisted. With two shaky steps, he closed the gap between us. "Listen. I know I said I don't envy you district hounds, but that was a lie. Actually, you've got it easy—a fertile district, citizens who like you, your own apartment. And me?" He spread out his arms. "I got nothing. I scrounge for meals. I sleep in alleys. I got so desperate once I wheedled a drunk Reaper into giving me a soul, and I've been on the run from him ever since. And now I have just one cycle after this one before I can retire from this gig and go home. You gotta help me out."

I glanced at his gateway valve, barely visible in the glow of the streetlamp. His cloak clasp hung loosely in the keyhole, a sure sign that the valve had not closed properly. Mex was losing energy. Without a recharge at the Gateway, he wouldn't last much longer. Still, I couldn't afford to trade a soul for a gold chain, and I had already taken too long. I had to check on Molly.

"It's not my fault you're a Jungle roamer. You did that to yourself."

I turned, but Mex grabbed my arm, spun me back, and jerked me close. "Why can't you show a little pity?" His bloodshot eyes widened. "Please! I gotta get a recharge! Just one more cycle!"

I knocked his hands away. The sudden shift sent him staggering backwards, and he landed with a thud on the sidewalk. As he sat with his head low, I straightened my cloak. "I saw a level two at the corner of Locust and Mohawk. She's probably still there. You can pick her up."

"A level two?" Mex climbed to his feet and stood shakily. "I can't reap her, not in my condition."

I looked Mex over. With his lack of confidence, he was probably right. Handling a level two required complete self-assurance. "Then go find her, and I'll meet you there to help you as soon as I'm done with Molly."

"Thanks, buddy. You won't regret it." A hand covering his valve, Mex skulked into the shadows.

When he faded out of sight, I took a deep breath and tried to settle my thoughts. I had to put his situation out of my mind. I couldn't trade a soul with just anyone who asked. I would never meet quota and get my own energy recharged. Every Reaper knew this, especially the roamers.

After repositioning my hood over my eyes, I strode up the stairs and knocked on the door. Footsteps pounded, drawing closer. The door flung open with a loud squeak. A dark-haired female, maybe twenty years old, stood in the opening, holding a glowing lantern at face level. Pretty and pale, tear tracks stained her cheeks.

"Oh, Phoenix! You're finally here!" Her Irish accent rode an unsteady voice. "Come in! Come in!"

Not bothering to ask how she knew my name, I entered the narrow foyer with steady, self-assured steps. The public persona had to continue. A Reaper must never appear flustered by impending death or frantic appeals.

"I'm Colleen." She gestured with a trembling hand. "Molly is this way."

I followed the lantern's glow toward the end of a dark hall. Through a doorway to the left, two redheaded preteen girls sat opposite each other on the floor in a dim room, their eyes wide as I passed.

I knew these girls—Molly's sisters, Anne and Betsy—but Colleen remained a mystery. Perhaps she was a distant relation who had been called to the family deathwatch. "Did you send a messenger for me?" I asked.

She stopped at a closed door, her eyes filled with the flickering flame. "We sent a neighbor to fetch you an hour ago. Brennan. An older man, maybe sixty-five. Didn't you see him?"

I shook my head. "He'll show up. He probably just got lost." I kept my tone calm. No use scolding them for sending a man of his age out at night. "We'd better see to Molly."

"Yes... yes, of course." Her hand again trembling, Colleen pushed the door open and led the way.

I entered the warm room and stopped just inside. Molly, dressed in a ballet leotard and skirt, lay on her back on a child-sized bed. Wheezing through labored breaths, she kept her eyes closed, her face slack. To the right of the bed, her mother, Fiona, sat on a stool, weeping as she brushed across Molly's dark hair with a leathery hand.

Lit candles stood in nearly every possible spot—from ivory votives in the tiniest nooks to tall red tapers embedded in rustic candlesticks in larger spaces on shelves. Only the sill in front of an open window leading to the back alley lacked a candle. A light breeze wafted in, carrying the late-night sounds of the city and troubling the tiny flames throughout the room.

Molly's father stood to the bed's left, shifting from foot to foot as he stared at me from under bushy eyebrows and balding head. Although only five-foot-six, his stocky build gave him a formidable stature.

"Colm," I said, nodding, "do you want your other children to witness the reaping?" I already knew the answer, but tradition demanded that I ask.

He gestured with his head toward the house's front room. "Her sisters said their good-byes." His brogue was thicker than usual. "They will stay where they are."

"A wise choice." I opened my hand. "Do you have the passage key?"

Colm extended a photo stick. His arm shook as if he were giving me a pen to sign Molly's death warrant. "This is…" He cleared his throat and blinked away tears. "This is all we could find."

I took the stick and wrapped my hand around it. As it warmed, azure light flowed between my fingers and down to the floor. The radiance collected in an animated hologram—Molly dancing in her ballerina outfit. Although her gap-toothed smile displayed joy as she pretended to dance under stage lights, her awkward steps and near spills reflected her lack of lessons. Even the tattered tutu was an apt sign that no one in this neighborhood could afford such luxuries.

Since this stick didn't have the expensive audio option, I imagined a tune from a music box guiding her movements and off-key notes accompanying her stumbles. Although she was likely a beautiful ballerina to her parents, to me she was a symbol of the city's futility—another hope-filled flower, now wilted and ready to be uprooted, an unkept promise.

When I opened my hand, the image disappeared. "This will do fine. Molly will dance with the stars for all eternity."

Her mother looked up. "Then is there really no hope for my little angel?" Her voice cracked. "If she dies, I'll... I'll..." She buried her face in her hands and wept.

Colm circled to Fiona's side of the bed and rubbed her back. "There, there, dearest. Remember you said you would be brave. You promised me and the children."

"I know. I know." Her hands muffled her voice. "But I can't believe there's really no hope."

I touched the pill-bottle pocket again. This could be the opening I was looking for. "There is always hope for the faithful." I gave Colleen a glance, hoping Colm would notice my concern. She gazed with teary eyes at Molly, seemingly void of any suspicion as she held the quivering lantern.

"You are among friends," Colm said. "Colleen knows about your, shall we say, unofficial profession. In our home, those who applaud death are the enemy, and those who cherish life are our friends. You are free to ply your trade."

"Very good." Trying to keep my hands steady, I slid the photo stick into my pocket and fished out the pill bottle. "Let's see what we can do for Molly."

CHAPTER TWO

I SHOOK THE BOTTLE, making it rattle. "Only two pills left. If they don't help, I brought something injectable, but it's way past expired so it has to be a last resort."

"We believe in you, Phoenix," Colm said. "You will make the right choice."

"Let's just hope a DEO doesn't show up, or all choices are out the door. Word on the street says that Molly's critical, so an officer might get wind of it."

"I have only the clothes on my back to barter with." Colm touched his shirt collar. "But I will gladly give them. Of course, if the worst happens, you can have Molly's shoes."

A pair of little-girl canvas shoes sat in a wall alcove. If Molly were to die, those shoes would likely mean the world to Colm and Fiona, though not much to me. "There's no need to discuss a Reaper payment now."

Something scuffled beyond the window leading to the backyard, a sound barely loud enough for my trained ears to pick up. Someone was listening, maybe a DEO agent.

I cupped the pill bottle in my hand and backed toward the window. "Molly will need water."

"I'll fetch it." Colleen set the lantern on the floor and rushed out of the room.

From the window, moonlight provided a good view of the backyard—a fenced square lot four paces wide that housed low-cut shrubs and sparse grass. Nothing stirred. Maybe a rat or a raccoon had made the noise.

I walked to Fiona and pressed the pill bottle into her damp palm. Leaning close, I whispered, "Be discreet. Unfriendly ears might be listening."

She nodded and pried the lid from the bottle, her hands hiding every motion. After dumping two orange pills into her hand, she passed the empty bottle to Colm and crouched at the bedside.

When Colleen returned with a mug, she, Colm, and Fiona worked together to force-feed the pills, coaxing Molly with hushed voices while I edged closer to the window again.

I peeked out. A cloaked shadow glided from one side of the yard to the other—sleek and lithe. No DEO could move with such agility. Sing, maybe? If so, why would she be here? This wasn't her district.

Molly choked on the pills and coughed them up. Her body stiffened, and she let out a moan. While the three patted her hands and stroked her head in futility, I swallowed hard. Even after more than three years as a Reaper, the sight of a dying child still tore a hole in my heart.

My cloak vibrated, sending hot prickles across my arms. The end was near. Only one hope remained—the syringe.

As I reached into my pocket, the rusty hinges at the front door squeaked. Everyone froze. Fiona whispered, "I heard no knock."

Colm shoved the pill bottle into his pocket. Fiona and Colleen rose and backed away from the bed, their eyes wide with fear. Molly's body loosened, and she breathed in gasping spasms.

The bedroom door swung open. A tall woman dressed in black leather stepped in and scanned the room. Piercing gray eyes set beneath a somber brow gave her the aspect of a bird of prey searching for a victim. With youthful face, trim body, and blonde hair draped over her shoulders, she looked nothing like the steroid-jacked male officer who normally patrolled at night. Yet, the leather pants and jacket with a Gateway insignia on the left breast pocket confirmed her status as a death officer of some kind.

Her shifting gaze halted at Molly. "A young one," she said in a low monotone. "My condolences."

I withdrew my hand from my pocket and, forcing an emotionally detached countenance, crouched next to the bed. "She's still alive, though the end is near."

"Quite near." The officer sat on the bed and stroked Molly's hair. Her hand trembled as her fingers passed over the little girl's locks again and again. "Such a beautiful princess. She will be a glittering star in the heavens. I am looking forward to seeing her drawn away from this broken shell so she can be set free to brighten the skies."

The family's terrified expressions shouted urgency. Somehow I had to get rid of this officer so we could try to save Molly.

I touched the officer's arm. "Because of this child's age and the high potential for extraction pangs, the reaping will cause an emotional upheaval, so if you wouldn't mind sitting in the front room, I will withdraw her soul in private and call you when—"

"Heightened emotions are normal and expected." She unzipped her jacket, revealing a form-fitting white T-shirt and a gun in a shoulder holster. "Pain is normal. Weeping is a necessary catharsis."

I drew back. "I suppose that's true, but—"

"My name is Alex." She extended her hand, though her expression remained stern. "And you're Phoenix."

"That's right." I shook her hand, again not bothering to ask how a stranger knew my name. "I guess you're not familiar with customary reaping procedures. Since the family requests privacy…"

"Familiar?" Anger flickered in her eyes. "I attended reapings before you were born, and I have followed your career ever since—" Her brow furrowing, she picked up a pill from the mattress. "What is this?"

"Candy," I said without hesitating. "I always bring some when a dying child has siblings. Molly has two sisters."

"Is that so?" She extended her hand, her voice calm, even in the midst of Molly's continuing gasps for breath. "May I see your supply?"

I rose and patted my cloak, trying to ignore Molly's travail and her family's looks of desperation. "I gave them all away."

"You are kind to give so much to the grieving siblings." She sniffed the pill, then wrinkled her nose. "Or perhaps not so kind." Pinching the pill at arm's length, she scanned the room again, her eyes shifting from the night table to Molly to the family trio as they stood stock-still. Finally, she nodded at Colm and spoke with tightened lips. "Empty your pockets onto the bed."

After a quick glance at me, Colm dug into his pocket, pulled out the pill bottle, and dropped it to the mattress.

Alex picked up the bottle. "An odd candy container,

don't you think?" Her tone carried only the slightest hint of sarcasm.

I focused on her gun, still visible inside her open jacket, likely a sonic gun—short-ranged, but deadly. Trying to disarm her meant I would have to kill her if I succeeded, or face execution if I failed. There had to be another way. "The pill bottle is mine. I traded for it at the shroud. I hoped to help Molly."

"Really?" She looked at the label, turning the bottle as she read. "Who is Barney Sexton?"

I shrugged. "Probably some rich guy who died before his meds ran out. The shroud doesn't reveal secrets like that."

"I suppose not." She closed her hand around the bottle. "The penalty for buying or selling medical contraband is death, but I assume the Council will take the family's desperate need into consideration."

"The family?" I pointed at myself. "But it's mine."

Alex let out a tsking sound. "Phoenix, I know you better than you realize. You'll do anything to protect the people in your district. And now you're lying to shift the blame to yourself, but once it comes time to testify, you'll change your story."

"Look…" I glanced at Molly again. As pale as a level-one ghost, she fought for breath, the scraping in her chest worse than ever. "Since you've already decided that the family's guilty, can't they try to see if the medicine will work?"

"Of course not, Phoenix. Unlike other officers you're familiar with who often shirk their true responsibility, I am not here merely to record a death; I am here to enforce it." The flicker in her eyes returned, as if kindled by her morbid words.

After sliding the bottle into a jacket pocket, she resumed petting Molly's head, smiling as she crooned, "It's time to go, little one. The Reaper awaits. Release your grip on life's fragile bonds. When you die, your family will finally have peace. The end of your suffering will mean the end of theirs. All pain will fly far away."

With every syllable Alex spoke and with every stroke of her hand, it seemed that Molly's face grew paler, as if Alex were drawing out life energy with her fingers and voice. "Although losing your bodily presence will be a tragedy, your mother and father will know that you have gone to a better place. And oh, what a ride it will be! You will soar into the heavens and be one with the stars. Never needing food, drink, or medicine, you will be a delight to their eyes without being a burden their poverty can no longer endure."

Molly's eyes opened. She blinked at Alex, then at her family. She smiled weakly for a moment, whispered an almost imperceptible "I love you," then closed her eyes and fell limp. Her head lolled to the side, and she breathed no more.

Fiona sobbed. Colm pulled her close and stroked her back. Colleen just stared, her mouth hanging open.

Her eyes still flickering, Alex rose and backed away from the bed. "Reaper... her soul awaits."

I boiled inside. This devilish woman had ushered death into the room, just as surely as if she had opened a coffin and rolled out the corpse. But I couldn't let anger get in the way. I had to do my job.

After raising my hood, I reinserted the clasp into my

valve. Warmth emanated from the connection, but no voices. Even Crandyke wasn't rude enough to speak during a reaping ceremony.

As the warmth spread down my sleeves, I sat on the bed next to Molly's hip, trying to ignore Alex's watchful eyes. "Has everyone witnessed an extraction?"

Colm and Fiona nodded, while Colleen gave her head a shake. "I always left the room," she said. "But I'll be brave for this one."

"For your benefit, I will explain each step." I pulled the cloak's sleeve over my hand and covered Molly's eyes with my palm as I recalled the usual speech. "The eyes are the gateway to the soul, and escape from the mortal shell comes through these orbs. Although the throes of extraction will be painful and cause you grief, it is better to weep gently than to wail in agony, for a soul is but a mist when it first emerges and is easily absorbed, but if it walks this world as a ghost, it thickens and becomes a viscous fluid that must squeeze into narrow paths in order to enter my cloak's fibers. The longer a ghost wanders, the greater its suffering when reaped, so we hope to minimize the pain by collecting it as early as possible."

All three family members nodded their understanding while Alex kept her gaze locked on me, her lips an even line and her forehead slack, no sign of approval or disapproval.

Looking straight at Colleen, I added an explanation that departed from my speech. "Since a soul usually tries to maintain a tight hold on the body for a short time, I will pry it loose in order to allow it to come into my cloak. When the moorings detach, the more violent souls sometimes attack the Reaper, but I'm sure we won't have to worry about that with a gentle soul like Molly's."

Colleen whispered, "I understand." Tears trickled down her cheeks. "Go on."

"Molly's life has borne its final fruit," I said, continuing the memorized ceremony, "so now I will reap the harvest. Prepare yourselves for the swinging of the scythe."

While Colm huddled with Fiona and Colleen, I mentally pushed my valve's warmth through my sleeve and into my hand. Energy poured into Molly's eyes and plunged into her brain. Closing my own eyes, I let the flow transform my physical arm into a ghostly appendage. From my elbow to the ends of my fingers, flesh and bone changed to vapor, enabling my forearm to pass through the cloak's sleeve and into Molly.

The end of the sleeve flattened, reflecting its empty state. As if putting on a glove, I slid my vaporous fingers into the energy flow and reached into Molly's brain. Probing with my energized fingertips, I searched for a tingling sensation, the unquenchable spark of life that would soon separate from the degenerating corpse.

I touched a buzzing spot and wrapped my hand around a pulsing sphere—the core of Molly's soul. Like an octopus, static-filled tendrils protruded from the sphere and tickled my hand. If her soul acted like others, many of the thin tentacles likely maintained attachments to her brain. As the seconds passed, most of the tentacles would let go in response to my warm grasp, though sudden sounds usually caused an instinctive reattachment.

I opened my eyes and focused on Molly's slackened brow. "I am now harvesting her fruit," I whispered. "Have no fear. Molly is safe in my hands. From this point on, complete silence is essential."

Fiona sobbed, then quickly covered her mouth with her apron and wept quietly.

With silence restored, I pulled, easing Molly's soul toward her eyes, but it stopped. The tentacles wouldn't let go—not unusual, but any delay might trouble her family. I pressed my free hand into her stomach, a common technique to encourage detachment. Air pushed through her voice box, making a moaning sound as the tentacles loosened.

"Stop!" Fiona shouted. "She's still alive! She's in pain!"

Molly's soul hung again. I grimaced but said nothing.

Alex lunged at Fiona and slapped her face. "Silence!" Alex hissed. "If you're too squeamish, then leave immediately!"

Fiona sucked in a breath and held it. Colm clenched his fists but kept them at his sides as he whispered, "We will be quiet."

After stepping back to the bed, Alex gave me a nod. "Proceed."

Forcing myself to ignore Alex's brutality, I closed my eyes again. Although silence ensued, Molly's soul whimpered inside. Her fragile sounds vibrated through my sleeve and into my ear, inaudible to everyone else. "Come, Molly," I said. "Your body can no longer hold you."

"The light out there is so bright." Her soul's voice trembled. "It hurts."

"I know, but darkness is not your friend. Come to the light." I caressed the curved surface of her soul with my thumb. "Let go, and I will carry you to a safe place."

"No. It's safe here. So peaceful. So quiet."

I pressed my lips together. Arguing with a reluctant soul had never worked in the past. In her confused state, Molly wouldn't be able to respond to reason, but jerking her out by force might incite another shout from Fiona and another slap from Alex, or worse. Still, I didn't have much choice. Waiting would just make the extraction more excruciating.

After establishing a tighter grip, I pried the tentacles from their hold. As each one snapped loose, Molly's soul cried out in pain. With the strength I had to use, the results wouldn't be pretty, but that couldn't be helped.

Finally, I forced the throbbing sphere through her eyes. As I relaxed my grip, her energy seeped between my fingers. Like a sponge, my cloak absorbed every particle. Molly's tingling warmth radiated up my sleeve, her thin vapor sliding easily through the fibers. The worst part was over for her. Now only a stuffy, cramped feeling would remain, along with a sense of detachment and loneliness. Her passage through the Gateway would relieve those discomforts, or so I always hoped.

A bright shimmer spread across my shoulders. As usual with the soul of a child, a surge of energy filled my muscles, but I couldn't let on that tragedy had provided me with a benefit.

My forearm returned to its physical form. Breathing a sigh, I lifted my hand. The cloak peeled away from Molly's skin. Her eyeballs bulged from their sockets, and black tears trickled from each corner, more severe than usual.

"Oh my God!" Fiona cried. "What have you done to her?"

I glared at Alex, mentally warning her to back off. Her

stare locked on mine. The fire in her eyes ebbed as she stood motionless and quiet. She got the message.

I returned to my Reaper's persona and shrugged to reposition the cloak on my shoulders. "She resisted. I did what I had to do."

Fiona dropped to her knees at the bedside and brushed away Molly's tears, smearing the black across her cheeks. "You Reapers are all alike," she growled as she closed Molly's eyelids. "So callous. So coldhearted. You use the Gateway to manipulate us all. No one has the courage to stand up and—"

"Now, Fiona..." Colm patted her shoulder. "If not for Phoenix..." He swallowed. "If not for Phoenix, Molly would be a wandering ghost."

She clasped Molly's limp hand, her face fiery red. "Then *you* thank him!" She kissed Molly's knuckles and spoke between sobs. "Reapers bring only... only death.... They give us nothing... nothing but false hopes. It's all a magician's trick."

"A trick, you say?" I fanned out my cloak. "Shall I prove Molly's presence within these fibers?"

"What do you mean?" Fiona brushed away tears. "How could you prove it?"

Alex crossed her arms. "Don't, Phoenix. This faithless woman doesn't deserve it."

"All the same..." I pulled the hood low over my eyes. "Ask me a question only Molly would know how to answer."

Fiona rose to her feet and took a step closer on wobbly legs. Her eyes wandered as if searching for Molly's presence in my cloak. Blinking away tears, she squared her shoulders and looked straight at me. "Who is her favorite dancer?"

I nodded, then closed my eyes. Contacting a newly absorbed soul required focus and drained a lot of energy, but bringing a measure of solace to Fiona would be worth it.

I probed the cloak with my mind and let my energy ooze through the fibers. As always, the draining sensation felt like someone had pulled a plug in my reserves and deflated my muscles.

"Phoenix," Alex called, her voice like a faraway echo. "You're trembling. Stop, or you'll collapse."

"I know what I'm doing." I took a deep breath and whispered, "Molly, it's Phoenix. Can you hear me?"

"I hear you." She sounded like a frightened child hiding under a bed, her voice muffled and shivering.

"Don't be scared. You're safe now." No time for chitchat. I had to get the answer quickly. "Who is your favorite dancer?"

"My favorite dancer? Why do you want to know that?"

"Your mother is asking."

"She already knows. It's Anna Pavlova. I read the old magazines all the time."

"Thank you. That's all I needed to know." As I drew back my energy flow, I slowly opened my eyes. I ached to talk with Molly a while longer, to soothe her fears, to bring light to her dark little corner. But she would acclimate soon. I had to move on.

After exhaling heavily, I looked into Fiona's worried eyes. "Molly says her favorite dancer is Anna Pavlova."

"Yes." As Fiona's scowl melted into a trembling smile, she brushed more tears away, but new ones quickly replaced them. "Yes, that's right." She laid her head on Colm's shoulder, and the three family members embraced, gently weeping.

Alex glided toward me with graceful steps. "Grief is a passing shadow. I'm sure you know that."

I nodded. "But it's a crushing shadow."

"For a season." She touched my arm. "I think now would be a good time to tell you why I am here instead of the normal patrol officer. The Gatekeeper himself sent me to offer you a special assignment. He has had his eye on you for quite a while."

CHAPTER THREE

I GAVE ALEX A noncommittal stare. Too many people used the Gatekeeper's title as a way to impress others. At this point, her only duty was to fill out the death form and send it to the Gateway attendants either by courier or by computer transmission. "Speak your mind."

The scuffling sounded in the yard again. I avoided glancing that way. If Sing was the stalker, maybe she could create a distraction and get this meddling death officer out of here.

Alex touched my cloak. "I have seen many reapings, so I know Molly's soul was a particularly stubborn case. Yet you collected her in mere moments. Your reputation is well deserved."

I kept my face slack. "Alex, I've been doing this too long to be influenced by flattery. Just tell me what you want."

"Very well." Alex sidled closer and whispered into my ear. "If you will do what I ask, I will process this poor family's tragic loss and forget that I saw their contraband."

I drew back and looked into her eyes. Her sparkling gray irises seemed unearthly, as if they had been dipped in ashes and still carried the fire's glowing embers. "What exactly are you saying?"

"I need your expertise, the same prowess I witnessed

here." She withdrew the sonic gun from its holster and held it casually at her thigh. "We are expecting, shall we say, a rash of deaths at a centralized location, so we will need a couple of proficient Reapers there to collect the souls. If you cooperate, you will be promoted to Cardinal status with all the benefits." She withdrew a shiny gold key from her pants pocket and set it close to my eyes. "After your stint at the scheduled reaping, you will move into your own furnished condo. No more rundown apartment. No more midnight death alarms. Your reapings will be scheduled for you without quota. A roommate of your choice, if you so desire." She gave me a knowing smile. "Aren't you tired of being alone all the time?"

I nodded. I couldn't deny that being alone was the worst part of a district hound's lifestyle. Yet, how could I leave my district? The citizens needed me. Another Reaper would just collect the souls of the dead without bothering to take care of the living. "Can you give me time to think about it?"

"You need time?" She smiled, though her lips quivered at one corner. "How much?"

"A couple of days, maybe?" I looked toward Colm. I had to get back to protocol. "Colm, I can collect my fee later, so don't worry about—"

Alex grabbed my arm. Her tight fingers trembled as she spoke through clenched teeth. "It is not considered polite to interrupt a conversation."

I spiced my reply with a growl. "It is also impolite to interrupt reaping protocol with your personal requests for my services."

"Oh. I see how it is." With sparks of red blazing in her eyes, she aimed the gun at Colm. "You asked for time to

make your decision. You have exactly three seconds....
One... Two..."

"Wait! Let me—"

A metal ball sailed in through the window. Attached to a thin line, it wrapped around the gun barrel in swishing arcs. The gun jerked from Alex's grip and flew outside.

Alex balled her fists. "Who would dare disarm me?"

"I'll check it out." I stalked toward the window. "They might be dangerous."

"No! Wait!"

I tucked my body and leaped through the opening. When I landed on my feet in the yard, something rustled above. A figure sat high in the branches of a willow tree. As the tree bent in the breeze, the stalker's feminine face appeared in the glow of a nearby streetlamp. Sing raised a finger to her lips, then scampered up into the darkness.

Alex leaned out the window. "Do you see anyone?"

"Not down here." I laid a hand on the tree trunk. "I'll take a look around." I leaped for a branch, swung up, and climbed high into the shadows.

When I drew even with the top of the building, Sing reached across from the roof, grabbed my arm, and pulled me over the parapet. Once I steadied myself on the roof's flat expanse, she whispered, "You okay?"

"For now." I peeked over the edge at the window below. Alex was nowhere in sight. "I just hope the family's safe. Alex isn't exactly the merciful sort."

A tall streetlamp buzzed like an annoying alarm clock and cast its light over the rooftop. Sing crouched next to the parapet, her cloak open, revealing her weapons belt with Alex's sonic gun in a harness. "I've seen her," Sing said. "She's a DEO, isn't she?"

I nodded. "But her real reason for coming was to recruit me."

Sing shifted her sparkling dark eyes toward me. "Recruit you for what?"

"To take part in a big reaping. You interrupted her before she spilled the details." I gestured with my head. "We'd better make ourselves scarce. It's too bright up here."

I turned to run, but Crandyke's voice made me pause. "I know Alex. She's an Owl, so you'd better watch your step. She's the specter of death with curves instead of a cloak, and she can draw life out of a lamppost. Some say she can even read minds, so if she's on your tail you'll soon be in big trouble."

"I'm already in big trouble." I glanced at Sing. She squinted at me but said nothing. "I'll just lay low for a while."

"You'll be a mouse in her talons in short order," Crandyke said. "You might as well do as she asks. You'll be a lot better off."

"I know, but I can't. It's not that simple."

"Is a soul talking to you?" Sing asked.

"You couldn't hear him?" I gave her a sideways look. "He's pretty loud."

Sing shook her head. "The buzz from that light's too noisy."

"His name's Crandyke. I don't get many souls as talkative as he is. Most are too scared." I refocused on my cloak. "Got any more information on this Owl?"

"Not really, but I'm sure she'll tighten the screws, if you know what I mean."

"You mean punish Molly's family." I crept to the front

of Colm's house, Sing following, and leaned over the edge of the roof. At the entry steps, the door opened, and Alex's voice rose from below.

"Pack one small suitcase for each member of your family. The bus will come for you soon, so get ready quickly. And don't try to escape. I already have someone watching your house."

"Bus?" Sing whispered.

"A camp bus. She's sending them to corrections." I heaved a sigh. "I guess I don't have any choice. I shouldn't have left them alone with her in the first place." I snapped the spool from my belt and handed Sing the weighted end of the line. "If you'll anchor this to your belt, I'll drop down and—"

"No." Sing grabbed my arm. "You can't."

I looked again at the steps below. Alex appeared, slowly descending.

"Colm and Fiona are too old for the camp," I hissed. "They'd never survive."

"I know." Her whisper took on an imploring tone. "You can't give in to threats. They'll just keep threatening you every time they want you to do something. You'll end up like a robot who'll do whatever the Gatekeeper asks. As long as you stay a district hound, you'll have freedom."

"Freedom?" I looked at the dark sky. "The only freedom is beyond the Gateway."

"Those are the Gatekeeper's words. You already sound like a robot. Hypnotized to the max."

I arched my brow. "And you sound like one of those Gateway deniers. Conspiracy nuts."

"I'm not one of them. I'm a Reaper, for crying out loud." She tightened her grip on my arm. "Listen. The family is her leverage against you. She's not going to hurt them, at least not for a while. Don't make a rash decision. You have some time to figure out what to do."

As Alex walked toward a motorcycle parked at the curb, I caught a glimpse of the gold key in her hand. Sing was right. I couldn't let them control me with bribes and blackmail. "Every option kind of stinks, doesn't it?"

Sing nodded. "Like rotten eggs."

"Or maybe…" I snatched the gun from Sing's belt. She lurched for it, but I jerked it out of reach. "This might work."

"What are you going to do?" Her face blazed with alarm. "You can't kill her. You know what happens to a Reaper if—"

"Don't lecture me on Reaper laws." I gestured toward the center of the roof. "You'd better get out of sight."

Sing backpedaled slowly, worry lines in her brow. Apparently she had never seen a sonic gun before, not having attended the executions. She didn't know I couldn't do any harm from this distance.

When Sing moved safely away, I slid to the roof's edge. Alex straddled the motorcycle and shook her hair back, getting ready to put her helmet on. I held the gun high and shouted, "Alex! I found it!"

When she looked up, I tossed the gun to the sidewalk. With a loud clatter, it settled close to her boots. "I think I'll stay up here awhile, you know, go for a relaxing stroll across the rooftops."

Alex stared at me long and hard. "And what of my proposition?"

"I told you I need more time. Three seconds isn't enough. Give me twenty-four hours."

She put the helmet on. Blonde locks flowed around the edges. "Molly's family members were charged with medicine trafficking, and they are going to the corrections camp. They will be safe there for twenty-four hours. After that, there are no guarantees."

"If I decide to accept your offer, how will I find you?"

"No need. I will find you before your time runs out."

I pushed back my cloak and set my hands on my weapons belt. "Just remember, I could have stopped you from reporting this family."

"You have more confidence in your abilities than you should." Alex picked up the gun and slid it into her holster. "Still, I will keep your restraint in mind. Just stay away from the family for now, and when we meet again, we can discuss their future." She steered the motorcycle into the street and zoomed away with barely a sound.

I followed her progress until she disappeared around a corner. An electric motorcycle. That explained her quiet arrival.

As I backed toward Sing, I mentally repeated Alex's words. She would keep my restraint in mind, and it seemed like Colm and family would be safe for now. "At least maybe we bought some time."

"I wouldn't trust a word she says." Sing shuddered. "She's as morbid as death."

"I know what you mean." I studied Sing's disgusted expression. She had saved Molly's family and had given me an excuse to vanish, but she had a lot of questions to answer. "So what brought you to Colm's window?"

"While I was out hunting down a death alarm, a DEO stopped me and told me he found a body, some guy named Brennan."

I winced. Molly's death messenger. "Bandits?"

"Looks like it. They stripped everything but his shorts and his photo stick." She shrugged. "I guess even bandits aren't cruel enough to take his passage key."

"Did you reap his soul?"

Sing nodded. "An easy one. His age, I suppose. He's the oldest I've ever reaped."

"Where was he? I didn't feel two alarms."

"A little ways inside my district. That's probably why I got the alarm instead of you." She lifted the hem of her shimmering cloak. "Anyway, his soul put me close to quota, so I was hoping to go to the executions and then to the Gateway with you. I knew you were at Molly's house. I didn't want to interrupt your reaping, so I waited outside."

"The DEO who stopped you. Was it Alex?"

Sing shook her head. "It was Judas. Why?"

"I was wondering how Alex knew to come to Molly's house." I looked toward the street again. "Maybe Judas followed you here and contacted Alex."

"Impossible. He recorded Brennan's death and left to get a corpse unit. Then he was going off duty. If he had followed me, we would've heard his bike."

"That's true." I looked down at the roof, imagining the family weeping as they packed their suitcases. They lost Molly, and now they faced extermination, all because of a coughed-up pill I neglected to recover. If only Alex had caught me with the bottle instead of Colm.

I kept my stare locked downward. What had Sing witnessed? Did she see me with the bottle before Colm took it? If she knew I was a medicine dealer, what would she do with that information? "I suppose you saw what got Molly's family in trouble, didn't you?"

"The pill bottle?" She nodded. "Sure. I saw it."

I looked her in the eye. "Do you know the penalty if a Reaper uses medicine to keep someone from dying?"

"Death, of course." She tilted her head. "Why do you ask?"

"To make sure you understand how important this family is to me."

"Don't worry. I get it. I saw you try to take the blame. You risked a lot."

I hid a sigh of relief. She must have shown up at the window too late to see me with the meds. "I guess I'd better get these souls to the Gateway. That'll give me time to think."

"How long is the train ride?"

"A couple of hours if I catch the high-speed. I can be back by noon."

Sing grasped my forearm. "Take me with you. We'll brainstorm. And I can help you rescue Colm's family. I know some people."

"What people?"

"Just..." She averted her eyes. "Just some people who can help Colm."

"And you'll call for their help if I take you to the Gateway." I nodded. "I get it. A little leverage of your own. I scratch your back, and you'll scratch mine."

"If that's what it takes." She pressed her fingernails into my back and scratched through the layers until a delicious shiver ran up my spine. "Phoenix..." Her voice lowered to a sultry purr. "Have you been alone so long that you can't... well... make a new friend? Haven't I already proven that I want to help you?"

The shiver transformed into heat prickles. I gazed into

her sincere eyes. I couldn't deny the truth in her words. "You're right." I stepped away from her massage. "But I can't take you to the Gateway while you're still short of quota. You'll get demoted to roamer."

"Like I said, let's go to the executions together. I need to learn." She closed the gap and began scratching my back again. "Friends teach friends, right?"

I twisted away from her touch. "Friends don't seduce friends."

"Seduce? I was just—"

"Never mind." I pulled out my watch and flipped open the lid—quarter past eleven. We would have to hurry. Sing gave my watch a curious glance but stayed quiet.

"We'll go to the executions," I said, "but I have one stop to make first. I promised to help Mex reap a level two."

"Mex?" She blinked at me. "I don't think I've met him."

"Best to stay away from him. He's a roamer."

"I'm not scared of roamers." Sing looked past me. "Where's the level two?"

I gestured with my head. "Back at our alley. You ran right past her when you left your apartment."

"Oh. Her." Sing ran her shoe over a tar-covered pebble. "She looked way too entrenched for me to reap."

"I guessed that. With the umbrella and suitcase, she was probably so confused—"

"We have a lot to do." Sing pulled my sleeve. "We'd better hustle."

"Okay, okay."

She jerked me into a quick jog parallel to the street. We ran from house to house, leaping over the gaps between the low parapets dividing the dwellings. As the light behind us dimmed, the obstacles became harder to see, forcing us to slow our pace. Yet, it was better traveling without help from the flashlight. No use signaling our presence with a beacon.

As we continued, heat rose from the roof's tacky surface, making the air even more stifling on this sultry night. Wearing a cloak with a long-sleeved tunic underneath added to the discomfort, but at least Crandyke wasn't complaining.

A half moon veiled by hazy vapor hovered over the skyline and provided a new frame of light around Sing—a flowing silhouette of cloak and curls running at my side. The daring rescue and her willingness to accept an unorthodox Reaper like me meant a lot. We would probably get along fine.

Yet, not everything made sense. Showing up at exactly the right time seemed too coincidental. And that speech about freedom and being a robot? Rehearsed. Her acting skills nearly glossed it over but not enough to quell suspicion. It would be best to keep her in sight, at least until after she called for help from her people, whoever they were.

Still, she could get in a lot of trouble hanging around me—a medical black-market trader who was trying to, as the Gatekeeper's Council often put it, "Interrupt the natural order of death and reaping." If she stuck around, she would eventually learn the truth and maybe get entangled in the danger.

I focused straight ahead. I would probably learn soon enough. The road to the Gateway might very well prove Sing's alliances.

CHAPTER FOUR

WHEN SING AND I approached the alley leading to our apartments, the ghost came into view, still standing at the curb with an umbrella over her head. Paul, our regular night-duty DEO, leaned against a nearby brick building, his motorcycle parked on the sidewalk.

With a computer tablet in hand, he scribbled notes with a stylus, his ample biceps flexing with the motion. His leather jacket lay across the motorcycle's handlebars, a reasonable sight considering the warm weather, but Paul would use any excuse to show off his muscles and his shoulder holster. These officers were among the few who could afford the time to indulge in frequent exercise.

I glanced around. No sign of Mex. Maybe he had already come and gone. We didn't talk about how long he should wait.

As we drew near, Paul looked up at me with an annoyed expression. "It's about time one of you got here. I put the word out about this ghost half an hour ago. I knocked on your door but no answer." He nodded at Sing. "Yours, too."

"We were busy." I whipped my cloak around, displaying its shimmer. "I had another reaping. You know how some nights are."

"Better than you." He glanced at his tablet. "Who took care of reporting it? There's no record."

"Alex. I didn't see a tablet, so she's probably doing it manually."

"Alex?" His eyes took on a sudden, fearful aspect. "Okay. That's cool."

"Do you know her?"

"Never mind. We have work to do." He pushed away from the wall and pointed at the ghost with his stylus. "Miriam Cruz, married to a Hispanic guy named Robert. They were killed in a traffic accident a couple of weeks ago. A roamer picked up Robert's soul at the crash scene, but we couldn't find Miriam... until now."

I walked in a slow orbit around Miriam and scanned her from head to toe. She seemed not to notice. The level twos were always unpredictable. "Two weeks is plenty of time to get entrenched."

"Definitely getting rooted," Paul said. "She's visible now, but she keeps fading in and out. I recorded her as a two point three. Since she's on the border between the districts, I don't care which one of you picks her up. Just get her off the street."

With hands on hips, Sing stood directly in front of the woman. "Why isn't she reacting to us?"

"Because she's loony!" Paul laughed and leaned against the wall again. "Phoenix, you gonna let the little darkie mutt earn her rookie wings?"

"Darkie mutt?" I shot him a warning glare. "Listen, jerk. You do your job, and we'll do ours."

Paul stalked toward me, his fists tight. "Okay, tough guy, that'll cost you."

I stood my ground. "It's two against one. Between Sing and me, we could put you six feet under."

"I'm not talking about fighting, you idiot." He reached for my cloak. "You're just paying a penalty so I don't put a mark on your perfect record."

I dodged his hand. "I don't have anything."

"If Alex was with you, the family must have been important enough to pay you pretty well."

"Shows how little you know."

He lunged and grabbed my cloak. Before I could twist away, he dug a hand into a pocket and jerked out the police scanner. As he backed away, he looked it over, smiling. "Pretty nice!"

I exhaled. At least he didn't find the syringe. I straightened my cloak with a hard tug. "Satisfied?"

"Not until you learn a little respect." He pushed me to the wall and wrapped his fingers around my throat. As he pressed me against the bricks, he squeezed, not enough to cut off my air supply but enough to let me know he could. "You're the collector. I'm the enforcer. You report to me. And I can call your mongrel friend anything I want. Understand?"

I glanced at Sing. She crept toward us with both fists clenched. I gestured with a hand for her to stand down. Although together we could handle Paul in a fight, we would lose in the long run.

Sing backed away. She likely understood that Paul's show of force was more for her benefit than for mine—the dominant ape letting the newcomer know who was boss. I squeaked out, "I understand."

"Good." Paul released his grip and nodded at the ghost. "Get to work."

I walked slowly toward Miriam. Could the night get any worse? No use trying to guide Sing through reaping this ghost now. I just wanted to do the job and get far away from this maniacal DEO. I could always transfer a soul to her after we got out of his sight. Still, it wouldn't hurt to give Sing verbal coaching while I worked.

"Okay," I said to Sing, "first I'll address this ghost directly. Then I'll use my acting skills to gain her confidence." I turned toward Miriam and spoke with a loud voice. "A fair evening, isn't it?"

She jumped back, startled. "Oh! I'm sorry. I was lost in thought." She looked up at her umbrella. "Actually, the weather is terrible. You must be getting soaked in this dreadful downpour."

"Indeed." I ducked my head, pretending to blink at the rain. "Is there room for me under there? My cloak isn't faring well. I think the rain's fallout content is pretty high today."

She glanced around, her glowing eyes brimming with fright. "I suppose we can share." She raised the umbrella higher. "But rest assured that my husband will be along at any moment. I expect you to continue acting like a gentleman."

"Have no fear about that." I edged underneath the umbrella and spread my cloak over her shoulder. "In fact, I will protect you until he arrives."

"Well, how kind of you." Smiling, she nestled close against my side. "You are very much like my husband."

I turned to Sing. Her mouth hung partially open. "This ghost is really just barely a level two," I said, "maybe two point one at the most. Higher levels are far more aware of reality, and they pay more attention to conversations that aren't directed toward them. She's probably oblivious to what I'm saying to you now, but ghosts like her are emotionally needy, and that allowed me to gain her trust."

"I can see that." Sing leaned to the side as if studying from a different angle. "What next?"

"We'll need photos for her Gateway passage." I nodded at Sing's belt. "I see you brought your camera."

When Sing reached for her belt, Paul called out, "The police got her photo stick at the crash scene, and they already sent it to the Gateway. But just in case it didn't get there, I took some pictures of her and saved them to a stick. Got some good shots. The Gateway guardians will be satisfied."

"That'll work." I looked at Sing again. "Now the hard part. You already know how much energy it takes to transform your hand. I have to transform as much of my body as possible and blend into her realm."

Sing nodded. "I heard the lecture in class. You have one minute, max. Right?"

"Right, so I'll leave an arm physical, and if I seem to lose contact with reality, grab me and pull me away."

"Will do."

I checked my clasp key, still attached to my sternum valve, then, looking into the woman's eyes, I spoke softly. "My name is Phoenix. What's yours?"

Her smile widened. "Miriam, but my husband calls me Bonita."

"Bonita?" As I drew my face closer to hers, I focused on the energy flowing through my cloak's fibers and let it seep into my body. "Bonita means pretty, doesn't it?"

"Yes, it does. My husband says I'm pretty, but he's kind of biased."

The transformation started at my hand and coursed across my shoulders. "He's not biased at all. You're very pretty."

"Oh... thank you." She furrowed her brow. "Actually, you look... you look a lot like my husband."

Her eyes took on a glazed aspect. She was nearly ready, and so was I. I glanced at Sing. She appeared fuzzy, as if standing on the other side of fogged glass. Rain pattered on the umbrella, and water ran around my shoes. With my energy dispersing, I had to hurry. "I know where Robert is. I can take you to him."

"Really?" She blinked rapidly. "I'm not sure I should travel with a stranger."

"You can trust me." I hated those words. I had uttered that lie too many times. Soon, Miriam would learn to hate them as well.

Her lips pursed, and her voice took on a childlike tone. "I do trust you."

Whispering "Trust me" again and again, I guided my cloak completely around her. Unlike the spherical presentation of Molly's soul, Miriam's had grown, thickened, and shaped into her physical appearance, spreading out into her umbrella and suitcase. Absorbing her might expend all of my reserves.

I pushed my energy flow through her body. As she grew more transparent, her outer edges seeped into my fibers. She let out a breathy gasp. "What... what's happening? Something is stinging me."

"The fallout rain can carry a bite." I pressed her close. The umbrella vanished. The suitcase dissolved. As Miriam's soul thinned, her face stretched into a hideous mask, her mouth gaping as she screamed. Her terrified eyes popped like tiny balloons and dispersed in sparkling fog, then her head exploded, followed by her body. The scream continued as if floating in the mist-soaked air, punctuated by fevered gasps.

I closed my eyes and concentrated on my cloak's absorbing pull as it sucked in Miriam's soul, now a pasty film lining the interior. I held my breath. Every micron of absorption felt like a stabbing knife, and the heightening screams proved that the torture was much worse for her than for me.

Finally, the film melted and fully assimilated into the fibers. A new shimmer flowed across the shoulders and down to the hem. Miriam was safe inside, though probably cursing me for the pain I caused.

Dizziness flooded my head. I staggered, trying to reabsorb some residual energy from my cloak.

Sing grabbed my arm. "Are you all right?"

Exhaling heavily, I looked at her. She was clear again. The rain had stopped. I was back in the real world. My legs still wobbled a bit, but my energy recovered to a functional level. "I'm fine. I always get a little dizzy after a journey into the ghost realm."

"Not bad." Paul walked toward us, again writing on his tablet. "I gotta give you credit. I think only Shanghai could've done it any better than that."

"Right. Shanghai." I resisted the urge to roll my eyes. The DEOs had been singing Shanghai's praises lately, as if she were God's gift to reaping. Sure, she was an excellent Reaper. In fact, her recent transfer to Chicago had ignited a string of reports about her prowess that had made her an instant legend. And who could bad-mouth a legend?

Since she was my childhood friend from training school, I certainly couldn't.

Paul nodded at my cloak. "When are you going to the Gateway? You look ready to pop."

"I hope to catch the morning train. We both do."

"I'll jot that down." After writing another note, he extended the tablet. "Need a thumbprint. I'll wire the data to the Gateway. They'll be expecting you."

I pressed my thumb on the screen in a small box next to an icon bearing my image, but nothing happened. "I think it's stuck."

"Blasted piece of junk." Paul slapped the back of the tablet. A message flashed across my image—*Data Validated.* "There it goes."

"Temperamental, huh?"

"Mine's one of the better units." Paul dug into his pocket and withdrew a photo stick. "Don't forget this."

"Right." I took Miriam's stick.

"See you next time, Phoenix." Paul took his jacket from his motorcycle, put it on, and climbed aboard. "And thanks for the radio."

When the engine rumbled to life and he rolled from the sidewalk to the street, I looked away. I couldn't stand the sight of him for another second. Sure, I had planned to use the scanner as a bribe if necessary, but the "if necessary" events always stung. I felt like a bug being squashed by a heel, a nobody who could do nothing to alter his dismal life. I just had to take the punishment and move on.

Sighing, I wrapped my fingers around the photo stick. A hologram of Miriam took shape above my fist. Carrying the umbrella, she stared into space, her eyes wide and tear-filled.

I whispered to my cloak, "Bonita, are you all right in there?"

Her voice filtered to my ears, weak but laced with anger. "You said I could trust you."

"And you can." I cleared my throat, hoping to keep my own voice in check. "The pain's diminishing, right?"

"No thanks to you."

I pushed the photo stick into my cloak pocket. "Listen. I'm a Reaper. I'm just doing my job. When I take you to the Gateway, you'll thank me."

Miriam didn't reply, though a prickly sensation ran along my skin. Angry souls often caused that. She would settle down soon. They always did.

I detached my cloak from the valve and looked at Sing. "Any questions about reaping a level two?"

She touched her cloak, as if imagining herself repeating the process. "Do you collect an entrenched male ghost that way? I don't think a woman would trust me the way Miriam trusted you. It was almost like seduction."

"I guess you could call it that. Really it's all just acting, no matter if you're reaping someone from a newly dead body or if you're collecting an entrenched ghost. We just do whatever it takes to get souls to trust us."

Sing's brow lifted. "Well, *shouldn't* they trust us? I mean, in the long run, since we're taking them to the Gateway."

I shrugged. "We promise them a better place, but keeping the promise is up to someone else. I've never seen what happens beyond the Gateway. No Reaper has."

A faraway look drifted across Sing's eyes. "Maybe one of us should."

I laughed. "Right. A Reaper will get sucked into the

collection station and ride into eternity. Good luck coming back to give the rest of us a report."

Sing shook off her daze. "So what you're saying is that you take each case individually and act according to whatever will gain the soul's trust."

"Exactly. Since Miriam was desperate to find her husband, I tried to take his place. You know, offer affection and security. You could have asked if she has a sister, a daughter, or a best friend, and you could have pretended to be that person. Level ones and twos are in a confused state. They want your act to be true, so they'll usually believe you."

Sing nodded. "I get it, but what about level threes?"

"Never tried one. I hear they know exactly where they are, and they're skeptical about everything."

"And always visible?"

"Only when they want to be. They're a big hassle, because a Reaper can't always tell if a level three is a ghost or a living person. Even when they're invisible to everyone else, they're visible to us." I touched my valve, still warm from the reaping. "Now that Paul's gone, I could transfer Miriam to you. Then I can make quota again at the executions."

"Transfer? Is that legal?"

"It's legal, but the DEOs don't like it. It messes up their paperwork."

Sing looked from side to side. "Out in the open?"

I nodded toward our alley. "Is over there all right? No one will see us. And no sign of bandits."

She gave the alley a skeptical glance. "I suppose."

"Let's go, then." I walked that way, watching Sing over

my shoulder. After taking a deep breath, she followed, her head low as if expecting to be struck by lightning.

When we made our way to a point below our apartments, I reattached the clasp to my valve. As soon as the cloak shimmered to life and radiated light throughout the alley, I pointed at Sing's valve. "You'll need to disconnect."

"Oh. Right." She fumbled with her clasp for a moment before unfastening it. Her cloak's shimmer faded to a dim luster.

Light from my cloak illuminated her valve's emblem, embedded a few inches under her throat. With her tunic buttons opened to just below the bottom of the emblem's circle, the entire symbol shone against her dark skin. Identical to the design of our clasps, the symbol looked like a double gate joined at the middle by two hands, their fingers curled to latch to each other. The central valve, circular and the size of a penny, lay embedded in the hands' knuckles, ready to be opened by the insertion of a key, such as another valve or a cloak clasp, or by depressing the valve to make its spring-loaded cylinder protrude.

When my clasp heated up, I touched its surface and mentally searched for Miriam's soul. Although my cloak had absorbed her throughout the fibers, she would have gathered herself in one spot by now.

After a few seconds, I found her brooding in the left sleeve. As angry as she was, it wouldn't do any good to talk to her, so I used the energy flow to guide her toward my clasp. When she drew close enough, I turned to Sing. Her expression seemed cautious, anxious. "Are you sure you want to do this?"

"It's okay." Keeping her eyes on mine, she gave a

nervous laugh. "So do you just plug my cloak into your valve?"

"We don't use the cloaks." I half closed an eye. "Since you didn't even know if this is legal, I guess you didn't see the training video."

She shook her head. "I was on the fast track. I doubt that a transfer is part of the core curriculum."

"Probably not." I pointed at my emblem and hers in turn. "I'll push Miriam through my clasp and into my valve compartment. Then we'll do a direct connect, valve to valve."

"Direct connect?" Her voice took on a tremor. "Is that the only way?"

"We could use an adapter tube to avoid close contact, but I don't have one. And no Reaper can use another's cloak. The genetics won't allow it."

"Right. I know about the genetics, but..." She looked toward the street as if searching for a way of escape. "It's just that—"

"Hey..." I touched her shoulder. "I know a connection's kind of... intimate, I guess. Don't feel any pressure to do it."

"How could I not feel pressure?" Her face took on a forlorn expression. "Can't we just go straight to the executions? I know you say it's dangerous, but I'm ready for it. I have to learn even the worst parts of being a Reaper."

I searched her eyes. She really seemed scared. "All right. We'll go."

"Good. I hope you don't think I'm..." She looked away for a moment before returning her gaze to me. "Prudish, I guess."

"Not at all." I feigned a confident tone in spite of my

doubts. Fear of intimate contact wasn't normal for a Reaper. In winter survival training, three of us had to huddle close under a single cloak to keep from freezing. Gender didn't matter. We were too cold to care. And Sing's willingness to scratch my back without prompting seemed to contradict her hesitance. With all the uncertainty about her odd behavior, maybe another test was in order.

I lifted her clasp. "Shall I reconnect your cloak?"

"Uh... Sure." She pulled her tunic open another inch and raised her chin. As I inserted the clasp into her valve, she closed her eyes, trembling.

I quickly locked it in place and drew back. "Done."

She opened her eyes. As her cloak's shimmer increased, the alley became as bright as the street. She wrapped her arms around me, stood on tiptoes, and whispered into my ear. "Thank you." She then kissed my cheek, letting her lips linger for a moment before drawing away.

"You're welcome." I touched the anointed spot. The warm tingle felt good, but her gesture added to the mystery. Was the affection real, or was she trying to cover up her fears? Too many unanswered questions hung in the air, but we had to get back to business. "Now to the executions."

She smiled, looking more relieved than the situation called for. "The crematorium, right?"

"Right, but wait a second." I focused on the cloak's fibers near my clasp and used the energy flow to send Miriam back to the sleeve. As she returned, she grumbled but said nothing. "Miriam's settled now. I'm ready."

Sing pulled me toward the street. "It's getting close to midnight. We'd better hurry."

CHAPTER FIVE

A S SING AND I jogged abreast, I let her set the pace. The difficult reaping and my temporary entry into the realm of ghosts left my head a bit dizzy. She glanced at me every few seconds, always smiling when I returned the glance. She was either incredibly open and honest with her affections, or she was pouring on deceptive charm. Maybe she thought she could gain my favor by piercing the shield every district hound had to wear. Since friendship and romance were forbidden, we couldn't allow emotional entanglements.

Still, taking a gun from an Owl was also forbidden, as was plotting to rescue citizens from a corrections camp. We both seemed willing to break a few rules. Maybe Sing hoped to secure a place at my side by forging a working bond between us, a Reaper alliance of sorts.

But why? This obsession with going to the Gateway in my company, and her willingness to add the risk of attending the night's executions seemed beyond the norm.

As we drew close to our region's crematorium, a one-story brick edifice that took up an entire block, Sing slowed her pace and stared at the spinning column of smoke rising from the brick chimney. A poster hung near one corner of the building—an advertisement for tablet computers, perhaps directed at the clinicians who worked there. No one in my district could afford such a luxury, though every officer in the death network seemed to have one.

Another poster displayed the Gatekeeper's face along with the usual statements about his benevolence. With youthful features that belied his long life—abundant dark hair, smooth skin, and bright smile—he certainly had a charismatic appeal. Since aging had no effect, his claims of being a demigod seemed believable.

Saying nothing, Sing accelerated. After rounding the corner, she slowed again. A line of three cloaked figures stood in front of the crematorium's rear entrance—a dark wooden door with a gray canvas awning. A nearby streetlamp cast its glow across a sign on the door—*Reapers Entrance*.

When we stopped a few paces away, a bearded man at the front of the line groaned. "I've been waiting three hours, and now a couple of district hounds are going to pull rank."

I glanced at the triangular patches on their sleeves. All three were male roamers, each one tall and wiry, definitely formidable. "Look," I said, raising my hands in a surrender pose, "I'm not planning to butt in line. I'm here to teach Singapore." I gestured toward her. "This is her first cycle."

The roamer at the end of the line pushed back his hood, revealing a twenty-something-year-old man with bushy hair and thin lips. I knew this scoundrel—Moscow. With his frequent attempts to trade stolen goods for souls, how he escaped being put on probation was anyone's guess.

"She can have my place in line," Moscow said in an alluring tone. A slowly emerging grin revealed a pair of sharp canine teeth. "I'll trade it for a cozy night with her in her apartment."

"In your dreams." Sing crossed her arms. "We'll wait our turn."

A click sounded at the door. I pulled out my watch and pointed the face at the streetlamp. Five minutes till midnight. Opening a little early was a good sign—probably plenty of executions waiting.

Sing and I took our places at the end of the line and filed in. As usual, only a bare bulb attached to a broken ceiling fixture lit the back entrance lobby—a cramped room with stacks of papers atop an old desk and empty urns on wall shelves. Ronald, the dour old attendant, stood next to a wall-mounted computer tablet near an interior door. "Enter your thumbprint and your desired number of souls," he said in monotone as he held the door.

The first Reaper pressed his thumb on the tablet screen, then entered a request for two souls and passed through the door. The second Reaper did the same, followed by Moscow, who entered a request for three. When he disappeared into the compound, I pressed my thumb on the screen and entered a zero, but the tablet beeped, and my entry flashed red.

"Zero?" Ronald squinted at me through thick glasses. "That's not allowed."

"I made quota already. I'm here to show Sing what to do. She needs only one."

"Our policy is to allow entrance to Reapers, not teachers or spectators." He pushed his glasses higher on his nose. "Enter your intent to reap at least one soul, or be on your way."

"But I just—"

"Rules are rules."

I heaved an exasperated sigh and entered a "one." As soon as it accepted the data, red letters flashed across the top of the screen—*Execution Total Reached.*

"What?" I turned toward Ronald. "Does that mean Sing can't get a soul?"

He shook his head. "Not tonight. Sorry."

"Can I let her have mine?"

Ronald pursed his lips. "I suppose I can make the transfer, but you'll have to wait outside. You can't just stand and watch."

"But I'm teaching her, not just watching." I clasped his shoulder and gave him a stern look. "Do you want to be the reason a new Reaper lost a perfect chance to receive crucial training?"

Ronald gulped. "Uh... no. Of course not."

"Good." I released him. "What can you do to help us?"

Sweat beading on his forehead, he tapped the wall tablet's screen and read a scrolling list. After a few seconds, he smiled nervously. "We're in luck. Another prisoner is available for execution. The judge hasn't entered the sentence in the system yet, but it's just a formality." He tapped the screen a few more times and nodded toward Sing. "Go ahead."

Sing pressed her thumb on the screen and entered a "one." I led her through the doorway and down a narrow corridor illuminated by flickering fluorescent lights above. A door at the end swung closed and clicked shut—probably Moscow entering the furnace room.

When we reached the door, I grasped the knob and pulled up my hood. "Get ready for an ugly scene. It's hot, dirty, and…" I glanced at the sign on the door—*Death Workers Only*. "And sad."

She raised her hood. "I'm ready."

When I swung the door open, a blast of hot air dried my eyes and slid the cloak's sleeves up my arms. About twenty paces inside, an open oven-like hatch at the back of the chamber revealed crackling flames burning deep within, making the brick wall look like a dragon's gaping maw. In fact, the workers here called the furnace *the dragon*, sometimes making jokes about feeding it as they disposed of corpses in its fiery belly.

Below the hatch, several foot-tall urns lined the base of the wall along with a shovel that leaned against a smaller, closed hatch. Firelight cast an undulating glow across a row of people kneeling on the concrete floor, their hands tied at their backs and their heads covered with dark burlap bags as they faced the flames. Since they didn't struggle or cry out, they had likely been drugged, the usual procedure to keep violent criminals in check, but once their souls detached from their brains, the departing phantoms might not be so docile.

I counted the condemned prisoners—eight, all apparently male and all wearing orange jumpsuits. Tim, a stocky DEO, paced in front of the line, tapping on a computer tablet. "Reapers, take your positions," he said as he pivoted and continued his switchback march. "Singapore will wait for the final prisoner to arrive."

I touched Sing's shoulder and whispered, "Stay close and watch. Don't be intimidated. That's the worst thing you can do."

We hurried to one end of the line. The other Reapers and I stood in front of the prisoners, our backs to the furnace. A photo stick lay on the floor in front of each victim.

Sing shifted nervously at my side. "What were their crimes?"

I shrugged. "No one ever tells us, but I've heard that most of them are murderers or rapists. They're the lowest of the low."

Tim withdrew a sonic gun from a shoulder holster and walked around to the back of the prisoner line. He set the barrel against the base of the skull of the first prisoner and pulled the trigger. A hollow pop sounded. The prisoner's head jerked forward. He grunted quietly, slumped over, and toppled to the side with a thud.

I looked on without blinking. The sonic gun had just obliterated a man's brain stem in unceremonious fashion, but I couldn't think of a single reason to feel sad. They were getting what they deserved.

Tim walked down the line and began shooting the remaining prisoners, pausing several seconds between each to let the gun recharge. With every pop, another head jerked and another body sagged or fell over. As if echoing the pops, Sing sucked in a series of short breaths. The furnace's flames revealed sparkling tears in her eyes, though her expression stayed calm.

When Tim executed the eighth man, he called out, "You have fifteen minutes, except for Phoenix. Since he's teaching, he can have more time."

The first three Reapers snatched up the photo sticks, dropped to their knees in front of the victims, and tore off their bags. Each Reaper drove a dematerialized hand into a prisoner's brain. Moscow pulled, grimacing. Mist boiled out from the prisoner's eyes and surged across Moscow's face, swirling like an angry tornado.

Moscow fell backwards to his bottom and clawed at the mist with his disembodied hand. With his physical hand, he whipped his cloak around and smothered the escaping soul. The other Reapers battled their souls as well, some souls with more ferocity, some with less. Screams filled the chamber. Tormented cries bounced off the walls before being drowned out by the roaring fire as the Reapers took charge of the resisting souls.

Sing drew in another sharp breath and held it. A single tear tracked down her cheek, but she quickly brushed it away with a trembling hand.

I hid a sigh. The first time I attended an execution, I had the same reaction. Without a trainer there that day, I had no one to guide me. I just copied what the others did, pretending to be callous as I ripped tethered souls from their bodies and battled their desperate attempts to escape from what the prisoners likely believed would be a terrifying afterlife. It didn't take long for real emotional calluses to develop. I hadn't shed a tear in this death chamber since that day.

While Moscow and the other Reapers worked on the remaining victims, I crouched in front of the prisoner at the end of the line. Still somewhat upright, his shoulders sagged low. I picked up his photo stick, untied the drawstring at his neck, and slid the bag off his head. A mop of scraggily blond hair fell to his ears and over his bearded face.

Sing knelt beside me and whispered, "He's so young."

"Younger than most. Maybe twenty-five or so." Grasping the photo stick, I raised the man's image. His three-dimensional form stood over my curled fingers, an arm wrapped around a woman's shoulders. Hunched over and shivering, both wore clothes that were not much more than rags. "Strange. They don't let violent prisoners stay with their spouses. He might have been part of the Resistance."

Sing brushed a finger over the woman's face. "His poor wife."

"First lesson. The sooner you detach your emotions, the better off you'll be." I let the hologram dissolve and stuffed the photo stick into my pocket. "Second lesson. Make the extraction quick. No one here cares how much the eyes bulge."

"But if he's not violent, can't you be gentle?"

"With this one, probably, but yours might be violent." I laid the man on his back, slid a sleeve over my hand, and covered his eyes. As soon as my forearm turned to vapor and my sleeve flattened, I slid my fingers under his lids and pushed into his brain. When I found his spherical soul, I grabbed it and pulled. The tentacles held fast.

A whispered cry ran along my cloak's fibers. "No. Please. Don't. I have to stay. I have to help Gail."

"Your wife?" I asked.

"Yes. Have you seen her?"

I called to Tim. "What's up with this guy's wife? Is she here?"

"She's next on the list." Tim tapped on his tablet. "She'll be out here in a minute."

I glanced at Sing. She seemed calm, apparently accepting the news without emotion.

"It's too late to help Gail," I whispered to the man's soul. "You're dead. You need to let go."

I pulled gently, not just for Sing's sake. With only one soul to reap, I had time, especially since this one didn't appear to be ready to fight. Maybe when Gail came out, Sing and I could reap the couple together.

While I massaged the soul's sphere, Tim stripped the jumpsuit off the first execution victim, hoisted the naked body over his shoulder, and hauled it to the furnace. Letting out a grunt, he heaved the limp corpse through the hatch. The body dropped a foot or so and disappeared in the flames with a thud and a chorus of loud crackles.

A new blast of hot air breezed by, carrying the unmistakable stench of burning flesh, though it diminished quickly as the inferno consumed skin and bones.

The first Reaper nudged the second victim with a shoe. "Finished." He wrapped his cloak close to his body, stalked to the door, and opened it. Another DEO bustled through from the other side, leading a jumpsuit-clad woman by a chain attached to manacles around her wrists. The officer bypassed the departing Reaper and pushed the woman to her knees next to my victim. Without a bag over her head, she scanned the furnace room. When she looked at the dead man's face, she whispered, "Mike?"

Sing knelt in front of the woman. The clarity in her eyes proved that they hadn't bothered to drug her. She would face the terror unveiled.

Letting out a shushing sound, Sing pushed back her hood. "Gail, my name is Singapore. Mike is dead, and my friend Phoenix is reaping his soul. When they execute you, I will reap your soul, and we'll take you both to the Gateway."

When their gazes met, Gail clutched her jumpsuit at the chest. "The Resistance will triumph!" she shouted.

"We speak for those who cower in fear, strangled by the Gatekeeper's tyrannical grip! He can't hold us down forever!"

Tim hoisted another body over his shoulder. "No one here cares, lady. Your preaching days are over."

"You don't care because you're part of the death society! You've been pampered!" As her shouts echoed, tears flowed from her anguish-filled eyes. "Try living in the slums. They're just a soul farm for the ravenous Gatekeeper. The poor are cattle he keeps in check by threatening their departed loved ones, and an uprising means a one-way trip to a death camp. Then the Jungle burns."

"Lady, you're crazy." Tim shoved the body into the dragon, again stoking the flames and creating another round of odorous exhaust. "But we'll shut you up soon enough."

"Singapore!" Gail clasped her hands and looked up at Sing in a pleading posture. "You must help the Resistance! We are a Reaper's friends, not a chain around your neck. Learn the truth! Help us set the souls free!"

"I understand, Gail," Sing whispered. "I will be your friend. Now prepare yourself to die. I'll be as gentle as I can."

"But Singapore, I—"

"Shhh. Everything's going to be all right."

The second DEO drew a sonic gun, set it against Gail's skull, and pulled the trigger. Gail's head snapped forward. As she tilted to the side, her eyes fluttered closed.

Sing grasped Gail's arm and guided her body down until she lay alongside her husband. After brushing another tear away, Sing pulled her sleeve over her hand and covered Gail's eyes.

While Tim and the second DEO stripped the remaining bodies and carried them to the furnace, the other Reapers departed, all with sagging shoulders and weary faces, exhausted by the battles. The furnace blaze erupted in greater fury, sending out a new blast of death-saturated air—hot, dry, and choking.

I blinked at the stinging smoke. Sing held her breath and closed her eyes. With her free hand, she clamped down on the end of her reaping sleeve, sealing the opening.

I refocused on Mike. "Gail is dead now, so let go. You'll be together again very soon."

The tentacles released their hold. As I drew his soul through his eyes, I glanced at Sing. A slight hint of mist seeped around her sleeve. The reaping process had begun. For some reason, she kept her free hand over her sleeve's opening, as if trying to prevent something from escaping. Her method seemed unorthodox, but apparently it worked for her.

When Mike's soul seeped into my cloak, I scooted closer to Sing. While the two officers worked together to strip Mike's body and carry him to the furnace, I watched Sing's sleeve. A shimmer rode along the surface, giving evidence of Gail's absorption. Within seconds, Sing would reach quota and qualify to go to the Gateway. We were fortunate to get cooperative souls tonight, though she didn't learn how to handle the battles we often had to face here.

Sing pushed her hand out of the sleeve and gave me a weak smile. "Are you ready to go?"

I looked at the DEOs. They had opened the furnace's lower hatch and were shoveling ashes into the urns. Of course, the ashes had mixed together, but the family members would never know the difference.

"This one's reaped," I called. "We'll be going now."

"Since I gave you some extra time…" Tim pointed at a pile of empty jumpsuits that lay between them and us. "Do me a favor. Strip off her clothes and throw them there. Marshall and I will toss her to the dragon after you leave."

"Uh… yeah. Sure." I concealed a swallow. I had been asked to do this a few times before but only once for a woman. Yet, what did it matter? She was dead. She wouldn't care.

When I reached for the jumpsuit's zipper just below Gail's throat, Sing grabbed my wrist. "I'll do it, Phoenix."

"It's okay. It's not like I haven't dealt with a female corpse before."

I pulled the zipper down a few inches, but she stopped me again, a hiss rising in her voice. "Just wait for me in the hall."

I glared at her. "If you don't want me to think you're prudish, you're not doing much to convince me."

Her grip tightened. "Phoenix, call me whatever you want, but I'm not going to sit idly by while you strip this poor woman nude. At least grant her a shred of decency. She's already lost everything else."

"Okay. Okay." I rose and stalked out to the hall. I closed the door and leaned against the side wall, crossing my arms. Decency? Seconds from now, Tim and the other DEO would carry Gail's naked body and throw it into the furnace, not caring where they touched her. Was that decency? Sing's inconsistency didn't make sense. Maybe Gail's speech had pricked Sing's emotions—the very thing I warned her to avoid.

A moment later, Sing opened the door and entered the

hallway. She grabbed my forearm, and pulled me into a brisk walk. "Let's go."

We hurried out the Reapers' entrance and onto the sidewalk. The questions burned in my mind, but now probably wasn't a good time to ask them. With a few hours to kill before the morning train, maybe we could sit at the station's coffeehouse and talk over a strong brew.

As we walked, we passed a convenience store sandwiched between a pawn shop and a plasma collection center. A ragged area of blood smeared the concrete a few feet in front of the door.

Sing stopped and pointed at an awning over the store's entry. "This is where I found Brennan. His ghost was floating under that canopy."

I studied the bloody area—the size of a blanket and still tacky. The bandits' daggers had done their dirty work. "Level ones and twos like the feeling of being covered. Remember Miriam had an umbrella."

"Good to know." Sing marched on, a hand in each cloak pocket. As I walked at her side, I glanced all around, wary for Brennan's attackers. Every few seconds, I peeked at Sing's expression. It never changed—always sober, eyes set straight ahead. Something held her thoughts captive.

We passed closed businesses and vacant offices, sometimes enveloped in shadows and sometimes in light. In this section of the city, half of the streetlamps hadn't worked in months, maybe years. The history books say this was a thriving community in better times but quickly deteriorated, especially after the meltdown.

Decades ago, no one thought that a single nuclear reactor could devastate the entire world's infrastructure, though rumors of what the power company was actually doing in that plant might have explained it… if anyone in the building had survived the disaster to tell the tale.

When we reached the street that bordered the park, I pulled the watch from my pocket and squinted at the dark hands pointing at the almost unreadable numbers. "Twenty minutes after one. We have plenty of time to go around and avoid the woods. We can get some coffee and wait for the five o'clock train."

Sing studied my watch again. "Is that a family heirloom?"

"A gift from a friend." I closed the lid and slid the watch back to my pocket. "Why?"

"Just wondering. Not many people have a watch like that anymore."

"I guess I'm not like many people. Kind of unconventional, I suppose."

"I like unconventional." Sing looked toward the train station, still too far away to see. "Why does it leave so early in the morning?"

"To give Reapers a chance to sleep during the ride. People tend to die at night."

She nodded. "I should have guessed."

"We could get a nap and catch the eleven o'clock, but that's a low-speed that won't get us home until late evening."

"Look!" Sing pointed across the street.

A cloaked figure carrying a wooden staff came into view, a hood over his eyes as he strode boldly into the park. The staff looked like a shepherd's crook, though bent in the middle and knobby on the curved end, an uncommon tool for a Reaper but not unheard of.

With his cloak's fibers dazzling, this Reaper must have

been carrying a dozen or more souls. As easy as he was to see, he would be bandit bait by the time he reached the center of the park.

I pulled Sing along and crossed the street. "Stay close."

"Are we going to help?" she whispered as she skulked at my side.

"Only if he needs us. Darken your cloak." After unplugging our clasps, we veered off the sidewalk and onto a narrow, tree-lined path leading into the park. Step by step, darkness enfolded us. Since every sane citizen knew to avoid this area at night, the authorities kept the streetlamps off to save electricity, leaving the park a haunt for bandits.

Still visible ahead, the mysterious Reaper marched on, clacking his staff on the walkway as if trying to invite attention. At this pace, we would emerge at the other end of the park in five minutes, and the danger would be over. Maybe the show of confidence intimidated the bandits. In another couple of hundred steps, we would know.

A glint of metal flew toward the Reaper. In a flash of arms and cloak, he swung his staff and knocked a dagger away. Several more daggers swished through the air. Like a whirling top, he blocked each one, his staff a blur. When the Reaper stopped spinning, the cloak's hood fell back. Long black hair spilled out, revealing the Reaper's Asian features, soft and feminine.

I stopped in my tracks. "It's Shanghai!"

Several voices erupted from the woods, each one echoing her name. Turning slowly, she probed the area with a menacing glare. For a brief second, she looked straight at Sing and me before continuing her scan.

"Shouldn't we help her?" Sing asked.

"Best to stay hidden until she needs us."

Shanghai dipped down, scooped up three daggers, and flung them one at a time, two to her left, one to her right. Each throw ended with a *thunk* and a cry of pain.

A weighted net flew over her head and knocked her to the ground. At least ten dark-hooded bandits stalked toward her in a semicircle, approaching cautiously with daggers drawn. Shanghai crouched under the weight, motionless, her eyes following her assailants.

"Phoenix!" Sing hissed. "She needs us!"

"Let's go. We'll use trip wires. Remember your training." Sing and I prowled toward the ambush site, both of us reeling out throw lines from the spools on our belts.

Shanghai rose slowly and grabbed the netting. Her shimmering movement locked the bandits' stares on her, obviously an intentional diversion. She knew we were coming.

After Sing and I handed each other the weighted ends of our lines, I popped all seven smoke capsules from my belt. Sing pulled out hers and gave me a nod.

When we drew within range, I whispered, "Now!"

CHAPTER SIX

I THREW MY CAPSULES, scattering them at the bandits' feet. Sing did the same. Plumes of smoke erupted around their legs. Holding tightly to our line weights, we split up and ran toward opposite ends of the semicircle.

As our lines reeled out, the spools squealed. We held the lines at knee level and swept them through the sea of legs. Shouts pierced the smoky air. Bodies toppled. Thuds and cracks sounded. Obscenities flew, punctuated by coughs.

Sing and I dropped our spools, grabbed the net, and threw it off Shanghai. In a blur of feet and fists, she flew at the bandits. I joined in, followed by Sing. I drove a foot into a man's side, cracking his ribs. Sing leaped and kicked a bandit in the face. As she dropped to the ground, she thrust an elbow down into his sternum, making him crumple.

We punched and kicked our way through the crowd. In the haze, Sing looked like a ghost herself, seemingly flying from bandit to bandit with her arms and legs twirling like propellers. A few bandits scrambled away, while others fell to our blows.

Another figure wearing a shimmering cloak joined the fray. Although slower than the three of us, he did his share of damage, punching one bandit in the nose and leg sweeping a second.

Soon, a breeze thinned out the smoke. Our Reaper foursome, now including Mex, stood in the midst of six or seven groaning and writhing bodies. Two bandits limped into the darkness like whipped dogs. Sing rubbed her elbow, though she showed no other signs of pain.

Mex, now illuminated by his cloak, bowed toward Shanghai. "It was a pleasure doing business with you."

"Is that so?" Shanghai raised her hood, shading her eyes. "You were late. If not for these two, I might have been sliced like a pizza."

Mex waved a hand. "I saw them coming. I knew they'd help."

"Whatever." Shanghai turned toward me and set her hands on her hips. As her expression warmed to a welcoming smile, her sparkling cloak billowed in the freshening breeze, revealing her athletic frame wrapped by form-fitting Reaper's attire. "Phoenix. It's been a long time."

I gave her a nod. "It has. Great to see you again."

"Same to you." Her gaze shifted to Sing, her smile intact though not quite as warm. "My thanks to both of you for your help, but let's save explanations for the station." She lifted each leg in turn. "I don't enjoy wading in bandit sewage."

I nodded again. "Agreed."

After Sing and I collected our spools and Shanghai found her staff, the four of us quick marched together, Shanghai's and Mex's cloaks providing enough light to see the path. I glanced again at Sing. Her smile spoke volumes. She was thrilled to have taken such a crucial role in helping

Shanghai. She performed flawlessly, and I hoped my own smile told her so.

When we arrived at the train depot, we slowed our pace and climbed the steps to the loading-platform level, then sauntered into *Jumpstart Café*, a coffee shop that catered to the city's night crawlers. A pair of gas-powered lanterns sat at each end of a service counter, and a third hung from the ceiling at the opposite side of the shop, making the place an oasis of indoor light. Since restaurants were allowed a higher gas ration than were home dwellers, such shops became haunts for human moths seeking the comfort of a warm glow.

As usual, the aroma of coffee blended with tobacco, beer, and sweat. Four of the café's six stools were occupied by old, badly shaven men hunched over steaming dark brews, as if inhaling the vapor might revive a long-lost dream. With their elbows resting on the sticky counter and their clothes a mishmash of castoff jeans and sweat suits, these hobos would likely beg for loose change through their remaining years. Their dreams of a better life would never come true.

A pair of hookers dressed in short, tight skirts sat on the other two stools, their rouged faces looking bored as they alternated between sips of coffee and drags on cigarettes. Five small tables lined two of the walls, all occupied by the typical customers—police officers, street sweepers, and utility workers. There would be no room in this café for four tired Reapers to sit.

After using the restrooms, we each ordered a *Vat*—the shop's euphemism for their extra-large size. While we waited for the coffee, a hum outside announced the arrival of the high-speed train.

I walked to the picture window facing the tracks. The sleek cars rolled to a stop. When the doors slid open, several men and women filed out to the loading platform, most looking bleary-eyed as they half staggered to the stairs leading to ground level. This was our train, and it would stay here until its departure at five.

Sing joined me at the window. "I wonder where they're going in the middle of the night."

I shrugged. "Never bothered to think about it."

"They look so tired." She leaned forward until her nose touched the glass. "It's like they're programmed, not really thinking about what they're doing."

A dime-sized medallion slipped past her tunic's opening, attached to a thin chain around her neck. The silvery disk sparkled, as if energized from within. She wasn't wearing it earlier when she opened her shirt for the soul transfer. Maybe she had it in her pocket. No matter. It wasn't any of my business.

When our Vats arrived, I nodded at the train. "Let's sit in our car. Plenty of seats, and it'll smell better."

The four of us walked out the café's back door to the loading platform and passed by the ticket machines without a second glance. Reapers always rode for free as long as we occupied our reserved car. Other passengers, few though they might be, were often scared of us—a reasonable fear considering the reputation of some of our clan. Most Reapers displayed a mean-spirited aloofness that reflected their hatred of their ball-and-chain service.

After tromping to the last car, we slid into a pair of bench seats facing each other, Sing at my right, next to the window.

Sitting at the window across from Sing, Shanghai laid

her staff on the floor and lowered her hood. She pushed back her dark locks, revealing a brown birthmark on the side of her neck. Oval in shape and the size of a penny, it was typical for Reapers, a mark with special properties that proved our genetic ability to reap souls, though the size and placement differed with each Reaper. The Council learned of my mark when I was three years old. That's when the ball and chain became mine to drag.

When we settled, I touched Sing's shoulder. "Shanghai, this is Singapore, better known as Sing."

Shanghai smiled. "Pleased to meet you, Sing. I heard from my trainer that you excelled in physical combat. Thanks for proving his opinion when I needed you."

"You're welcome." Sing gave her a polite nod. "I am honored by his assessment."

I kept my face expressionless. Sing and Shanghai had the same trainer? That was news. My trainer was a drunk. I had to learn most of my skills on my own.

Mex extended his hand toward Sing. "I'm Mexico City, but that's a mouthful. Everyone calls me Mex."

After they shook hands, I sipped my coffee, strong and bitter. Perfect. As soon as the others had sipped theirs, I leaned closer to Shanghai. "What was that bandit-fishing expedition all about?"

Shanghai winked at Mex. "We had a deal. I transferred a soul to him in exchange for help with clearing out the park. I was tired of hiking around it. Let the bandits find someplace else to terrorize."

"And now I made quota." Mex touched his valve and looked at me. "Sorry about skipping out on our date with the level two. My energy is just about kaput. I didn't think I could handle it."

"It worked out all right. I reaped the ghost." I nodded toward Sing. "First Gateway trip for her, so I'm showing her the ropes."

"Good to have an experienced guide." Shanghai laid a hand on my knee. "I heard that you two have bordering districts and your apartments practically rub shoulders. Is that true?"

"It's true." I glanced at Shanghai's hand, still on my knee. "She's just across the alley from me. We could probably jump from one fire escape to the other if we wanted to."

Shanghai pushed my leg. "I would love that. I could hop over to see you, and we could talk all night. No one would ever know." She rolled her hand into a fist. "Hang the solitary-confinement rules. We're not felons, right?"

I took a long sip of coffee. Shanghai's complaint echoed the thoughts of many district hounds, but words never changed reality. "True, but it would be a distraction, just like they say. Sometimes I can barely feel the death alarms even when I'm alone."

Shanghai slid her hand into mine and locked gazes with me. "That's what I like about you, Phoenix. You're the most dedicated Reaper in Chicago. I'm glad we're finally on the same train to the Gateway."

"Wow!" Mex said. "What award are you shooting for, Shanghai? Bootlicker of the year?"

"No, freak." Shanghai elbowed his ribs, then turned back to me. "I'm serious. Ever since we graduated, I've wanted to tell you how much I admire you. I heard how you rescued ten people from an apartment fire last year. Most Reapers would have poured fuel on the flames while waiting for ghosts to pop out. But not you. You're the real deal. You get your souls honestly."

I shifted my stare to our clasped hands. Mex was probably right. Something more than a Reaper-to-Reaper encouragement speech was going on. "Thanks for the pat on the back."

"No problem." Shanghai withdrew her hand. "I just wanted to give you a heads-up in advance."

"A heads-up? What do you mean? In advance of what?"

Shanghai lowered her voice, as if someone might be listening. "I got recruited by an Owl for a special reaping. I'll be a Cardinal by the end of the week."

"An Owl?" I glanced briefly at Sing. "Is her name Alex?"

Shanghai blinked. "Oh. You know her. That's good. Anyway, during the reaping, I'll stay in an on-site facility, and then I'll move to a cool condo in a safer neighborhood. After that, my reapings will be assigned to me. No more hunting down death alarms. And best of all…" She looked at Mex and Sing before continuing. "Best of all, I can choose a roommate to come and live with me, and I'd like you to be my roommate."

I drew my head back. "I… I don't know what to say."

"Well, think about the benefits. No more wandering through the city streets searching for tragedy. No more fighting bandits." Her full lips pursed into a comely pucker. "And no more long and lonely nights."

My ears turned hot. "That's kind of… well… a private matter, don't you think?"

Shanghai glanced at Sing and Mex once more. "Oh. I see. Well, even if news gets around, it won't exactly hurt your reputation. But who cares about street gossip, right?"

"My reputation? What do you mean? And what do the gossipers say about me?"

Mex cleared his throat. "What she's trying to say, Romeo—the word on you is that you're not AC or DC. You're a flatliner. Your pulse wouldn't pop even in a porn shop."

I tried to speak, but my throat caught. My ears burned hotter than ever.

"Just shut up!" Sing said. "Both of you!"

"Why?" Mex grinned. "It's true until he proves otherwise."

"Then we'll prove it." Sing leaned over and kissed me on the lips, warmly, tenderly. As she pulled away, she ran her soft fingers along my cheek and whispered, "There's more where that came from."

I felt my mouth drop open, but I couldn't help it. My heart pounded. A tingle raced from my lips to my shoulders and down my spine. I could barely breathe.

Mex grabbed my wrist. "I take it back. He's at about two hundred beats per minute. Definitely not a corpse."

I jerked my arm away, almost spilling my coffee. "Of course I'm not a corpse!" The shout surprised me. Getting worked up about Mex's joke made the embarrassment even worse. Still, Sing's words echoed in my mind. *There's more where that came from.* The thought kept my heart racing.

Shanghai firmed her lips, obviously trying to keep from laughing. "Well, I'm glad to know that your body is fully functional." She touched my knee again. "Seriously, Phoenix, I've been alone for more than three years. You know what it's like." A genuine smile replaced her smirk. "Remember the talks we used to have after our training fights? From the time we were both seven years old, we would sneak out of our rooms and meet in the pantry because we weren't allowed to have friends. We'd munch on crackers while we nursed each other's wounds, even though we had inflicted them ourselves, and we'd talk about our fighting techniques and how we would beat each other next time."

Her brow shot upward. "Oh! And our pets! You had a field mouse you caught in a dresser drawer, and I had a bunny I rescued from a cat. And we had to leave them at home when they took us away, so on cold nights, especially if our trainers had just shaved our heads, it felt good to talk about how soft and warm our pets were. And then we'd talk about our families and how much..." Her voice faltered. "How much we missed them." She gazed at me with teary eyes. "Do you remember?"

Her words deflated my anger and calmed my voice. "I remember. Those were good days."

She sniffed, blinking through her tears. "I'd like those days to come back, so when I become a Cardinal, I'd like to request you as my roommate, but I won't unless you agree."

I looked at Sing. She folded her hands in her lap, her expression blank. She needed no words. She didn't like the situation one bit. "Give me some time to think about it." I infused as much sincerity into my tone as I could. "I mean, I'd like those days to come back, too, but I have... well... a lot going on." I wasn't lying. It would be great to be with Shanghai instead of sneaking around the city streets scavenging medicines and sitting alone waiting for my neighbors to die, but the Mollys of my district needed me.

I rubbed my pewter ring with my thumb. And my covenant wouldn't allow such freedom... or comfort.

"That's fine." Shanghai's smile wilted. "When I get promoted to Cardinal, I'll come looking for you. Maybe you'll get things straightened out by then."

"I know what's eating him," Mex said. "Word on the street says the Fitzpatricks were hauled to the corrections camp by the river. He's probably plotting a way to rescue them."

"The camp? That's where Alex told me to go." Shanghai pinched her hood. "I'm supposed to show up this afternoon with an empty cloak."

"A rash of deaths at a centralized location?" I asked.

"That's exactly what she said." Shanghai furrowed her brow. "Did she recruit you?"

I nodded. "She gave me twenty-four hours to decide."

"Two Reapers?" Shanghai's frown deepened. "They're clearing out the whole camp, aren't they?"

"Clearing it out?" Sing said. "Do you mean…"

Mex slashed a finger across his throat. "Terminating the residents. Punching their tickets to the afterlife. Killing them is cheaper than feeding them."

"And I'm supposed to reap the convicts." Shanghai grasped her cloak and shook it. "I feel like a sewage drain."

"Why so surprised?" I asked. "What did you think you were going to do there?"

"When she said a rash of deaths, I thought she meant ten, maybe twenty. You know, execute the worst criminals. But since she wants to add you within twenty-four hours…" Her cheeks reddened. "Wow!"

"So what are you going to do?" Sing asked.

Another Reaper shuffled into the car, his hood up and his head low. When he settled into a bench seat a few rows away, Shanghai answered in a whisper. "I'm going to reap the souls, of course. Someone's got to do it. Who can stop the Council, anyway? And when the prisoners die, which Reapers would you want to be there? I don't mean to toot my own horn, but I can reap twenty in an hour if I have to, and no bandit's going to take one from me. That's another reason I staged that little show of strength in the park. Word will get around that I'm not going to back down from anyone, and the souls in my cloak are going to get safe passage to the Gateway. I want everyone in Chicago to know about me. A potential bandit will be a dead bandit."

"Brava!" Mex clapped his hands. "Brilliant speech!"

"Stuff it, Mex. I'm not looking for approval." Shanghai breathed out a sigh. "Listen, Phoenix, most of the people in the camp are criminals. You've reaped at the executions, right? It's not like it's fun reaping murderers and rapists and carrying around their foul souls in our cloaks, but we're doing the city a service keeping their ghosts off the streets. It's our job."

"I know, I know." I shook my head. "But *most* isn't enough. Colm and his family aren't criminals. I have to get them out of there."

"Technically, they *are* criminals," Mex said. "I heard they got caught with unauthorized drugs."

I growled under my breath. "It's not a crime to try to save a little girl's life."

Mex raised his hands. "Look, I'm just stating the facts. What they did is illegal. You can argue all you want about whether the law is right or wrong, but we Reapers still have to pick up the souls, no matter what. We can't wait for justice before we service a soul."

"No," I said, "but it doesn't mean we can't have both."

Shanghai squinted. "Both?"

"Justice and service." I pressed my lips together. I wanted to say more, but I couldn't be sure Shanghai and Mex would be on my side. The fewer people who knew what I was thinking, the better.

Mex laughed. "Phoenix, you're such a boy scout. You hope for the impossible." He shrugged. "You'll never get it, but at least you have ideals."

"And that's why people in his district trust him," Sing said. "They know he's there to help them, not just to do a job."

Heat rose to my cheeks. If Sing knew that the contraband was actually mine, would she still support me? In any case, there seemed to be just one real option, and Sing might be the only Reaper I could trust, at least for now. "Shanghai, I guess you're right. If people are going to die, we need to be there. I'll go to the camp."

Sing swung her head toward me. "What?"

I whispered, "Just trust me. I know what I'm doing."

Shanghai pumped a fist. "That's great! You and I will make an amazing team. We'll carry a truckload of souls to the Gateway, and no bandit will dare come near us."

"Maybe so, but I have an idea I'm working on. I'm going to see if I can swing a deal with Alex."

"Why would she make a deal with you?" Mex asked.

"Let's just say she owes me a favor."

"Okay..." Shanghai ran a finger along the rim of her coffee cup. "But what about the roommate question?"

I leaned close to her. "What are your accommodations at the camp?"

"There's a building in one corner that used to be a dorm of some kind, and it has suites, like motel rooms. You know, two bedrooms with a bathroom in between.

Anyway, most of them aren't used anymore, but for reapings they keep a suite ready for two Reapers. And there's camera surveillance. After all, it's a prison compound."

"Then we'll be suite mates," I said. "And we'll insist on privacy. No cameras allowed."

Sing's mouth dropped open. "Phoenix?"

"Well..." Shanghai settled back in her seat. "That's an unexpected turn of events."

Mex withdrew his valve adapter tube and swatted my knee with it. "So much for wanting to keep your distance."

"Back off." I kicked his shin. "That's not what I have in mind."

Shanghai leaned close again. "So what *do* you have in mind?"

Another Reaper walked into the car and sat at an empty bench. The first Reaper had fallen asleep leaning against a window, but the new one shifted toward us, his hood shadowing his eyes. He seemed to be looking at Mex, but after Mex's story about a Reaper trying to hunt him down, it could have been my imagination. Either way, a hunter wouldn't bother four Reapers sitting together.

"I don't want to talk about it here," I said, "but if you trust me, then play along, at least for now. If Alex doesn't agree to my proposal, then the deal's off."

"I'm in," Shanghai said. "How could I lose? No more lonely nights."

Mex slid his adapter tube back into his cloak pocket. "I wish I could help, but they wouldn't let a roamer close enough to the camp to spit into it. I'll be busting tail trying to get souls to finish my last cycle, and Shanghai won't be around to barter with."

"I'll figure out something. We'll work together to make

sure you get enough." I turned to Sing. "You're directly involved in my plan. Are you in?"

"I don't know, Phoenix." Wringing her hands, she looked out the window at the Chicago skyline. "Can we talk about it privately?"

"Sure. No problem." Sing's vibes felt cold. And why not? She probably thought I was ready to abandon my district, that I was trashing my principles. And might she be just a tad jealous? If so, I could easily squash that feeling. I just needed a chance to tell her the rest of my plan, but not with Mex listening.

After four more Reapers entered the car and settled into their seats, Mex tossed his empty cup to the floor and yawned. "I don't know about you guys, but I'm beat. We've got a few hours to kill, and I plan to snooze them away."

"Same here." Shanghai guzzled the rest of her coffee, leaned against the window, and closed her eyes, the cup still in her hand. "If anyone wakes me before we get there, I'll whack him with my staff."

"No worries." Mex drooped his head. Within seconds, both began breathing in heavy, rhythmic pulses. Like most Reapers, they had learned the art of sleeping whenever and wherever they could.

I whispered to Sing, "I guess we'd better sleep, too."

"Sleep?" Her brow dipped low. "If you *can* sleep."

"What do you mean by that?"

She looked me in the eye, her whisper sharp. "Didn't that kiss mean anything to you?"

I glanced at Shanghai and Mex. They hadn't stirred. "I thought it was just to shut them up."

"It wasn't." She scooted closer to the window. "But if you want to shack up with Shanghai, that's fine with me."

"Wait a minute." I glanced at the Reaper who had stared at us earlier. He was now leaning against a window, his hood covering his face. "I know it sounded like that, but there's more. I want you to come with us. All three of us in the suite with you and Shanghai sharing her bedroom. Alex doesn't need to know. That's why I don't want cameras."

"Oh." Her brow lifted. "But why do you want me there?"

"To help me get Molly's family out. I need someone who has the skills to spring them, someone who can fly under the radar. Shanghai and I will probably be busy reaping, so I'll need you to do the sneaking around. I'm not sure what you'll do yet. We'll have to play it by ear."

"What about our districts?"

"Alex will probably get a replacement for mine, and Mex can handle yours. You heard him. He'll be glad to be a hound again. It's an easy way for him to finish his last cycle. I just don't want him to know where you'll be. That's why I didn't spill the details. We can make up an excuse for your temporary absence."

Sing gazed into my eyes, her features softening. "I'm sorry, Phoenix."

"Sorry? You mean you won't do it?"

"No, I'll do it. I'll be glad to do it. And maybe the people I know can help us." She swallowed. "I'm sorry for not trusting you. I said that people trust you, but I didn't for a while. So… I'm sorry."

I looked into her eyes—weary and wet. "No problem. I'm sure it sounded pretty strange."

"It did, but I didn't want to say much. You know. The prudish thing. If you really want to be with Shanghai—"

"I don't!" I cringed inside. That came out too harshly. Still, it communicated my thoughts. I had no romantic feelings for Shanghai or any other Reaper for that matter. At least I couldn't let any feelings break through. Misty was waiting, so I had to wait. Besides, Reapers had to construct an impenetrable shell. Witnessing tragic deaths and the resulting wounds of savage grief had taught me that long ago.

I slid the pewter ring up and down on my finger. Mex was right. In some ways, I really was a flatliner. Although Sing's kiss had stirred my emotions, I could control them. I *had* to control them.

After a deep sigh, I whispered, "I didn't mean to bark at you."

Sing smiled, though she appeared a bit wounded. "It's okay. I understand."

"You will understand… eventually. After you handle a few dozen more deaths, your nerves will get frayed, too."

"I believe that. They're already unraveling." Sing glanced at Shanghai. "When are you going to tell Shanghai about me coming?"

"As soon as the three of us are alone." I stifled a yawn. "Think you can sleep now?"

She laughed softly. "Just try to stop me."

"Couldn't stop Mex." I nodded at him. With his chin nearly touching his chest, his neck's angle looked uncomfortable at best. "At least Shanghai's got the window to lean on. I'm used to riding alone, so I usually use the window as my pillow."

"Here." Sing angled her body toward me. "Lean your head against mine."

"Uh… all right." When our heads touched, her curls fell

across my face. They tickled my nose, but I didn't bother to brush them away. I'd be asleep in no time. Besides, her hair smelled nice, like flowers in a meadow, not overwhelming, just a gentle blend of petals and grasslands—sweet and natural.

I took in the aroma and let my mind drift away. Sing's shoulder pressed against mine, providing a sturdy foundation. And she was like that—strong, supportive, someone I could trust without reservation. I had been stupid to question her motives earlier. She was new, scared, vulnerable. She didn't have a deceptive bone in her body.

Rumors about her history came to mind, played out in mental images. I let my thoughts melt into the daydream. Thinking about Sing would be a pleasure, even if the details of her life were sketchy. I had pieced a lot of it together from the gossip network, throwing out whatever Mex didn't corroborate. Although Mex's character had a few rough spots, he was usually a reliable source of information.

One fact was certain. Everyone knew about Sing's mother's reputation. Tokyo was considered the most powerful Reaper the world had ever known. She could enter the ghost realm and reap a level three without batting an eye. That power, along with her acting prowess, fostered distrust among the Council members, giving rise to a popular theory that they conspired to bring about her untimely death.

As I allowed sleep to overtake me, the images morphed into a dream. Sing knelt at a graveside, her hands covering her face as she wept. A setting sun, veiled by haze, cast long tree-shaped shadows across her kneeling form, painting her dark dress an even darker shade. Block letters etched the tragedy across the tombstone: *Takahashi Fujita (aka Tokyo—Reaper Divine)*. Below that, Japanese characters filled the remaining space, most likely spelling out the name and perhaps dates of birth and death.

A black man wearing a dark suit spread a cloak over Sing's shoulders and knelt beside her. "Your mother would have wanted you to have it."

"I don't want it." Sing shrugged the cloak off. As it slid down her back, she lowered her hands and looked at the man. "Being a Reaper is what killed her."

"No, sweetheart. Her willingness to sacrifice herself for those she loved led to her death, but being a Reaper did not kill her." He picked up the cloak and draped it over his arm. "I'm not sure you'll have any choice about taking the cloak. When you hear my news, you might understand."

She squinted at him. "What news?"

He pushed a finger through her hair, brushing back her signature curls. "The ultraviolet tests came back on that mark. I didn't tell you while we were waiting to see if Fujita would survive, because—"

"You mean I'm a Reaper?" Sing pointed at herself. "Me?"

"Why are you so surprised? It doesn't always skip a generation."

Sing rose to her feet. "But I'm almost fifteen. The marks are supposed to be there from birth."

"It's probably been there all along. Your hair's as thick as your mother's, and your skin's almost as dark as mine. Genetics kept your birthmark hidden."

Sing backed away. "But you can keep it a secret, right? A father can still hide a minor child's medical records, can't he?"

"Not this record. The only facility qualified to make the determination automatically reports all positive tests to the Gatekeeper's Council. They already know."

"Then why did they even do the test? We shouldn't have asked for it!"

"I didn't. The doctor who ordered the biopsy didn't tell me he was screening for anything else. I thought he was just ruling out cancer. But since I had to bribe so many people to get the simplest tests, I couldn't make too many demands."

"But..." Sing stared at her father, tears coursing down her cheeks. "But I don't *want* to be a Reaper."

"Sweetheart..." He reached around and draped the cloak over her shoulders again. With loving hands, he fastened the clasp and smoothed out the folds. "It's in your blood. There's a lot of good you can do."

While looking at the clasp, she touched her sternum just below her throat, exposed by the V-neck dress. "Will I have to get one of those valves?"

He nodded. "And you'll have to go through an accelerated training course that lasts about a year and a half. Most Reapers are taken when they're very young, so you'll have a lot of catching up to do. At least you already have a cloak spun from your mother's hair, so the close genetics should allow you to reap with it. And you won't have to go through the head shavings to get a cloak of your own made."

Sing's chin quivered. "So I'll have to leave you."

"For twenty years, yes. Then you can decide whether or not to continue as a Reaper."

Sing grasped the cloak with both hands and pulled it close. New sobs broke through. She hugged herself and twisted her body back and forth, making the cloak spin. "I'll... I'll miss you, Daddy."

He wrapped his arms around her, stopping her motion. "And I'll miss you, little flower. But I'll do everything I can to help you, even if I have to do it in secret. I promise."

As they cried together, fog blew across the gravesite. The scene faded to gray, then black.

I blinked my eyes open. The train had left the station and was now rumbling along the tracks, rocking from side to side as it negotiated a curve. Sing's hair swayed with the motion. Neither of us had moved a muscle, nor had Shanghai, though Mex's head bobbed with the train's jostling. They slept on, oblivious to the brightening sky—the sun veiled, as always, by the meltdown's vaporous shield.

The dream scattered into fragments in my memory, though Sing's turmoil-twisted expression stayed front and center, and her sobs echoed like a dying lament. Of course, her father's face wasn't clear in the dream. I didn't know what he looked like. According to the gossip, he died the day after Sing left for training school, so I would never find out. What was worse, his promise died with him. It seemed that Sing had become an orphan indeed.

I crossed my eyes and looked at Sing's head, trying to penetrate the curls to get a glimpse of the birthmark, but her hair was too thick, just as the dream had said. Who could tell how true it was? Mex surely told the story exactly as he had heard it, but whenever mysterious deaths were involved, cover-ups abounded. Someone was always hiding something.

I let my gaze drift to her chest. The chain led behind her tunic, the medallion now hidden from sight. Farther down, her hands lay folded in her lap. The dream provided a good reminder—Sing was really a lonely orphan. Tragic circumstances threw her into this dangerous job against her will and after only a year and a half of training. No wonder she didn't know all the tricks of the trade, and no wonder she was so nervous about rule breaking and intimate contact. She was just trying to survive.

After taking a deep breath, I shut my eyes and nestled closer to her. In spite of the rules and my flatline ways, I would be her friend. From now on, that would be my sacred duty, and nothing could keep me from fulfilling it.

CHAPTER SEVEN

SCREECHING TRAIN WHEELS woke me from a dreamless daze. On the opposite bench, Shanghai stretched and yawned. Mex was already standing in the aisle, his eyes bleary and his face ashen.

Shanghai scooped her staff from the floor and used it to vault up and slide toward the aisle. "Rise and shine, you two."

Sing pulled her head away from mine, blinking and smacking her lips. I looked out the window at the gloomy sky looming over the forest. Two outhouses stood a few paces beyond the far side of a raised wooden platform, the only structures in the remote station. A sign with twin two-by-four standards had been nailed sloppily to one edge of the platform. Its black hand-painted letters read *Gateway Depot #3*. Since only Reapers boarded and disembarked here, no one bothered with constructing ticket counters or courtesy shelters.

"Looks like rain," Sing said.

"Let's hope not. Fallout rain makes the souls jumpy." I rose and stretched. "The concentration usually isn't as bad in the rural areas, but you never know."

Sing nodded at my pocket. "What time is it?"

As I reached for the watch in my trousers, my hand

brushed across a cloak pocket. It was empty. But was it supposed to be? Wasn't something there when I went to sleep?

My mouth dried out. The syringe! I had forgotten all about it. It would be insane to bring it to the Gateway. Maybe I moved it without remembering.

I searched around my seat and reached into all my pockets but found only the souls' photo sticks in the other cloak pocket and the watch in my pants pocket. I pulled out my watch and read the face. "It's seven-twenty."

"You look kind of pale." Sing said. "Is something wrong?"

"Maybe." I looked at the aisle. The Reaper who had stared at us earlier stood at the end of the line waiting for the door to open. If he stole the syringe to fence it at the shroud, he was risking a lot by taking it with him to the Gateway. I averted my eyes. Best to just let him keep it.

I gave Sing a weak smile. "It's probably nothing."

We pushed behind Shanghai and Mex. When the car door opened and our foursome tromped onto the platform, Shanghai blocked us with her staff. The other Reapers shuffled past and trooped down the two steps that ended at a gravel path leading to the Gateway depot. A few took advantage of the outhouses before beginning a slow march along the path.

Once we were alone and the train began its squealing departure, Shanghai lowered her staff. "We'll let the others deposit their souls first, just in case."

"In case what?" Sing asked.

Mex raised his hood. A slight tic in his face gave away his fear. "In case they give me a hard time for the transferred soul. Some of the Gateway attendants get miffed if their data doesn't match what we're carrying, and they're more likely to punish me if a bunch of Reapers are around."

"To set an example," Shanghai said. "Besides, there aren't enough Gateway stations for all of us."

After we took turns using the outhouses, a light drizzle began to fall. I nodded toward the path. "At least let's get under tree cover and let the branches leech out some of the contaminants. Then we can take our time."

"How long till the train comes to pick us up?" Sing asked.

"About an hour and a half. We'll be back without a problem."

I led the way along the path, Sing immediately behind me. Shanghai stayed close, but Mex trailed by several yards, grimacing with every step as the gravel crunched under our shoes on our way to the checkpoint.

With tall oaks creating an arching canopy over our heads, the drizzle altered to larger, more sporadic drops that left splotches on our cloaks. Since we were plodding slowly, we would probably get pretty damp and give my captured souls more discomfort. I checked my clasp—unplugged. Good. I preferred avoiding Crandyke's complaints.

The path narrowed and bent to the right, bringing into view a black wrought-iron gate and a uniformed female attendant about fifty paces away. Designed to match the look of the Gateway as well as our clasps, including the joined hands at the fastening point, the gate was more ornamental than functional. Since the frame attached to a head-high chain-link fence that encircled the fifty-acre grounds, a potential intruder could climb in just about anywhere, though few would be bold enough to venture close to the mysteries that lay at the center of the compound.

About fifteen paces in front of the gate, an old man sat on a stump at the side of the path. With his shoulders slumped, he hooked an arm around the base of a picket sign that read *Reapers Beware. The Gateway Leads Souls to Torture.* With his other hand, he extended a pamphlet, a multipage tract no one ever bothered to take.

I nodded as I approached. "Good morning, Bill."

"Morning, Phoenix." From beneath bushy gray eyebrows, Bill stared at Sing, his head swiveling as she drew close. Sing kept her gaze low, obviously avoiding eye contact, but when she passed by, she took the pamphlet and stuffed it into her cloak pocket.

"Her name is Singapore," I called as I continued walking. "First cycle."

"I know who she is." Bill picked up a compact umbrella and opened it over his head. "I have my contacts."

"Yeah, yeah, I know. That rag you call a newsletter."

When we stopped at the gate, I stood in front of the attendant—Erin, a thirtyish redhead who wore navy blue coveralls over her trim form. "This is the easy part, Sing. Erin will read your birthmark DNA and send a message ahead so the attendants will know you're coming. You'll see why when we get there. She'll also check your energy level and refill your blood reservoir if you need it."

"Okay," Sing said with a less-than-confident nod. "I'll watch and learn."

Erin reached a hand toward me. "Valve first."

I spread my tunic opening. Using a fingertip, she depressed my valve, making it protrude, and inserted a silver pen-like probe. When she twisted it, a sharp tingle ran into my chest reservoir and from there to my heart. Within a few seconds, a meter on the probe's side flashed.

"Your energy level is twenty-five percent." Erin withdrew the probe and touched my clasp. "How's your blood supply?"

"Pretty low. I reaped a level two and an execution. They're always a drain."

"Sounds like a tough cycle." Erin's tone matched her expression—mechanical and indifferent—as she tapped the information into a computer tablet hanging on the gate. "Birthmark check."

I leaned over and rolled up a pant leg, exposing the birthmark on my calf. While Erin drew the probe close to the mark, I looked at Sing. "It's routine, but they want to make sure no one is posing as a Reaper. Sometimes we have new checkpoint workers and, of course, new Reapers."

"Routine for you," Mex said. "I know a Reaper who has the mark on his butt."

Erin shook her head. "I know who you're talking about. It's not a pretty sight." She pressed a button on the probe. A light flashed from the tip, sending a narrow beam over my mark—an oblong brown splotch just above my ankle. After a few seconds, the mark glowed purple. "Positive identification." Erin tapped an entry into the tablet. "Your image will be ready when you arrive."

"Image?" Sing asked.

I winked. "You'll see."

Erin opened a short drawer embedded in the gate and withdrew a syringe. "Arm, please."

I rolled up my sleeve. Erin wrapped an elastic band around my upper arm and jabbed the needle into the crook.

While more raindrops fell from the sodden branches, she pulled back on the plunger and filled the syringe.

"How's your blood supply?" I asked Sing.

"Fine, I think. My quota's low, so I don't have to worry about it yet."

"Mine's wasted." Mex let out a long yawn. "I need blood and energy."

"Same here." Shanghai began rolling up her sleeve. "I'm carrying thirteen souls, so—"

"Twelve," Mex said.

"Right. Twelve. I've been a busy girl."

Erin handed me a cotton ball. While I pressed it on my vein, she pulled out the needle and inserted it into my clasp. As she filled the tiny reservoir, it grew warm and began to glow with a reddish hue.

Sing folded her arms in front and furrowed her brow, apparently less than excited about the prospect of being probed and poked by Erin.

"Done." Erin pulled out the needle, not quite emptying the syringe. "I'll store the rest in your blood-bank account."

I rolled down my sleeve. "Blood-bank account?"

"It's new." Erin inserted the needle into a tube and ejected the rest of my blood into it. "We've developed a detection device that can track your blood from a long distance. I can't explain the science behind it, but it has something to do with a Reaper's DNA. Soon we'll be able to find our Reapers wherever they go."

"Another way to keep us in line?"

"No, Phoenix. It's for your safety. You'll wear a signal beacon that you'll receive sometime during your next cycle. Since you'll be able to remove the beacon whenever you want to, you don't have to be paranoid about us tracking you when you want privacy. The point of the device is to find you if you get in trouble."

I gave a light shrug. "Sounds okay, then."

Shanghai took her turn, registering twenty-one percent, followed by Mex. When Erin announced his two-point-five-percent level, she shook her head but said nothing. After scanning their birthmarks, drawing their blood, and filling their reservoirs, she extended her hand toward Sing. "Next."

"I guess that's me." Sing spread her shirt's plackets. As she lifted her chin, she licked her lips. "I'm ready."

"First timers." Erin shook her head again. "You'd think I was going to rip her heart out."

"Give her a break," I said. "The Jungle is tough for a rookie."

"If you say so." Erin lifted Sing's medallion, still attached to a chain around her neck. "What's this?"

"Just a keepsake," Sing said. "It's harmless."

"It might get in the way of the collection tube." Erin pulled the chain over Sing's head, momentarily catching it in her hair. "Pick it up on your way out."

"Okay. No problem."

Erin inserted the probe into Sing's valve and turned it. Sing flinched. When the probe flashed, Erin withdrew it and read the meter. "Eighty-five percent. You're above the normal range."

Sing released her shirt. "I think it's because... well, it's just that..."

"She reaped an old guy," I said. "Easy stuff. And like she said, her quota's low."

Erin gave me a skeptical look. "Again, if you say so."

"Then can we skip the blood?" Sing touched her clasp. "I'm sure it's fine."

"It's your life." Erin flicked on the probe's light. "Where's your birthmark?"

Sing used both hands to spread her hair apart between her ear and the top of her head. "It's kind of hard to see."

"This will read it." Erin pointed the beam at the spot. After a few seconds, the glow from Sing's head spilled over Erin's fingers. "Positive ID for Singapore."

When Erin drew the probe away, Sing flopped her arms at her sides. She looked at me and smiled, obviously relieved that the procedure had ended.

After entering the information into her tablet, Erin disengaged the gate's center bolt, slid it to the side, and walked the right-hand half of the gate to its fully open position.

Shanghai pushed her staff into Mex's hand. "You look like you need this more than I do."

"Thanks." Mex braced himself on the staff and plodded forward on the trail, now flattened grass instead of gravel.

As we followed, Bill called out, "Don't feed Leviathan! His hunger will never be sated. His thirst will never be quenched."

"Freak," Shanghai muttered. "Don't pay any attention to him, Sing. He makes flat-earthers look normal."

Sing raised her hood, shading her eyes, but said nothing. I lifted mine and walked at her side. Since the three of us might soon become suite mates, it would be best to temper Shanghai's words. "She's right, you know. Those Gateway deniers think if we stop reaping, the souls will travel where they're supposed to go without our help. But you've seen for yourself—"

"I know what they think." Sing kept her head low. "I might be a rookie, but I know what's going on in the world."

"Right. I guess you do." I cleared my throat. "Sorry."

She looked at me from her hood's shadow. "Sorry for what?"

"For assuming you didn't know what the deniers think. It was like calling you ignorant, but you wouldn't be a Reaper if you were ignorant."

"Thank you for saying that." Keeping her gaze on me, she slid her hand into mine and held it as we continued walking. "You don't mind, do you? No one's looking."

My cheeks blazed. I resisted the urge to look at Shanghai to verify Sing's claim. Either way, a fellow Reaper wouldn't report the violation of friendship rules this far from our districts, and Misty would probably be all right with it. We were just holding hands, like I might with a sister... if I had one. "I don't mind."

"Good." She shook her head, making her hood fall back. A few droplets pelted her curls, making them shimmer. Her eyes seemed brighter somehow, more alive, as if walking into the Gateway sanctuary had made her prettier than ever.

Soon, we crested a rise. Sing released my hand and folded both of hers at her back. The other Reapers came into view, walking toward us single file along a grassy clearing. With their hoods up and heads low, it was impossible to tell much about them, though they all appeared to be male. Their cloaks no longer shimmered, and they strode uphill with vigor. Apparently the Gateway had provided their recharge.

Once they passed by, we reached the bottom of the

slope and began trudging up another rise, still maintain-
ing Mex's crippled pace. I glanced from the path to Sing. I
hoped to catch a glimpse of her face the moment she saw
the Gateway depot for the first time.

When we made it to the top, Mex and Shanghai halted,
Mex breathing heavily. Sing and I joined them, and all four
of us stood abreast. A clearing spread out in a circle the
size of a city block with surrounding trees arching overtop
like a dome. Perfectly trimmed grass formed a ring around
a smaller circle of gray-streaked white marble. At the far
end of the marble, foot-high cylindrical pedestals stood
in a semicircle, seven in all, curved so that the ends of the
semicircle were closer to us than was the center.

Immediately behind the central pedestal, the represen-
tation of the Gateway shimmered. As tall as a house and as
wide as two city buses, this manifestation of pure energy
floated at the same level as the tops of the pedestals. Like a
fence attached to the gate, channels of light extended deep
into the forest in both directions.

I gave Sing another glance. Her jaw loosened, but her
lips stayed together.

"We have to leave our weapons belts here." I unfastened my belt and lowered it to the ground. Shanghai and
Sing did the same, while Mex set his belt and Shanghai's
staff down side by side.

Shanghai waved a hand. "Enough dawdling. Let's get
it done."

We walked toward the marble circle. As soon as
Shanghai's foot touched the surface, a shining hologram
took shape on the pedestal to the left of the central one. It
quickly formed into a perfect replica of Shanghai, cloak

and all, though semitransparent. When Mex followed, his image appeared on the pedestal to the left of Shanghai's.

Sing and I stepped onto the marble at the same time. My hologram appeared to the right of the central pedestal and Sing's to the right of mine. All four Reaper images stared straight ahead with their hoods raised and their cloaks shimmering, though waves of static rippled through mine, warping the presentation.

Sing's mouth dropped open. Her wide eyes completed her look of awestruck wonder.

As we walked on, light flashed at the central pedestal, and the image of a tall man formed. Cloaked in white, radiance poured from his face, making his features impossible to see.

"The Gatekeeper," I whispered to Sing. "Just a manifestation. He's not really here. But I suppose you guessed that."

"Don't worry about insulting me." Her whisper carried a distinct tremor. "Tell me everything you know."

"Well, this is one of five Gateway depots on this continent. The Council tried to locate them as centrally as possible, but there's more to it than just geography. There is one *real* Gateway, the place where every soul gets transferred to the afterlife. It's a central hub, and the depots are nodes in an energy network, sort of like an electrical grid with transfer stations. Those fence-like channels on both sides of this depot are like connecting wires. Anyway, the depots have to be set where there isn't so much interference from the fallout, points they call radiant gaps. Reapers sometimes have to travel for more hours than we do to get to one, but it's the only system we've got."

"Where is the real Gateway?" Sing asked.

I shrugged. "Beats me. As far as I know, no Reaper has ever been there. I suppose if you followed the grid, you'd eventually find it, if not for the security guards at the outposts who would shoot you on sight."

A few seconds later, two men dressed in ivory robes with gold trim walked from behind the Gateway, one at each side. Both sporting neatly trimmed white beards and flowing white hair, they looked like stereotypical angels from a biblical movie. "That's Bartholomew with the hooked nose," I whispered. "And Thaddeus is the one who walks with a limp. No idea why."

"All bow!" they called. When their voices died away, thunder rolled across the sky, as if in response.

Shanghai, Mex, and I lowered ourselves to one knee and bowed our heads. Sing quickly did the same at my side. I leaned close to her. "Hold the pose until they say to stand. They know you're a rookie, so they're going through all the formalities. They're far more lax with regulars."

"Are they trying to impress me or scare me?" Sing asked without looking up.

"Both."

She shuddered. "They're doing a good job."

"All stand!"

We rose and stood in a row again, now fewer than ten steps from the closest pedestal. The two attendants walked toward us in a stately march, Bartholomew carrying a computer tablet laid over his hands as if it were a serving tray. When they stopped in front of us, he nodded. "Photo sticks, please."

All four of us dug into our pockets and withdrew one or more sticks. I inserted one of mine into an interface in the tablet's side. Molly's image appeared on the screen, dancing in her ballerina costume. Once the tablet down-loaded the photo, Bartholomew removed the stick and pushed it into his pocket. After I did the same with sticks for the other souls, Bartholomew studied the screen for a moment before nodding. "Quota met."

With a hand in my pocket, I fingered Crandyke's photo stick, the only one with an embossed DEO emblem, mak-ing it easy to distinguish without looking at it. Normally I would go ahead and transport him even though I had already met quota, but his knowledge of the death industry could help us rescue Colm and his family.

I released his stick and withdrew my hand. He would be furious, but what could he do except complain? Since he didn't know I kept his stick, he wouldn't figure out that he had been left behind until after the soul-withdrawing pro-cess. Yet if Bartholomew noticed a mismatch between the number of souls I provided versus the number the DEOs reported, he might give me a hard time. If so, I would have to come up with an excuse.

After Shanghai and Mex downloaded their sticks, Sing inserted her first one. An old man appeared on the screen, posing with a bowler hat pressed against his chest, most likely Brennan. The next stick brought up Gail, standing with Mike in the same position his stick had displayed earlier.

Before pushing in her third stick, Sing glanced at me but quickly refocused on the tablet. When she slid it in, she coughed loudly several times. As the spasms continued, Bartholomew patted her on the back. "I think the damp weather doesn't agree with you." While her coughs and patting continued, the screen displayed an Oriental woman sitting at a desk with a pen in hand. Seconds later, the image disappeared.

Her coughs easing, Sing drew back. "Thank..." She cleared her throat. "Thank you. I apologize for the interruption. I think I feel a cold coming on."

"You need not worry. These are mere formalities to show you the details of the procedures here." Bartholomew withdrew the photo stick and slid it into his pocket. "You will find future visits to be much more relaxed."

Bartholomew hooked his arm around Shanghai's, Thaddeus hooked mine, and they escorted us to our respective pedestals. We stood in front of the pedestals at ground level with our backs to our images, raised our hoods, and locked our clasps into our valves.

After escorting Mex and Sing to their holograms, Bartholomew and Thaddeus positioned themselves in front of the Gatekeeper's image. "Rise to your pedestals," Bartholomew said.

I nodded at Sing. "Just do what I do." I took a backwards step up to my pedestal and settled within my hologram, though the static made it hard to conform perfectly to the hologram's undulating frame. Shanghai and Mex did the same on their pedestals.

Sing rose to hers. As soon as she set herself inside her image, a click sounded, then a hum. At the front edge of each pedestal, a metallic pole rose and stopped at chest level. A flat, rectangular sheet of metal sat on top of the pole, similar to a music stand.

"Connect," Bartholomew called.

I grasped a flexible tube protruding from a hole in the center of the stand. While looking at Sing, I removed my cloak clasp. She did the same, watching while copying my motions. I plugged my clasp into one branch of a T-adapter at the end of the tube, then plugged the other branch of the T into my valve. A sudden suction locked it in place. Until the process ended, I was stuck there. Trying to leave would tear the valve out and my heart along with it.

Once all four of us had connected, Bartholomew returned to the central pedestal and set his tablet on a stand similar to ours. He reeled out a tube that protruded from the stand and walked with it behind the pedestal toward the Gateway. When he arrived, he plugged the tube into a hole at the center of the gate's clasped hands. Light flashed at the connection point, and a brief sizzling sound pierced the air.

He stepped up to the central pedestal again and poised his finger over the tablet. His brow bent downward. After a few seconds, he called, "Valve check. We have a leak."

Thaddeus joined Sing on her pedestal. While she lifted her chin, he wiggled the tube's adapter.

I smiled at her, hoping to communicate that such a check was normal for a new Reaper. During my first journey to the Gateway, I hadn't connected properly. The fastening procedure wasn't exactly obvious.

"It's flush," Thaddeus said. "She did it correctly."

As Bartholomew stared at the tablet, his frown deepened. "The readings still indicate a leak. Check them all."

Thaddeus stepped up to my pedestal, wiggled my connection, and nodded. "His is tight." He then limped to Shanghai's and announced the same result. When he stepped up to the final pedestal, Mex shifted his connector. "I've been having trouble with my valve."

Bartholomew stroked his chin. "When the suction increases, the leak might seal on its own, and to make sure it seals, I could increase the suction in your tube beyond the normal level, but too much could endanger your life. It's risky."

"I'll just hold it in place. I've done it before." Mex patted Thaddeus on the back. "You've seen me do it, Thad. Tell him."

"It is true." Thaddeus looked at Bartholomew. "Is that acceptable?"

"Hmmm…" Bartholomew stared at the tablet's screen. "You have only one more cycle after this one."

"Yeah." Mex licked his lips. "My valve is kind of worn out. I'm looking forward to retiring and getting it removed."

"I can adjust your clasp to make it fit better." Bartholomew extended a hand. "Bring the cloak to me."

"Wait!" Mex laid a hand over his clasp, his smile trembling. "I'm fine. It's just one more cycle. I can make do. Just let me—"

"So you've been a Reaper twenty years?" Bartholomew asked.

"Right. Like you said, I have one more cycle after this one."

"So you will be anxious to fulfill quota and return here as quickly as possible."

"Well… yeah." Blinking, Mex cocked his head. "Wouldn't you?"

"Not enough to violate protocol. And your years of experience do not match your nervous demeanor." Bartholomew nodded at Thaddeus. "Check him for another photo stick. Perhaps he is holding back a soul."

I hid a swallow. Of course Mex didn't do that. He barely made quota. Yet, that was exactly what *I* was doing. The attendants wouldn't like it, but I had no idea they might punish someone caught in the act.

Mex turned his pants pockets inside out. "Look. Nothing. I wouldn't keep back a—"

"But what is this?" Thaddeus reached into Mex's cloak pocket and withdrew his valve-adapter tube. Nodding, he looked Mex in the eye. "Now I understand." He hobbled to Bartholomew and laid it next to the tablet.

While Bartholomew examined it, I glanced at Sing. She pulled in her bottom lip, her hands trembling. I had told her that transfers were legal. Maybe they were clamping down for some reason.

Bartholomew touched the tablet. "I see now that you are carrying a transferred soul." He slid his finger across the screen. "From Shanghai."

"Right." Mex laughed nervously. "It's legal. I've done it before."

"Of course it is, but I prefer that you report your transfers when you arrive." Bartholomew looked up and nodded. "The extraction will proceed. Mexico City may hold his connector in place."

Mex blew out a sigh. I smiled at both Shanghai and Sing. Everyone seemed relieved. Mex had gotten by unscathed.

"Okay," I said to Sing. "You don't have to do anything. The computer will match the images to what's in your cloak, and the vacuum mechanism will draw them out. This is the worst part. You'll feel backwards pressure, like something is trying to suck your insides out, and when each soul emerges..." As Sing's brow wrinkled deeply, my mouth grew dry. "Well, I guess you heard about it in training. It's going to hurt."

Sing's eyes reflected a hint of fear. "Don't worry. I can handle it."

Bartholomew pushed a finger across his tablet screen. The suction against my clasp's connection point spiked, and my valve grew warm. The tingling sensation spread across my skin. My heart vibrated, making my pulse race. As the cloak's shimmer brightened, waves of radiance rode the fibers toward my clasp, each wave signifying a different soul.

I kept an eye on my cloak. Since my clasp wasn't directly connected to my valve, Crandyke's soul wouldn't cause a shimmer unless the computer drew him out. That would keep his presence a secret, at least for a while.

When the first soul reached the clasp, pain jolted my heart, as if trying to rip it away from its attaching vessels. Sharp stabs knifed into my bones—my legs, my hips, my arms. Spasms clenched my thighs, abdomen, and biceps. I tried to relax my muscles, but they wouldn't respond. I just had to endure the torture, as usual.

After the second soul pushed through the valve, the pain decreased—a brief respite while I waited for the third. I took a breath and sneaked a peek at the other Reapers. Similar waves crashed across their cloaks and through their valves, like tsunamis breaking on a fragile coastline. The face in Shanghai's hologram altered with every change of expression in her real face—widened eyes and grinding teeth, then sudden slackness as she waited for the next peal of pain. Mex's image did the same, a time-lapsed collage of fluctuating emotions.

To my left, Sing kept her head low, sucking in short gasps with each pulse. Her image stared straight ahead as if disconnected, but the shimmers rippled from cloak to connector all the same.

After souls three and four entered the Gateway system, a final wave shimmered along the cloak's fibers toward the valve. Molly's voice filtered into my ears, stretched out and pain streaked. "I thought... I could trust you... Phoenix."

More knives stabbed my body. "It'll be okay soon, Molly. You'll see."

Her voice came through again, but I couldn't pick up the words. Whatever she had said, it sounded lost and forlorn... betrayed.

Seconds later, my muscles unclenched. The stabs eased. I exhaled and took in a cleansing breath, sweat now dampening my tunic. As my heart steadied, a wave of sorrow flooded my mind. Molly hated me, at least for now. Soon she would awaken in a new world and maybe change her mind, but these moments of terror and uncertainty for departing souls never failed to skewer my heart.

I reached out and took Sing's hand. "Are you all right?"

"I... " She swallowed, tensing her facial muscles. "I have one more soul to go. It's really hard."

I nodded. "They say it's like childbirth, only worse."

Across the way, Shanghai let her shoulders droop, her hair in disarray. Mex just closed his eyes, as if thankful that yet one more cycle had ended. After twenty years of reaping and traveling to the Gateway, he was probably dreaming of going home to Abilene, finding his family, and forgetting about roaming in Jungles and hunting for the fallen fruits of death.

When all the cloak shimmers faded, a new click sounded. The suction slowly eased, then reversed. New energy flowed into my valve. I inhaled deeply. Heat radiated through my limbs and down my spine. It felt so good. As the energy's healing effects coursed through my body, every muscle ache diminished. The flow would continue until my reservoir filled, an amount calculated based on the reading Erin took.

I looked again at Sing. Since she requested no energy, she just watched me, a smile emerging. Shanghai closed her eyes and swayed, her head tilted back as if she were listening to beautiful music.

Mex, still holding his clasp, blinked at Bartholomew. "Hey! I'm not feeling any energy flow."

"There is a reason for that." Bartholomew shook the adapter tube. A syringe fell out of the end and dropped to the ground.

I gulped. *My syringe!*

Mex cocked his head. "What? Where did that come from?"

Bartholomew set the tube down. "I was going to ask you that."

Mex looked at me, his face pale. I kept my expression calm. He could easily accuse someone of planting the syringe on him, but with no proof, what good would that do? No one would believe him.

After heaving a sigh, Mex squared his shoulders and folded his hands behind his back. "I don't know where it came from."

"Yet you admit to a soul transfer, so this must be your adapter."

"It is my adapter, sir, but I didn't put the syringe in it. I think someone else must have done it while I was sleeping on the train." Mex looked at me as if begging for help.

I tensed. Only one option remained—the truth.

"Bartholomew! That syringe is mine. It's filled with an antibiotic I hoped to use to heal a little girl in my district. There's a Reaper who's been hunting for Mex because of some kind of grudge, so he must have waited for us to go to sleep on the train. Then he took the syringe from me and put it in Mex's tube to get revenge."

Mex gave me a thankful head bow, though fear still bent his features. Now he seemed more worried about me than himself.

Bartholomew chuckled. "Leave it to Phoenix to come up with a cockamamie story to protect a friend. You're not stupid enough to transport contraband to the depot."

"But it's true. I just forgot—"

"Nonsense. A certain Owl has entered a note in your records indicating your willingness to lie for such a purpose. Your loyalty is well-known, Phoenix, but I cannot allow you to suffer for someone else's offenses." Bartholomew tapped his screen a few times in various places. "Smuggling of medicine is a capital crime. If essential supplies are siphoned and misdirected, deserving citizens will suffer. The fact that Mexico City was hiding the syringe so carefully is proof enough of his offense."

A sucking noise filled the air. Mex's tube stiffened, and his eyes shot open. "What are you doing?"

"Administering the penalty. A trial would take far too long."

"No!" Mex grabbed the tube and pulled, but it didn't budge. "You can't! I have just one more cycle!"

My own tube clicked. I let go of Sing and grasped it with both hands. Locked tight. Shanghai and Sing also pulled on theirs to no avail. We were trapped.

CHAPTER EIGHT

M Y BELT LAY on the ground, way out of reach—its tools useless. "Bartholomew!" I shouted. "Stop! Let him go!"

"All in good time." Bartholomew kept a finger on the pad, his expression flat.

The hum increased. Mex fell to his knees. His face paler than ever, he tipped to the side, but the taut suction tube kept him from falling. With his mouth hanging open, he dangled like a fish on a grappling hook.

"Mex!" Shanghai reached for him, but her fingers brushed air only inches away.

As Sing stood shakily on her pedestal, a tear coursed down her cheek, sparkling in the hologram's radiance.

Finally, the hum ceased. Our connectors clicked. I jerked the suction tube away from my valve and cloak, leaped from the pedestal, and dashed toward Mex. When I arrived, Shanghai was already crouching next to him. While I supported his body, Shanghai detached his tube, and we lowered him to the ground in front of his pedestal. Sing joined us and knelt close to his head, holding her breath.

I pressed my ear against Mex's chest. No heartbeat. I

felt for a pulse at his throat. Again, nothing. I whispered, "He's dead."

"No!" Shanghai set her hands on Mex's chest and pushed down again and again. "He's been out only a few seconds. Maybe we can—"

"Don't waste your time." Bartholomew walked our way, his tablet's screen facing us. "His soul has already migrated into the Gateway. You can see for yourself."

On the tablet, three icons filled the screen from left to right—an image that looked like a Reaper standing on a pedestal, a second image resembling the Gateway, and a third mimicking sunlight penetrating a gap in the clouds. Several faces hovered over the clouds, including Molly's and Mike's, while just to the right of the Gateway, only one face appeared—Mex's.

"Mexico City is just inside the Gateway waiting for me to send him to eternity with the others." Bartholomew dropped the adapter tube on the ground. "He cannot be returned to his body without a replacement."

I scowled at him. "A replacement?"

"Ah, yes. Reapers are ignorant of how our transport mechanism works." Bartholomew pointed at the middle icon. "Your friend is on the eternity side of the Gateway, and it will not open for any disembodied soul on that side. Yet, while he is there, if it opens from our side by means of sending another soul through, he could come back, as long as his body is still intact enough to revive."

"How long does his body have?" I asked.

"Under normal conditions, perhaps several minutes. I could, however, use our energy reserves to put him in a state that would minimize deterioration, though without a soul, he would not revive. He would merely be preserved."

I laid a hand on Mex's cheek—already cold. As Thaddeus pushed buttons on the stand, our holograms faded. It seemed that death itself had draped the forest in a dark shadow. "So when the next soul goes through, the Gateway will open and allow Mex to come back."

"Not just *any* next soul. Transferring requires Reaper training. If one of you chooses to die, I can send your soul to the Gateway. There you may attempt to transfer your friend back to this side. If you succeed, he can be restored to his body."

"And what happens to that Reaper?"

"He or she will go on to eternity, unless, of course, another Reaper wishes to perform the same transfer, but such a cycle of redundancy would be absurd. Someone has to go on to eternal rest. The Gateway will not allow a void."

I glanced at Shanghai and Sing. Tears streamed down their cheeks, their expressions torn.

Bartholomew laughed. "I have been calling Mexico City your friend, but it seems that I have overestimated your relationship with him. It appears that you three are not willing to lay down your lives for him."

I averted my eyes. I couldn't stand to look at his smug expression as he continued in a mocking cadence.

"And what a shame that you pride yourselves on taking souls to the delights of never-ending comfort while not believing in those comforts enough to risk going there yourselves. It should be a place you *want* to go."

I boiled inside. As if Bartholomew would ever die for someone else. He was the one who sentenced Mex to death, and now he laughed at us for not wanting to suffer the same fate. This Gateway attendant was too callous for words, a glorified clerk who let his power turn him into a pompous, self-important prig.

"How about this?" I rose, stepped close to him, and fanned out my cloak. "Since you're so sanctimonious about sacrificial acts, how about if Shanghai, Sing, and I arrange for you to visit the Gateway so you can enjoy the delights of never-ending comfort? Being the senior Gateway attendant, I'm sure you believe in those delights. You must be *dying* to experience them."

Bartholomew backed away a step. "Young man, are you threatening me?"

I mimicked his earlier mocking tone. "Of course not. I am offering you transport to a place you surely *want* to go."

Bartholomew gave me a hard stare. "Sarcasm doesn't become you. If not for my friendship with your father, I would write up an order to demote you to roamer status. Don't let anger be your downfall." He tapped on his computer screen, his eyes darting. "Seeing that Mexico City has no Reaper friends in this world, I am sending him along now. I will call for someone to dispose of his body."

The radiance in the Gateway flashed, then dimmed. "And don't think I didn't notice what you're hiding, Phoenix. After today, I will grant you no further pardons. My friendship with your father will stretch only so far." Bartholomew pivoted and marched toward the central pedestal with Thaddeus following.

I raised a hand and called out, "Wait!"

The two attendants turned. "What?" Bartholomew asked.

"Can I take Mex's cloak?"

Bartholomew squinted. "Whatever for?"

"To send to his family in Abilene."

He waved a hand. "Go ahead. Since no genetically compatible energy will be flowing through it, it will eventually deteriorate. We have no use for it." He turned again. After a few seconds, he and Thaddeus disappeared behind the Gateway.

I stooped with Shanghai and Sing and stared at Mex's body. His cloak lay spread out underneath him. Blood oozed around the edges of his valve, evidence that he had pulled furiously to detach from the vacuum tube that sucked the very life from his body.

"Give me a hand." I unfastened Mex's clasp. With Sing and Shanghai helping, I rolled his body enough to slide the cloak away. When we pulled it free, I draped it over my shoulder, the triangular roamer's patch hidden from view.

"Are you sure his family will want it?" Sing asked as we continued crouching at Mex's side. "It might just remind them of the system that killed him."

"It's made from his hair, so I think they'll want it. I'll ask them before I send it."

"What was that Bartholomew said about stretching a friendship with your father?"

"I violated protocol, and he noticed. I'll tell you about it later." I pulled the watch from my pocket and checked the time—eight forty. Sighing, I picked up Mex's adapter tube and shoved it into my cloak pocket. "We'd better get back to the station. Twenty minutes till the train comes by."

Shanghai retrieved her staff from where we left our weapons and returned to Mex's body. Bending low, she set the staff in his hands and kissed his ashen cheek. "Safe travels, my friend."

We shuffled slowly to our belts. While Shanghai and Sing refastened theirs, I picked up mine and Mex's and put them both on, one above the other. I reached out to Sing and Shanghai. Their eyes teary, they linked hands with me, and we began the walk back to the station.

For the first few minutes, everyone stayed quiet. The light rain had stopped, though the boughs above still pelted us with drops now and then. I hoped my two fellow Reapers would forget about the protocol breach. Apparently Bartholomew noticed that I had kept Crandyke but didn't want to do anything about it. His excuse seemed lame. As far as I knew, he and my father hadn't seen each other since my final shaving ceremony more than three years ago. He probably didn't want to bother with the reports he would have to fill out.

Finally, Sing spoke up. "Has something like this happened before… a Reaper getting killed at the Gateway?"

I shook my head. "Not during any of my transfers. Bringing smuggled medicine to the Gateway is absurdly risky, so I can't imagine it's happened before."

"I've never heard of it," Shanghai said, her voice low and somber. "But I keep hearing rumors of a crackdown, so maybe we'll see more stuff like that."

I rubbed a thumb along Shanghai's hand. "You and I will be part of the crackdown. We'll be reaping the souls of executed criminals."

"Criminals," Sing repeated with a huff. "It's not a crime to try to save your daughter's life."

"Not that again." Shanghai raised a hand. "Look, I'm not getting into politics, so leave me out of the discussion. I'm willing to try to help the Fitzpatricks escape, but that's as far as I'll go. The system is the system, and there's nothing we can do about it."

"That's a cop-out," Sing growled, "And you know it."

"You're right. I admit it. I'm copping out. But what're you going to do? Overthrow the Gatekeeper? He's been in control for two centuries. It's not like you can topple a god from his throne."

Sing gave Shanghai a hard stare. "He *calls* himself a god."

Shanghai returned the stare. "Well, if he's not a god, then what is he? No one can live—"

"Okay, okay!" I looked at them in turn. "Listen, we can't do anything about the Gatekeeper. God or not, he is what he is. All we can do is work within the system to keep people from getting hurt. We'll collect souls like always, but maybe when we get to the camp we can figure out how to do a little more."

As we continued walking, Sing drew her hand back and plugged her cloak's clasp into her valve. "I just wish we could somehow contact Mex."

"Right. You want a Reaper to go there and come back to report." I laughed under my breath. "We might as well wish for chocolate drops to fall from the sky instead of acid rain. It ain't gonna happen."

"Oh, let her dream." Shanghai plugged her clasp in as well. "It won't hurt anything. I daydream about stuff I can't have all the time."

All three of us quieted, leaving rustling leaves and our footfalls as the only sounds. After nearly a minute, Sing said, "Like what, Shanghai?"

"Well…" Shanghai spoke in a wistful tone. "Like being able to go home and see my parents, so they can have a daughter to fill the void my brother left behind when he killed himself."

Her voice pitched higher. "Like quitting this whole

Reaper thing so I don't have to watch another pneumonia-stricken old man drown in his own fluids. Or try to be stoic while a little girl curls in her daddy's lap, crying in horrific torture because no one has any drugs to keep her from feeling the cancer that's eating her brain. Then she finally dies in a violent seizure while her daddy weeps... no, he wails in inconsolable torment, and I have to tell him that it'll be all right, that she'll go to a better place, even though I have no way to prove it."

Another pause ensued, filled only with water dripping from leaves and more shuffling. Sing broke the hush. "If we could figure out a way to prove it, we'd all be better off—the Reapers and the grief-stricken."

"Yeah, right." Shanghai held out a hand. "Feel any chocolate falling?"

For the rest of the walk to the checkpoint, we stayed silent. Sing kept her head low, apparently in deep thought. It seemed that her idea to learn the secrets beyond the Gateway wouldn't give her any peace. She was right that it would be great to know, but it was just an idea, a child's hope for chocolate rain.

When we arrived at the checkpoint, Erin scanned our birthmarks to register that we had left the compound. We told her about Mex, but she said in her unflappable manner that she had already received word about his death and the need to remove his body. She took no notice of Mex's cloak, still draped over my shoulder, or his belt around my waist.

She also returned Sing's medallion. For some reason it no longer carried the luster it had before—probably just my imagination—or maybe its battery-powered inner light had faded. Everything seemed duller now—the sky, the trees, my mood.

As we drew near the station, the other Reapers were milling about on the platform, though no one seemed to be conversing. The screeching of wheels rose in the distance. We picked up our pace. It was arriving a little early, so we had to hustle. The engineer wouldn't wait for stragglers.

We climbed the stairs to the platform. With the rain bringing cooler air, the Reapers kept their hoods up and cloaks close to their bodies. I scanned the group for the Reaper who had been watching us earlier, but with every face partially hidden, the effort was useless. Even if I found him, what could I do? I had no proof that he did anything wrong.

I touched my clasp, still loose from my valve. Now was not a good time to energize my cloak. Crandyke might get loud enough for others to hear, and his presence would raise a lot of questions I didn't want to answer.

After the engine and lead cars blew by, whipping us with a cool blast, the last car slowed to a stop at the platform. We let the other Reapers file in first, then entered and slid into the same facing benches we had occupied before.

When the train began a squealing departure, Sing reached into her pocket and withdrew the pamphlet she had taken from Bill. As she slowly flipped through the pages, I scanned some of the text. The first part appeared to be an account of the history of the Gateway, including what I told Sing earlier about the location of the depots. It went on to explain how Reapers become soul carriers and that each Reaper chooses a name of one of the cities that collapsed and burned under the burden of "An oppressive regime," a dictatorship that prefers to let people die than to allow freedom.

Of course there aren't enough dead-city names to go

around, so there are many Reapers named Detroit, Hanoi, and Shanghai, though only one of each is allowed in any given Jungle city, the Jungle designation assigned based on certain statistics—poverty level, crime rate, and death-to-birth ratio. Nearly all of the history appeared to be factual with only a few oblique barbs directed at the Council and other members of the ruling class.

From that point, the pamphlet diverged into the Gateway-denier theories, what "really" happens to souls that enter the Gateway—crazy stuff about becoming dinner for soul eaters who feed on life energy. Their only proof was pure conjecture—"How else do you explain a world leader who seems to live forever? Why else would he encourage procreation and not allow enough medicine to take care of growing families? And the reason younger people are more valuable to Reaper quotas? They have more life energy to consume."

I shook my head. Utter nonsense. Although the pamphlet raised intriguing questions, its answers sounded like fairy tales. Soul eaters? Did the pamphlet offer any evidence of such a creature beyond the fact that the Gatekeeper lived a long time? No. Nothing.

And regarding our quotas, right or wrong, young souls were more valuable because their removal from the population meant a bigger relief on the government—no education needed; no medicine for the years they would live; and a lighter burden on the family, making the survivors more productive. And procreation was encouraged in order to increase the supply of workers. If the children were healthy, great. If they were sickly, it was better for them to die. The policy was callous and cold, but it reflected reality.

Sing closed the pamphlet and slid it into her pocket. "Anyone else hungry?"

"A little bit," I said. "More sleepy than hungry. We can find something to eat at the station when we get back."

Sing leaned her head against my shoulder. "Then let's sleep."

Shanghai ran a hand along the empty space next to her. "I can't believe I called him a freak."

"Don't go there," Sing said, straightening. "Save the beating up for the people who really deserve it. Those Gateway attendants are callous killers. At least Mex should have had a trial."

Shanghai shook her head, lament in her tone. "I like your spunk, Sing, but if you keep talking like that, you'll be next. You haven't been around long enough to know how the system works. As long as protestors just carry signs and hand out pamphlets, the Council doesn't worry about them, but let one of them take a step of real aggression, and it's lights out." She nodded toward me. "Ask Phoenix. He'll tell you."

Sing looked at me, waiting for my affirmation, but I didn't really want to contribute. Although Shanghai was right, why should I try to bridle Sing's anger at the system? It might be better to let her vent. Besides, Sing had already seen two other resistors executed. She knew what "lights out" meant. "Maybe we should all sleep for a while. We probably won't have time when we get back."

"You're right." Shanghai leaned against the window, blinking as she stared at the dreary sky. She seemed lonely, disconnected, worried. With several windows partially open in the fast-moving car, cool air circulated. Shanghai drew her hood up and shivered.

I took Mex's cloak off my shoulder and slid toward the window, scooting Sing as I shifted. I patted the space on my other side. "There's room for one more."

Shanghai crossed to our bench and sat next to me. I spread the cloak over all three of us, and we huddled underneath. Shanghai looped her arm around mine and leaned her head on my shoulder, while Sing and I leaned our heads against each other's and held hands.

Warmth radiated from body to body—the soothing warmth of friendship I hadn't felt in three lonely years. Yet, why had Mex's death incited this call to comfort? None of us knew him well. We didn't treat him like a close friend before he died. Now it seemed that his sudden departure had torn our hearts open and exposed secret fears.

Maybe we were commiserating. Maybe we didn't really believe in the joys of the afterlife, just as Bartholomew had chided. Maybe we didn't really believe in the Gateway at all. Could our roles as Reapers be something less than the beneficial transport that dying citizens longed for? Were we providing false hope to the bereaved and instead taking their loved ones to a place of eternal horror? Maybe our lot in life had been a lie. To whom could we turn except to each other?

Now, in spite of the rules against friendships, we had become close allies. It felt good and right. So what if the other Reapers in the car could see us? They could report an infraction if they wanted to. And with Mex's triangular patch now in plain view, they would figure out what happened and guess that we were sympathizers with a crooked roamer. But I didn't care. The pleasure of sharing a consoling touch with these two girls was worth it. In a way, it felt like Mex was covering us. Now we were all roamers, and no one could stop us from grieving together over the death of a friend.

While I rested, an image came to mind—Misty huddling with me under a blanket while sitting on a two-person bench. Before my initiation as a Reaper, I had been given a week at home for Christmas. One evening I went for a walk, supposedly to "enjoy my freedom," but instead I sneaked over to Misty's foster home. As we watched the snow fall from her front porch, I felt the same comfort Sing and Shanghai now provided. Misty and I didn't say a word. We just enjoyed each other's warmth and companionship. Why ruin the moment with awkward conversation? Our friendship needed no words.

CHAPTER NINE

AFTER SLEEPING ON and off during the trip back to Chicago, I awoke to the usual squeal of the slowing train. Now that it was close to noon, a crowd of people walked in and around the station, many of them out-of-work men and women hawking homemade goods and food to travelers. I took in the aroma of spicy soup, mustard, and freshly baked bread. My stomach growled for lunch.

When we disembarked, we walked behind the line of other passengers through the turnstile leading to the street, letting them take the brunt of shouting marketers and waving arms.

"Beef stew! Hot and hearty on this cool day!"

"Bread! Fresh from the oven! Meat for sandwiches at my cart!"

Sales transactions created a bottleneck, giving me time to survey the city block. Dozens of men and women poured out of three-to-four-story office buildings, a few in business suits, most in service-personnel clothes. The damp, blustery wind funneling between buildings hurried them along, sweeping skirts and flapping jackets. It seemed that no one paid attention to their fellow Chicagoans. They just wanted to buy their lunches and get out of the breeze and back to work. With unemployment so high, they knew they were expendable.

I spotted the cart I frequented standing well away from the bustle—*Flo's Odds and Ends.* Taking Sing and Shanghai by the hand, I pushed through the crowd, ignoring the bleating calls from other vendors. When we arrived, we stood in line, two customers in front of us. I folded Mex's cloak and waited.

Flo, a thin-faced lady with silver hair and deep laugh lines, stood behind a counter loaded with sandwich meats and breads; pots of soup; and bowls of lettuce, pickles, onions, peppers, and the like. In the midst of slicing through a sub roll with a long knife, she noticed us and smiled. "Phoenix! Welcome!"

The other two customers—a young bearded man in a coat, tie, and turban and a middle-aged woman wearing a smock dress and baseball cap—turned and backed out of the way.

I waved a hand. "No. Go ahead. We can wait."

Smiling, the man spread out an arm. "By all means, take my place. I will not be the one to delay a trio of Reapers." The woman nodded, though she didn't smile.

When I stepped up, Flo wiped her hands with a towel. "What'll it be, Phoenix? Corned beef on wheat, lettuce, mayo, and pickles, right?"

"Good memory, Flo. And a cup of your chicken soup."

"Colder, isn't it? A foul wind, it seems." Flo lifted her brow. "And for the ladies?"

Sing joined me at the counter. "I'll have the same, except no mayo."

"Just soup," Shanghai said from behind me. "Thank you."

"Something to drink?"

I nodded. "A large bottle of water. We'll share it."

While Flo prepared our food, I punched my Reaper's code into a numeric pad attached to her cash register. After Sing and Shanghai did the same, I turned and again scanned the street. A dark-skinned man stood alone at the opposite corner, leaning against a building. Kwame? Why would he be here?

Kwame gestured with his head, as if beckoning me to follow. I nodded at the cart, hoping to indicate that I'd be along after we got our food. He nodded in return and sauntered away, his short sleeves making him appear immune to the buffeting breeze.

We gathered our food and walked toward the park between the station and my district, Shanghai on my left carrying the water bottle, and Sing on my right. Sing gave me an elbow nudge. I needed no explanation. It was time to tell Shanghai the rest of my plan.

After I swallowed a bite of my sandwich and took a sip from my soup cup, I turned to Shanghai. "We might as well get our plan going right away. You go to the camp and tell Alex you want me to help you with the reapings. Since you'll eventually get a permanent roommate afterward, ask her if it's okay to request me now."

A smile emerged on Shanghai's face. "That's fine with me, but how does that help us get the Fitzpatricks out?"

"It's a stepping stone. Get Alex used to the idea of putting us together so when I ask to get rid of the cameras, it won't sound so bold. The key is for us to be able to plan in secret, so the cameras have to go."

"Got it." Shanghai drank the rest of her soup and tossed the cup into a trash can. "Then what?"

I took in a breath. It was now or never. "Then we'll figure out how to get Sing into our suite at the camp. You and she can share your room."

"Sing's joining us?" Shanghai's smile tightened. "Well... um... that's great. When did you two decide that?"

"On the train. While you were sleeping."

Her cheeks reddened. "Okay. That's cool. So Sing can sneak around while we're reaping and report her findings to us."

"Exactly what I was thinking."

Shanghai halted and pushed the water bottle into my cloak pocket. "You keep thinking, Phoenix. That's what you do best." She spun away and jogged down the sloping sidewalk, her cloak flowing behind her. Soon, she turned a corner in the distance and disappeared from sight.

"Well," Sing said as she stared in the direction Shanghai had gone. "That was... abrupt."

I nodded. "She felt out of the loop. She'll get over it."

"I hope so." Sing wadded her sandwich wrapper and thrust it into the trash can with more than the usual force.

"What's bugging you?" I asked.

"Let's get moving." She pulled the bottle from my pocket. "We'll talk when we're alone."

As we walked through the park, we finished our soup and tossed the empty cups into a trash receptacle. When we passed by the spot where we fought the bandits, we slowed our pace. Our expended smoke capsules lay strewn about, and divots in the grass gave evidence of a struggle, but it seemed that no bandits lurked. On such a cool, blustery day, neither they nor any park visitors wanted to brave the elements.

Now well away from the bustle, I brushed my shoulder against hers. "Still upset about Mex?"

"Of course, but not just because he died." She kicked a pebble on the walkway. "Obviously you're still going through with the plan, but what about my district? Now we don't have Mex to cover it."

"Good point." I glanced at Mex's cloak, once again draped over my shoulder. "I'll have to think about that. Maybe you won't be able to join us in the condo after all."

"No!" Sing bit her lip. "I mean, like you said, you and Shanghai will be busy with the reapings. You'll need me. I'll be like a ghost who'll appear and disappear whenever I'm called upon."

"But you can't just abandon your district. If souls don't get reaped there, you'll get busted to roamer. I don't mean to offend you, but you're not experienced enough to survive on the streets like Mex did."

"I'm not offended. You're right." She stopped and coughed, covering her mouth with her sleeve. The episode lengthened into a series of hard spasms that added more color to her face. When she finished, she held up the bottle of water. "I guess I shouldn't contaminate this."

I waved a hand. "No. It's yours. I'll be fine."

She smiled thankfully, took a drink of water, and slowly recapped the top. As she swallowed, her brow knitted tightly. "What if I just disappear?"

"Disappear?"

She began walking again. "They'd have to get a replacement, right? And I wouldn't be around to get busted."

I kept pace at her side. "But you'd still have to collect souls no matter where you go. I know you didn't expend much energy this cycle, but that'll change. Even if you don't reap, you'll eventually leak out. We all do."

She pointed the bottle at me. "Maybe you and Shanghai could give me enough souls to make quota."

"Transfers? I thought you didn't want to—"

"I didn't, but desperate times, you know."

"That still won't work. If you disappear, you won't be assigned a quota to make." I gestured with my head toward the train station. "What'll happen when you show up at the Gateway to deliver the souls and recharge your energy? You'll get busted."

Sing breathed a sigh. "I guess you're right."

After walking quietly for a minute, I looked in the direction of Kwame's home, still twenty blocks away. "Tell you what. I have a friend who gets insider information about the Gateway. Let's talk to him and see if he has any ideas."

"You'd tell this friend about your plans? You trust him that much?"

"He's kind of like a Gateway denier." I nodded at Sing's cloak pocket. "Not like the loony who wrote that pamphlet, but he has a lot of questions about the system that I can't answer. He wouldn't rat us out. He'd get in trouble himself."

"Okay." Sing's dark eyebrows scrunched together. "But I'm skeptical."

"Good. In the Jungle, skepticism keeps you alive."

Sing lowered her head for a moment before looking at me again. "Since it's okay to be skeptical, you won't mind if I bring up something I'm wondering about, right?"

"Sure. Go for it."

"I watched your photo downloads into the Gateway

computer. They were all female except Mike. But earlier you said you were talking to a guy named Crandyke."

"Right. Him." Still walking, I withdrew his photo stick from my cloak pocket and showed it to her. "This is what Bartholomew was talking about."

"The protocol violation?"

I nodded. "Since Crandyke worked in a DEO office, I thought he could provide some information, so I kept his soul."

"What?" Her eyes widened. "You're delaying his passage to the Gateway just to get information?"

"For Colm's family..." I thrust the stick back into my pocket. "Yeah."

"Isn't that a punishable offense?"

"Why? You wouldn't report me—"

"No, no. Never. And I'm not saying you're wrong." She lowered her head. "It's just that... well..."

"You might as well tell me, Sing. No use holding back."

"Okay. Here goes." She took a deep breath. "I'm surprised that you're telling me about this offense when you won't trust me enough to tell me that you're a medicine smuggler."

"A medicine smuggler?" I bent my brow. "What did you really see through Colm's window?"

"I told you I saw you try to take the blame. That was true."

"But you saw more. You saw me give the pills to Molly's family."

"Let's just say—"

"Don't start with a 'let's just say' dodge." I halted and grabbed her arm. "If you know I'm a smuggler then tell me how you know. If I'm going to risk my life with you, you have to be honest with me."

"Honest? Like you've been with me?" Sing glared at my grip. "I'm supposed to help you rescue people who'll be executed because you smuggled medicine to them, and you haven't told me that you're the one who got them in trouble." She jerked her arm away. "If you call that honesty, then I'll keep a few of my own secrets, thank you very much."

Heat crawled across my skin. "Touché. I deserved that one."

"You did." She brushed the wrinkles from her sleeve. "But we've known each other for what? Two weeks? We never really talked before last night. Trust takes time."

"Okay. I get that. But how did you know?"

She glanced away for a moment before refocusing on me. "The people I mentioned who might help us. They told me. But I don't know how they know. Maybe they'll tell you when you meet them."

A sharp pain drilled into my stomach. All this time I thought I had kept my activities hidden, but Sing's "people" had been secretly monitoring me. "Okay. I'll look forward to meeting them."

"Don't worry, Phoenix. They're on our side." She tilted her head and looked at me as if searching for light in my eyes. "Still friends?"

"Sure." I couldn't help but smile. "Now I know why they say Reapers can't be friends. We'd probably fight each other all the time."

"No way." Sing gave me a hard shove from the side. "You wouldn't last two minutes with me."

"Only because you'd be begging for mercy." I shoved her back. "I couldn't stand watching you cry."

As we walked, we continued the playful pushing and teasing. Our cloaks fanned out, flitting against each other as if mimicking our antics. With each push we eased up on the force and drew closer and closer together. Finally, she gently bumped my arm with hers and said, "You'd better break the news to Crandyke."

"I suppose so, but he's going to be spitting mad." Letting out a sigh, I plugged my clasp into my valve. When my cloak energized, I listened for Crandyke, but no sound rode up the fibers. "Crandyke? Are you there?"

"As if you didn't know." A growl rumbled in his voice.

"Yeah, well, I can explain, you see—"

"Sure. Explain away. I'd like to hear why you kept a dead man from going to his eternal resting place. This ought to be good."

"Don't get bent out of shape, Crandyke. I kept you here because I need you."

"And that's supposed to make me feel better?" His tone changed to a girlish squeal. "Oh! Phoenix needs me! I'm so honored! I think I'll jump up and click my heels together!" After a high-pitched giggle, he reverted to a growl. "Give me a break."

"Listen, Crandyke, I'm actually doing you a favor. I heard from a..." I glanced at Sing's cloak pocket where the pamphlet lay. "From an unnamed source that the Gateway is dangerous for souls."

"The crackpot soul-eater theory?" Crandyke laughed. "Lousy effort, but I'll give you points for amusing me."

"Well, believe this." I withdrew his photo stick again. "Like it or not, you're stuck with me. If you cooperate, I'll

take you to the Gateway when I meet quota again. If not…
well… I might just lose track of your photo stick."

"You wouldn't dare!"

"Try me." I tossed the stick in the air and caught it. "I'll
do anything to save Molly's family, including manipulating
a stubborn ghost."

After a moment of silence, Crandyke gasped. "I figured it out. I didn't miss the Gateway. I went through it,
and now I'm in hell. I'm trapped inside a lunatic Reaper's
cloak, and I'll suffer through an eternal cycle of promised
trips to the Gateway only to be thwarted every time by a
new sadistic reason for not taking me there."

"Think what you want, but if you don't cooperate, your
photos are going for a swim in the closest portable toilet.
Got it?"

Crandyke moaned. "Why did I decide to eat that triple
cheeseburger while walking through your district? I was
just asking to have a heart attack. Now I have to put up
with—"

I unplugged my cloak and let the clasp dangle. "That
was… interesting."

"That's one word for it." Sing smiled. "Do you think
he'll help?"

"Probably. He doesn't have much choice." I slid
Crandyke's photo stick back to my pocket, but it stuck
to my sweaty palm. With a quick shake, I broke contact.
More sweat moistened my back. No surprise. I was using a
dead man for my own purposes, a real breach of protocol.
I was breaking the Reapers' pledge. Reaped souls came
first, regardless of my motivations. My trainer hammered
that principle into me from day one. Even a drunk like him

wouldn't break that covenant. So what did that make me? Something worse than a drunk.

And guilt over Mex's death only added to my burden.

I tightened my grip on his cloak. Regardless of protocol, I had to end this nightmare once and for all. Since souls came first, I had to make sure they ended up in a safe place, no matter what.

CHAPTER TEN

A FTER EXITING THE park, I led Sing back to my district and entered a residential area near the river. We passed by dilapidated row houses where elderly men and women sat on front steps, staring at us from under dark leathery brows. Normally they might be worried about the presence of a Reaper, but our lowered hoods signaled that we weren't on official business today. Their stares communicated curiosity. Why would two Reapers be walking together so far from the train station? Almost unheard of.

We continued our quick march. Children ran here and there, sometimes stopping in front of us, then backing away with awestruck stares. Their playful screams barely competed with a stereo blaring classical music through an open window.

"Beethoven?" Sing asked as we drew near the house. "Kind of unusual, isn't it?"

"Not from that place." I pointed with my thumb toward the window. "Noah is a classical music nut. He's twelve, almost thirteen, and he has a beat-up cello he uses to jam with while he listens. I don't hear him now, but you'll know it when he tries to tune that scratchy old thing."

"How did you get to know him so well?"

"He's a Reaper in training. He invites me over for sparring whenever he's home on leave." As we passed by a motorcycle chained to a lamppost, I ran my hand along its contoured seat where a Gateway insignia had been stitched into the leather-like material. "Why would a DEO be here in my district? I didn't get an alarm."

The music stopped. "Phoenix!" a woman called from Noah's window. "You're here! I knew you'd come!"

The front door flung open. Georgia, Noah's mother, ran out. As she hustled toward the street, her short legs carried her stocky frame at a surprising rate. When she stopped, she laid one hand on my shoulder and the other on her ample bosom. "Give me a minute to catch my breath."

"Of course." I nodded at Sing. "Singapore, this is Georgia Taylor. Georgia, this is my Reaper associate, Singapore, better known as Sing."

Sing bowed her head. "Pleased to meet you."

"And the same to you, young lady." Georgia's smile stretched her cheeks. "Well, I hoped and prayed for one Reaper to come, and I got two!" She shifted her hand to Mex's cloak. "But you didn't need to bring a cloak. We're almost finished making Noah's. He looks so cute with his head shaved."

"Today's his initiation?"

Georgia bobbed her head. "Turned thirteen yesterday."

"Why didn't you invite me?"

"Oh, Phoenix, I wanted to, really I did, but Noah's trainer said if an older Reaper shows up at the initiation without being invited, it means the new Reaper will be blessed beyond measure."

I nodded. "I've heard that, too, but Sing and I are going—"

"And since two Reapers showed up, well I guess that means Noah's gonna have blessings overflowing!" Georgia gripped my forearm and led me toward her house. "Noah's going to be so excited to see you."

As I let her pull me along, I looked back at Sing and shrugged.

She followed, flashing an amused grin. It seemed that we didn't have much choice.

Georgia opened the door and ushered us in. Walking slowly through a narrow hall, we drew near a combination living room/TV room where Noah sat on a straight-backed chair at the center, his shaved head erect and his shoulders straight. With his training-enhanced muscles filling out his beige long-sleeved tunic, he looked sharp indeed.

Judas, tall and lanky, leaned against the far wall, yawning as he studied his tablet. Although his real name was Jude, we Reapers used our nickname for him when he couldn't hear us. No one trusted this DEO.

Three couples stood about, all in their Sunday best. One lady wearing a purple-on-white floral shawl sat on a sunken sofa cushion, hand sewing a hood to a cloak at a furious rate. Bright smiles on dark faces abounded, but when they saw Sing and me enter the room, several mouths dropped open.

"Reapers," a wrinkle-faced man in a gray suit said. "They actually came!"

"Just like I told you." Georgia introduced us and rattled off the guests' names, but most of them flew in one ear and out the other. I did catch the name of the woman stitching the cloak together—Valerie Evans, a fortyish woman with a few threads of graying hair around her pink bonnet, a dress fit to be worn at a royal wedding, and nimble fingers that whipped through the thick cloak material as if they were attached to an industrial machine.

"I'll be done in two minutes," Valerie said. "I spun his hair with flax just yesterday, but it came out tougher than I expected."

Georgia laid a hand on Valerie's shoulder. "Two minutes is perfect. That'll give Phoenix and Sing time to administer the Reaper's pledge." She turned to the man in the gray suit. "You don't mind, do you Harold?"

"Of course not." Harold held a tattered sheet of paper covered with handwritten text and extended it toward me. "I don't suppose you need this, do you?"

"The pledge?" I shook my head. "It's still memorized, but Noah's trainer should administer it." I scanned the room. "Where is he?"

"He was supposed to be here thirty minutes ago." Georgia pointed at the sheet. "We don't have a handbook, so Noah wrote the pledge on that paper from memory."

"Is Hanoi your trainer?" I asked Noah.

He nodded, his head now low.

"Then we shouldn't wait for him. He probably got sidetracked at a bar." I motioned for Noah to stand and whispered, "You're a bigger man than Hanoi will ever be."

"Thank you, Phoenix." Noah rose from his chair. No taller than Sing, his tunic lay partially open, exposing his valve. Although his dark skin tones hid much of the surgical trauma, the skin around the valve's edge looked raw and blood-tinged. "I'm ready," he said, lifting his right hand.

"Wait a minute." Judas pushed away from the wall and pointed his tablet at Noah. "Gotta get this on video." After tapping a couple of keys, he nodded. "Go ahead."

"Sing, if you'll join me." I faced Noah and raised my right hand, as did Sing, now standing at my side. "Repeat after me.... I, Noah, do solemnly pledge to uphold the principles of the Reaper's Code."

Noah cleared his throat. "I, Noah, do solemnly pledge to uphold the principles of the Reaper's Code."

After Sing and I recited each phrase, Noah echoed it with fervor.

"To have compassion for the dying, the bereaved, and the disembodied souls; to keep souls in my care safe from all harm no matter what the circumstances; to consider their needs before my own and those of all others, whether living or dead; to ensure that they are treated with the respect due to all humans; and to deliver them safely to the Gateway even at the risk of my own life."

Every word burned a hole in my conscience, especially when repeated by a new Reaper who looked up to me as a perfect model. I kept reminding myself that my running afoul of the pledge was actually good for Crandyke in the long run, but I wasn't very convincing.

When Noah finished, I shook off the pangs of guilt, picked up the now-completed cloak from Valerie, and laid it over his shoulders. "Have you chosen a city name?"

He nodded. "Cairo. The one in Africa burned, but the one here in Illinois is still alive. That's where my family is from. It's pronounced different, but I don't care."

"Very well." I plugged the clasp into his valve. "Cairo, you are now an official Reaper. You are free to collect souls as long as you adhere to the pledge."

Cairo lifted his hood over his head. "Thank you, Phoenix. It's a great honor that you came."

"My pleasure."

Judas held the tablet in front of Cairo. "Press your thumb in the box. I'm creating a secure Reaper file for you."

Cairo set his thumb in a square at the corner of the screen. The tablet clicked, and an image of Cairo appeared above the box.

"That'll do." Judas swept the tablet away and began tapping on the screen.

"Has he been assigned somewhere yet?" I asked.

"No, but when he is, you'll never find out where. It'll be far away and secret, as usual." Judas shook the tablet. "It's not transmitting. I'll have to take it to the office and plug it in manually."

I bent to the side, trying to see the screen but to no avail. "When will he find out?"

"Probably about a week. One of our head clerks died recently, so the paperwork's backed up."

I nodded. Crandyke. So he was a head clerk. He probably did know a lot about the system.

Judas tucked the tablet under his arm and offered a shallow bow. "I have to be going." He strode from the room without another word.

Georgia hugged Cairo. "I'm so proud of you!" She brushed away tears. "I know you have to go away, but you'll be like an angel from heaven, carrying souls across the great divide. Those thoughts will keep me company."

"In the meantime," Harold said as he picked up a wide-brimmed hat from a coffee table, "we have a week to raise half the money for his weapons and belt." A few dollars and several coins sat in the bottom of the hat, not nearly enough to pay their share. As was true for other Reapers, once Cairo proved himself and made quota the first time, the Council would pay for everything thereafter, but the family had to contribute at the beginning.

I unfastened Mex's belt. "Well, Georgia, it seems that your prayers have been answered in more ways than one." I wrapped the belt around Cairo's waist. "I'm sure the former owner would be pleased to see this put to good use."

Georgia clapped her hands. "Will you look at that? We're gonna do some celebrating tonight!"

I fastened the belt and whispered to Cairo, "Wear it well, my friend."

Cairo pulled a dagger partway from its harness, then slid it back in place. "I will, Phoenix. Let me know if there's anything I can do for you."

"Just be kind to the people in your district. That's all I ask."

After we said good-bye, Sing and I hurried through the neighborhood. We soon crossed a railroad track and entered a retail area within view of the Chicago River. A black man with a five-day beard sat against a liquor store wall, his hand strangling the throat of a bottle partially wrapped in a brown paper bag. I knew this man quite well—Murphy, a regular patron at the liquor store whenever he could panhandle enough quarters to get a cheap bottle of wine.

As we walked by, Murphy stared at us with bloodshot eyes. "What're you... you doing here, pretty boy? Come to take... my soul to heaven?" He belched, then laughed. "Funny thought, ain't it? Someone like me going to... to heaven? I'd be a sight standing next to those... those preachers with their poofy hair and slick suits."

Sing halted and crouched in front of him. "We take everyone to the same place. Where they go from there isn't up to us, but I don't think fancy suits will get anyone to heaven." She took his bottle, set it down, and slid her hand into his. "My name is Sing, what's yours?"

"Mur... Murphy." His eyes watered as he stammered on. "But... but you can call me Murph. All... all my friends do."

Sing shook his hand. "Pleased to meet you, Murph."

"First girl Reaper... I ever met." He sniffed and ran a finger under his nose, smearing mucous. "When I die, I hope you're the one to... to collect my soul."

"You're not in my district, but it could happen. Sometimes we Reapers transfer souls, so Phoenix might let me take you for a ride."

I stooped next to Sing and whispered, "Murph and I have talked several times. He won't remember this conversation tomorrow."

"That's all right." Sing released Murph's hand. "Nice meeting you."

He picked up his bottle. "Any day I get... get to talk to a pretty girl is a good day." He nodded in the direction we had been heading. "The other ladies won't... won't give me the time of day."

"Dancers," I whispered. "A couple of doors down. And they don't dance to classical music."

I took Sing's arm and helped her rise. We walked past a window emblazoned with bold letters—*EZ Cash*—and stopped at a door—a combination of a rotting wood panel and a broken window.

"Your friend lives here?" Sing asked.

"Yeah. He doesn't have anything to steal, so no one bothers him."

"Ain't nothing in there," Murph called. "No... no pick-ins at all."

"Like I said." I opened the door and guided Sing into a waiting room. Four mangled chairs and a desk with a cracked top littered the floor, and at a rear corner, an interior door stood ajar. I walked to the door and called through the gap. "Kwame? Are you home?"

"Phoenix?" The call came from somewhere inside.

"Yeah."

"What took you so long?"

"I got sidetracked." I smirked at Sing. "He's not exactly the easiest guy to get along with."

Sing grinned. "Don't worry. I know a lot of people like that."

We walked into the back office, a spacious chamber with most of the walls stripped to the studs, allowing a view throughout. I ducked under a dangling ceiling panel and pushed up a cluster of wires to allow both of us to pass.

In a side room, Kwame sat in an easy chair, his feet resting on a green ottoman with orange stains. Springs and stuffing protruded from the chair's arms, but Kwame seemed comfortable all the same. "Now that you're finally here..." Muscles rippled on his forearms, as dark as the chair's chocolate-brown upholstery. "We have a lot to talk about."

"Sure. I've got some news, too." I slid a folding metal chair in front of Kwame and motioned for Sing to sit.

"I... uh..." She gave the rickety chair a sideways glance. "I'm okay, thanks." She coughed quietly into her sleeve.

"Are you sure you're okay?" I asked.

"I'm fine." She licked her lips. "Seriously. It's just a cold."

"She looks as nervous as a mouse at an owl convention," Kwame said.

I laughed. "Believe it or not, that's a relevant quip."

"All my quips are relevant."

"Yeah. Sure." I nodded at Sing. "Kwame, this is Singapore."

Kwame ran a hand through his short hair, salted by his sixty years. "Well, Singapore, I am pleased to finally meet Chicago's third female Reaper. I assume it must be hard walking in the shadow of your illustrious mother."

"It's an honor to be in her shadow, sir." Sing's eyes didn't quite focus on Kwame. For some reason, she seemed scared to death of this man. "And it's an honor to meet you as well."

"And she's polite!" Kwame grinned. "Well, I must say that Phoenix's prospects are looking up. I've been telling him for a year to find a girlfriend, but he's more concerned about hearing the death alarms than about soothing his lonely heart."

I waved a hand. "Kwame, I never said I was lone—"

"You didn't have to. I can see it in your eyes. You need a sweet young lady to kiss away the shadows of death." Kwame folded his hands in his lap. "Now tell me your news, and then I'll tell you mine."

For the next few minutes, I related our story—from the time I heard Molly's alarm to our return from the Gateway, including the Fitzpatricks' sentencing to the camp, Alex's proposal for me to help with a reaping, Mex's death, and our idea to infiltrate the corrections camp to rescue the family. At times Sing gave me a nudge, warning me not to provide some of the details, but she didn't know Kwame like I did. He wouldn't be on Alex's side.

When I finished, Kwame pressed his fingers together. "So you need Sing to be in two places at once—at the camp with you and in her district responding to death alarms. That is a difficult obstacle."

"Difficult?" I laughed under my breath. "Get real, Kwame. It's impossible. We'll have to come up with—"

"Oh, no. It's not impossible." He nodded toward my shoulder. "You have Mex's cloak. All you need is a courageous young person who is willing to masquerade as Singapore. That person can let herself be seen in Sing's district, and she can rely on the gossip network rather than death alarms. When she learns of an impending death, she can contact the real Sing to handle the reaping."

"Or contact a roamer if I'm busy," Sing said. "They're always glad to pick up a soul."

Kwame pointed at her. "An excellent addition to my brilliant plan."

I let the idea roll around in my mind. It had merit, but a problem remained. Who would play the role of Sing? Cairo came to mind, but being bald and male disqualified him. "Does your brilliant plan include a candidate for masquerading as Sing?"

Kwame snorted. "Do you expect me to solve all your problems? I'm a penniless hermit. I don't know anyone around here besides you."

"Don't con me. You have all sorts of contacts in the Council's bureaucracy."

"Ah, yes! The Council. This is true. And now I should tell you my news." Kwame leaned back in his chair. "We've all heard about the crackdown on smuggling, but that's merely a smoke screen to throw as many people as possible into the corrections camps. The reaping you have been called to participate in is a new experiment, though it is an echo from the past. The Council hopes to flood the Gateway with souls, and Chicago will be the swollen river. Within a few months, this city will become the next Phoenix, the next Singapore, the next Mexico City. In a word, it will burn."

I shook my head. "Why would they do that? It doesn't make sense."

"It makes perfect sense if you suspect the Gateway of being something other than what they claim it to be."

I rolled my eyes. "Here we go again."

"Maybe it's time you listened for a change." He waved as if dismissing me. "Go ahead. Live in your Reaper dream world. You play goody two-shoes by running around trading boots for balms and pants for pills, but at the end of the day you go home to the apartment and food the Council provides, the very same Council that condemns the people of your district to their impoverished conditions. While you sleep, parents sit at bedsides trying to comfort children who cry out because of fever-induced nightmares."

Kwame gestured toward the street as he continued. "They all have to live in those nightmares every day. You simply visit them, provide the means to prolong their suffering, and then go home. You don't clean up their vomit. You don't lie awake at night worrying that their halting breaths might halt for good. You just go home."

I clutched a section of Mex's cloak and strangled the fibers. "Are you saying I shouldn't give them medicine?"

"Not at all. You should try to help. But what you're doing isn't enough. You're watering a lily in the desert.

You help it survive, but for what purpose? To suffer more?" He waved an arm as if clearing chess pieces from a board. "You have to wipe away the sand, till new soil, and make Chicago an oasis in the midst of the surrounding wilderness." Clenching a fist, he infused his voice with passion. "You have to cut the head off the serpent who encourages these people to breed only to arrange for them to die so he can inhale their souls and become fattened by their life energy."

I glanced at Sing. She shifted from foot to foot, her eyes darting.

"Look," I said, focusing again on Kwame, "I'd love to do all that, and I admit a lot of things don't add up, but without proof that the Gateway is phony—"

"Proof? You say you want proof?" He clapped his hands. "I was waiting for that. You've been demanding proof for months, and now I can finally hang it on a banner and bop you on the head with it."

Sing covered her mouth, stifling a laugh.

"Is that so?" I crossed my arms over my chest. "Okay. Let's hear this head-bopping evidence."

He shook a finger at me. "Not so fast, my eager friend. This is evidence that must be discovered at a slower pace." He leaned forward. "Of course you know that a Reaper is able to partially merge into the realm of ghosts."

I nodded. "Right. I've done that."

"Of course you have. Now hush a minute." He lowered his voice to a whisper. "I recently learned that if a Reaper allows himself to completely blend into the realm of ghosts, he can travel into the Gateway and see for himself what happens beyond. As long as he can stay in control of his mind, he can explore the beyond and return with whatever information he needs to expose the Gatekeeper. In fact, I have heard that one Reaper has already crossed the barrier and returned."

He stared at me for a moment as if milking his own dramatic pause.

"Okay," I said. "Go on."

He spread out his hands. "There isn't any more."

I stared at him. "That's it? That's your evidence?"

"Seeing is believing, isn't it?"

"Well, yeah, but I'd have to believe it first before I'd risk doing something so dangerous just to see your stupid evidence."

"Don't call it stupid just because you're a coward." He nodded at Sing. "Maybe she's brave enough to go."

"Don't play the competition angle on me." I pointed toward the train station. "The only way to know if your story's true is for me to go through the Gateway and come back. If a Reaper's done it, why would you need me to do it?"

"Because the Reaper who did it is the son of a Council member. He's a pampered Cardinal who isn't about to expose the Gateway for the cruel hoax that it is."

I crossed my arms over my chest. "And exactly how do you know this?"

"I go places most people don't. I keep my eyes and ears open. The snobby folks who run the show tend to be free with their words when an old derelict like me is around. Their noses are turned so high they can't even see me."

"That part I can believe." I leaned closer. "Do you have a name for this Cardinal?"

Kwame shook his head. "Only that the Cardinal is male and that his mother is a Council member."

"Okay, that's something to go on, but it'll have to wait." I pulled the cloak from my shoulder and let it hang from my hand. "For now, I have to find someone to masquerade as Sing."

"Surely you know someone who is bold, brave, and loves a challenge." Kwame nodded at Sing again. "Someone like Singapore, also known as Akua."

"Akua?" I looked at Sing. "Is that your real name?"

She slid a step back, her eyes wide. "How could he know?"

"I told you I get around." Kwame laughed. "It wasn't that hard to guess your name. Even though your mother kept her maiden surname when she married, it's a simple matter to search records to learn about her husband. Since your own status as a Reaper allows for your birth date to be known, I learned where your parents were when you were born. From that combination of data, I simply deduced your name. Perhaps you will explain my most excellent guess to Phoenix."

Sing's lips tightened. Clearly she didn't want to respond.

"Okay, you've proven your point. You get around." I let out a sigh. "We still need to find a fake Sing, but what girl her size would be safe roaming the streets in her district, especially one who isn't trained in self-defense?"

"Who says it has to be a girl?" Kwame said. "With a hood raised, a boy could pass for Sing."

Sing set her fists on her hips, her elbows pushing back her cloak. "Well, thanks a lot!"

"I meant with the cloak closed in front." Kwame laughed again. "Don't worry. Standing there like that, no one would ever mistake you for a boy."

Sing whipped her cloak to the front, a sheepish smile on her lips. "Okay. I should've seen that coming."

"Wait a minute," I said. "Sing, raise your hood."

She wrinkled her brow. "Why?"

"Just humor me."

As Sing slowly pulled her hood over her head, I studied her profile. Kwame was right. With the hood up and the cloak covering her curves, she could pass for a boy. "Cairo's about your height, and his voice hasn't deepened yet. He's itching to get started as a Reaper."

Sing touched her cheek. "But he's darker than I am."

"Only a shade. With the hood up, no one will notice the difference."

"He's freshly shaven." Sing teased her curls with her fingers. "He would need a wig."

"His mother has a wig she sometimes wears. The hood will keep it shadowed."

"You forgot one thing," Kwame said. "Incentive. What's in it for him? We're talking danger here. The Jungle's a tough place for a rookie."

"Good point." I painted a mental picture of Noah's home. I had gone there to reap his sister Tanya who died of pneumonia on a bitterly cold day in January. It was snowing so hard I nearly got lost in the whiteout, but Georgia's grief enhanced the death alarm and guided me through the blizzard. With her gratitude for keeping Tanya's soul from wandering in the storm, and the promise of a private apartment for Noah, we might have enough incentive. "I think I know a way to persuade him."

Sing took in a deep breath. "Okay, then. Let's see what we can do."

I gestured with my thumb. "I'm heading back to my

place to get showered first. Then I have to talk to Alex to make sure it's all going to work out with the suite mate thing. No sense in involving Cairo until everything's set."

"Sounds good," Sing said. "I need a shower, too. Let's talk across the alley when you know more."

Kwame shooed us away. "You're right. You both stink. Now go. You have a lot to do."

CHAPTER ELEVEN

AFTER SING AND I said good-bye to Kwame, we
jogged toward our alley, Mex's cloak still in my grasp.
The broken and crumbling sidewalk and the need to dodge
passersby forced us to employ agile footwork, adding to
our exhaustion. Still, we talked in spurts between breaths.

"How did you meet Kwame?" Sing asked.

"Reaping a soul right about where Murph was sitting.
He just walked out of that office and started talking to me."
I raised my brow. "Why?"

"Since you trust him so much, I was just wondering.
He obviously knows a lot." She glanced behind us. "How
old do you think he is?"

"Considering the gray in his hair and the amount of
wrinkles, I'd say sixty or so. What do you think?"

"I don't know. I was asking because his voice sounded
kind of familiar, like someone I knew who would be fifty-
five now if he hadn't died."

"Let me guess. Your father."

She smiled. "Good guess."

"Maybe they sound alike because they're both African,
maybe from the same region."

"Exactly. For some reason, he brought up my name
intentionally. Kwame is Ghanaian, meaning 'born on

Saturday.' My father was from Ghana and had the same name. Since a seventh of the population were born on Saturday, you can imagine there are a lot of men named Kwame."

"Don't they get confused?"

"We also have what we call Christian names, so there's no problem."

"And Akua means..."

"Born on Wednesday. My father called me Akua, but my mother called me by my Christian name and used it on all my official documents, so that's the name I remember most from my childhood."

I angled my head, trying to see her eyes. "Mind telling me that name?"

"Kind of. I like Singapore better."

"I'm the same way. I've gotten used to Phoenix." I slowed to allow a bicyclist to veer past us. "Does this Kwame look anything like your father? Besides being an African male, of course."

Sing stared straight ahead for a moment as if comparing images in her mind. "The voice was the only similarity I noticed."

"But we still don't know why he brought up your name."

"Right," Sing said. "It was almost like a signal, like a coded message. I'll have to think about it."

"If you figure it out, let me know."

When we stopped at Sing's apartment building, I stood with her at the door. People approached on the sidewalk from both directions, each one staring at us. Few ever passed by a Reaper without taking notice. We had to maintain decorum. Attempting an aloof air, I nodded at

Sing. She nodded in return, her expression solemn. That exchange would have to be enough of a good-bye.

I hurried to my building, ran up the interior stairs to my room, and fished the keys from my belt. I turned the first two deadbolts, as usual, but the bottom one felt loose, as if already unlocked. Since I exited through the window last night, I last locked them from the inside. Could I have forgotten one?

After stowing the keys in my pants pocket and tying Mex's cloak around my waist, I withdrew my dagger, slowly turned the knob, and pushed the door open a sliver. With daylight pouring in from the window, much of the interior lay in view. Everything seemed in order, though my reading chair was out of sight.

As I widened the opening, the hinges squeaked. I cringed. I never bothered to lubricate them because they acted as a great burglar alarm, but now they threatened to backfire on me.

"Come in, Phoenix." It was a woman's voice, low and calm. "After all, this is your apartment."

With my dagger still drawn, I walked in, loosening and dropping Mex's cloak along the way. Alex sat in my chair, a business satchel at her side and my book open over her leather-clothed lap. With a finger twirling her hair, she flipped through the pages. "*Nineteen Eighty-Four* by George Orwell. How fitting."

"I thought so. It's a favorite of mine."

"Really?" She closed the book with a snap and stared at me with her steely predator eyes. "Until they become conscious they will never rebel, and until after they have rebelled they cannot become conscious."

"That's from the book." I slid the dagger into my belt

and stood in front of her about three paces away. "What are you trying to say?"

Her stare stayed riveted on me. "Are you conscious, Phoenix? Have you ever thought of rebelling?"

Crandyke's warning about Alex being able to read thoughts returned to mind. Maybe it would be best to answer boldly. "Of course. Who hasn't? Is thinking about rebellion a crime?"

"Not yet. But we can't be sure the Gatekeeper will allow freedom of thought to continue. You had best keep dissident thoughts squelched."

"Like your thoughts about the Gatekeeper?"

"I am merely stating facts." She withdrew a sheet of paper and a pen from her satchel. "Let's get to business. I talked to Shanghai a little while ago. She is in line for pro-motion to Cardinal and made an advance request to have you as a roommate." She showed me the paper.

I took a step closer. The page contained text prompts and lines, handwritten entries on the lines, and two places for signatures at the bottom, one signed by Shanghai and the other blank. "Her request surprised me," Alex said. "I was unaware that you and she were so close."

"We grew up in the same training facility. We talked a lot when we were kids, but that was years ago."

"Then why would she ask for you now after so long?"

I shrugged. "I suppose she wants someone she can trust. She's a district hound, so she's a loner like me. Maybe she's worried she'll get someone... well... weird, I guess."

"Fair enough. From my viewpoint, you do seem to be a principled young man." She set the sheet on my book and poised a pen over the blank signature line. "Are you recep-tive to her request? I could order the arrangement even without your consent, but I am willing to consider your preferences as well, that is, if we can come to an agreement about..." She smiled. "Other issues."

"You mean about my participation in the reaping."

She reached out and grasped my hand. As her fingers touched mine, her gray eyes took on a brighter metallic luster. "That and another issue or two."

"Another issue?" I resisted a cringe. How could I guard my mind from this sly Owl? I glanced briefly at the wall panel behind the radiator—undisturbed. My medicine cache was still safe. "Let's put everything on the table so we'll both know what each other wants."

"Patience, Phoenix. Let's start with the bottom line." She released my hand and slid the form and the pen back into her satchel. "Have you decided to accept my invitation to join the reaping effort? Shanghai will be there, and she suggested that you join us. You would share a suite, so you'll have a friend close by. Since we have twenty-four hour camera surveillance in the suite, you won't have privacy, but we can't risk compromising prison security."

I exhaled. The loss of physical contact cleared my mind. Whatever her power was, I had to steer away from it. "I'll go on one condition—that you drop all charges against Colm and his family and release them."

Alex laughed. "Come now, Phoenix. They're the only leverage I have. If I let them go, what could I use to persuade you to stay?"

"My word isn't good enough?"

She locked stares with me again. "Maybe it is; maybe it isn't."

A feeling of weakness crept into my muscles. "But you just said I'm principled."

She offered a tight-lipped nod. "Principled is a fair description. Yet I witnessed you lying about who owned the pill bottle. A principled man will sometimes lie to protect a friend, so I need Colm in custody to ensure that you aren't lying now just to get him released."

I studied her eyes—steady, almost fierce. "Then let's do this. I'll go to the camp with Shanghai if you'll take out the surveillance cameras in our suite."

"Take out the cameras?" Alex's brow lifted. "There will be plenty of time for that kind of privacy when you move in with Shanghai later."

"No, seriously. Shanghai and I aren't going to—"

"Spare me the denials." One eye closed halfway. "The only reason you want to get rid of the cameras is to hide something, and I'm more concerned about subversive behavior than whether or not you and Shanghai engage in romantic activity."

"Like I told you before, I could've stopped you from taking Colm's family, and no one would've been the wiser. I've proven that I'm not subversive."

"And as I told you before, you overestimate your skills." A scowl tightening her face, she opened her jacket, revealing her gun. "As I said, the only reason for privacy is to engage in some sort of deception, and your persistence is lowering my estimate of your principles."

The weakness vanished, but anxiety spiked. When she slapped Fiona, she proved that she was a powder keg ready to explode. Yet, she wouldn't dare shoot me. I was too valuable. "Listen, either trust me or don't trust me. I want to try to help my friends, but that's as far as it goes. I'm not trying to rebel against the system. I admitted to thoughts of rebellion, but I'm not crazy enough to try anything."

Her scowl eased, but only slightly. "Okay, then why no cameras?"

"Simple." I intentionally relocked our stares. I couldn't back down now. "I want to enlist Shanghai to help me save Colm and his family from the corrections camp, and I don't want you to hear what we're planning."

Alex chuckled under her breath. "Well, I must say that's a refreshing approach. Throwing down a gauntlet, so to speak."

I nodded. "It's only fair. I would be joining you because you're holding Colm, but you won't release him because you want me to stay. In that scenario, there's no way they'll ever go free, so there's really no incentive for me to help you. Give me a fair shot at rescuing them, and I'll have all the reason in the world to stick around."

"Very clever, Phoenix. It seems that my stellar evaluation of you is accurate. And this little challenge might be an excellent opportunity to continue examining your skills." She picked up the book and rifled the pages. "Yet, I require one additional test to prove your loyalty."

"And that is?"

She snapped the book closed again. "Who was your helper behind Colm's house, the person who snatched my gun away?"

I took a step back. "What makes you think that person was my helper? I just found your gun on the roof."

"I have my sources. They tell me that you have a Reaper friend helping you."

I sharpened my tone. "Give me a break. District hounds don't have friends."

"An ally then. Semantics aren't important."

"Just for the sake of argument, let's say that I did

BRYAN DAVIS | 159

have an ally. Why would I do anything to get an ally into trouble?"

"Because betraying an ally will prove your loyalty to me." She touched her satchel. "As an incentive, I am willing to add to my offer. I have been authorized to shave ten years off your term as a Reaper."

"Ten years!" I bit my lip. That outburst damaged any hope of further negotiations. She had picked up my gauntlet and thrown it back in my face.

"Think of it, Phoenix." Her tone softened to an alluring hum. "You'll be finished at the age of twenty-three, a perfect time to begin a new life, get married, start a family. You'll be free."

Alex paused. Her offer seemed to hang in the air, like a tasty fruit ready to be plucked. Misty's words returned to my mind. *Just promise me you'll do everything you can to get out early. I hear there are shortcuts.*

"A shortcut," I whispered. This could be my chance. Alex already knew I wanted to get the Fitzpatricks out, and yet she still made this offer. Maybe I could get everything to work in my favor.

"Now tell me. Who helped you last night?" Alex fingered her gun's grip. "I already have my suspicions, but I want to hear it from your own lips."

"Then from my own lips…" I strode to the place I had dropped Mex's cloak and brought it back, letting gravity unfold it. "Mexico City helped me. We call him Mex. This is his."

She eyed the cloak. "Mexico City? The roamer who can barely reap a level one?"

"*Could* barely reap a level one. He died at the Gateway depot this morning. He was carrying medical contraband, so Bartholomew sucked the life out of him. They let me keep his cloak."

Alex touched the frayed material. "What a shame."

"Really?" I tossed the cloak to the floor. "Are you sorry they did your dirty work for you?"

Alex shot to her feet. She grabbed my arm, bent it behind my back, and shoved me against the wall, rubbing my cheek on the rough plaster. Cold steel pressed against my skull. Her breaths blew past my ear, hot and heavy. "You think you're so smart, don't you? Three years on the street, and you know it all. You think you're bucking the system being Mr. Nice Guy Reaper, looking down your nose at loyalists. You think I'm just an enforcer who gets her jollies inflicting pain." She twisted my arm, sending shock waves to my spine. "Well, you're wrong. There is method to my madness. Pain is just one tool in my arsenal of ways to get what I want. And what I want right now is for you to realize that you're dealing with someone who could jerk your soul out of your skull and hurl you into the abyss without a second thought. And if I find out you've been lying to me, that's exactly what I'll do."

I grimaced but refused to grunt. "What's the abyss?"

"A place no one wants to go." She spun me around and pressed the gun barrel between my eyes. "You have nothing to worry about if you'll keep that smart-aleck mouth of yours shut."

I gave her a shallow nod. My stupid mouth nearly cost me my life. But did it cost me a reduced term as a Reaper?

"In any case..." She backed away a step. "I agree to your conditions. Pack your things. A new district hound will take your place and this apartment as soon as possible.

I will meet you at the camp facility at sundown this evening."

I nodded, using all my strength to keep from shaking. "Sundown. I'll be there." I gave her a sideways glance. "Is the deal about the ten years still intact?"

"That part is set in stone."

I suppressed a celebratory shout. I needed to keep the conversation businesslike. "You said there was another issue or two."

"There are, but you're not ready to discuss them. If you prove yourself at the camp, I might change my mind." Alex slid the gun behind her jacket, picked up her satchel, and strode out, closing the apartment door with a loud click.

As soon as her footsteps faded down the hall, I locked the door and thrust a fist into the air. Yes! Ten years off my ball-and-chain sentence! If only I could tell Misty. We would dance together like a couple of kids. We got our shortcut, sealed in stone. All I had to do was survive.

Still, Alex's "Another issue or two" nagged at my mind. What could she have meant? I shook my head. It wouldn't do any good to dwell on it.

I hurried to my medical cache. Since I wouldn't be living here, at least for a while, I had to get rid of it. Besides, I probably wouldn't need it anymore, and everything would expire soon.

After I pried the panel away, retrieved the box, and put the panel back in place, I looked out the window at Sing's apartment. Through her fire-escape-access door's window, only a linoleum floor and a gas cookstove lay in view. She was probably in the shower.

I threw the box across the alley. It clanked on Sing's

metal landing and slid against the threshold. That would do for now. I could tell Sing to hide it later.

I rushed through a shower and shave, changed to a fresh set of Reapers' travel clothes, and hauled a suitcase from a storage shelf in my closet. After throwing in all my toiletries, clothes, and Mex's cloak and adapter tube, I walked around my apartment, looking for any other belongings. With only one room, it didn't take more than a couple of minutes. The next resident could keep the dishes and bed linens. After all, they belonged to the Council. I would probably get new ones at the Cardinal condo.

I ran a hand along the top of my dresser. The tri-fold picture frame was gone. Had it fallen into a drawer while I was packing my clothes? I jerked open the top drawer. Two mothballs rolled inside. I slammed it shut and yanked open the middle drawer, then the bottom. Empty.

After a quick search around the dresser, I looked at my old chair where Alex had sat. Might she have taken my photos before I arrived? She could have easily hidden the frame in her satchel. But why would she want pictures of Misty and my parents? That made no sense at all, unless she planned to contact my father to learn more about me, maybe to find out how "principled" I was when I was younger. But even that didn't make sense. If she wanted to use my parents as leverage against me, why would she need the photos? Didn't the Council know where they live now?

I caressed my pewter ring, smooth except for a few bumps and notches. At least Misty's gift would keep memories alive. I could ask Alex about the frame later.

I walked to the window again. Sing sat on her fire-escape railing with the medical box on her lap, the lid open as she peered inside. With her windblown hair freshly washed and dried, her face clean of tear tracks, and laundered clothes fitting close to her athletic form, she looked amazing.

When she saw me, a bright smile lit up her face. "I got a present at my doorstep."

I leaned out. "Since I'm leaving I had to get rid of it. Didn't want anyone seeing me carrying it out the door."

"So is everything set?"

I nodded. "Alex came by. We made the arrangements for Shanghai and me."

"No cameras?"

"No cameras."

She grinned. "I would like to have been a fly on the wall to hear how you swung that deal."

"Trust me. It wasn't easy." I climbed out and plunked my feet down on the fire-escape landing. Leaning over the railing, I could almost reach Sing's swaying shoes. "I'm all packed. When I get there I'll figure out the best way to sneak you into the camp and then come and get you, probably in the middle of the night."

Sing closed the box. "When are you going to ask Noah... I mean, Cairo?"

"Now. If he's up for it, I'll bring him here." I pulled out my watch and checked the time—four thirty-two. "What are you going to do until then?"

"Get my apartment ready for Cairo and pack my stuff. I suppose I can't bring much."

I shook my head. "Sneaking you in might not be easy, so you'd better travel light."

As we gazed at each other, she lifted her hand, kissed her palm, and blew over it. A freshening breeze flapped my cloak. Goose bumps ran along my arms. It seemed that her gesture reached across the gap and tickled my skin with a teasing caress.

Keeping my eyes locked on hers, I kissed my own palm, but I didn't blow the kiss. How could I send her that kind of signal, especially now that my wedding had drawn so much closer?

A tear glimmered in Sing's eye. "I'll see you soon, Phoenix." She tucked the box under her arm and hurried into her apartment.

When the door closed, I climbed onto the railing and looked at the pavement below. For some reason it seemed farther away than ever before. Of course my mind was playing tricks on me. With the dangers that lay ahead, my better judgment was probably trying to warn me to reconsider our insane plan. But I couldn't. Too many lives depended on the outcome.

I leaped and plunged into the alley, maybe for the last time.

CHAPTER TWELVE

I WALKED ALONG THE street toward Cairo's house, this time with my hood up. The eyes of several families perched on front steps followed me, nervous, likely wondering who in their neighborhood might be ready to die.

With the cloud-veiled sun sinking toward the horizon, time was running short. I couldn't stop and explain why I had raised my hood—not because the temperature had dropped; I needed to display a measure of coolness and wear my aloof persona. My own confidence might be contagious enough to help Cairo decide that he could endure a short stint in a dangerous Jungle district.

I climbed the three steps to Cairo's door and knocked loudly. As before, classical music boomed from speakers inside, Mozart this time, if I remembered my music history correctly. "Requiem Mass" would have been perfect background music, but it sounded like a lively violin concerto. That would have to do.

When the door opened, Georgia appeared. The moment she recognized me, her brow lifted. "Phoenix? Back so soon?"

"Yes. I need a favor."

"A favor?" She fanned her face. "Heavens' sakes,

Phoenix, you scared me half to death. I thought you had come to reap my soul. I've been having chest pains, and I thought they were from indigestion, but when I saw you, I was sure a heart attack was on its way."

I pushed back my hood. "I apologize. I just want to talk to Cairo. I have something important I'd like him to do."

"Then I'm not about to die?"

"Not that I know of." I leaned closer and lowered my voice to a whisper. "But I've learned some things that worry me. I'm on a mission to find out more. I'm suspicious about how the Council is using the Gateway. If the worst is true, then Tanya's eternal existence is at stake."

She gasped. "Tanya? My baby?"

I slid my hand into hers. "And Cairo can help me."

Tears in her eyes, she nodded. "Then you name it. He'll do it." We walked into the room where we had performed the initiation. Still wearing his cloak, Cairo sat on the sofa plucking his cello, apparently satisfied with playing pizzicato instead of sawing the strings with his ragged bow. With the boom box now turned down, his out-of-tune notes dominated the soundscape.

"What's up?" Cairo stared at me with vibrant eyes. "Got a soul for me to reap?"

I maintained a stoic expression. "Not yet, but something related to reaping."

Georgia and I sat next to Cairo, one of us on each side. "Now, listen," Georgia said, "you pay attention to Phoenix and do what he says. He's your mentor, so he'll steer you right."

"Sure." Noah slid his cello to the floor and again stared at me. "Let's hear it."

His eager eyes told me that I could drop the persona

and speak candidly. "Okay," I said, spreading out my hands. "Here's the deal. You met Singapore. Well, she has to leave for a while, but she doesn't want the people in her district to worry about no one being around to reap souls while she's gone. You see, we have some suspicions about what really happens at the Gateway, and that means we're not super confident that the souls we've reaped, including Tanya's, are in a safe place, so we're going to do everything we can to find out."

"Okay. What do you want me to do?"

I pinched the edge of his cloak. "We need you to live in Sing's apartment until further notice. I'll let your mother know where it is in case she receives word of your new assignment. Once in a while you'll walk around Sing's district with your hood up and your head down so people will think the district's covered, and no one will be the wiser that you're not Sing. It won't take you long to start picking up death alarms, but keep your ears open for street gossip about someone dying and your eyes open for a death messenger. Someone or something will lead you to whoever the victim is. Then you can reap the soul."

I paused to take a breath. "I know it sounds dangerous, but—"

"No, no!" He grabbed my wrist. "The more dangerous, the better. I'm in."

Georgia fanned her face again. "Oh, Phoenix, this makes me so nervous, but if you say he can help Tanya, we'll both do whatever it takes."

"Perfect." I pushed Cairo's hood back and rubbed his bald head. "We have a lot to do."

For the next hour, Georgia and I worked on transforming Cairo into Sing by teasing Georgia's wig into Sing-like curls and fastening it onto his head with poster-board adhesive. While Georgia packed Cairo's essentials in a backpack, I used the last few minutes to help him mimic Sing's silky voice. He caught on quickly, his ear for music and his youthful vocal cords providing the perfect blend of talents. When we finished, we said good-bye to Georgia. She cried for a moment but quickly calmed herself and sent us away with a blessing.

While I walked with Cairo, I coached him on how to move in Sing's graceful manner. Again he picked up the new skill without a problem. After I explained how to get information from the gossip network, I glanced at the descending sun. I had to hurry.

We jogged the rest of the way to my apartment, bustled inside, and climbed out the window. As soon as our feet touched down on the fire-escape landing, Sing opened the door and peered at us from her apartment. "I'd better not show myself while you're out there." She gestured with her head. "Come over through my building's front entrance. I'm in two nineteen."

With his hood raised, Cairo clutched the straps of his backpack and jumped up to the railing. "I'll just take the shortcut." He leaped across the gap, landed with one foot on Sing's railing, and dropped to her fire escape. When he settled, he spun toward me and grinned. "Piece of cake."

I gave him a thumbs up. "I guess there's nothing to worry about."

Sing ushered Cairo inside. After he disappeared within, she cast a worried look at me.

I leaned forward against the railing and tried for a comforting tone. "It'll be all right. Just be ready to go at a moment's notice. Someone will be knocking at apartment two nineteen in the middle of the night. I hope it's me, but it might be someone else."

She nodded. "The entry code for the main door is six, nine, one, four."

"Got it." As soon as she went inside, I climbed back through the window, grabbed my suitcase, and hustled out, locking the door behind me. The camp lay in an abandoned industrial district about three miles away, an easy walk under normal conditions, but lugging a suitcase would make it difficult to get there before sundown.

When I arrived at the street, I broke into a quick march toward a busy thoroughfare at the next block. I could try to hitchhike once I got there, but most people hesitated to give anyone a ride, much less a Reaper. Picking up one of us probably felt like inviting death itself into the car, so standing with my thumb in the air would likely be a waste of time.

As I walked, the rain returned in a spitting drizzle. I raised my hood and accelerated a notch. Maybe I could pass the time by checking on Crandyke and seeing how he could help my cause.

I plugged the clasp into my valve. When the cloak energized, I probed the fibers with my mind. "Crandyke? How's it going?"

"What do you think? I'm a disembodied slave to a tyrannical master who refuses to complete his sacred duty to set me free."

I waited for a woman to pass me on the sidewalk before answering. "That's pretty close to the mark. But maybe if you think of yourself as a genie in a lamp, you'll deal with it better."

"And you want three wishes, don't you?"

"It's for a good cause. Rescuing an innocent family… and securing your ticket to the Gateway."

"All right. All right. But if you don't send me through the Gateway soon, I'll become your worst nightmare. You won't be able to plug in your cloak without hearing me screaming bloody murder at the top of my lungs."

"As if you had lungs." I stifled a laugh. "Don't worry. You'll get through the next time I'm there."

"I suppose I'll have to trust you," he grumbled. "Not that I have a choice."

"No. You don't."

"What's your first wish?"

I glanced at the river to my left. Every few seconds, a car or truck whizzed by, blocking my view for a moment and raising a racket. Following the grayish-green water upstream would take me straight to the camp. "What do you know about the corrections camp near the river? I've passed by it, but I've never been inside."

"Quite a bit. I toured it once with a high-security clearance. While I worked at the enforcement office, I procured equipment and supplies for them, and I hired their security personnel, you know, interviewed candidates, did background checks, that sort of thing."

"Is there an unguarded door? Any way to enter and exit without being seen?"

His voice took on a sarcastic bite. "Well, being able to leave like that would pretty much ruin the whole prison motif, don't you think?"

"I don't mean for a prisoner. I'm going there for a mass reaping, and I assume my temporary quarters will be close by or maybe inside the compound itself."

"A mass reaping? Imagine that. A Reaper who won't do his job gets a cushy assignment."

"Stay on topic, Crandyke. The sooner I get my answers, the sooner you'll get what you want."

"Yes, master. I will obey your every whim." Crandyke's tone altered to that of a proud know-it-all. "The camp complex is surrounded by a tall fence with razor wire on top. It used to be a manufacturing facility that housed a few employees in an old dorm they called the Hilton, a joke, I assume. It's pretty rundown. Anyway, the security is high even there—motion-sensitive cameras in nearly every room. But guards in that building are few and far between. If memory serves, there is a rear entrance for residents that allows direct access to the outside without having to pass through a gate, though there is an armed guard posted there. I doubt that he would check a Reaper who is going in, but going out is a different matter, as you might expect."

"They don't want a prisoner to leave disguised as a Reaper."

"Right. Prison guards tend to want to keep prisoners inside. They do their jobs, unlike some people I know."

"Cut the commentary. It's getting old." A truck breezed by, flapping my cloak. After waiting for it to settle, I probed the fibers again. "What else can you tell me?"

"Can't you get out of this weather? Between the wind and the rain, I'm getting dizzy and itchy."

"I'm moving as fast as I can. Just answer the question. It'll get your mind off the weather."

"Okay, okay." Crandyke's voice reverted to his pompous persona. "It's a work camp. Until recently the prisoners made pine-box coffins, but since most corpses are burned to save resources, they retrofitted the plant. I'm not sure what they make there now. I wasn't in the loop, and I didn't really care. But the new production started only a couple of months ago, so they probably haven't rolled much out yet."

"Interesting." I imagined an assembly line at a table surrounded by workers, each one vanishing from his station as the seconds passed—a bizarre scene. Why would they retrofit a plant if they were planning to kill the laborers? "Maybe I'll get a chance to see the operation and figure it all out."

"If you have time. My guess is that you'll be busy collecting souls, and not just because of new executions they're scheduling. Past executions have a way of haunting the axe men, if you know what I mean."

"A lot of ghosts around?"

"Rumors. Just rumors. But from what I heard, some aren't shy about poking their non-physical noses where they don't belong. Hard to punish a ghost, you know."

"Right. All we can do is annoy them." I unplugged my clasp and let it dangle at my chest. Crandyke had already proven his usefulness, but now I had to refocus on my job.

When I finally arrived at the camp, I set my suitcase down and pushed my fingers through the chain links in the entry gate. The attached fence encircled a collection of old factory-like buildings—two-to-three-stories-high structures made of pale bricks and dirty glass.

Five feet above my head, razor wire ran in loops along the top of the fence. Ripped fabric intertwined with the wire here and there, and attached threads stretched out in the breeze.

At the far end of the paved entry driveway, a

concrete-and-glass watchtower loomed roughly thirty paces inside the gate. About fifty feet tall, it looked like a miniature air-traffic-control tower with two rifle barrels protruding from partially open windows that wrapped the upper third of the tower.

A searchlight sat on top inside a bowl-shaped structure that looked like a concrete bird's nest. A ladder on the tower's exterior wall stretched from the ground up to the bowl—an odd design. Did that mean there was no access to the searchlight from inside the tower? Maybe the searchlight was added after the tower was in use for a while.

Inside the camp, the wet breeze swept through an empty yard, an expanse of sparse grass with a well-beaten path around the perimeter, perhaps an exercise trail, barely discernable in the failing light. Except for the whisper of the wind, all was quiet... eerily quiet. Considering the early evening hour, maybe the inmates were taking a meal in one of the buildings, but no lights or movement indicated which one.

A solitary woman emerged from the base of the watchtower, her back toward me as she locked a metal door. With long lines of leather and flowing blonde hair, she had to be Alex. When she turned, she looked at her wristwatch, then at me, a smile emerging as she set a hand on a hip. "I should have known you'd be right on time."

"I have principles." I picked up my suitcase. "And one of them is to keep my friends alive."

Carrying her satchel, Alex hustled across the hundred-foot space between us. She whistled and twirled a finger in the air. A man looked out of one of the tower's windows and nodded. Seconds later, the gate began dragging across the entry road. When the gap grew to about three feet wide, it stopped. Without hesitating, I marched in.

"Shanghai is in the dorm eating her dinner," Alex said as the gate closed again. "I'll take you there."

"I heard they call it the Hilton."

"They do." She tucked the satchel under her arm. "How did you know?"

"I did some research." I inhaled deeply. The odor of dead fish tinged the air—the river's contribution to the ambiance. "When does the reaping begin?"

"The reaping?" Her brow bent. "Interesting angle, Phoenix, and well played. Feigning enthusiasm for this assignment, however, will not alter my watchfulness over you or Colm's family."

"It's not enthusiasm. It's information gathering. I told you I was doing research." I gave her a hard stare, focusing on her eyes. They no longer displayed a metallic glint. "And watch me all you want. You can't intimidate me."

"Perhaps not." She set a hand on my back and guided me toward a building at a far corner, a dormitory-like edifice with red bricks and clean windows—the Hilton. "There are others who might be able to intimidate you, but I will spare you that experience, at least for now."

A human shape flitted past a second-floor window in one of the factory buildings. When I turned to focus, nothing was there. It appeared to be a little girl, but if everyone was having dinner, why would she be wandering alone in a prison factory?

As we walked, I glanced at Alex's satchel, now in her hand, swinging with her gait. Might my photos be inside? I had to ask. "Alex, after you left my apartment, I packed all my stuff, but something was missing."

"A picture frame with three photos," she said without missing a beat. "I took them. Once you finish the reaping, you will be allowed to see your family again. Since another branch of government scrubs their data, I needed the photos to make sure I could find them."

My face grew hot. "You could've just asked."

"I wanted to surprise you." Still looking straight ahead, she kept her expression blank. "I suppose the surprise is ruined now."

I tried to read her voice for any hint of deceit. She probably thought Misty was my sister, so that might be a way to get her to tip her hand. "Do you know if all three still live together?"

"Not yet." A smile bent her lips. "I still have more research to do."

I suppressed a wince. That didn't work. I tried to think of another way to get her to spill information, but nothing came to mind.

She opened one of the Hilton's double doors and ushered me into a small lobby where three high-backed chairs and a sofa surrounded a low table. Fluorescent lights in the ceiling flickered, and worn spots and stains marred the flat carpet. Apparently "the Hilton" had seen better days. A camera mounted on a corner wall bracket followed our movements, letting out a soft whir as it rotated.

A clinking sound drifted from a hallway to the left. We followed it to a dining area where Shanghai sat at a two-person table just a few steps inside. At least six other tables of various sizes and shapes stood to the left and right. Chairs perched upside down on the empty tabletops, many with cobwebs strung from leg to leg. Another camera sat in a bracket on the back wall, but it stayed motionless.

With a fork poised over a circular meat patty, Shanghai pushed back her hood and smiled. "Would you like to join me, young man?"

I nodded. "Assuming Alex approves."

"I do. I'll get the cook to send a meal for you." Alex took my suitcase. "While you're eating, I'll put this in your room and personally check to make sure there are no cameras. Shanghai can escort you to your suite when you're finished. She'll fill you in on what I've told her so far."

When Alex departed, I slid into the chair across from Shanghai and leaned forward. "I got some good info on this place, so—"

"Shhh!" She glanced at the camera, then whispered, "There's a microphone hidden somewhere close by. I found out the hard way."

"How?"

"I muttered something about the meat being as tough as shoe leather. The cook came in later with a new plate and said, 'Try the other shoe.'"

I grinned. "Actually, that's pretty funny."

"True, but it kind of shook me up. They can probably hear our whispers now."

I leaned back. "I'm not worried about it. I actually told Alex we're going to try to spring Colm and his family."

Her eyes shot open. "What! Are you crazy?"

"I traded that info to get rid of the cameras. I'll tell you more when we get to our rooms."

She touched her valve, fingering the clasped hands. "I'll look forward to that."

A man wearing a dirty apron over a white T-shirt walked in, clanked a plate down in front of me, and grumbled "Bon appétit" as he shuffled away.

I stared at the meat patty, stiff mashed potatoes, and string beans. "Is any of this worth eating?"

"Only if you want to vomit." Shanghai slid a fork to me. "You might have a stronger stomach than I do."

"Well, I need to eat something. The potatoes look edible."

"Maybe. If you like them crunchy."

For the next few minutes, I force-fed myself the potatoes. They had no discernable taste, and I had to swallow hard to get them down. Still, they filled the void in my gut, and I was giving Alex time to check on the camera situation.

When the last bite hit bottom, I pushed my chair back and rose. "Let's go."

Shanghai led me up a flight of stairs lit by a single flood lamp in one corner, then through a second-floor entryway and down a dimly lit hall until we stopped in front of a worn wooden door with an elliptical metallic label—205. "This is your room," she said, handing me a key. She pointed several steps farther down the hall. "And two-oh-seven is mine. We can pass through the bathroom in between. No kitchen, though. We'll pick up our meals in that dining area."

I searched the hallway's ceiling and walls—no cameras so far. "Got it."

As I inserted the key, Shanghai padded along the carpet toward her room. "I'm going to get out of this costume. I'll knock on your bathroom door in a few minutes."

"Sound good." I entered and flipped on the wall switch. Across the room, a bulb in a shaded lamp flashed to life, providing only a little light. Partially spent candles standing here and there along with several matchbooks proved that electricity shut-off time included the Hilton, and a lack of windows made the dismal situation worse, especially since the room felt warm and stuffy. Getting some fresh air from outside wasn't an option.

After tossing my cloak and weapons belt on the bed, I scanned the room for cameras. An empty bracket, similar to the camera brackets downstairs, hung at one upper corner. The walls were bare except for a few cracks in the plaster, an ironing board folded into a nearby recess, and a framed painting above a two-person sofa. The oil rendering showed the Gatekeeper sitting on a park bench with a little towheaded boy in his lap. Both smiled while other children frolicked on playground equipment—a fantasy, really, at least for the people in my district.

A door stood closed to my right. I opened it, letting light into a bathroom. The size of a walk-in closet, it had the typical setup—a linoleum floor, toilet, sink-and-vanity combo, mirror, and curtained shower stall. The faucet in the sink leaked with a steady drip, and the toilet gurgled every few seconds. Another door stood closed on the opposite side—Shanghai's access to the bathroom.

I shut my door and sidled to a waist-high dresser where my suitcase sat. I flicked open the latches and distributed my clothes and Mex's cloak in the three stacked drawers, two of which had a knob only on one side. Changing into shorts and T-shirt would be more comfortable, but with a journey still ahead to retrieve Sing, it would be best to stay clothed for travel, minus my cloak. I could put it back on later.

When I lifted the final garment, the adapter tube slid across the bottom of the suitcase. I breathed a deep sigh. Poor Mex. Just a few more weeks and he would have been home in Abilene, maybe sipping iced tea with his parents and his younger brother. His nightmare service as a roamer finally completed, he could have lived in peace, far from the dark Jungle that turned him into a desperate soul trader.

I grabbed the tube and shoved it into a drawer. Those pigs! They murdered him! No trial. No witnesses allowed to testify. They wouldn't even listen to me. They didn't care about him or anyone else! If only there was a way to crash the system, unplug the Gateway, and send all the Reapers home.

I slammed the drawer. No. It couldn't happen—not as long as lost souls wandered around unable to get to their destination. Mom, Dad, and Misty would have to keep waiting for my return.

Letting out a huff, I sat heavily on the double bed. Something bounced under my cloak. I dug out a dark flat object and turned it over—a computer tablet. I never had a tablet of my own, but I knew how to use one. Hanging around Paul and other DEOs provided some benefits.

When I tapped the power button, the screen blinked on, showing my face with "Phoenix – District 19" underneath. I pressed my thumb on the screen's security box. The image's eyes flashed. My face disappeared, replaced by a bright blue background and three application icons labeled *Schedule, Map,* and *Messages.*

At the bathroom, a light glimmered under the door then disappeared. Maybe Shanghai had opened her access door, though no latch sounds had come through.

I tapped on the *Schedule* icon. Nothing happened. I tapped it harder. Still nothing. Mimicking Paul's fix-it technique, I slapped the back of the tablet. The screen cleared, and a document opened showing times and activities for the coming week. Each day listed breakfast at eight, lunch at noon, dinner at six, and curfew at eleven.

Tomorrow's schedule included a short tour of the compound in the morning, a session called *Demonstration* in the afternoon, and finally, in the evening, *Entertainment in Jail Yard*.

Reaping filled the rest of the week's spaces. At the bottom, a note said to wear our Reapers' cloaks and traveling clothes for every session.

The light in the bathroom glimmered again. I set the tablet on the bed and tiptoed to the door. With a knuckle, I gave it a light tap. "Shanghai? You in there?"

No one answered.

I opened the door slowly, silently. A dim glow emanated from behind the shower curtain. With my fist tightened, I set a foot gently on the floor and eased my way in. The glow, twin clouds of pale blue haze, vibrated on the curtain, like candles flickering in a fog. As I reached for the edge of the curtain, I listened. What was that sound? A hum? A whimper?

I jerked the shower curtain across the rod. A girl no older than eight stood on the other side. Barefoot and wearing a dirty, ankle-length dress, she stared at me, her eyes glowing. With tears dripping and disappearing before they struck the drain at her feet, she sniffed and said, "Do you know where my mommy is?"

CHAPTER THIRTEEN

I DON'T KNOW WHERE she is, but maybe I can find her." I bent over and looked her in the eye. She appeared to be a level two plus. A few questions would determine how entrenched she was. "What's your name?"

"Tori."

"And how old are you?"

She pushed dark stringy hair from her eyes. "Seven."

"Well, Tori, maybe we can work together." I straightened and gestured for her to follow.

As she stepped onto the linoleum, the opposite door opened, letting in more light. Shanghai entered carrying a computer tablet. When she saw Tori, she halted and reared her head back. "Well! Who do we have here?"

"Tori. I'm guessing a two-point-four, maybe higher." I waved for Shanghai to follow as well. "Let's see what we can find out about her."

When the two entered my room, Shanghai, now dressed in black shorts, white T-shirt, and ankle-high red socks, sat on the bed with her tablet in her lap, crossing her legs under it. The red socks drew my eyes to her legs, lean and toned.

I wrenched my gaze away, sat on the sofa, and patted the space next to me. "Tori, sit here."

She climbed up, her hands and knees not quite touching the seat. This ability to adapt her non-physical body's position with respect to furniture meant that she was, indeed, higher than level two, though her glowing eyes gave evidence that she hadn't quite reached level three.

Once she settled, I slid my arm around her, hoping to pose as a family member. "Tori, where was the last place you saw your mommy?"

"At the grinding station." She pointed toward the hallway. "In one of the other buildings."

"Oh, yes. I should have known."

Tori squinted. "How could you know? I've never seen you working there."

"Two point seven," I whispered to Shanghai before focusing on Tori again. "You're right, but I would like to know more. What does she grind?"

"She grinds the glass for the…" She wrinkled her button nose. "For the lenses."

"Ah! The lenses!" I sneaked a glance at Shanghai and gave her a quick head gesture. She picked up my signal to join in. Since she went through the training, she would know to take the role of the ignorant bystander while I maintained familiarity.

"Tell me about the lenses," Shanghai said. "I don't know anything about them."

Tori formed her fingers into circles around her eyes. "They're bigger than glasses. We put them into the white circle things."

Shanghai nodded. "How big are the white circles?"

"Big enough to stand on, like a trash can lid, only a little taller."

I lifted an eyebrow. They sounded like Gateway pedestals. "What does your mommy do at the grinder?"

"Well, it's a big wheel that spins real fast, and Mommy makes the lenses smooth and the right shape."

"Can you remember the last thing she said to you?" I asked.

Tori touched her scalp. "She was telling me to keep my hair away from the grinder."

Shanghai cringed but said nothing.

"The next thing I knew," Tori continued, "I was standing in the middle of the square where we put everything together."

"The assembly room," I said.

She nodded. "But I couldn't find Mommy anywhere, and no one would talk to me."

Shanghai prodded me with a finger. "Do you think her mother was reassigned?"

I lowered my voice. "More likely reaped. She might have tried a bit too hard to rescue her daughter, if you know what I mean."

Shanghai's cringe returned. "Unfortunately, I do. They aren't likely to send a condemned prisoner to a hospital."

"Right. No one is supposed to leave this camp alive."

Shanghai shifted closer to Tori. "Well, sweetheart, would you like me to take you—"

"Wait!" I held up a hand. "Tori can help us."

Shanghai narrowed her eyes. "How?"

"She seems to know the layout of this place, so maybe she can—"

"Be a guide," Shanghai whispered. "And if no one would talk to her, she's probably invisible to non-Reapers, so that's even better."

"If she can control her visibility, that would be best. She could run interference for me when I go out tonight."

"Distract the guard, you mean. Pretend to be an escaping prisoner. But the only way she can consciously control it is if she learns that she's... well... passed on."

"Exactly." I gave Shanghai an approving smile. "You haven't changed at all. You're just as smart as I remember."

She offered a thankful nod. "As are you, Phoenix."

I gazed into her glistening eyes. It felt good to be with her, to renew a long-lost friendship. I wanted to tell her so, tell her how much I enjoyed her company, but now wasn't the time. "So we have to figure out how to inform Tori of her condition without scaring—"

"I'm going," Tori said as she slid out of her seat. "It's been nice talking to you, but I still have to find my mommy. She's probably worried about me."

"Wait." I instinctively reached for her, but my hand passed through her body.

She turned and blinked at me. "Why does that happen?"

I pulled my hand back. "You mean why do things pass right through you?"

"Uh-huh. It happens a lot. It's scary."

"Sit down, please." I patted the seat again. "I'll tell you where I think your mother is, but there's a lot to explain."

"While you do that..." Shanghai pressed her thumb on her tablet screen. "I'm going to study the map of the compound."

"Thanks." I smirked. "I get the easy job."

"Hey, someone's got to tackle the tough stuff. I'll brief you when I get the layout memorized."

For the next several minutes, I talked with Tori and

eased her into an understanding about her status as a dead little girl and the likelihood that her mother had died trying to rescue her, allowing her to come to the conclusions herself. She took it surprisingly well, probably because she had a growing suspicion all along. Once she accepted her condition and realized that we would eventually take her to the Gateway to be reunited with her mother, the rest was easy.

"So," I said, settling back in my seat, "if you can learn to control being visible or invisible, you can help us."

Tori wrinkled her brow. "I think I already did once. A guard saw me a little while ago. I was looking out the window when you got here."

"Ah!" I winked. "That was you I saw spying on me."

"Yup." Her grin revealed two missing front teeth. "I ran away, but there wasn't another door, so I stopped. I was afraid the guard would catch me, but he just walked right past me. He called me a..." She covered her mouth. "I shouldn't say it. It's a bad word."

"Don't worry. I don't need to hear it." I drew a mental picture of the confrontation, though I had no idea what the inside of that building looked like. "Do you know how you disappeared?"

Tori nodded. "I just wished I could, real hard, like when I wished my daddy wouldn't die. Wishing didn't work for Daddy, but it worked for me."

I wrapped my fingers around Tori's hand, pretending to hold it. "And do you know how to become visible again?"

She cocked her head. "What do you mean? You can see me."

"We're Reapers, so we can see invisible souls. You

might be visible to others now, but we can't tell. Since you managed to get across the camp's yard without being noticed, you're probably still invisible."

Shanghai shifted closer. "How'd Tori get here without one of us seeing her?"

Tori pushed a ghostly finger through my chest. "I heard Alex talking to you, so I followed her here. While she was standing on the sofa and reaching to the ceiling, I sneaked into the bathroom and watched her."

"How?" I asked. "The bathroom was closed when I got here, and you can't open doors."

"It was?" Tori blinked. "How could that be? I walked right in."

"And the shower curtain was closed." I looked at Shanghai. "She still has awareness issues. She doesn't know she walked through a curtain and a solid door."

Shanghai nodded. "I picked that up."

"Still at least a few days short of level three." I turned back to Tori. "Did Alex do anything else?"

Tori tapped her chin. "Let's see. She put your suitcase on the dresser, but then she dropped something and pulled out the dresser to look for it."

Shanghai's brow shot up. I gave her a nod. That sounded suspicious.

I signaled for Shanghai to continue the conversation. As I padded toward the dresser, she set her tablet down, detached the camera from my weapons belt, and shifted to the sofa. "And then Alex left?" she asked.

"Uh-huh. But she never saw me."

I leaned over the dresser and looked behind it. A walnut-sized disk microphone adhered to the back panel. Alex was likely listening in. That meant she heard our plans to use Tori as a distraction and a guide.

I raised my thumb and pretended to speak into it, hoping Shanghai could figure out the signal.

She nodded and focused on Tori again. "Then I guess Alex didn't put a hidden camera anywhere."

Tori shook her head, making a lock of hair fall over her face. "Not that I saw."

As I walked back to the sofa, Shanghai pointed my camera at Tori. "Do you mind if I take a picture of you? We'll need a photo stick."

She straightened, pushed back her hair, and smiled, her eyes glowing brighter. "Okay."

"Good idea." I aimed my voice directly at the microphone. "Since Tori doesn't know how to become visible again, she can't distract the guard. I'll just go ahead and reap her and take her to the Gateway as soon as I'm allowed."

"That's what I was thinking." Shanghai snapped the photo, raising a click and a flash. "She'll be happier with her mother anyway."

"Goody!" Tori bounced in place. "And I'll see Daddy, too, I'll bet."

I slid my dagger from the weapons belt. "Listen, I'm pretty tired, so—"

"Want me to reap her?" Shanghai rose to her feet. "You can go to bed. I'll reap Tori in the bathroom where we won't disturb you."

I concealed a wince. With Tori's entrenchment level, the process would be excruciating. Alex would know that and listen for yelps of pain. "Down the hall would be better. And maybe I can sneak out tomorrow night after I get a better feel for this place. Without a decoy, it'll be impossible tonight."

"Fair enough. Go on to bed." Shanghai led Tori to the bathroom, stopped just inside the door, and peered around the jamb, pressing a finger to her lips to signal for Tori's silence.

I shuffled around, opened and closed two dresser drawers, and pulled back the bedcovers. I then tapped the dagger's blade against the wall hoping to mimic the sound of a clicking light switch.

After waiting a few seconds, I tiptoed to the dresser, slid the blade behind the adhesive that kept the microphone in place, and quietly pried it from the panel. With the microphone pinched between my fingers, I studied the surface. A tiny diode emitted red light next to an equally tiny rocker switch. Using the point of the blade, I tipped the switch the opposite way. The diode blinked off.

I quietly made a quick sweep of the room and checked every possible surface for another microphone. All clear. I slid the now-deaf one into my pocket and gestured for Shanghai. When she reentered with Tori and closed the door, I look past her, imagining the surfaces in her half of the suite. "You'll need to check your room," I whispered. "And the bathroom."

"I will," she whispered in return, "but I think it's cool that Alex's microphone backfired on her. Now she'll think we're taking Tori to the Gateway instead of using her as a decoy."

"What?" Tori asked. "You're not taking me?"

Shanghai turned to her. "We're taking you, honey. Just not right away."

"There's one problem." I sat on the sofa. "Do you remember if we mentioned our plan to bring Sing here?"

Shanghai shook her head. "I don't think we did. Alex probably heard that you want to sneak out, but she doesn't know why."

I reached for my camera. "Let's see the photo stick."

"Right. The visibility issue." Shanghai removed the stick from the camera and handed it to me. "We could just take her to the bathroom mirror."

"This is quicker." I wrapped my fingers around it. An image of part of the sofa formed above my hand, but no Tori.

I tossed the stick to the bed. "She's invisible."

"I am?" Tori climbed onto the sofa. "So how do I become visible again?"

"Wishing," Shanghai said. "Maybe if you try real hard, like you did to disappear."

"She had incentive, an absolute need to hide." I set my hand behind her head and pretended to stroke her hair. "Listen, Tori. Here's the fastest way for you to get to your mommy and daddy. If you can become visible, you can help me bring someone here who will take you to the Gateway sooner than I can."

Tori balled her fists. "Oh, I want to help you. I want to see Mommy and Daddy again."

"Then come with me." Shanghai walked toward the bathroom. "Quickly now."

Tori hopped up and hurried along. I followed as well. Once inside the bathroom, Shanghai closed both doors and flipped on the lights. We checked all the surfaces for a microphone and found nothing.

The three of us looked at the mirror hanging on the

wall opposite the shower. Although Tori stood between Shanghai and me in reality, she didn't appear in the reflection.

She pointed. "I'm not there."

"Then wish yourself there," Shanghai said. "Wish with all your heart."

"Okay." Tori scrunched her brow. "I'm wishing."

Again I stroked Tori's nebulous hair. "Just think. In a little while, we'll be able to take you to your mommy, but you have to become visible so you can help us. I have to bring Singapore here, but I can't do it without you."

Tori's whole body shook. "I'm trying!"

For a moment, nothing happened. Then, a wispy human frame took shape in the glass, growing clearer by the second.

"You're doing it, Tori," I said. "You're almost there."

After a few more seconds, her reflection matched her ghostly visage—pale face, glowing eyes, and nearly opaque body.

"You did it," Shanghai whispered.

Tori relaxed her muscles. "I know how to do it now. Watch." Smiling, she stared at the mirror. Within two seconds, her reflection vanished. Then two seconds later, it appeared again. Her grin widened. "This is fun."

"Perfect." I opened the door to my bedroom. "Let's make our plans. When it gets late enough, I'll go and get Sing."

After I lit three candles and set them on my dresser, we all sat on my bed and talked. Sometime during our two-hour conversation, the electricity shutoff arrived and dimmed the room. The flickering wicks and soft glow added a hushing mood, causing us to whisper and slow our speaking cadence to a relaxed rhythm.

Once we had made plans for my exit and return, Tori filled us in on her story, though Shanghai and I had to interpret quite a bit. Since Tori's father died, her mother started her own business—"being a nurse," Tori called it, which we translated as "smuggling medicine." They worked together in the corrections camp for three months before the grinding accident, so Tori knew everyone and what they all did.

After we exhausted our stories, I pulled my watch from my pocket. Eleven-fifteen. Probably late enough.

I put on my belt and cloak and blew out the candles. Shanghai and I skulked down the hall, Tori trailing and copying our furtive postures, though her footsteps made no noise at all.

Using my flashlight, Shanghai led us downstairs and through another hall that ended at a metal door. A sign on the wall instructed non-incarcerated residents to notify security personnel and gain approval before attempting to leave.

I peeked through a tiny square window. It provided only a narrow view—just a street about a hundred feet away with parked cars lining the curb. A guard could be standing near the wall out of my line of sight.

I grasped the door's lever and gently tried to push it down. Locked. Bending low, I whispered, "Okay, Tori, you disappear, stick your head through the door, and come back to tell me if you see a guard."

Tori grinned. "This should be fun."

Shanghai gave me the flashlight and backed away,

whispering, "I'll go to my room. It'll be dark, Tori, so I'll look for your eyes when you come."

As soon as Shanghai walked out of sight, Tori pushed her head through the door. After a few seconds, she drew it back in. "I saw a guard smoking a cigarette." She stuck out her tongue. "Yuck."

"Okay. Now go visible. You know the plan."

Tori crouched in the corner. "I'm ready."

"Good." I turned off the flashlight, knocked on the door, and pressed my body against the corner opposite Tori's.

A husky voice penetrated the metal. "Who is it?"

I waited, saying nothing. Tori's eyes glowed more brightly, whether from delight or fear, I couldn't tell.

After a few seconds of silence, I reached from my hiding place and knocked again.

The guard called out, "Listen, no one's on the list for pre-authorized exits, so if it's an emergency, go to the main gate and report."

I waited a few more seconds, then knocked a third time and squeezed again into the corner. I imagined the guard looking through the window, his shifting eyes unable to catch sight of either of us.

"Some prankster in there is going to be in big trouble." Beeps sounded, then metal scraping on metal. The moment the door opened, Tori jumped up and ran outside.

"Hey!" A tall guard gave chase and faded quickly in the darkness.

Just before the door swung closed, I slid through the gap and ran across a strip of grass, illuminated by the glow of two searchlights that swung toward the direction Tori had run. When I reached the street, I ducked behind a parked car. The guard stood near the side of the Hilton, scratching his head under his cap, the two searchlights locked on him.

I rose slowly and backed away. So far, everything had worked perfectly. The plan was for Shanghai and Tori to pull a similar stunt to get me in, but success seemed unlikely now, unless the guard was unrealistically gullible.

I flicked on the flashlight and ran toward my apartment. Since it was nearing midnight, only a few cars and trucks traveled the riverside road. I hadn't bothered to plug in my valve, so Crandyke's laments wouldn't slow me down. Still, bandits were a concern, though my rapid pace might keep them at bay.

In less than half an hour, I arrived at the alley. After catching my breath, I strode to Sing's apartment building, stopped at its shallow entry alcove, and pulled the knob. The door just rattled. I found a keypad on the right and punched in the code—six, nine, one, four. No beeps sounded. I pulled the door again. It stayed locked.

Back at the street, the lampposts shone brightly, but power to the building had been cut off by now, killing the keypad. Electricity was always off by this time of night. We should have remembered that.

I retreated to the alley and stood under Sing's apartment. The fire-escape ladder hung horizontally about ten feet over my head. After fastening the flashlight to my belt, I backed up a few paces, sprinted forward, and leaped up. My fingers wrapped around the end rung, and my weight dragged the ladder down, raising a loud whine.

As soon as the angle allowed, I climbed hand over hand until my feet pressed on the lowest rung. Then, I ran up the ladder, keeping my footfalls as quiet as possible.

When I reached Sing's level, I knocked on the access door. A flashlight beam shot through the window and shone in my face. Blinking at the brightness, I hissed, "Sing! It's me!"

The door flew open. Sing leaped out and threw her arms around me, making her cloak twirl. "You're here!"

"Of course I'm here." I returned the embrace and patted her on the back. "Did something happen?"

She drew away and looked at me face-to-face. With her flashlight pointing at her chest, the glow made her eyes sparkle. "I was standing out here watching for you, and Alex rode by on her electric motorcycle. I think she stopped at the front of the building, but I can't see the door from here, so I'm not sure. Anyway, I thought she might have been waiting for you in the lobby."

"I couldn't get in. The keypad wouldn't work. No electricity."

"Right. I forgot about that. I should have told you about the night entrance in the back. Maybe Alex found someone to open it for her."

I gazed toward the lobby. "If she was waiting inside, she might have heard me rattle the door."

Sing turned off her flashlight and pulled me down to a crouch. I peered through the metal slats in the railing. At alley level, a rat skittered from one trash can to another, but no humans roamed anywhere.

I whispered, "I didn't see her motorcycle, but she might have taken it inside. It's pretty small."

"She's not stupid enough to leave it out in the open," Sing said.

"But why did she go to your building? She doesn't know you're involved."

Sing laid a hand on my shoulder and rubbed it gently. "It wouldn't take much snooping to find out we've been together a lot lately."

"Who would tell her? Bartholomew, maybe?"

Sing looked away. "Or Erin."

"Erin didn't take a liking to you, did she?"

"Not really." Sing slid her hand into mine. "I don't know why. Maybe because I'm new. I upset the routine."

"Maybe." I focused on our hand clasp, smooth and warm. My heart accelerated, though not as much as when she kissed me. She had said there was more where that came from, and her soft lips beckoned me to ask for more.

I closed my eyes. I couldn't ask. My promises had to keep my shell intact.

Alex appeared at the end of the alley, looking in. Sing released my hand. "Stay down. I'll see what I can do to put her off your trail."

Sing rose, turned on her flashlight, and aimed the beam at Alex. "Are you a death messenger?" Sing called.

"No." Alex strolled into the alley, her hands in her jacket pockets as she angled her head upward. "My name is Alex, and I'm looking for Phoenix. I heard someone trying to get into your apartment building, but whoever it was left before I could get to the door. I thought it might be him."

Sing shone the light on the fire-escape ladder below. The spring-loaded hinges had brought it back to its horizontal perch well above the alley pavement. "Some guy tried to climb that ladder a few minutes ago. It makes quite a racket, so I came out here to see if a death messenger was trying to contact me. I scared him away, whoever he was, but he wasn't Phoenix. Too short and scrawny."

"When was the last time you saw Phoenix?"

"Maybe five or five-thirty." She shifted the flashlight beam to my former apartment's window. "He was over there. He wanted me to come and help him with a rescue mission at the corrections camp. I told him no way. I'm not risking my life for a crazy stunt like that. So he left."

Alex tapped her foot on the pavement. "Interesting."

"Why are you looking for Phoenix?"

Alex set a hand on her hip. "He was supposed to be doing something for me, and he went missing, so I'm concerned about him."

"I see." Sing shrugged. "Well, maybe you could check at the corrections camp."

Alex glanced toward the street before looking up again. "Thank you for the information."

"No problem."

As soon as Alex turned to leave, I whispered, "We can't let her get back to the camp before I do."

"I'll go down and distract her." Sing clipped her flashlight to her belt and climbed to the top of the railing.

"Do you know where the camp is?" I asked, still crouching.

"By the river, right?"

"Right. There's a building on the camp's southeast side with a door you can get to without passing through the perimeter fence. Go there and hide behind a car, then keep your eye on the door. When you see me there, come running."

"Got it." Sing leaped from the railing and plunged. When her feet struck the alley floor, she rolled into a somersault, then bolted upright and ran, calling, "Alex! Wait!"

Alex pivoted. When Sing caught up, the two of them

strolled out of the alley together, Alex touching Sing's shoulder.

I clutched the railing. I should have warned Sing about Alex's power. If she could really drain energy or read minds, talking to her unguarded could ruin everything.

As soon as they turned out of sight, I climbed up to the railing and looked down. Only hours ago I thought I had taken this plunge for the final time, but now it seemed that many more plunges awaited, perhaps of a different nature. With Alex knowing that I had broken curfew, I might become one of the camp prisoners at the reaping.

I took a deep breath and leaped into the darkness.

CHAPTER FOURTEEN

I LANDED ON THE alley floor and ran toward the street. When I reached the corner, I stopped and peeked around it. Sing stood in front of her apartment building's door talking to Alex, who had her back toward me. I turned the opposite way and jogged silently until I found a side street to dash into.

From there, I chose a path that stayed clear of the main thoroughfare and sprinted toward the camp. Fewer streetlamps dotted the side roads. No matter. I again ran at a fast enough clip to discourage bandits.

When I neared the camp, I stopped behind a car and caught my breath. Sweat dripped everywhere, dampening my clothes from top to bottom. I mopped my brow with a sleeve. A few streetlamps and the camp's searchlights illuminated the Hilton's rear entry. The same lanky guard leaned against the wall, smoking a cigarette.

A few steps away from the guard, Tori bounced on her toes, apparently in her invisible state. When she saw me, she ran to the car, walked right through it, and stood at my side. "Shanghai can't come. Alex put a guard in your hall."

"She's tightening the screws. I'll have to come up with a new plan." I plugged my cloak into my valve. When it energized, I whispered, "Crandyke, do you have any info on the Hilton's guard at the back door? He's tall and thin. Chain smokes. About forty years old. Maybe six foot two."

"Have you been swimming? It's itchy in here."

"Just sweating. I'll be dry soon. Now pay attention. Do you know the guy?"

"All right, but try not to sweat so much." Crandyke sighed. "He's probably Herman Stanskey. Only smoker I know in the guard detail."

"Got anything on him I can use for leverage?"

"He's clean as a whistle, a by-the-book guy, if you catch my meaning."

"High morals, huh?"

"Not really. Just scared to death of getting in trouble. He lost a security-guard position at the phone company for sleeping on the job, but we gave him a chance. He's supposed to be assigned to posts where he's not allowed to sit."

"That could be helpful." I crouched next to Tori. "Just stay close to me. I might need you again when we get back to my room."

She nodded. "I will."

After waiting for one of the searchlights to sweep past the guard, I walked straight toward the Hilton's rear entrance. When the guard caught sight of me, he nodded. "May I help you, young man?"

I stopped in front of him and read his name tag— Stanskey. "My name is Phoenix. I'm in residence here for the reapings."

"Ah! So *you're* the one."

I tried to read the guard's tone—a bit irritated. The trouble had begun.

He withdrew a miniature tablet from his pocket and

read a message on the screen, too small for me to make out. "Alex said to watch for you." He talked with the cigarette in his mouth, making ashes fly. "She's been delayed, or she'd be here herself. She said to escort you to the dining room. You're supposed to wait for her there."

I noted a radio at his belt next to a set of handcuffs. "Am I in trouble for some reason?"

"Probably, but not in as much trouble as the guard at the watchtower after you explain that she's the one who let you out tonight. You couldn't have gotten out through this door."

"Catching some heat, huh?"

"Yeah. Your little tomcat prank could get a lot of people in trouble." He began tapping out a message on the tablet's screen. "I'll just tell Alex you're here and—"

"Wait!" I pushed the tablet down.

He narrowed his eyes. "Wait for what?"

I glanced at the searchlight. Its beam would return soon. "Well, I suppose I could decide not to point the finger at the watchtower guard, couldn't I? Then you'd have to get out of trouble on your own."

Stanskey threw down his cigarette and mashed it with his foot. "Are you trying to hustle me? Because if you are—"

"No." I dodged his puffs of smoke. "I'm just trying to make a point. Hear me out before you contact Alex."

"Okay." Giving me a skeptical stare, he slid the tablet back into his pocket. "I'm listening."

I swallowed. I had to summon my best acting skills, and fast. "Look, if you take me to the dining room, you'll leave the door unguarded, right?"

He nodded. "It's locked, so it's no big deal. The

prisoners work hard so they're glad to get some sleep. No one ever tries to get out this way."

"Really? No one ever tries?"

"Not since I've been here." He pulled a new cigarette from his shirt pocket and slid it into his mouth. "Besides, it has an alarm."

"That's odd. I saw this door open a little while ago, and no alarm went off."

He flicked on a lighter and lit the cigarette. "I disabled it before I opened the door and—" He blew a stream of smoke into my face. "Did you sneak out when that little ghost ran by me?"

I coughed through my reply. "What little ghost?"

"A girl ran out a couple of hours ago. I reported it, of course, but since she vanished into thin air, we decided she was a ghost."

Tori grinned at me, but I kept my face slack. "That makes sense. Living people don't vanish."

"Don't get smart with me, kid. What's your angle?"

I fanned the smoke away, again glancing at the search-light. Probably less than thirty seconds until it would return. "Simple. You let me back in, I tell Alex I got lost exploring the compound, and no one gets in trouble, not you, not me, and not the watchtower guard. It was all a big mistake."

After glaring at me for a second, he let out a sigh. "You got me by the short hairs, don't you?"

"True, but it's probably best for all of us."

"But how do I know you won't go alley catting again?"

"Because you're going to let my friend into the Hilton, the girl I went to visit."

His tone sharpened. "Now that's going too far. I'm not going to contribute to your—"

"No, it's not like that." The searchlight beam was closing in. I spoke rapid fire. "She's a Reaper, and she'll stay with another female. She's having a hard time meeting quota, so she wants to get involved here. I sneaked out to set it up, and I'll get her to reap the little ghost, so that problem will be out of your hair. You just have to keep it all a secret."

Stanskey looked over the Hilton's wall at the top of the watchtower. He, too, seemed nervous about the searchlight's approach. "All right, all right. If it'll keep you and that spook from getting me in trouble." After disabling the alarm on a wall-mounted keypad, Stanskey pulled a ring of keys from his belt, unlocked the door, and opened it.

Tori and I hurried inside and waited for the door to close. I flicked on my flashlight. Her eyes glowed brightly again. "So what do we do now?" she asked.

"Go out to the car where you saw me and wait for Singapore. She's shorter than me, has dark skin, and she'll be wearing clothes like mine. When she comes, tell her what I said to the guard. My guess is that the hall guard will leave when I get there, but if not, you'll have to figure out a new plan to sneak her into the room." I gave Tori a reassuring smile. "You're smart. I know you can do it."

Her gap-toothed grin returned. "You bet I can. I'll make sure Sing gets there. I want her to take me to my mommy."

"Good girl." I pointed the flashlight at the exit. "I'll see you in a little while."

Tori scampered through the door and disappeared.

With the beam leading the way, I hurried to the stairwell and up to the second floor, then stopped at the door to my hall. I looked through the windowpane. Another flashlight beam wandered from side to side, coming toward me. Its glow illuminated a woman gripping a police nightstick.

"Crandyke," I whispered. "I have a female guard patrolling my hall. Can't tell her age. She's about five eight. Plump but not obese. Too dark to determine hair color."

"And you want me to get you out of trouble again." A tsking sound followed. "Phoenix, now I know the real reason you kept me around. You have no conscience to guide you, so you have to lie and deceive."

"Crandyke, I'm not a kid who's lying to steal a cookie. Give me a break."

"Not this time. Even if your nose is as long as Pinocchio's, I'm not going to play Jiminy Cricket. You'll have to get out of this mess by yourself."

"I'm trying to save lives!" I hissed. "You know that!"

"Tell that to the guard. Maybe she'll believe you."

I leaned my head against the door. What a bad time for Crandyke to pull the ethics card on me. Still, his advice to talk to the guard might be a good idea. The straightforward approach had worked before. Why not?

I unplugged my clasp, opened the door, and strode into the hall. The guard's flashlight beam jerked toward me and landed on my face, blinding me. "Phoenix?" the guard called.

"Yeah." I squinted, blocking the light with my hand. "Is there a problem?"

She slid the baton into a sheath and grasped my arm. "Where were you?" Her voice was gravelly, though not harsh. "Why weren't you in your room?"

"I was checking out this place. You know, exploring my home away from home." I swung my beam toward the stairwell. "Would you believe there are more stairs on this side of the building than on the other side? I would've thought—"

"You're supposed to be in bed. There's a curfew." She shifted her beam to herself, illuminating a pointed chin and severely dipping eyebrows, but her compassionate tone softened her appearance.

"Right. I read about the curfew. I thought it meant I couldn't leave because of bandits outside."

"That, too. But you're not allowed to wander anywhere you want. This is a prison, not a shopping mall."

"I noticed." I tried to read her name tag, but darkness covered it. "What's your name?"

"What's it to you?"

"Just wondering. You're one of the nicer guards I've met."

"Don't brownnose me, kid." She shone the flashlight on her name tag—Andrews. "Theresa. Theresa Andrews." She withdrew a miniature tablet from a pocket and began tapping on the screen. "I'm notifying Alex so she can stop looking for you."

"You do that." I let out an exaggerated yawn. "Can I go to bed now?"

"Go ahead." She frowned at the tablet and muttered, "Everything's down. I'll have to use the radio."

"Well, goodnight, Theresa."

"One more thing. We altered your lock. Alex's orders. You can't get out from the inside. We'll open it in the morning. Same deal for Shanghai."

"So we're prisoners now."

She wagged her flashlight at me. "It's your own fault."

I pulled the room key from my pocket. "Are you going to stay on this floor?"

She shook her head. "I'm normally a perimeter guard. I walk the grounds outside the camp. But I'm staying here until you're locked in. Alex will have my head if you sneak out again."

"Sure. I understand." I unlocked my door, stepped inside, and pivoted back. "Seriously, I'm glad you're here. You're doing a good job."

"Well... thanks... I guess. Sorry about the prisoner thing. I wish I could do something about it, but... you know."

"Yeah, I know. It's not your fault. Good night again." I closed the door. The knob rattled—Theresa checking to make sure the lock engaged.

"You're a smooth operator, Phoenix."

I aimed my beam toward the voice. Shanghai stood a few steps away holding a lit candle. Three more candles burned on the dresser behind her. "Listening in, I presume."

"Every word." She joined me near the door and laid a microphone in my palm. "Attached to one of my bedposts. No others, though. Even in the hallway. I checked every inch before Theresa showed up."

"Good job." I pushed the microphone into my pocket with the other one.

She leaned her shoulder against mine. "What're we going to do now? We're trapped."

"No worries." I showed her my key. "I'll slide it under the door when Sing comes."

I gave her a quick rundown of what happened with Sing, Alex, and Stanskey and how I planned for Sing's entry. When I finished, she nodded at the key. "So Sing can let herself in, we'll keep the door from latching, and we're free birds again."

"We'll let it latch. We need some sleep." I unfastened my cloak and tossed it onto the bed. "After tonight, maybe we'll keep it unlatched until just before they come for us in the morning."

Shanghai tapped her socked foot on the carpet. "Okay. It's all kind of fragile, though."

"Right now, everything feels fragile. Since Theresa's patrolling outside, Sing has two guards to worry about."

"Don't worry. She can fly under any radar."

"Let's hope so." I leaned my back against the door and slid down to a seated position. "Get some sleep. I'll doze here. When I hear Sing, I'll push the key under."

Shanghai rubbed my shoulder. "All right if I snooze in your bed? I want to be here when she comes."

"Well… actually…"

"Right. Sing wouldn't like it." Shanghai stooped in front of me. "Tell her to crawl into bed with me. There's plenty of room."

"Thanks for understanding."

"Hey, we're all friends." Shanghai kissed me on the cheek, lingering the same way Sing had. The touch was electric. A buzz raced along my spine to my fingers and toes. Her minty breath and berry-scented hair swept through my senses. My heart thumped harder than ever. When she drew back, she whispered, "Goodnight, friend."

With a graceful turn that accentuated her athletic form, she sashayed into the bathroom. Light from the candle swept away with her, leaving three other flames undulating in the background, as if echoing her moves.

My skin tingled. Heat sizzled within. My heart seemed to rise into my throat, pounding like a hammer. The shell was cracking, and either Shanghai or Sing could easily smash through. I had to patch the cracks. Remember my promises. Stay focused. Stay away from those two girls. My heart thrummed in protest, but I didn't dare pay attention. Too much was at stake. Just seven more years to wait. I could do it.

After climbing to my feet and using the bathroom, I settled at the door again and closed my eyes. As the sensation of Shanghai's touch came back to mind, I let myself smile. And why not smile? Wasn't it okay to enjoy her affection as long as I didn't betray Misty? Getting reacquainted with Shanghai was like a dream come true.

For more than three years I had been alone, constantly monitoring for a death alarm, never letting my senses tune to another frequency for fear that a little Molly somewhere might die without my knowledge, and her soul would wander in confusion. And medicine smuggling was too dangerous to allow for close friendships. A false friend could betray me. A true friend could be accused as an accomplice.

Now, finally, a friend had risen as if from the dead. And Sing made a trio. With both of them here, maybe enduring the next seven years as a Reaper wouldn't be so bad.

I slept for a while, maybe an hour or so, until a whisper crawled into my ear.

"Phoenix? It's me, Tori."

"Tori?" I opened my eyes. Tori stood in front of me, her expression anxious. "What's wrong?"

"Nothing, maybe." She pointed at the door.

"Singapore's in the hall. I brought her, just like you told me to."

"Great!" As I climbed to my knees and turned, my leg muscles tightened, complaining about the recent run. I slid the key under the door and whisper-shouted, "Sing, take this key and open the door."

I rose and backed away. Two seconds later, the lock disengaged. Sing bustled in carrying a flashlight and a small hard-shell suitcase. Blood trickled from an inch-long cut on her forehead, and a deep bruise darkened her cheek. She dropped the suitcase and threw her arms around me. "I made it!"

CHAPTER FIFTEEN

"WHAT HAPPENED?" I took her flashlight and shone it on the bruise. "Bandits?"

"Three of them." She caressed her fist. "Two won't be walking anytime soon. They might even be dead. But the third one got away with my cloak."

I looked at her back. "Your cloak!"

She nodded, tears welling. "It was my mother's… and… and they must have thought souls were in it, because it always shimmers. But when they find out it's empty, they'll probably sell it as a souvenir. I'll never get it back."

Laying a gentle hand on her arm, I pushed her toward the bathroom. "Maybe you should clean up those wounds, and then we'll talk."

She pulled away. "I'm all right. My heart hurts more than the wounds do."

"I can imagine." I turned off the flashlight. Now only the three candles and Tori's glowing eyes illuminated the room. "Maybe if I get word to some friends I know in the shroud, they can be on the lookout for it."

She offered a thankful nod. "But be careful. Since Cairo is patrolling my district, we can't let it be known that my cloak's missing."

"Good point. Any other ideas?"

"I can try to contact my people." She brushed tears from both eyes. "They know I was coming here, but I don't know what they're planning. They said we'd find out soon."

"I hope so."

I took the next few minutes to give Sing a summary of discoveries at the camp—the schedule on the tablet, the microphones, the altered locks, and other details, including how I found Tori. When I finished, I exhaled loudly. "Tomorrow we're supposed to learn more about what we're doing here, so we can make plans after that. Tomorrow night you can start snooping after electricity cutoff, so get plenty of rest during the day."

"I will." Sing looked toward the bathroom door. "Shanghai is that way?"

I nodded. "She said just crawl into bed with her. There's plenty of room."

Sing wrapped her arms around me again and pulled herself close. She stayed quiet for a moment, so quiet I could hear my own heartbeat. After several more seconds, she whispered, "Sometime soon I need to talk to you about something important."

"Okay. Why not now?"

"Too much has happened." She dabbed at her cut with a fingertip. "Maybe I'll feel better in the morning."

"Don't worry. I understand." I pushed her away and laid a hand over her bruise. "If you need me anytime during the night, you can wake me up."

"I'll remember that." She glanced at Tori, then stood on tiptoes and kissed my cheek. "Good night, Phoenix."

I touched the tingling spot. The warm sensation was all too familiar. "Good night."

She picked up her suitcase. As she headed into the bathroom, I got a better look at the cracked and dented shell. Maybe she had bashed a bandit or two with it. When battling three men at once, any weapon would do, though it seemed strange that she had managed to keep her suitcase but not her cloak. The cloak was far more valuable.

I shook my head hard. I couldn't let doubts enter my mind. Her wounds proved her story. Questioning it was stupid.

After washing my face and hands in the bathroom and changing to baggy shorts and T-shirt, I tossed my traveling clothes onto the floor next to the dresser. Tori sat on the end of the bed, twiddling her thumbs. Of course she wore the same ratty dress as before. Except for fully entrenched level threes, ghosts never appeared with clothes other than what they were wearing when they died.

"Where have you been staying at night?" I asked. "I know ghosts don't sleep."

"In the room where my mat used to be. They rolled up my mat and my mommy's and took them away, but I didn't have anywhere else to go, so I just laid on the floor. I didn't sleep, but hearing everyone else sleep made me feel better."

After blowing out two of the three candles, I slid underneath the bedcovers and patted the space next to me. "You can lie here with me if you want."

Without a word, she climbed onto the bed and settled at my side. Since her body didn't sink into the mattress, she again proved her high-level ghost status. She could control whether or not she passed through certain solid objects.

I closed my eyes. "Comfortable?"

"Uh-huh."

"Good, but you'll need to stay quiet so I can sleep. There aren't many hours left in the night."

"Okay." After a few seconds of silence, she whispered, "Phoenix, can I ask one question?"

"Just one?"

"Uh-huh. Why couldn't Singapore see me?"

I opened my eyes. Tori stared at me almost nose to nose. The remaining candle's light flickered across her nebulous face. "Couldn't see you? What do you mean?"

"She came to the parked car, just like you said, but when I talked to her, she couldn't see me until I turned visible."

"Did she actually say she couldn't see you?"

"No." Tori rose to her knees and wagged her head. "But she was shaking her head like this, like she was looking for me, and when I turned visible, she looked right at me. I thought it might be because she wasn't wearing her cloak."

"No, I've seen plenty of ghosts while not wearing my cloak."

"She was fine later, 'cause I turned invisible again to get past the guard. After he let her in and closed the door, she talked to me all the way here, even though I stayed invisible."

"Well, I've noticed that you're not always aware of where you are. Maybe you were standing inside the car, and it was blocking her view of you."

"Maybe. I can't remember."

I closed my eyes again. "We'll ask her tomorrow. I'm sure she'll be able to see you after she gets some rest."

"Okay. Good night, Phoenix."

"Good night."

"And Phoenix?"

I opened my eyes. "Yes?"

She snuggled close and brushed her pale lips against my cheek. "Thank you for taking care of me."

As goose bumps crawled along my back, I resisted the urge to shudder. A tear crept to my eye. "You're welcome, Tori. I'll do whatever it takes to get you safely to your parents."

The candle extinguished on its own. I fell asleep quickly. A dream formed, a familiar one, a dream I welcomed. Some recurring dreams reflected death, the pain-filled screams of extracted souls, and I would wake up troubled and morose. This dream made up for all of those moments.

Misty stood in front of me in our backyard next to a makeshift picnic table, her eyes sparkling with tears. Wearing a calf-length skirt, a frilly short-sleeved top, and a newsboy cap that allowed her silky red hair to spill over her shoulders, she looked beautiful, as always.

My initiation ceremony's potluck table had been cleared, and my parents and our guests had gone inside. I stayed in the yard, hoping to delay wading into the nearly shoulder-to-shoulder conditions in our modest home and the many voices that would pepper me with questions. As usual, Misty stayed with me.

She took my hand in hers. "I have something to show you," she said with her Scottish lilt, "A gift for your life as a Reaper."

"Thanks." I leaned to the side and looked around her. "Where is it?"

"Here." She glanced toward the house, then slid a gray ring over my left ring finger. "It's pewter. I couldn't afford silver."

I stared at the ring. Although a few slight bumps

marred the surface, it was smooth and lustrous. "Did you make this?"

She nodded. "It took me a month, but I made two of them." She slid a similar ring over her own finger. "They'll help us remember our promise."

I, too, gave the house a furtive glance. If anyone in my family found out about our covenant, I would get the same lecture I had heard a hundred times before. Supposedly we were young, inexperienced, infatuated. But they couldn't understand how the rigors and sacrifices inherent in Reaper training could mold a boy into a man. They couldn't fathom how raising a younger sister practically by herself could fashion a mature woman out of a little girl. Yet, they didn't have to understand. It would be twenty years before we could complete our covenant. By then, no one would mind.

"Misty, it's amazing. I love it." I held her hand. "But it's not going to be hard to keep the promise. I'll be alone, and I'll be thinking about you every day."

"You think so now." A tear trickled down her cheek. "We both need the rings. Twenty years is a long time."

"Twenty years," I repeated, almost in a whisper. "It's hard to imagine."

"I know. I lost my parents, and I lost my brother. I don't want to lose you." She stood on tiptoes and kissed the top of my freshly shaved head. "I'll wait as long as it takes, and my ring will never leave my finger."

The back door creaked open. I stepped away from Misty. My father, dressed in a navy blue suit, descended the trio of steps, his graying hair askew in the breeze. His trim body belied his years, but his weathered face gave evidence of all five decades.

As he lit a cigarette in a casual manner, I recognized his pretentiously noncommittal expression. He had seen Misty kiss me but didn't want to let on.

"Better get inside," I whispered.

Misty nodded and hurried past my father without giving him a glance. When the door closed, he sauntered closer to me, took a deep draw on his cigarette, and blew the smoke into the breeze. "I see that you decided to dismiss what I told you."

I leaned away from the smoke, forcing myself not to cough. "It was a good-bye kiss. And it was on my head. No big deal."

"I'm not stupid, son." He flicked the cigarette. Ashes fell close to my shoes. "Look, I like Misty. She's a good girl—sweet, hard-working, pretty as a daisy. But you're both only thirteen, for crying out loud. You're too young to make promises to each other."

"Promises? What promises?"

"Like I said. I'm not stupid." His jaw tightened, but his voice stayed under control. "I specifically forbade you from pursuing a relationship with her."

I pressed my lips together. It wouldn't do any good to talk to him until he finished having his say.

"But now you belong to the Council, so I suppose you'll answer to them for your decisions." His face relaxing, he nodded at my ring. "Looks like pewter. Am I right?"

"It's pewter." I rolled my hand into a fist and rubbed the ring. "So she gave me something to remember her by. What's wrong with that?"

"For you? Nothing. In fact, it'll help keep you out of trouble." He took another draw on the cigarette and continued, smoke puffing with his words. "Since it's becoming clear that you inherited your grandfather's curse, the ring's probably a good idea."

I blinked at the smoke. "Wait a minute. What curse? What kind of trouble?"

"Something Bartholomew explained to me." He set a hand on my shoulder, a gesture that meant he was about to say something I probably didn't want to hear. "Grandpa Maxwell was a lot like you—independent, confident, principled in his own way. But he had a weak spot. His Reaper genetics were part of it."

He took another drag on his cigarette. "If a woman could break through his defenses, he became like a devoted slave to her, even if he knew she was evil." He touched his chest. "The valve attachment to his heart added to the problem. I think it makes some Reapers more vulnerable to emotional upheavals. Kind of messes with their minds."

I glanced down at my valve, exposed by my V-neck shirt. The skin around the metal still looked raw, though the bleeding had stopped days ago. "So you think Misty's got that kind of hold on me?"

"It's obvious to everyone but you. You're only thirteen, but you made a promise to be true to her for the next twenty years. Who in his right mind would do that? Still, like I said, it'll probably help you. You're not allowed to be with girls anyway, and because of your commitment to Misty, you won't let another female get her hooks into you."

He averted his eyes. "In the meantime, Misty can break the promise and gallivant with a dozen guys, and you'll never know it. All the while, you'll be mooning for her until your Reaper years are over." He dropped the cigarette and let the butt smolder on the walk. "Then you'll come home and find her married. You'll be crushed, of course, but at least you'll have been protected. Bartholomew says only obvious betrayal or death of the female can break the hold. At least that's the way it was for Maxwell."

Heat rushed into my cheeks. "No," I said, backing away. "You don't know Misty. She won't betray me. I know she won't."

"Of course you think that way." He nodded at my hand again. "Since she has you wrapped around her finger more tightly than that ring, you can't think otherwise."

I fumed within. My mind wasn't playing tricks on me, and he didn't know Misty like I did. I just tightened my fists and stayed quiet.

"In any case," he continued, "I asked Bartholomew to keep an eye on you. He thinks you have a special talent that will make you a target, so he'll give you advice when you need it."

"What talent? A target for who?"

My father shrugged. "He wouldn't say. But I can tell you this. Grandpa Maxwell had an obsession with finding the actual Gateway and learning what it was all about. One day he set off on a journey to locate it, and he never returned."

"Mom told me he died of a heart attack."

"Quite true. That's what the telegram said." He withdrew a pack of cigarettes from his shirt pocket, pulled one out part way, then, after pausing for a moment, let it slide back in. "Whatever you do, son, don't put yourself in unnecessary danger. Do your job and lay low. Don't try anything foolish like Maxwell did. The Gatekeeper is immortal for a reason. Better to live as long as you can and come home in one piece. If Misty really does wait that long, you'll be glad you did."

The scene faded, though my father's voice echoed in my awakening mind. Until tonight, the dream had always ended with Misty's kiss. My father's entry signaled something new. When the episode happened in reality, his advice didn't make much sense. Now it made all the sense in the world. I was Alex's target. But for what reason? What was my talent? It had to be more than simply collecting souls. Any Reaper could do that.

I opened my eyes to darkness. Tori's glow was nowhere in sight. Maybe boredom had prompted her to explore the compound.

Her absence and the dream's memories drilled a hole in my heart. Loneliness flowed in, making the room seem darker. Maybe my father was right after all. Misty and I were only thirteen, old enough to think we knew what love was all about and too young to realize that the coming years would strip the blinders of naiveté from our eyes. Our promise made us feel good then, but living in the Jungle and witnessing tragedy after tragedy quickly taught me that even the most heartfelt promises are as fragile as a candle's flame.

I let out a quiet sigh. The winds of change blow through every life, sometimes with a ferocity no one can predict. I could keep my promise to wait for Misty. My life as a Reaper demanded solitude. But Misty had likely met plenty of attractive young men who would love to ease her loneliness. Maybe her pewter ring soon felt like a lead weight, and the words of promise took on the tone of childish hope. When she realized the limitations of our youthful vision, maybe the loss of blinders led her to remove the pewter shackle and deposit it in a jewelry box, a place for shiny baubles and pretty keepsakes… and a coffin for our dreams.

I curled my fingers, feeling the tightness of the ring. A new weight of reality burdened my heart. I had learned so much in three short years… too much, really. Visions of death and grief do that to every Reaper. We grow into adults before our time, and solitude provides too many hours to reflect and ponder. In only a few years, Reapers become poets, mentally writing bitter verses that reflect bitter hearts.

I brought the ring to my cheek and rubbed the cool metal against my skin. No matter what Misty did, I would keep my promise. I couldn't let those bitter winds infect my heart. Although Sing and Shanghai were both beautiful young women inside and out, giving in to their charms would break my only attachment to the days when love still thrived through any storm—days of innocent ignorance, to be sure, but days when I looked forward to each coming dawn. If I broke that connection, all hope that those days might return would be shattered forever.

I shifted the ring to my lips and kissed it. *Yes, Misty, I will keep my promise. I have to keep it. I can't survive without a lifeline to your love.*

CHAPTER SIXTEEN

A MELODIC HUM WAFTED through my mind, gently awakening me. I opened my eyes. The floor lamp filled the room with light. A Reaper's tunic and trousers lay folded neatly on the bed near my feet, and a cloak draped the sofa, its fibers straight and shiny. A computer tablet sat on the dresser, and my suitcase was nowhere in sight.

The hum emanated from the bathroom, a feminine lilt, a wordless song of peace and contentment. Sing was giving voice to her nickname. Even after getting ambushed by thugs and losing her cloak, she still maintained a buoyant attitude.

A knock sounded. The humming stopped. Someone called from the hallway, "It's time to get up! I'm unlocking the door. Get something to prop it open."

Theresa's voice. I jumped out of bed and grabbed one of the candles. "I'm ready."

The lock clicked, and the door opened a crack. I laid the candle on the floor and slid it into the gap. "Got it."

Theresa's eyes appeared at the slit. "Breakfast in thirty minutes. Alex says to be on time. She wants to have a word with you."

"Yeah. More than one word, I'm sure." I gave her a smile. "Don't you ever sleep?"

"It's still night shift. I get off soon." As she walked away, she called, "Thanks for asking."

When her footsteps faded, I turned to get my clothes. Sing and Tori stood next to the open bathroom door. "Good morning, Phoenix," Sing said, now dressed in fresh traveling attire. Although her cut had closed, the bruise still looked pretty bad.

"Shhh." I took her by the arm and guided her away from the hall door. "Let's talk over here."

When I sat on the bed, Sing sat next to me and laid my clothes on my lap. "I found them in your drawer."

"Thanks." I checked the pockets. Sing had transferred the watch and the microphones from the dirty set of clothes. "How much sleep did you get?"

"A couple of hours. I'll snooze again when you leave."

"You can ask Tori to stand guard in the hallway."

Sing nodded. "I already discussed that with her. If someone comes, she'll warn me in time to hide under the bed."

Shanghai walked in from the bathroom, also wearing a clean set of Reaper clothes. Her cloak looked freshly brushed. Apparently Sing had spread her favors around. "Get dressed, amigo," Shanghai said in a chipper tone. "Let's hunt down some breakfast. I'm starved."

I grabbed my clothes. "I need to take a shower. Theresa said Alex is waiting for me. Maybe you can try to cool her down before I get there."

"Will do."

When Shanghai left, I opened the bathroom door, my clothes still in my arms. Sing grabbed my wrist. "Can I talk to you a second?" She glanced at Tori. "Alone?"

"Sure." I bent toward Tori. "Would you please guard

the hallway for a little while? You can come back when you see me leave."

"Okay." She ran through the door.

I focused on Sing. "What's up?"

She showed me a folded piece of paper. "Someone slid a note under your door. My code name was on the outside, so I read it."

"Your code name? But no one knows you're here."

"My people do." She unfolded the paper. "Take a look."

I studied the hastily scrawled script, whispering as I read. "Raven, we have a tweeter in the cage. Watch for signs. The Eagle is coming."

Sing refolded the note. "It means we have someone working inside the camp."

"I figured that out. Kind of risky to make it so obvious."

"The tweeter probably didn't have time to encode it," Sing said. "I don't know who it is."

"I'm guessing Theresa, but who's the Eagle?"

"The head of our organization."

"Organization? You mean the people you've been talking about?"

"Right." Sing looked at the floor and ran her shoe along the carpet. "I think it's time to tell you some secrets I've been holding back from you."

"Okay. That's worth keeping Alex waiting. Let's hear them."

"It won't take long." After heaving a sigh, she whispered, "Like I told you before, I'm not a Gateway denier, at least not like some who are on the kook fringe. My people believe..." She glanced away for a moment before looking at me again. "*We* believe that something isn't right about the Gateway story. My mother was one of the first to start the investigation. You see, when she retired after twenty years as a Reaper, the Gatekeeper recruited her to become a member of his inner circle, a ring of six former Reapers who now serve him as disciples."

"You mean the Council."

She nodded. "Since Council members stop aging when they join, it's considered the most glorious appointment possible. It's literally like heaven on earth. So when my mother declined the invitation, trouble started. Assassins showed up everywhere. She fled to Ghana and lived there. That's where she met my father. They married, and I was born soon after. While in Ghana, my parents began an organization that hoped to unravel the mystery of the Gatekeeper, the Council, and the Gateway. There are too many reasons to go into right now, but here's the bottom line." She paused, biting her lip. "First, do you know the story about how I became a Reaper?"

"They found your birthmark late, when you were around fourteen or fifteen, during a cancer screening or something like that."

"Close enough." She crumpled the note. "Our organization decided to use me to infiltrate the system to get clues about any falsehoods in the Gateway story, but when we moved to North America, an assassin caught up with us and killed my mother."

I stroked my chin. "Interesting. Mex told me she died before you learned about your birthmark."

"There are several versions of my story going around. Anyway, the Gatekeeper was satisfied with getting revenge for the rejection insult. He didn't know anything about our organization, so he didn't pursue my father or me. Not long after that, my father put me into Reaper training, but he died in a car accident, so the next in line in our organization took over, and she watched over my progress."

"She? I assume you know her name."

"I do, but I'm not allowed to tell anyone. I'm sure you understand."

"Okay." I nodded. "Go on."

"Since my mother was considered such an important Reaper, everyone assumed I inherited her talents, so our organization pushed to have me assigned to the Jungle right away. In fact, they specifically asked for the district I'm in."

"Because they knew it's a tough district?" I shook my head. "That's a killer assignment even for the daughter of Tokyo."

"That's not why." She pressed a fingertip against my chest. "They asked for that district because it's next to yours."

I blinked at her. "They put you next to me on purpose?"

"I told you my people knew about your medicine smuggling." She set her hands on her hips. "They hoped that meant you're no friend of the Council. Since you're willing to risk your life and your quota to help others, it means you're not a typical Reaper."

"But I've never been a Gateway denier. It works. I've seen it. Souls really go into it."

She lowered her head and whispered, "I saw it, too."

"Exactly. So now you know. Denying it is useless."

She looked up at me. "But we don't know where it takes souls. That's why I think a Reaper needs to go there and find out."

I shook my head. "You're asking the impossible. You heard Bartholomew. Even if a Reaper goes through the

Gateway, another Reaper has to pull him out, and the one who pulls him out will get stuck."

Sing propped her chin with a hand. "So we need a Reaper who's willing to take a huge risk to bring someone back."

"A huge risk? You're talking about dying. That's more than a risk. And besides, who would be the first one to go? You need one dead Reaper to make the trip and another one to transfer him back."

"That's true, but a dead Reaper already made the trip. We just need one to bring her home."

"Her?" I half closed an eye. "Who?"

Sing bit her lip again. As she stared at me, her chin quivered. "My mother."

"Your mother! But how? If she died almost two years ago—"

"I'll tell you more later." Sing pushed my arm. "You'd better go. You don't want Alex to get angrier than she already is."

"All right, all right." I hustled into the bathroom, brushed my teeth, and took a quick shower. A few minutes later, I was dressed and ready to go.

When I left the bathroom, Sing stood near the door holding my cloak. With a dramatic twirl, she wrapped it around my back and fastened the clasp in front.

"Lock it in?" she asked as she poised the clasp over my valve.

"Go ahead. Now that I know Theresa's name, I should ask Crandyke what he knows about her."

She pushed the clasp key into the valve and locked it in place. The fibers shimmered, brighter than usual, likely due to Sing's brushing job.

I slid my arms into the sleeves. "Thank you."

"You're welcome." She wrapped her hands around one of mine. "And thank you for trusting me, Phoenix. It means a lot."

"Of course I trust you. Why wouldn't I?" Even as I uttered the words, I regretted them. I still hadn't asked why she couldn't see Tori last night.

"I hope you keep that attitude." Letting a smile break through, she laid a hand on her stomach. "By the way, if you could find something for me to eat, that would be great. Maybe at lunchtime?"

I returned her smile. "I'll do my best." I grabbed the tablet off the dresser and breezed out the door. As I strode down the hall, I spoke into my cloak fibers. "Good morning, Crandyke. I hope you had a good night."

"I had an amazing night." His voice came through bright and cheery. "Someone brushed your cloak for nearly an hour. It was resplendent. Better than one of those chairs with the thousand-fingers massage. If that keeps up, I won't be in any hurry to get to the Gateway."

"I'll give your compliments to the masseuse." I hustled through the door at the end of the hall and jogged down the steps. "That guard in my hall last night was named Theresa Andrews. Know anything about her?"

"No. She must be recent. Not my hire."

"Recent, huh? That makes sense. She didn't act like someone who hated her job yet." Theresa's face appeared in my mind. She could easily be the tweeter. I would have to keep my eye on her. "Thanks, Crandyke. I'll get back to you in a little while." I unplugged my clasp and hurried on.

When I arrived at the dining area, Alex stood at the doorway, dressed in her usual leather getup, a Styrofoam cup of coffee in her hand. Before I could get a look inside, she threw the cup into a trash can, grabbed my arm, and pushed me to the lobby. "That stunt you pulled last night nearly got two guards fired."

"What do I care about your guards?" I jerked away and straightened my sleeve. "I already told you I'm trying to figure out a way to spring Colm's family, so I went exploring. You shouldn't act so surprised."

"You think you're so smart." Alex lifted a hand as if to slap me but quickly lowered it. With her jacket open, the holster and gun came into view. "If a guard catches you out past curfew, the orders are to shoot to kill. Got it?"

"I'm in lockdown now. I couldn't leave my room at night if I wanted to."

She pushed my valve button, making it protrude. As energy leaked out, she grabbed a fistful of my hair and slammed my head against the wall. "Just remember our deal. You'll cooperate with the reapings. No complaints, or I'll make you shrivel." She let go of my hair and pressed my valve stem back in place. "Understood?"

"I remember the deal." Ignoring a blossoming headache, I dug into my pocket and pulled out the microphones. I grasped her wrist and slapped them into her palm. "I'm not the one with the bad memory."

Alex clenched her fist around them. Lines dug into her brow, etching a menacing scowl. "It's going to be a pleasure watching your smart-aleck smirk wilt when the prisoners start dropping like flies. You have no idea what you're in for."

My throat tightened, but I resisted swallowing. "I'm a Reaper. I'll do my job."

She stared at me for a moment, then nodded. "We'll see

about that, Phoenix." She patted me on the cheek. "I have something in mind that will test your words."

Her touch felt cold, like death itself. I refused to cringe.

"I'll be back very soon." She walked past me and exited the door leading to the prison yard.

Holding a hand on the back of my head, I walked to the dining area. Shanghai stood just inside the door. "She's a witch without a broom."

"You heard?"

Shanghai massaged my head's tender spot. "I sneaked up and eavesdropped. I hope you don't mind."

"Not at all." I winced at the pressure—a good kind of pain. "She's also a witch with a wallop."

"I tried to talk to her before you got here, but she told me to buzz off." Shanghai kept a finger on the lump. "Want some ice for this?"

"No. I'll be all right."

She lowered her hand. "Breakfast is just a bagel with an egg and a sausage patty, but it's not bad."

"That'll do."

We entered the dining room together and sat at the same table as before. Shanghai's bagel lay half eaten on a paper plate next to a tall Styrofoam cup of coffee. I set my computer tablet on my side of the table and slid into the chair. My own bagel sat askew on its plate as if slapped together by a blind man. "Where'd you get the coffee?"

Shanghai pointed at a table near the door. A coffeemaker dripped black liquid into a pot next to a stack of cups. I got up, poured a cup, and began sipping as I walked back to my chair. The coffee was hot and bitter, a fitting wake-up alarm for a place like this.

"I found a microphone under this chair and got rid of

it," Shanghai said. "Maybe Alex won't bother with bugging us anymore."

I nodded. "After our little episode just now, you're probably right."

After I ate about half of my bagel and Shanghai nearly finished hers, Alex walked in and called, "Turn on your tablets, pull up the map on the screen, and follow me."

We downed our coffee, grabbed our tablets and partial bagels, and filed out after Alex. As I passed through the doorway, I smiled and nodded at a gray-haired woman wearing an apron, apparently the clean-up person. She turned away without acknowledging my gesture. Maybe she was a prisoner assigned to this detail, and seeing Reapers fueled rumors that many of them would die soon. Who could blame her for worrying? Or for hating us.

When we entered the central prison yard, I took a bite of my bagel and blinked at the misty air. The cool breeze made me glad for the long sleeves and cloak, though the moisture would irritate Crandyke. He'd just have to deal with it.

Eating while we walked, we tucked our tablets under our cloaks and continued following Alex toward one of several squarish buildings that surrounded the complex. Just as I swallowed my last bite, a male teenager exited the watchtower and walked toward us. Wearing the signature tunic, trousers, and cloak, he appeared to be a Reaper, especially considering his expression and body language—aloof, restless, serious. Blond and clean-shaven, he strode with confident steps. His muscles, evident in his bulging sleeves, proved that he was a force to be reckoned with.

I studied his profile. Something about him seemed familiar, but I couldn't pinpoint it.

When he caught up with Alex, the two walked side by

side, whispering. No expressions or inflections gave away their moods.

When we arrived at a building's rusted door, already open enough for us to pass through, the new Reaper entered first, followed by Alex. After we all had taken several steps inside, they stopped and turned toward us, though they kept their heads low and continued whispering.

Behind them, an assembly line formed a square, the closest corner only a few steps away from us. Men, women, and children, including Colleen, stood at stations on the outside of the square, some assembling and some passing objects along.

Several workers within the square, ranging from about five to fifteen years old, including both of the Fitzpatrick girls, ran from cardboard boxes at the center to the stations, distributing thin wires of various colors, white disks the size of a manhole cover, and tiny hardware that looked like nuts, bolts, and screws.

In one corner, a huge disklike stone stood on edge, spinning clockwise so fast the perimeter blurred. A woman sat on a stool holding a curved piece of glass against the disk, shifting the glass every few seconds. Close by, a little boy squirted mist over the stone from a spray bottle. The bottom edge whirred about a foot above the floor, clearly a death trap for anyone caught underneath.

I swallowed hard. So many children! Were they planning on killing the adult criminals and sending the children to orphanages, or were the children to be victims as well? I scanned the square. Colm stood near the far corner at a welding station wearing dark, protective glasses as he held one of the nearly completed pedestal-like disks in place for the welder. With sparks flying all around, he didn't seem to care that some landed on his cap and shirt.

A swarthy, middle-aged man walked slowly around the square, looking on at each workstation, perhaps a foreman assigned to help out wherever possible.

I scanned the faces again. No sign of Fiona. She must have been stationed elsewhere.

I leaned close to Shanghai and kept my voice as low as possible. "What do you think of this new Reaper?"

"Let's see..." She rolled her eyes upward. "Handsome, mysterious, handsome, strong, and did I mention handsome?"

"A couple of times. I get the picture."

She slid her arm around mine. "But not as handsome as you, gorgeous."

"I appreciate the compliment. But does he look familiar?"

"Now that you mention it." She gave him a hard stare. "Wasn't he with us on the train to the Gateway?"

I added my own stare and tried to match his features to the shadowed faces on the train. Yes, he was the second Reaper who boarded the car after we did. I curled my fingers into a fist. "He was watching us. I was wondering if he planted the syringe on Mex."

"A spy trying to sabotage us?"

"Maybe. I wouldn't put anything past Alex."

Alex cleared her throat loudly. When we focused on her, she spoke like a tour guide giving a memorized talk. "This is the facility's assembly room. Look for the central rectangle on your map."

I withdrew my tablet and pressed my thumb on its screen. When the icons appeared, I tapped on the map. The screen drew the left half, then froze. I slapped the back, but it just shut off. The odor of burnt wires rose to my nostrils.

"Look on with me." Shanghai held her tablet where I could see it. "Mine's been acting funky, too. I guess we got the bottom of the barrel."

Alex continued in a lively tone. "Since this has been a corrections facility for the past three decades, the Gatekeeper insisted that the inmates do something educational and practical, so the Council converted the former factory into a plant that produces what we need to create a new Gateway depot. Reapers in our area will no longer have to endure a long train ride. You will deliver souls here, and they will be conducted to the central Gateway as usual."

I whispered to Shanghai, "The prisoners are building their own soul transports, and they probably don't even know it."

Alex nodded toward the new Reaper. "Go ahead."

He folded his hands behind his back, his brow low. "My name is Peter, short for Saint Petersburg. I was a Reaper in Miami's gang district for three years and have been a Cardinal in Chicago for the last two. Alex asked me to speak because I took part in a special reaping in Miami that's similar to what you'll be doing here. The bottom line is simple. A mass reaping can be intimidating, but don't worry. I got through it. So can you. It's all for the best." He added a nod and backed away.

"Thank you, Peter." Alex stepped in front of him. "Now, go out the way you came in and turn left. Next we'll see the prisoners' dining area and sleeping quarters."

As we exited, Shanghai whispered, "Why was Peter talking about reaping with so many prisoners around?"

I shrugged. "My guess is he and Alex don't care what the workers hear. They can't do much to stop a reaping."

We passed into a light drizzle and raised our hoods. "This is getting creepier all the time," Shanghai said. "These are families. No one looks like a criminal."

"You're right. This isn't a tour. It's a conditioning drill to see if we're squeamish."

"So the demonstration this afternoon is going to be—"

"Shhh." I looked over my shoulder. Alex and Peter exited the building and breezed by us without a glance, hurrying to take the lead. When they passed out of earshot, I continued in a low tone. "Let's just keep our eyes open. Memorize everything—potential weapons, hiding places, exits—everything. Whatever they're planning for the demonstration, you can bet it's not going to be good."

CHAPTER SEVENTEEN

WHEN WE ENTERED the next building, Alex and Peter stood several steps inside, again whispering to each other. Carried by a draft, the odor of urine and sweaty bodies assaulted my nose. A concrete floor extended a hundred steps straight ahead and to the left. Sleeping mats and wadded sheets dotted the expanse, and fifteen or so burnt-orange picnic tables and adjoining wooden benches stood in haphazard array near the right-hand wall. At least a dozen people roamed the floor or lay on the mats. Their glowing eyes and semitransparent bodies gave away their status.

"Ghosts," I whispered to Shanghai.

"Mostly level ones and twos." She nodded toward an open door near the right rear corner. "Except for her."

At the door, a woman wearing a gray smock pulled a lever on a bucket to wring out a mop, then began mopping tiles inside the corner room. No ghost could do that.

I moved a few steps closer. The woman's sloping shoulders and lackluster effort gave away her sorrow. Fiona. Apparently she had been assigned to clean a community bathroom while everyone else worked in the assembly area.

Fiona looked our way. I pulled my hood lower over my eyes. It would be best to avoid contact for now.

"As you can see," Alex said, waving her arm toward the interior, "you already have souls to collect. More than thirty ghosts wander throughout the compound, though most congregate here."

"How many ghosts are visible to you?" Shanghai asked.

Alex squinted at her. "That's an odd question."

"Well… I heard that you were once a Reaper, so…"

Alex nodded. "So you're checking on my abilities." She scanned the room. "I see one, two, three, four, five, six level ones. One, two, three, four level twos. And the level threes?" She swiveled as she pointed directly at each one. "A little shirtless boy, a woman lying on a mat, an old man sitting at a table, and…" She pulled her hand back. "No. The woman with the mop is a worker here." As she turned toward us, she riveted her stare on me. "She is very much alive… for now."

I stared back at her. I couldn't let her intimidate me with a thinly veiled threat.

"So," Alex continued, "not only will you be reaping newly emerged souls, you will also be searching the facility to find those who passed away before you arrived."

Shanghai spoke up again. "What's the demonstration this afternoon? Collecting ghosts? We've done that plenty of times."

"Not collecting ghosts." Alex's smile widened, looking mysterious, almost sinister. "Let's just say that you will be introduced to a technique that you have never seen before, so your attendance and careful observation are essential."

Peter sidled close to Alex and whispered into her ear. She nodded, then turned to us. "Sandwiches and soup will be delivered to the dining area at noon, so you may pick up your lunch at that time and eat wherever you wish. Just be sure to meet me in the lobby at one." Without another word, she and Peter strode to the door and hustled away across the field.

"Well," Shanghai said as she scanned the spacious room. "This is interesting."

"Interesting is right." I stared at the open door. The breeze caressed my cheeks with tiny droplets—a blend of refreshment and a slight sting. "This smells like a setup."

"You're ahead of me on this one, Phoenix. What's Alex planning?"

"She's baiting us with Fiona. She expects us to stay here and talk to her." I fished the room key from my pocket. "Let's see what's going on."

We hurried out of the building and jogged across the field. Ahead, Alex and Peter opened the Hilton's door and disappeared inside. When we neared the building, we slowed to a quick march, walked in, then hustled up the stairs. I stopped at the top and looked through the hallway door's window. Alex and Peter walked toward my room, their backs to us.

"They're checking us out." After catching my breath, I opened the door and walked into the hall at a leisurely pace. I stopped and feigned surprise. "Alex? Peter?"

Alex spun toward us, a key in hand. "Phoenix!"

"I was just heading to my room." I narrowed my eyes and continued toward them, Shanghai keeping pace. "What are you doing here?"

Alex showed me the key. "I came to change your lock situation. Peter convinced me that it doesn't make sense to punish you for exploring when eventually you're going to be hunting the compound for ghosts."

"Just trying to help you out," Peter said, flashing a disarming smile. "And, by the way, there was a little female ghost in the hall when we came. She ran into your room, so you might want to check on that for the sake of privacy. They've been known to tell others what they've seen, so… you know."

"A little tattletale, huh?" I walked past them and pushed my key into the lock. Tori had had plenty of time to warn Sing. She was likely under Shanghai's bed by now.

I opened the door, flipped the light switch, and walked in. My bed had been neatly made, the candles stood perfectly aligned on the dresser, and my other set of traveling clothes lay folded next to them. The aroma of soap wafted from the open bathroom door.

I held the door for Shanghai. After she entered and headed for her room, I nodded at the lock. "It's all yours."

"I don't have the tools to change the lock right now." She withdrew two more keys from her jacket pocket and pressed them into my palm. "One for your interior lock and one for Shanghai's. I don't have spares, so don't lose them."

I wrapped my fingers around the keys. "They're safe with me."

Alex fastened her stare on me. Her eyes once again took on a silvery gloss. "You can come and go as you please, Phoenix. Just stay in the compound."

"No problem."

"I'll see you at the demonstration." Alex took Peter by the arm. "Let's go."

As they left, Peter offered a saluting wave. "Nice talking to you, Phoenix."

"Same to you." When they walked out of sight, I closed the door from the inside and leaned against it. Sing and Shanghai walked in from the bathroom together, Tori trailing them.

Shanghai gestured with her head toward the hallway. "She wasn't here to change our lock situation."

"No. That was to save face." I laid my interior key in Sing's hand and gave Shanghai hers. "Lucky break, really. We prevented a search and picked up some freedom at the same time."

"You can bet Alex will keep snooping," Sing said.

"Probably not anytime soon." I sat on my bed. When Sing and Shanghai joined me, I gave Sing a rundown of what we had seen in the assembly and prisoners' residence rooms. Once again we chatted about home and families, though Sing added only tidbits of information about herself.

After a while, I withdrew my watch and read the face. Nearly noon. "Maybe we can pick up our lunches and eat with the prisoners."

We rose from the bed and walked to the door. I opened it carefully and peeked out, then entered the hall with Shanghai and looked back at Sing. "I'll bring some food soon."

Holding the door from inside the room, Sing rubbed her stomach. "Thanks. I'm getting famished."

"No problem." I studied her eyes—anxious, nervous. "Is something wrong?"

She glanced at Shanghai. "It's okay. I can deal with it. You two go ahead."

"I detect a need for some privacy." Shanghai pivoted on the carpet. "I'll see you downstairs."

When she disappeared through the stairwell door, I turned again to Sing. "What's up?"

"Just a minute." Still holding the door, Sing looked at Tori. "Would you please go to Shanghai's bedroom for a minute? I'd like to talk to Phoenix alone."

"Sure." Tori half bounced and half floated away.

"Look at this." Sing pulled a folded piece of paper from her pocket. "I got another note while you were gone this morning." She opened it, revealing the same hurried script.

I read it out loud. "Raven, no time for disguised words. Alex suspects that Phoenix is hiding someone in his room. Think about who could have told her. Trust no one."

Sing pulled the note away. "Do you think the guard at the back door told her?"

"Probably. No one else knows."

"Shanghai knows."

"Shanghai?" I backed farther into the hallway. "Wait a minute. Don't even go there. I trust her as much as I trust you. All three of us are in this together."

"You're right. I'm sorry." She gazed at me with tear-filled eyes. "Phoenix, I can't afford to mess this up. It's too important. My mother's somewhere in the Gateway system, and if she didn't go to the afterlife, we have to help her."

"Her and everyone else we Reapers have taken to the Gateway."

She nodded. "So since someone reported me, Alex will keep looking. If she finds me, everything I've planned will be ruined."

"So what are you saying?" I stepped close to the door again. "Do you want to leave the camp?"

"No. I have to stay and help." Sing ran a finger along the door jamb. "I can find a better hiding place, somewhere other than this room."

"Maybe Tori can recommend a place where the guards never go."

"Or even better, I could pose as a prisoner. Alex probably doesn't take a second glance at any prisoners besides the Fitzpatricks, so she won't notice me."

"Don't be so sure. With those Owl eyes, she's pretty sharp. You should have seen her analyze the ghosts in the sleeping quarters. Faster than I could have done it."

"Then I'll stay out of her sight. And I can alter my clothes to help me fit in." Sing pushed the door until only a narrow gap allowed a view of her eyes. "While you're having lunch, I'll try to get a nap. Then if you'll bring me something to eat, I'll be ready to work on my disguise the rest of the afternoon."

"Sounds like a good plan." When the door latched, I hurried to the dining area. Shanghai met me just inside the door. A pair of brown paper bags, Styrofoam bowls with attached lids, and bottles of water sat on our usual table.

Shanghai picked up a bag and whispered, "We'll share one and give the other to Sing."

"That'll work." I grabbed a bag, a bowl, and a bottle. "She's catching a nap, so let's go back and talk to Fiona. Since it's lunchtime, Colm might be there, too."

We hustled across the yard to the prisoners' living quarters. Along the way, I told Shanghai about Sing's plan to disguise herself. She listened intently, nodding but saying nothing.

Inside the quarters, the families sat on the picnic table benches, each person facing a small bowl that couldn't hold enough to feed a house cat much less a hungry laborer. Some prisoners bent close and scooped spoonful after spoonful while others lifted their bowls and slurped down the contents.

I spotted Colm sitting with Fiona, Colleen, and the two girls at the table closest to the bathroom. As we passed by the other prisoners, it seemed that every head turned to follow our progress. When we arrived at Colm's table, two men rose from the benches with bowls in hand and stalked away, grumbling.

"Please, sit." Colm gestured toward the newly empty spaces. "And please excuse those gentlemen. With rumors flying about mass executions, Reapers aren't exactly a welcome sight."

"I can't say I blame them." I slid in across from Colm, to the left of the girls, and set Sing's lunch at my side. Shanghai sat on the opposite bench between Fiona and Coleen and withdrew a sub sandwich from her bag. She used a dagger from her belt to slice it in half through its paper wrapping, then passed a section to me.

After introducing everyone to Shanghai, I leaned forward and whispered to Colm, "I'm afraid the rumors are true. I volunteered to join the reapings so I could get you and your family out of here."

"We guessed that to be the case." Colm nodded toward Fiona. "She saw you when you were here earlier."

"I did indeed." Fiona slid her half-empty bowl across to the girls. "Divide the rest fairly between yourselves."

As the girls traded spoonfuls, I glanced at Shanghai.

Her eyes glistened with tears. No doubt she was thinking the same thing I was.

I handed Anne my half of the sandwich while Shanghai placed hers and the soup bowl in front of Betsy. "We have another lunch," I said, "so please share this. We'll have plenty to eat this evening."

Fiona reached across the table and stroked my hand. "Phoenix, you and Shanghai do a mother's heart good. As long as you're here, we have hope."

"There's always hope." I gave her a nod, trying to smile, but my lips wouldn't cooperate. "At least Molly's safe. I delivered her to the Gateway without a problem. She spoke to me as she left my cloak." My heart thumped. I couldn't bear to tell this bereaved mother what her precious daughter said as she departed.

A tear trickled down Fiona's cheek. "Bless you, Phoenix. In the midst of sadness, we see a glimmer of light."

Tears slid down Colleen's cheeks as well. "The Gateway ushered another star to the sky. 'Tis a shame that we so rarely see them."

"Speaking of the Gateway..." I pointed with my thumb over my shoulder. "Can you tell me more about what you're putting together in the assembly room? They look like the platforms we use for transferring souls at the Gateway."

"I wouldn't know about that," Colm said, "but I can tell you that the disks project holographic images, sort of how photo sticks create such images, and the disks expand vertically into platforms, maybe a foot high. They also have connection points for hose-like tubes. I have seen the tubes, but they are fabricated in another location, so I don't know much about them."

"Does the tube have a T-connector on one end?" I asked.

"Most do not, but I have seen a couple that do."

"How many disk platforms have they made?"

"The assembly line produces about four in a day, and the facility has been working on them for maybe eight weeks. Start-up was probably slow, so I guess the prisoners might have made a hundred and fifty or so by now."

"A hundred and fifty." I looked around the room. Many heads quickly turned away. A camera in an upper corner rotated slowly from right to left. Might it be unsafe to reveal our plans here?

The moment the camera angled away, I bent over and looked under the table. A microphone disk had been attached to the underside. Alex never gave up.

When I straightened, I gave Shanghai the same microphone-is-present gesture I had the night before, then leaned over the table and whispered so only Colm and Fiona could hear. "They're listening in, so I'll try to throw them off. Believe the opposite of what I say."

Before the camera turned back toward us, I settled to my seat. "We tried smuggling a friend into the compound, even got her past the guards, but we're pretty sure Alex heard about it, so we smuggled her out again. I don't think we'll have anyone to help you besides us."

Colm nodded. "So if someone comes to us claiming to be your ally, we shouldn't believe them. It will be a trap."

"That's right." I gave him a brief head nod. He had caught on perfectly. "What measures do they take to keep you here, I mean, besides the fence and razor wire? Can you go inside my residence building?"

"We cannot. The guards lock us in this room after

dinner, usually just after dark. The door you entered is the only way out."

I scanned the room. Indeed the front entry proved to be the only door. Huge dirty windows ran along the walls at least fifteen feet above, far too high to reach. Some were open for ventilation, and cracks drew jagged lines across several others. A long pole stood in a corner, apparently the tool to open and close the swivel-mounted panes.

Sing could use the pole to vault to a window or else climb a spool line. Since it would be dark in the room at that hour, the camera wouldn't see her. After dropping on the guards and subduing them, she could snatch the keys and let Colm and his family out. From there, getting them outside the prison through the Hilton would be easier. She could overpower Stanskey without a problem.

"Well," I said with a fake sigh, "it looks impossible, but we'll try to figure out something."

Fiona glanced at her daughters. "I hope so. If what we hear is true…" Her face twisting, she clutched her spoon and turned away.

I leaned forward again. "Colm, I always thought this camp held criminals, you know, murderers, rapists, thieves, but what's up with all the children?"

"There are no murderers here. No rapists. Thieves?" He shrugged. "Perhaps a few. Most parents were caught dealing in the medical black market, and the police brought the children along. It's much more efficient than putting them in an orphanage."

"True." My heart thumped again. There was more to the children's presence than efficiency. This was a test of loyalty to the Gatekeeper. If we were willing to participate in this reaping of innocents, we would do anything for him.

A bell rang from the ceiling. The prisoners stood and filed toward the door, heads down and feet dragging. A few stayed put in their seats, and their glowing eyes revealed the reason. Ghosts didn't have to respond to the bell.

I checked my pocket watch—twelve thirty. We still had some time. "I guess you have to go." I rose and shook Colm's hand, then Fiona's and Colleen's. After bidding them all good-bye, I picked up Sing's lunch and waited with Shanghai for the prisoners to leave. Now each man, woman, and child took on a new character. They weren't criminals at all. Not a single one deserved to die. They needed to be rescued every bit as much as Colm and his family did.

I let my shoulders sag. It seemed that energy drained from my body. Three Reapers couldn't sneak a couple of hundred people out of a camp surrounded by razor wire, searchlights, and tower-mounted guns. It was impossible.

When the cavernous room emptied, except for the ghosts, Shanghai and I walked abreast toward the door. "I think I got the message across."

"You did," Shanghai said. "Colm's a smart guy."

We exited and walked across the prison yard toward the Hilton. As light drizzle continued, dampening the grass and giving it a slippery feel, I plugged my clasp into my valve. When the cloak energized, Crandyke immediately spoke up. "You're getting wet. Don't you know enough to get out of the rain?"

I forced a tone of levity. "Are you my mother now?"

"Don't worry. If you catch a cold, I won't be wiping your nose. You're on your own."

"Listen, I don't have much time. How many guards

patrol the inside of the camp after dark, especially around the prisoners' living quarters?"

"I think ten are on duty, some in the watchtower, a couple on the outside of the fence, maybe four walking the grounds inside. I don't know how many would be at the living quarters at any given time. Depends on the access points."

"There's one access, a single door."

"That matches my memory." Crandyke hummed for a moment. "My guess is two guards would watch that door, but it's just a guess."

I nodded. A surprise attack from above could take down two guards, but when a searchlight scanned the spot, other guards would run there in a hurry. Someone would have to shut the lights down somehow, at least long enough to get Colm's family to the Hilton.

When Shanghai and I arrived in the second-floor hallway, we found Tori sitting between our two doors. Smiling, she jumped up and rushed into the wall in a blur. By the time we reached Shanghai's room, the door opened revealing a bleary-eyed Sing.

"We don't have much time to talk," I said as I walked past her and set the lunch items on Shanghai's bed. Tori sat on the sofa. Her eyes barely glowed now; she would be a full level three soon.

After Shanghai closed the door, she and Sing joined me on the bed. I told Sing about the conversation with Colm and that he would be watching for an ally. I added the details about the camera, windows, and pole, and we agreed that Sing would join the inmates tonight by sneaking into the living quarters just before the guards locked it up. With reapings starting tomorrow, the sooner Colm and family escaped, the better.

The next obstacle would be sneaking back across the open yard after knocking out the two guards. Dodging the searchlights might be possible for a Reaper as nimble as Sing, but not with a family tagging along. I asked Tori to study the searchlights and report if they have a power switch. Of course she wouldn't be able to turn them off herself, but she could lead Shanghai or me to take care of that task.

The final obstacle would be getting the family out the Hilton's rear exit. We decided that Sing should try the door-knocking trick again, but since Stanskey would be ready this time with his gun drawn, she would have to overpower him and knock him out the moment he disabled the alarm and opened the door.

After we set the plans, I looked at Sing. "We should be able to come back here between the demonstration and dinner, and we'll see how your disguise is coming along."

"That's fine." Sing rose from the bed and opened her beat-up suitcase on Shanghai's dresser. "It shouldn't take more than a couple of hours."

I glanced at the suitcase's contents and caught a glimpse of a dark glass bottle with a prescription label, half buried under clothing. "Where did you get the medicine?"

"One of my people picked it up at the shroud." Sing pulled the bottle out and showed it to me. "It's for my cough. It helps a lot. If I cough like a seal while I'm here, someone's bound to find me."

I leaned forward to try to read the label, but her hand covered the words. No matter. It was just a cough suppressant. "Good thinking."

Tori jumped up from the sofa. "I'm going to the search-lights now."

"And we'd better get going, too." After Shanghai and I said good-bye to Sing, we walked slowly down the hall toward the stairwell. "What do you think our chances are?" I asked. "Do you think the plan can work?"

Shanghai shook her head. "Plans never work the way you expect. Something always goes wrong. We have to be ready to adjust. You know, think fast. Be quick on our feet."

After a few seconds of silence, I leaned toward her. "I'm glad I have you at my side. I've never seen anyone as sharp and quick as you are."

"The feeling's mutual." Shanghai brushed her hand against mine. "But will you stay at my side?"

I stopped at the stairwell door and faced her. "What do you mean?"

"I mean..." Looking into my eyes, she took my hand and compressed it with both of hers. "Once we're done here, will you stay with me? Just like now? Roommates, so we won't be alone again."

Shanghai's gaze pierced my heart, and her touch sent pulses of heat surging through my body. She was so beauti-ful, so intelligent, so electric. Every other guy in the world would jump at the chance to be with this amazing girl.

Without looking, I rubbed the pewter ring with my thumb. Misty. She still waited. "Shanghai, I can't make promises like that. We're sprinting headlong into a charg-ing bull. We might not be alive tomorrow. We might have to die for this cause."

"I know. We always have something to die for, but I want something to live for, something to look forward to." As her eyes misted, her voice cracked. "If I have to keep living alone, maybe I won't... I won't..." She bit her lip and turned away.

My mind begged to ask "Won't what?" but I bit my own lip and touched her shoulder. "Can we talk about it later?"

"Um..." She turned back to me, brushing a tear, her head low. "Sure. We'll talk later."

I angled my head to catch her gaze. "No hard feelings? We'll talk about it. Really."

"No hard feelings." After brushing another tear, she hooked her arm around mine, her voice resuming its perky bounce. "I won't bring it up again."

"You won't have to." I leaned close and kissed her forehead. "Trust me. I really want to be with you. I just have to figure some things out first. Is that all right?"

"It's all right." Shanghai returned the kiss to my forehead. "I'll wait as long as it takes."

CHAPTER EIGHTEEN

A LEX LED SHANGHAI and me across the prison yard toward the assembly room. The drizzle had stopped, though the grass remained damp and spongy. The searchlight on the watchtower stood dark and motionless. Another dormant searchlight sat atop a taller factory-style building I hadn't entered yet. With nearly every window broken and a double door standing open on rusted hinges, it was likely abandoned.

Inside the assembly room, the workstation square had been cleared, replaced by three white disks, similar to the pedestals at the Gateway, though only half as thick. The foreman stood fidgeting near a wall, the only prisoner remaining.

Alex crossed the room and crouched with Peter next to the largest disk. She pointed at a bowl-shaped depression at the center of its otherwise smooth surface. They exchanged whispers before Alex rose and turned toward us. "Each of you take one of these and carry it outside. It looks like the rain will hold off for a while."

I chose one and lifted it. Weighing about twenty pounds, it wasn't too heavy. Shanghai picked up another, the same size as mine.

I glared at Alex. She had a purpose for this visit other

than to get help carrying disks. She wanted us to see that the work was finished. The prisoners had served their purpose. Their next assignment would end with their disembodied souls locked inside the fibers of a Reaper's cloak.

Alex picked up a slender rectangular box, similar to one that might hold long-stemmed roses, and walked toward the exit, motioning for the foreman to come along. Peter carried the largest disk and followed.

When we arrived at the middle of the yard, Alex directed the placement of the disks in a triangle, separating them by about three paces. When Peter set his disk on the ground, he stood on it for a moment, apparently checking its stability.

As soon as Alex approved the setup, she withdrew a miniature tablet from her jacket pocket and tapped on the screen. "Since this demonstration is the first of its kind anywhere in the world, we will have a special guest in attendance to monitor the results."

I stepped close to Shanghai. "Any guesses?"

"Someone who could approve a Gateway test?" Shanghai rolled her eyes. "A certain pompous windbag we both know all too well."

I let out a quiet groan. "Not Bartholomew."

She elbowed my ribs. "Hush."

While we waited, I scanned the grounds once again, looking for a ladder or rope or any way to scale the abandoned building that held the searchlight, but no climbing devices lay around. A spool and line would have to do.

My gaze paused at the foreman waiting outside the pedestal triangle. He shifted his weight from one foot to the other, apparently unaware of the reason he had been called to join us, and rightly so. No one had yet asked him to do anything.

After a couple of minutes, the camp's front gate dragged open. A white stretch limousine breezed through and drove across the yard, its tires pressing into the soft turf. The driver, a man wearing a dark blazer and chauffeur's cap and sporting a gray goatee, kept both hands on the wheel, his expression stoic. A curtain behind him and tinted windows prevented a view of the rear passenger compartment.

The limo stopped several paces away from our Gateway setup. When the motor shut off, the chauffeur got out and opened the rear passenger door on his side. A woman in a hooded white cloak emerged with a silver box cradled in her palms. When she straightened, her hood fell back, revealing red hair and a familiar face.

"It's Erin," Shanghai whispered.

"I know, but she's just a checkpoint clerk."

"True, but that's a job that requires a lot of trust from on high, if you know what I mean. Maybe she's not alone."

Keeping her eyes fixed straight ahead, Erin strode directly to the largest disk. She set the box down, then reached inside and withdrew a glowing sphere. Its alabaster radiance washed over her face, turning her skin pale blue.

She placed the sphere in the disk's bowl-shaped depression. The sphere's glow diminished from top to bottom, as if absorbed by the underlying surface. Emanating a hum, the disk expanded vertically into a circular foot-tall slab, the same size and shape as the Gateway pedestals.

Alex walked to one of the two other disks, touched a button on the side, and inserted a photo stick in a port at the base, then repeated the process with the third disk. As the two disks grew in height, holograms took shape over their surfaces. Within seconds, they clarified into cloaked Reapers that looked like Shanghai and me.

"Each of you stand on your pedestal," Alex said. "You know the drill."

I stepped up and meshed with my hologram. Shanghai did the same with hers. Because of the disks' triangular arrangement, we faced each other. I glanced at Peter, who stood at Alex's side next to Erin. Since no hologram appeared on the third disk, his part in this demonstration remained unclear.

Once we were in place, Alex focused on the computer tablet. "The pressure hasn't stabilized yet. Just another minute or so."

The chauffeur opened the limo's other rear door. A man stepped out, straightened to a six-foot-plus height, and looked around. His blue eyes sparkled in spite of the dreary sky. The breeze blew back his collar-length black hair, making it brush against his pullover sweater. Wearing jeans and athletic shoes, he walked toward us, his skin nearly as radiant as the glowing sphere. "Well," he said with an energetic voice, "it is certainly a pleasure seeing these fine Reapers here."

Alex dropped to one knee and bowed her head. "The pleasure is ours, Exalted One." Erin and Peter copied Alex's pose, and the two holograms knelt in the same way.

I stayed on my feet. No one had ordered a bow or even introduced the visitor, though I recognized him as the Gatekeeper from the many portraits and posters throughout the city. I had never been a conformist before, and I wasn't about to become one now, though standing in the midst of my own bowed form probably made me look like a stubborn rebel.

Shanghai bent for a moment, but when she noticed me, she straightened again. Although her lips stayed taut and even, her eyes darted nervously.

The Gatekeeper walked to me and extended his hand. "I am Melchizedek. What is your name?"

"Phoenix." I bent slightly and slid my hand into his. The moment our skin made contact, a pulse of energy ran up my arm and through my body, as if I had plugged into a human electrical outlet. Yet, instead of hot and painful, the sensation was warm and soothing.

"Alex told me about you." As we shook hands, he smiled. "I trust that you know my position."

I nodded. "The Gatekeeper."

He drew his hand away. "Then why did you not bow?"

"I assumed you honor deeds rather than show. I am here to reap souls, as requested." I straightened. "Is it my duty also to pay you genuflecting homage?"

Still smiling, he spoke in a low tone. "Phoenix, I applaud your courage. I always prefer sailing in a sturdy ship over a rickety showboat. Moorings are far more important than colorful banners. Yet I do expect proper decorum. A bow of respect is sufficient."

"I understand." I gave him a half bow, as did Shanghai. "If your character matches your marketing, I respect you highly."

"Courageously stated." He pivoted toward Alex, Peter, and Erin. "Rise, my friends. I am looking forward to this demonstration."

When the trio rose, Alex studied her computer tablet. "One moment, if you please."

"Take your time. I see no reason to hurry."

While they waited, I looked at my hand. My palm tingled, and the energy surge ebbed. The fading sensation left a void, a hunger that gnawed within. My cheeks flushed hot. My body ached with desire. It wanted more, another touch, another taste.

I clenched my fists. Maybe this was how Melchizedek controlled his minions—with a sip of his power, a narcotic that instantly addicted. The handshake was designed to bring me to my knees, if not in body, then in mind. I had to resist.

Shanghai cocked her head, blinking. I showed her my palm and shook my head hard, hoping she would interpret the signal. She had to avoid contact.

She gave me a nod.

The gnawing hunger eased. I let my muscles relax. I had fought off the influence, at least temporarily.

"We're ready now, sir." Alex laid a hand on Peter's shoulder. "Let's proceed."

Peter stepped in front of the Gatekeeper pedestal. Alex opened the "flower" box, and she and Erin began withdrawing flexible tubes from inside, identical to those we used at the Gateway depot.

Peter gave Melchizedek a head bow. "Since you have overseen the project, sir, I have no need to explain the principles, but for the sake of the other two Reapers, I will include a brief description." He fanned an arm across the triangle of pedestals. "We have constructed a new Gateway depot, the first portable one in the world. Yet portability is not its only important innovation. The alterations we have made to the energy delivery system will greatly enhance a Reaper's abilities."

While Peter spoke, Alex and Erin attached the pedestal bases together with flexible tubes, plugging one end into a base and the other into an adjacent base to form a triangle of connected pedestals. When they finished, they brought two other tubes, one for my pedestal and one for Shanghai's, and attached one normal end to a valve on the pedestal surface and a T-connector end to our clasps.

Peter gestured for the foreman to come. His back bowed as if ready to receive a lashing, the foreman hurried to Peter's side.

"What we have here," Peter said, nodding toward the foreman, "is a full-fledged level-three ghost." He pushed his hand through the foreman's back until it protruded from his chest.

I gave Shanghai a glance. With her mouth partially open, she looked as surprised as I felt.

The foreman leaped away and stood with his back bowed again, trembling. "I'm sorry, sir. I just wanted to help. I offered a lot of advice in the assembly room. Ask anyone."

"I know you did," Peter said in a soothing tone. "You have nothing to fear. In fact, I asked you to join us so you can be rewarded."

The foreman straightened. "Thank you, sir. Thank you very much."

"During our earlier tests," Peter continued, "I consumed an augmented form of energy and practiced an enhanced ability we had theorized. After several attempts, I was able to reap a level-three ghost with ease. Our new disks are able to deliver the Gatekeeper's energy in this purer and more powerful form, so once all Reapers begin energizing this way and learn the techniques, we will be able to reap wandering souls more efficiently and thereby help them go to their eternal homes, giving their families peace and assurance that all is well for their departed loved ones."

A vague aura formed around Melchizedek's head, like that of an angel in early religious art. "Excellent. Please proceed."

Peter turned to the foreman. "I understand that your name is Zeke."

He nodded. "Yes sir. Yes sir, it is."

"Well, Zeke, let's talk about your reward." Peter fanned out his cloak and set it over Zeke's back. Instead of falling through, the cloak spread out neatly on his shoulders.

I leaned closer and studied Peter's appearance, paler, definitely transformed. He had joined the ghostly ranks on a whim, including everything he wore from his clothing to his cloak and belt. It had always taken me much longer.

"Do you trust me?" Peter asked Zeke.

"Uh... " Zeke's eyes began to glow as if he were reverting to a level two. "Sure. I trust you.... Who are you again?"

"A friend." Peter draped his cloak completely around Zeke and pulled him close. Zeke's body thinned out into vapor and flowed into the fibers. Seconds later, without so much as a whimper, he was gone.

As Peter turned to face us again, his cloak shimmered. "I am still in the realm of ghosts, as Alex will demonstrate."

Alex pushed her hand through Peter's back. When she stepped away, she took on the tour-guide persona again as she addressed Shanghai and me. "If Peter were to return to physical form now, we could transfer the soul from his cloak in the usual way, but instead he will demonstrate a new method that is less painful." She lifted the loose end of the largest pedestal's tube and pushed it into Peter's body. "We're ready."

Erin walked closer, now tapping on Alex's computer tablet. "Turning on the vacuum."

A hum sounded. Peter's body stretched out and rushed into the tube.

Erin studied the tablet. "Peter and Zeke are separating," she said in monotone. "The sphere is absorbing Zeke's soul, while Peter is resisting the pull."

A few seconds later, the sphere's radiance brightened.

"Zeke is now in place, and the lock is secure." Erin slid a finger across the tablet's screen. "Peter is ready to return."

"Bring him back," Alex said.

Erin tapped on the screen. "Reversing the flow."

The hum returned. Mist appeared at the end of the tube, poured to the ground, and collected in a vertical column. Within seconds, Peter's body took shape. After staggering for a moment, he closed his eyes, took in a deep breath, and exhaled slowly.

"Good work, Peter." Alex patted him on the shoulder, proving that he had returned to the physical realm.

"Thanks." Still looking a bit woozy, he backed away. "You can finish, Mother."

Alex flashed an angry look, then laughed. "As the other Reapers know, transfers to and from ghost status can cause temporary dizziness and confusion. It seems that Peter thinks he's at home with his mother, but he'll soon recover."

I studied Peter's expression. Yes, he was confused, but probably just enough to forget about hiding who his mother was. So Peter was the Reaper Kwame mentioned, and Alex wasn't just an Owl; she was really a Council member, which would explain her apparent youth in spite of her twenty years as a Reaper.

"The confusion is a drawback," Alex continued, "so we make the transfer as quick as possible in order to minimize the effect. Also, the drawback is outweighed by the benefit of convenience. Since this is a portable station, the sphere Erin brought can be carried to the actual Gateway and the souls therein transferred to the afterlife. We can have one of these stations in every major city, and death officers can facilitate the transfers. No more long train rides for weary Reapers."

I nodded. Less pain and more convenience sounded good to me.

Alex touched her sternum. "You might be wondering why we attached the tubes to your clasps. This will be the next step in our demonstration. Since the Gatekeeper graciously filled the primary pedestal with abundant energy, you will receive his gift in a purer form, as if he has breathed his very soul into yours, enabling you to more easily collect the ghosts that reside here."

Alex nodded at Erin. "You may proceed."

"One moment." Erin began tapping on her tablet again. "The Reapers need to connect their valves so I can check for pressure leaks."

After locking clasp to valve, I stared at my palm. The physical tingling had stopped, but the memory persisted. If the new pedestal system infused me with a potent form of the Gatekeeper's energy, might it have the same effect as the handshake? Maybe even stronger since it would go straight to my heart?

Shanghai gave me a curious stare. But this was no time to explain my concern.

Erin tapped the screen once more. "No leaks. Energy transfer commencing."

I tensed my muscles. The hum returned. As usual, energy flowed through my valve, bringing an invigorating sensation. Tingles ran along my skin. My heart raced. I gazed at Shanghai. She closed her eyes and spread out her arms like an angel in flight—majestic, beautiful. Her dark hair shone, her trim and toned body flexed with vigor, and her face's lovely features magnified. In a word, she was dazzling.

After several seconds, Erin called out, "Shutting off the flow."

The hum ceased. I exhaled. My smile locked in place, making my cheeks hurt. The dismal prison yard brightened. Even Alex looked like a decent human being. Maybe this reaping job wouldn't be so bad after all.

Erin gave Alex the tablet. "Congratulations on a successful demonstration."

"Thank you, but we're not finished. There remains another step." Alex set the tablet on the primary pedestal, withdrew her sonic gun from the inner holster, and called toward the prisoners' living quarters. "Bring him out!"

I shuddered. Something in Alex's voice belied her pleasant appearance, something sinister.

A guard led a man our way. As he drew closer, his balding head and bushy eyebrows clarified—Colm Fitzpatrick.

I glanced between him and the gun. My heart thumped harder than ever. Would Alex really use the gun on him as part of the demonstration? Nearly laughing, I shook my head. She wouldn't. She was just trying to scare me.

Though a voice deep inside screamed to break through—a warning, a desperate cry that something terrible was about to happen.

When the guard arrived, he pushed Colm down to his knees. I looked at Shanghai. Her smile remained, though somewhat wrinkled. Apparently the unfolding events perplexed her, too, as if we both swam in the same murky haze.

Alex circled behind Colm and set the gun at the base of his skull. He looked straight at me. Although his expression betrayed no fear, his eyes pleaded for rescue. But what could I do? I couldn't take on both Alex and Peter. Besides, this had to be a scare tactic, a test of some kind. Alex wouldn't—

A muffled pop sliced through the air. Colm's eyes rolled up into his head. He toppled to the side and hit the ground with a sickening thud.

CHAPTER NINETEEN

I SANK TO MY knees. With my entire body quaking, I whispered, "What... what happened?"

Alex smiled as she lifted the sonic gun. "This is a lovely weapon—quiet and lethal. Its only drawback is its recharge time." She walked toward me with a cocky stride. "Phoenix, you seem ill."

My throat tightened. I could barely spit out a word. "He's... dead?"

Her brow furrowing, she glanced at Colm. "Of course. I'm sure you've seen this gun's efficiency at the executions."

"But Colm is my... my..."

She bobbed her head in an exaggerated nod. "Oh, I see. You don't understand why I executed someone from your district." She slid the gun to her shoulder holster. "It's complicated, Phoenix, especially for someone in your confused state, but I'm sure you can figure it out. In one stroke I have proven what I am capable of doing without hesitation and at the same time preserved the remaining assets that keep you from shirking your duties. I have also enhanced our demonstration by showing how our energy boost has encouraged all who partake of it to acquiesce to, shall we say, unpleasant necessities. Even a principled Reaper like you did nothing to stop me."

The words flowed in, but they jumbled in a messy pile. As I pieced them together, her malice became clear. If I didn't give in to the energy's influence, she would kill the entire family.

"Shanghai," Alex said, extending a photo stick toward her, "kindly reap this man's soul, then return to your station. I think Phoenix is in no shape to do so at the moment."

"Yes ma'am." Bowing her head, Shanghai jumped off her pedestal, snatched the stick from Alex, and knelt at Colm's side.

I blinked. *Yes ma'am?* What happened to Shanghai? Did she surrender to the influence, or was she just playing along?

While I watched in silence, Shanghai turned Colm onto his back. "Come with me," she said, her voice like an alluring song as she laid her cloaked hand over his eyes. "Let me take you away from this world of pain and torment to a place where you can lay down your burdens and rest." After a short pause, she let out a deep sigh. "Yes, I know you're concerned about your family, but there is nothing you can do for them now. You must release that responsibility and transfer it to Phoenix and me. We will do all we can to protect them from harm. You have been a wonderful husband and father, and your duty has come to an end." Then she whispered something too quiet to hear.

A shimmer flowed into her cloak and covered her shoulders. A few seconds later, Shanghai lifted her hand and rose to her feet. Colm's eyes bugged out but not much, and no dark tears stained his face. This was an easy reaping.

Shanghai slid the photo stick into her pants pocket. "Yes, Colm. I will tell Fiona when I see her."

While Shanghai shuffled to her pedestal, Alex grabbed my wrist and helped me stand, whispering sharply, "Colm is dead because of your earlier antics. If you decide to cooperate from now on, the rest of the family will live. Got it?"

I steeled my body. The urge to break this witch's neck spiked, making me curl my fingers into a strangling pose. But I had to play it cool, pretend to be under her control, though her Owl eyes seemed able to pierce my thoughts. "I understand, Alex. You've made yourself perfectly clear."

"Good. I'm glad to see you're coming to your senses." Alex backed away and reprised her tour-guide tone. "Since this depot doesn't directly transfer souls, you don't need a photo stick at this point. Still, the final Gateway needs the images. You can deliver the stick to Erin at any time before she transports the sphere to the actual Gateway."

I kept a wary eye on Erin as she studied the tablet screen, her white cloak flowing. Her security clearance had to be super high to be able to deliver souls and images to the Gateway. Since she was chosen for this duty, she must have risen quickly in the Council's good graces.

"Thank you for your participation," Alex continued. "After dinner we will have an entertainment event here in the yard, but I'm keeping the details a secret for now. Feel free to use the time before dinner to experiment with your newfound abilities."

As I detached my clasp from the connector and stepped down from the pedestal, I focused on Shanghai as she dismounted and walked slowly toward me. Her face had changed somehow. Instead of radiating bright-eyed optimism, she now looked morose, downtrodden.

Alex bowed her head toward Melchizedek. "I hope the demonstration met your expectations."

He clapped his hands. "Very much so. I must say that you proved your theory to the utmost." He gave Shanghai and me a quick glance before continuing. "I trust that your Cardinals are, shall we say, birds of a feather?"

"They are, Exalted One." Alex, too, glanced at us. "They realize that your energy is a sublime infusion of peace and joy. As you saw, the execution did nothing to significantly ruffle their feathers."

"Excellent, because it takes only one dissenter to ruin the nest, if you don't mind the stretching of the metaphor."

"I understand completely. You need not be concerned."

"Very well." Melchizedek nodded at the glowing sphere still sitting in the center disk's bowl. "Since you will be collecting so many souls tomorrow, Erin will return in the morning to retrieve this sphere and replace it with a new one."

"Thank you." Alex's tone dripped with nauseating submissiveness. "We all appreciate your participation and generosity."

With Erin again at his side, Melchizedek extended his hand toward me. "It was a pleasure meeting you, Phoenix."

I stared at his hand. Could I overcome yet another infusion? I had fought off the other energy spikes, but a third shot might make me lose control.

"Why the hesitation?" He pushed his hand into mine and shook it. "I assume that the newness of this experience has overwhelmed you, so I will not take into account this second breach in decorum."

Energy surged through my body. I gasped for breath. My knees buckled. Pure pleasure pulsed through ever fiber, though my heart felt as if it were about to explode. Pain joined the pleasure in a crushing duet of bittersweet agony.

Melchizedek let go of my hand and walked with Erin toward the limo. As they conversed, their words warped into unintelligible ramblings.

"Shanghai," I whispered, "help me."

She wrapped her arms around my torso and propped me up. "I've got you."

Her touch sent shivers crawling across my skin, pure delight, excitement. "Get me..." Words caught in my throat. "Somewhere I can rest... and fight this thing."

"I will. Don't worry."

Erin and Melchizedek boarded the limo. When the engine purred to life, Shanghai helped me hobble toward Alex. "Phoenix isn't feeling well. I'm going to take him to his room."

Alex clasped my arm. "The Gatekeeper blessed you with an extra burst of energy. The effect sent your body into overdrive, but it will soon settle down. Feel free to rest until dinner. You'll want to be wide awake for our entertainment tonight."

I managed a nod but nothing more.

She lowered her voice to a whisper again, her grip tightening as her eyes narrowed. "I know that you didn't really acquiesce to my actions, but don't worry. More tests are coming." She released me and walked away.

With help from Shanghai's supporting shoulder, I shuffled toward the Hilton. Every contact point with her sent warmth blazing into my body. "You know something, Shanghai?"

Still propping me with one hand, she opened the door with the other. "What?"

I pushed my fingers through her dark silky hair, so

soft, so perfect, matching her angelic face. "You're really beautiful."

"Thank you." She cast a wary glance behind us. "I hope you still think so when you recover."

"Recover?"

"Yes. Recover." She led me inside and closed the door. "That energy has pumped you full of joy juice. You're so soused, if you were behind a wheel, you'd be DUI, my friend."

"Right." Closing my eyes, I shook my head. "I'm sorry."

"Sorry? For calling me beautiful?" She grinned. "Are you taking it back?"

"No, no, that's not what I mean. I was trying to—"

"Phoenix, I was just kidding." She set a hand on her hip. "Listen, I had a shot of that stuff, too, and it's a heavenly trip. When I looked at you standing on that pedestal, I was thinking… well, never mind what I was thinking, but you looked better than any movie star. Anyway, you need to come back down to earth, so just remember what Alex did to Colm." Shanghai pretended to pull a trigger and mimicked the popping sound. "That devil woman killed him in cold blood."

The memory rattled my brain, again clearing some of the fog. "Yeah. Thanks for the jolt."

"No problem."

I drew a step away and looked her over from head to toe, intentionally letting her see my eyes conduct a full body scan. With her cloak shimmering behind her as a sparkling frame, her bright smile bending her lovely Asian features, and her hands on her hips accentuating her toned physique, she really did look amazing. "The effects are wearing off, and I still think you're beautiful."

"Well, thank you, sir, but you still look pretty dazed to me." She hooked her arm through mine and guided me toward the stairway. "Come on, handsome. You need to sleep it off for a while."

Dizziness returned, forcing me to shift some weight to her. She held me up without a problem. "So you really think I'm handsome? Or are you under the influence?"

"Trust me. Even though I didn't get two handshakes from the Exalted One, I'm still feeling the high, so give me some time to come up with the right word to describe you."

"Sure. Fair enough."

We climbed the stairs in silence and walked along the second-floor hallway. When we reached my door, Shanghai pushed me against the wall and scooted nearly toe to toe. "I've had enough time, Phoenix," she whispered as she slid her hands behind my head, "you're much more than handsome. You're a dream come true."

Her lips drew closer, soft and moist. My cheeks burned. My own lips ached to join hers, but how could I let it happen? My ring. My promise. I had to preserve the lifeline.

Just as her breath warmed my lips, a call pierced the moment.

"Shanghai?" Tori poked her head out through Shanghai's door. "Is Phoenix all right?"

Shanghai stepped back, brushing my tunic as if smoothing it out. "He just had a dizzy spell, so I helped him walk here."

"Oh," Tori said. "I hope he feels better soon."

"He'll be fine."

I exhaled heavily. Sweat dampened my back. I had almost lost control. The infusion of energy had blown my concentration to pieces. I had to redouble my resolve—fight Melchizedek's power.

"Where's your room key?" Shanghai asked.

"In my cloak pocket."

Shanghai dug into the pocket, withdrew the key, and unlocked the door. "Tori, please tell Sing we're coming into Phoenix's room."

"Okay." Tori's head disappeared.

After fumbling with the door, Shanghai guided me through, laid me on the bed, and began untying my shoes. "I'll stay here with you if you want. You know, keep you company while you rest."

Every move she made sent my heart racing at hyper speed. "Stay," I whispered, touching her hand. "Fight it with me."

"Why fight something that feels so good?" She pulled off one of my shoes and tossed it to the floor. "Phoenix, I've already made it clear. I want us to get together, so that's the side I'm fighting for."

I swallowed through a narrowed throat, unable to say a word.

She punched my pillow, fluffing it up. "Just rest. You'll be fine soon."

Led by Tori, Sing staggered in from the bathroom, rubbing her eyes. "Phoenix! What's wrong?"

Shanghai pulled off the other shoe. "An overdose of energy from the Gatekeeper. He got zapped three times, twice by contact with the Gatekeeper himself."

Sing sat on the bed at the other side of my socked feet. She, too, looked more beautiful than ever, her skin tones raising images of milk chocolate, almonds, and caramel. "The Gatekeeper was here?"

"In the flesh." Shanghai pulled off my socks and wiggled one of my toes. "This little piggy needs to rest while I tell you about it."

"Little piggy?" Sing blinked at her. "Are you sure you didn't get zapped, too?"

"I did get zapped. Never felt better in my life."

After Shanghai and Sing helped me take off my cloak and belt, Shanghai related the events of the past hour. I closed my eyes and relived them, especially Colm's execution. Again and again that horrible pop echoed in my mind, followed by an image of Colm's fall. And Alex's callous contempt made me want to tear her tongue from her throat.

As before, the vision of brutal death cleared my thinking. I opened my eyes. Although Sing and Shanghai still looked beautiful, they seemed to transform into weapons, their toned arms and shoulders flexing whenever they moved in response to peaks and valleys in Shanghai's story.

When Shanghai finished, Sing shifted her gaze to me and back to Shanghai again. "That little demonstration wasn't just to show you how the portable Gateway works. It was to show them how well their energy works."

"You mean how it knocked us for a loop?" Shanghai asked.

"Put it all together." Sing crossed her arms over her chest. "No offense, Phoenix, but I don't think Alex wanted you for this reaping because of your skills. That was her pretext, how she wooed you. Sure, you're good at reaping, fantastic even, but there are a couple of dozen Reapers who could do the job, and they'd jump at the chance. Alex wouldn't have to make roommate or camera concessions to convince them to participate."

I gave her a questioning look. "Then why did she make concessions?"

"Phoenix, think about it. The reason she sent Colm's family to the camp was to ensure that you'd come. Would an Owl really care about one little pill? The concessions meant nothing to her. She just wants you here. She has everything under control."

"I get part of their reasoning," I said. "They wanted to see if the energy influence was strong enough to keep me in line while I witnessed Colm's execution. She knows it didn't really work, though. I was just too dazed to stop her. She said more tests are coming, so she still has a target painted on my back."

"Am I a target?" Shanghai asked. "Why did Alex choose me to be here?"

Sing shrugged. "A physical attraction? Maybe Alex used you as bait. How many guys can resist a girl like you?"

Shanghai frowned but said nothing.

"Let's drop it." I shifted my body higher so I could get a better view of Sing and Shanghai. "We'd better focus on Colm's family."

"Do you have a plan?" Shanghai asked.

"Sort of." I nodded at the computer tablet on my dresser. "Like the schedule says, the entertainment is supposed to take place in the jail yard. The prisoners will be locked in their quarters, and Alex, Peter, the guards, and the searchlights will be focused on whatever the entertainment is. No one will notice Sing working backstage getting Colm's family out."

Sing nodded. "I'll arrange for them to be waiting for me at the door. Once I unlock it, I'll pull them out and lock it again so the other prisoners don't rush to join us. It'll be hard enough getting four people across the compound without anyone seeing us. But two hundred?" She let out a short huff. "Impossible."

I gave her a nod in return. "Right. You can only do so much." A pang of guilt gnawed at my heart. My admission felt like a cowardly surrender, but I couldn't deny reality.

Sing touched her weapons belt. "And when I get the family to a safe place, I can send up a flare to let you know."

"Then we'll need our own escape plan," Shanghai said. "Once everyone sees the flare, we'll have to fly like bats out of hell."

Sing reeled out a few inches from her spool. "After I get Colm's family to safety, I won't be able to disable the alarm at the Hilton's back door, so I'll station myself on the roof. By the time you see the flare, I'll have dropped a line for you. Just use your smoke capsules and run. Easy escape."

"Easy?" Shanghai half closed an eye. "Ever tried to climb a line while guards are shooting at you? I don't want a bullet in my backside."

"Who would?" Sing grinned. "You'd better use an extra smoke capsule."

While waiting for dinnertime, Shanghai, Sing, Tori, and I sat and talked once again, mostly about life before becoming Reapers. After nearly an hour, I mentioned the possibility of never seeing my mother and father again. Tori got up abruptly and hurried into the bathroom, saying she wanted to be alone for a while.

"Poor girl," Shanghai said. "She misses her parents. I wish we could help her."

"Maybe we can." I slid off the bed and lifted my legs in turn. No dizziness. The energy's negative effects had greatly faded. Now would be a good time to test the benefits. I grabbed my cloak from the bed and slung it over my shoulders. "I'll check on her in ghost mode."

"Want me to be your lifeline again?" Sing asked.

"Let me test it here and see if I need one." I fastened my clasp, closed my eyes, and concentrated. I had partially crossed into the realm of ghosts a few times, but now I should be able to imitate a level three. Yet, no one had said exactly how to do it. We had talked to Tori about changing states by wanting it to happen. Maybe that was the trick, to focus on my desire to make the transition. I wanted to be with Tori, to touch her, hold her, comfort her as she grieved. She needed to know that someone cared.

I drew a mental picture of her. In my mind, she sat on the bathroom floor, her legs crossed and her head low as she fiddled with a loose string in her dress's hem. After a few seconds, the sound of weeping reached my ears. Yet, the girl in my mental picture wasn't crying. That had to be the real Tori. She was heartbroken.

With my eyes still closed, I lifted my arms and reached out. I had to be with her, dry her tears. Taking care of bodiless souls was my job, but for lost little girls like Tori, it was more than a job; it was life, the very reason I was born, to wrench away tragedy and transform it into joy. I had to help her. I just had to.

I reopened my eyes. Sing and Shanghai still sat on the bed, but now a thin haze covered them, as if fog had settled in the room. I spread out my arms. "Am I a ghost?"

Shanghai laughed. "Phoenix, you're looking a bit pale. Are you sick?"

I touched my cheeks. They felt physical, though cold. "Are my eyes glowing?"

"Not a bit." Sing slid across the bed and pushed a hand through my chest. "You're definitely a level-three ghost."

"Good." I patted my torso. It felt as solid as ever. "Shanghai, maybe you could try going to ghost mode while I visit Tori. But you have to concentrate on really wanting it. It's not that easy, but maybe it gets easier with practice."

Shanghai nodded. "I'll see what I can do, but you saw what happened to Peter. He came back off-kilter, like his brain was affected."

"Another good point. It takes time to recover." I walked to the bathroom and stopped at the closed door. I had never passed my body through something solid before, so this would be an interesting test.

Keeping my eyes open, I stepped into the dim bathroom, feeling nothing more than a slight drag on my clothes as I crossed the barrier. The partially open door on the other side provided a shaft of light from Shanghai's room. Even that appeared misty, as if someone were blowing dry-ice vapor through the light.

Tori sat on the sink countertop, her hands covering her face as she rocked in time with spasmodic sobs, her whimpers not as loud as earlier. The steady dripping from the sink faucet added a gentle percussion to her sad song.

"Tori?" I whispered.

She lowered her hands, exposing a tear-streaked face. Her eyes no longer glowed. "Yes?"

"Are you all right?"

She nodded. Then, as new tears sprang forth, she wagged her head. "I'm not all right! I miss my mommy! I miss my daddy! I don't want to be dead! I don't want them to be dead! I'll never see them again."

"Yes, you will."

"No, I won't. You keep saying that, but I'm still here and—"

"Shhh." I slid my arms around her, lifted her from the counter, and pressed her against my chest.

She gasped. "Phoenix? What's happening?"

"I'm showing you what it will feel like when you see your parents again." I held her close and swiveled back and forth. "This is what your daddy will do."

Tori threw her arms around my neck and kissed me again and again. "Oh, Daddy! I missed you so much!"

Laughing between kisses, I rubbed her back. "And I missed you, too, sweetheart."

She pressed her cheek against mine and held it there. After mutual sighs, I stood quietly with her in my arms. The sounds and odors seemed so odd. How could Tori's breaths whistle across my ear? How could the scent of dirt in her dress enter my nostrils? How could we embrace? She had no lungs, no clothes, no physical existence. And neither did I, at least for the moment. This sharing of impossible contact defied explanation.

I pushed my fingers through her tangled hair. "I have to go for now, but soon we'll be together and never part again."

"Don't go! Please, don't go!" She drew her head back and pressed my face between her hands. "I know you're not my real daddy, but I can't stand being alone anymore." As tears dripped from her chin, her voice altered to a lament. "I'm so lonely, Phoenix. Please stay with me. Just hold me until it's time to go to the Gateway."

I set her gently on the counter. "I can do that. You can ride in my cloak."

She brushed away tears. "Are you going to reap me?"

Her hopeful tone sent a shiver through my body. "Yes. If you're willing."

"Oh, please do!"

"It might hurt." I caressed her cheek. "But it won't last long."

She nodded, her brow deeply wrinkled. "I'll be brave."

"Very well." I grasped her hand and pulled it close to my clasp. "Ready?"

"Ready."

I wrapped my cloak around her and laid it over her shoulders. The fibers latched to her body and adhered like flypaper. As the cloak began absorbing her, she sucked in a breath, her face locked in a grimace, but she stayed quiet. Apparently the new energy was easing the transition process. Otherwise she would be screaming in pain.

My clasp hissed, indicating an energy leak, not unheard of during a ghost collection, but more noticeable than usual. A tingling sensation ran through the valve's wires to my heart—not bad at all.

Tori flattened out against the inside of my cloak. Whimpering softly, she thinned to a mist and disappeared, her eyes the last to vanish.

My heart pounded furiously. Each beat sent tingling waves through every nerve. A new shimmer penetrated my cloak and spread across the outside. A halting voice emanated from somewhere near my shoulders. "I feel... funny."

After taking a cleansing breath, I nodded. "That's normal. Don't worry." A twinge lingered, though not as sharp as typical reaping pangs, more like the simmering hunger I felt after shaking hands with the Gatekeeper. It would probably pass soon.

Feeling dizzy again, I turned and walked toward my bedroom. My forehead banged against the door. I back-pedaled, regained my balance, and shook my head hard. Somehow I had returned to the real world without knowing it. With wobbly legs and trembling arms, it seemed that I was standing in raging floodwaters.

I sat on the toilet. Maybe the dizziness would go away soon.

Crandyke's voice broke through my mind fog. "Finally, some company. We can commiserate about how you handle souls like an unwanted litter of puppies. I'm surprised you haven't tied us in a bag and thrown us into the river."

I rested my arms on my thighs. "Crandyke, what put you in such a foul mood?"

"When you were hooked up to that Gateway contraption, you could have requested to send me through, but you kept me imprisoned. And when that new kind of energy came in, it carried a foul stench. It shook me out of my usual good humor."

"A foul stench? That's interesting. Did you notice it at the other Gateway station?"

"Nothing at all. That stench was the first odor I've noticed since I've been in here. It's not like I have a real nose to sniff with, you know."

I nodded. "I'll have to think about that one."

"Well, while you're thinking, think about getting me out of your cloak. I'm tired of hearing excuses."

I rose from the toilet seat. "But I didn't give you an excuse this time."

"Well, good. I'm glad you've come to your senses and… Wait a minute."

"Talk to you later. Signing off for now." I unplugged the

clasp, opened the door, and staggered into my bedroom. "Whew! That transition is a beast!"

Shanghai lay on the bed, a hand over her eyes. "Tell me about it. I nearly fainted."

"She did it, though," Sing said as she finished sewing a stitch in her disguise. "She was a level three for more than a full minute."

"Good. So was I." I shook my head to cast off the remaining fog. "I think."

Sing nodded at my cloak. "It's fading now, but it looked like it was shimmering brighter when you first walked back in here."

"I reaped Tori." I twirled part of my cloak to the front. "I couldn't stand seeing her cry."

"I suppose it's for the best." Sing tied off the thread, broke it, and slid the needle into her belt. "Tori did a great job guarding the hallway, but we don't need her there anymore."

I sat on the bed and touched Sing's handiwork. "Did you finish?"

"Yep." She gathered her disguise and headed toward the bathroom. "I'm going to try it on."

While I waited, Shanghai lay motionless, exhaling heavily from time to time. I put my socks and shoes back on and fastened my belt in place. The pressure of the weapons felt better than usual, as if I had put on a superhero costume. I was ready to go to war. Maybe that infusion of energy did some good after all.

A few minutes later, Sing emerged wearing a calf-length beige skirt, navy blue polo shirt, and a gray scarf tied over her head to keep her curls in check. Torn at the hem, stained with grime, and patched with ragged squares, the skirt looked like a hungry dog had gotten hold of it. The short-sleeved shirt bore some of the same flaws, though not as much dirt.

Sing touched the skirt. "I had to slice up my Reaper pants to make some of the patches, so I'm wearing what's left of them as shorts underneath this skirt."

Shanghai sat up and whistled. "Girl, you look positively chic, though you're way too gorgeous for that grungy prison theme. The bruise helps, but you might want to ugly up a little more."

Smiling, Sing dabbed at her bruise. "Maybe I'll get into another fight."

I twirled my finger. "Let's see the whole outfit."

Sing spread her arms and rotated slowly. "Do you like it?"

"You look..." As she continued turning, I searched for the right word. In one way she was a lost waif who needed protection. In another way she was a spy on a rescue mission—strong, confident, seductive. Again her medallion had slipped out and dangled in sight, though still not as lustrous as the first time. "You look fantastic."

"Thank you." She stopped her spin, tucked the medallion behind her shirt, and picked up her weapons belt. "Tori helped me find a place to hide my old suitcase, so you don't have to worry about Alex finding that, and I buried the rest of my clothes under Shanghai's in her dresser."

"Good thinking." I helped Shanghai to her feet, and the three of us walked slowly toward the room's exit door. "Sing, are you going to try to blend in with the other prisoners during dinner?"

"That's my plan." She strapped on her belt. "I'll hide my belt in a place where I can pick it up later. Then I'll sneak out of this building while you're eating. If I'm caught, they'll probably just assume I'm a prisoner and send me to their dining area."

"And Shanghai and I will go straight to the entertainment function after dinner." I stopped at the door. "So I might not see you again."

Sing's lips drew a thin line. "That's true."

I clasped her wrist. "I just want you to know…" My throat tightened, but I managed to keep my voice from squeaking. "I think you're an amazing Reaper. I know I can count on you."

She gripped my wrist in return. "Thank you. Your trust means everything to me."

Shanghai rolled her eyes. "What is this? Act two of Night of the Melodrama Twins?"

"No, Shanghai," I said. "Get a clue. This could be the end of the line for all of us. We're allowed a little melodrama."

"If you plan to die, you *will* die." Still standing near the room's door, she laid an arm around each of us and pulled us close. "Listen. I'm all for hugs and smooches and sappy good-byes, but let's save them for weddings and funerals. We need to get real. Sing's about to risk her life by sneaking into death row. You and I are going to try to escape from an Owl, a Cardinal, and guards with guns. We're kids with toothpicks trying to slay a fire-breathing dragon. If we're going to survive this thing, we need to walk out there with some swagger, not with our tails tucked between our legs. This is serious business."

"So what are you saying?" I asked. "No hugs? No kisses?"

She nodded. "Phoenix, when all of this is over, I'm

going to plant history's biggest kiss ever on that gorgeous face of yours, but until then, I'm not going to do anything that'll make me think we might lose this battle. This isn't good-bye. This is go-get-'em time. We can't afford one second of doubt."

"She's right." Sing slid from our huddle and backed away, her eyes wet. "Stay strong, Phoenix." She kissed her fingers and blew across them. With a quick spin, she opened the door and hurried down the hall.

When the door to the stairwell closed behind her, the click resounded through the corridor.

"Well, Phoenix," Shanghai said, holding the suite's door open, "since death is stalking our every move, we'd better stay a step ahead of it."

As I looked at her, dizziness again crept in, but I forced my body to stand erect. I had to display a confident pose. "What do you want to do now?"

"No use waiting around here." She hooked my arm with hers and pulled me into the hallway, letting the door close behind us. "We've got lives to save."

As we walked toward the stairwell, Shanghai tightened her grip on my arm. "Just so you know, Phoenix, no matter who you choose, as long as you're happy, I'll be happy."

"No matter who I choose? What are you talking about?"

She slid her hand down to mine and intertwined our fingers. "That's good, Phoenix. Keep your mind on the battle. We can't afford to think about anything else."

I let her cryptic words sink in. Was she talking about choosing between her and Sing? Maybe. But with the new energy still in our system, it might be better to ignore the romantic notions it had ignited, at least until our minds cleared.

As we walked hand in hand, I focused on the energy's lingering effects. Yes, it had created a spike in emotions that were hard to control, but it had also awakened something deep inside. Was it courage? Compassion? Love? Whatever it was, it burned like an inferno. Not even death itself would douse the flames.

When we reached the stairwell, I let go of Shanghai's hand. "Maybe we really can do this."

She blinked. "Do what?"

"The impossible." I checked the stairwell through the door's window. No one was around. "You know, climb Sing's line before anyone can catch us. We'd get demoted, but maybe we can be roamers, you and me together, and we can barter for food and fight bandits. We could make it."

"Now I know the joy juice is talking. That's pure romantic pulp. If we pull this escape off, we'll be on the run every day. We'll be branded as criminals, and we won't be allowed to go to the Gateway and recharge. Our energy will leak out, and we'll die a slow and excruciating death. I'm not exactly keen on a Romeo-and-Juliet ending."

"We could find a surgeon and get our valves—"

"Death penalty for any doctor who does that before a Reaper's retirement. No one would dare."

"A back-alley doctor might be willing—"

"Stop it, Phoenix." Shanghai's voice spiked. "Just stop it. It's an impossible dream."

I looked into her sparkling eyes. The sadness leeched every ounce of optimism from my heart. The reality of surrender again settled in. I exhaled slowly, as if deflating. "So I guess there isn't much hope for us. Whether we succeed or not, we'll die."

She nodded, a tear in her eye. "If we're going to die either way, maybe we should chase a different impossible dream, something that'll help the world."

"You mean Sing's impossible dream," I said. "Going through the Gateway and coming back again."

She gave a light shrug. "It's choose your poison. Run away as a roamer or break through the Gateway. We might be Romeo and Juliet after all."

"Hey." I laid a hand on her cheek. "Don't lose your swagger now. Hang on."

"I know, I know." A warm tear trickled over my thumb. "I'm trying."

I brushed the tear away and grasped her fingertips. "Will you make me a promise?"

She narrowed her eyes. "Don't rope me into that, Phoenix. Spill the promise first."

"Fair enough." I interlocked our thumbs. "When we get Colm's family out, let's at least think about running away and trying to make it on our own. We'll have a fighting chance to survive as long as we're together."

She nodded slowly. "I have to admit that sounds romantic. Running away with you is like a dream come true, but I have a feeling…" She averted her gaze.

"What?" I angled my head. "What feeling?"

She looked me in the eye. "When the energy wears off, you'll be singing a different tune. Your principles will come roaring back."

"Principles? Which principles would make me choose suicide over running away with you?"

She touched my ring. "Do you really think I haven't guessed what this is all about?"

The metal seemed to sting my skin. The promise had

completely slipped my mind. Was the energy influence that strong? How could it make me forget something so important?

"Well..." My throat narrowed. No coherent words came to mind.

"Don't worry about it." She smiled, her lips trembling. "Whatever you decide, I'm with you. I think we're joined at the hip. If we have to die, let's do it together."

I pressed my palm against hers and threaded our fingers. "Together sounds good to me." I teased with a grin. "But let's not get matching bullet holes in our backsides, okay?"

CHAPTER TWENTY

I SAT AT OUR dining-room table and studied the foil tray in front of me. A chunk of dry meat loaf sat in one compartment, stiff potatoes and lumpy gravy in another, and eight shriveled green beans in a third. Everything looked three days old.

Shanghai picked at her food in silence, her head propped by a hand, an elbow resting on the table.

After swallowing a green bean, I nudged Shanghai's arm. "Are you all right?"

"No." She set her fork down. "Not even close."

"What's wrong?"

She looked at me with reddened eyes. "I'm not sure I can describe it."

"Okay." I glanced around. No one was in sight, but the camera aimed its probing lens at us. Although its built-in microphone probably couldn't pick up our conversation, I kept my voice low. "Can you try?"

She leaned closer. "It feels like a monster's inside me. Like my emotions are out of control. Love. Jealousy. Pure rage." She strangled her napkin. "So now I'm scared. The feeling's nothing like when I first got infused. Back then it was a trip to heaven, but now I'm in hell."

"Are you afraid the monster will control you?"

She nodded, tears spilling to her cheeks. "What if they try to make me do something awful?"

"You wouldn't do it. You're too strong."

"I wish I had your confidence." She pressed a fist into her stomach. "You're not feeling what's going on inside me." Averting her eyes, she wiped tears with a wadded napkin and said nothing more.

I stared at the meat loaf. I didn't have much confidence at all. I felt the hungry beast. It had no cage or leash. We were both vulnerable. Maybe the worst was yet to come.

Several quiet minutes later, Alex and a prison guard walked in. Alex carried something tucked under her arm that looked like folded clothing. The guard gripped a rifle that he kept pointed toward the floor, a frown communicating readiness to shoot without mercy.

Alex stopped next to our table. "I assume," she said, "that you've been wondering about the entertainment I've been promising for tonight."

"We have," I replied in a noncommittal tone.

Alex withdrew something small from her jacket pocket and displayed it between her thumb and forefinger. "I'm sure you remember this."

I squinted at the object—one of the microphones we found in our suite. "I remember."

She pushed it back into her pocket. "When I first stopped receiving audio signals, I went to investigate your rooms, but, as Peter mentioned earlier, a little ghost prowled the hall, warning you whenever someone is coming, so I didn't go in. Just now while you were eating, I decided to try again. I found something very interesting." She pulled the clothing from under her arm. "This." The material unfolded, revealing Sing's Reaper shirt.

Shanghai flinched. I kept my face slack. The situation was going from bad to worse.

"As you can see," Alex continued, "this is too small to fit either of you. It seems that you have conspired to smuggle in a Reaper, a female, judging by the garment. Guards are searching the prisoners' residence building as we speak. Because certain events have transpired that allowed me to deduce her identity, they have an excellent description of her."

I kept my stare on Alex. "If you mean Singapore, then yes, I smuggled her in here, but it got too dangerous, so I smuggled her back out. She's long gone."

"I'm not stupid, Phoenix. I heard you say that to Colm, but you found the microphone in his dining room, didn't you? If you found the ones in your suite, you were sure to look for others, like the one I put under Shanghai's chair. You lied to throw me off track, just like you're lying now."

"You have a vivid imagination," I said, keeping my voice calm.

"Don't play games with me!" Alex wadded up the shirt and shook it in a tight fist. "You two have conspired to infiltrate this prison with a spy from the Resistance, a rogue Reaper who hopes to destroy our ability to more easily transport souls to the Gateway through the new portable system."

I slid my chair back and rose to my feet. "You're the one playing games, Alex. Everything we've done has been out in the open." I pointed at the shirt. "Singapore just left her spare one behind. You didn't find any other parts of the uniform, did you? That's because she's not here. Check her district if you don't believe me."

"We already have. We found a Reaper named Cairo

impersonating Singapore." Alex tossed the shirt onto the table. "A valiant effort to conceal your friend's activities, Phoenix, but you and Shanghai have been exposed. We doubled the guards at every exit point, and we will find Singapore. She won't get away."

My cheeks burned. What had they done to Cairo? The poor kid was just a brave volunteer. "Look, I don't know what Singapore is doing, but she's obviously not here. You found part of a uniform with no one wearing it, and you jumped to a bizarre conclusion that a spy is here to destroy your precious experiment. You make the Gateway deniers look like rational people."

"Another bold stroke, Phoenix, but still inadequate." Alex swiveled her head toward the lobby. "Ah! Peter. Perfect timing. Bring him in."

Peter walked into the room with a glowing sphere cradled in his palms, similar to the one Erin had placed in the Gatekeeper's disk outside. "Your witness is safe inside," Peter said as he handed Alex the sphere.

She held it aloft for everyone to see. "Peter captured a level-three ghost who is of great importance. We will release him to allow you to hear what he told us. Then I will reveal more unpleasant surprises for Phoenix." After turning an abrupt about-face, she strode out of the dining room.

Peter nodded at the guard. "Make sure Phoenix and Shanghai come."

"Let's go," the guard said, nudging me with the rifle barrel. "The easy way or the hard way. Your choice."

I rolled my eyes. "We're coming."

As Shanghai and I walked, she popped a few smoke capsules from her belt and slid them into her pocket, then popped a few more and, while holding my hand, stealthily transferred the capsules to me.

Once I had them in my grasp, I squirreled them away in my pants pocket. We might need them sooner than later. The situation was plunging downhill faster than ever. Alex proved to be the ultimate schemer. She had everything under control from the first moment she walked into Molly's bedroom, and now she was ready to reveal yet another surprise move. But maybe she hadn't figured out our plan yet. If we played it right, Sing still had a chance to rescue Colm's family if she could get them out in time.

As we walked toward the trio of pedestals, the searchlights swung that way and locked on the area, illuminating the white disks. Next to my pedestal, someone sat in a chair. A Reaper's cloak and hood covered his entire body, including his face, hands, and feet, hiding his identity. Ropes bound his wrists to the chair's arms and his ankles to the legs. Smaller than a full-grown man, he squirmed and thrashed to no avail.

I whispered to Shanghai, "I'll bet it's Cairo. They're going to use him to try to get information from us."

"What information? We're not part of the Resistance. We don't know anything."

"But Alex doesn't know that. She isn't leaving anything to chance. She's hiding him to keep us guessing."

Shanghai kept her whisper low. "So what'll we do?"

"We're stuck. We can't trade lives. The best we can hope for is to set him free in the scramble. He's a Reaper. He can run and climb with us."

"Okay, but what if it's Sing? Our plan is shot."

"No way," I said. "Sing lost her cloak."

"But Alex was snooping through our rooms. If she found Sing's shirt, she probably also found Mex's cloak."

"Mex's cloak?" I squinted, searching for a triangle on the sleeve. "I don't see a roamer patch."

"Alex might have taken it off, or maybe the sleeve is twisted. Or it might be Cairo's cloak wrapped around Sing."

"Well, we'll cut whoever it is loose. We can all three run or fight or do whatever it takes to escape. But I'm still betting it's Cairo."

Shanghai gave me a grim nod. "Agreed."

When we arrived within the pedestals' triangle, I looked past the squirming figure in the chair and scanned the yard. Twilight had descended, making it difficult to see the prisoners' living quarters, especially with the search-lights nearly blinding us to everything beyond the make-shift arena.

By now, Sing was probably inside the quarters, and with the spotlights already frozen on the center of the yard, she could make her escape move at any time. Since the guards had been doubled, she would have to overpower two guards twice—once at the door to the quarters and again at the Hilton's rear exit when they opened the door in response to her knock. With each passing moment, every step in our plan seemed more unlikely to work.

Still, if anyone could do it, Sing could. I had to keep my hopes alive, though trying to free Cairo really complicated matters. Our chances of escape were as thin as the smoke in our capsules.

Alex set the sphere in the central disk's depression and held the vacuum tube at waist level. Peter stepped close to the nozzle and nodded at her. "Ready."

Keeping the vacuum tube tucked under her arm, she tapped on the tablet's screen. The hum returned. Peter diffused into a ghostly cloud and streamed into the tube. After several seconds, she slid a finger across the screen. "Peter has him. Reversing now."

Soon, a stream of vapor flowed from the tube and transformed into Peter standing with his hand locked around someone's arm. As they congealed, the captive's details clarified—a black man with short, salt-and-pepper hair.

I hid a swallow. Kwame! But how could that be? He wasn't a ghost. Maybe Peter killed him, but Kwame's eyes weren't glowing. He couldn't have become a level three so quickly.

Peter kept his hold on Kwame's arm. "I'll stay in this state until we're done. We can't afford to let him escape."

"Very well." Alex pointed at Kwame while looking at me. "We discovered this rebel agent by following you to his home in an abandoned building, proving the alliance between the two of you. Since Peter can physically connect with ghosts, he was able to... shall we say... pressure the spy into talking."

I had to force my jaw closed. Kwame looked the same as always. Since he was a ghost now, maybe he always had been, at least since I had known him. But why the secrecy?

Peter patted Kwame's shoulder. "Now tell everyone what you told Alex and me. We already have your confession recorded, so you have nothing to lose. I don't want to use the same persuasion methods I did before."

"I guess I don't have much choice." Kwame glanced at me for a split second before folding his hands at his waist. "I am part of a group that has worked to infiltrate the Gateway system in order to determine what really happens to souls when they are transferred there."

While the captive in the chair continued to squirm, Alex walked closer to Kwame, a strut in her step. "And how is Singapore involved?"

"She is our number one agent." Kwame's voice carried the heaviness of resignation, quiet and monotone. "She delivered a soul to the Gateway, a departed Reaper who hopes to return to report her findings."

Alex tapped on her tablet again, glancing between the screen and Kwame. "Since you told us that story earlier, we searched the data and learned the identity of the Reaper Singapore delivered. Tokyo has traveled beyond the point of no return. She will not be coming back."

I curled my fingers into a fist. So that was how Sing's mother got to the Gateway. Sing delivered her herself—the Asian woman on Bartholomew's screen. That meant the Resistance kept Tokyo's soul around until Sing was ready to deliver it—a brilliant but dangerous plan.

Alex gave the screen a final tap and tucked the tablet under her arm. "Your conspiracy theories are pure lunacy, and you have wasted valuable resources. In pursuing this ridiculous idea, you endangered your wife's journey to the afterlife and you risked your daughter's life by making her an anti-Gateway agent. Your insanity is monstrous."

My heart skipped a beat. His daughter? Kwame was Sing's father? How could that be? Sing said she didn't recognize him. The only resemblance was his voice. They had the same name, but so did thousands of other Ghanaians.

"I make no apologies for my beliefs." Kwame looked straight at me. "My only apology is to Phoenix. He knew nothing about this plan, and now he faces punishment for no reason."

"Do you expect me to believe that?" Alex paced in front of Kwame, her hands folded behind her. "Phoenix willingly broke the law to smuggle Singapore in here. He allowed himself to be taken in by her seductive ways. He was friendless, and she used his vulnerability to sweep him into her scheme. It's not hard for someone as pretty and charming as Singapore to put a lonely boy under her spell. Your spies arranged to have her stationed in the district next to Phoenix's, to live in an apartment directly across an alley so she could seduce him."

She huffed a sarcastic laugh. "Oh, how clever to put her so close yet just out of reach. This is pure seduction at the highest level. And once she gained his trust, her mission was to learn about the Gateway as quickly as possible, though she cared nothing for the fact that as he followed her come-hither advances, he might find himself dangling with his neck in a noose."

Shanghai slid her hand into mine and whispered, "I still love you, Phoenix. Never forget that."

I grasped her hand weakly. It seemed that all strength had drained away. On one side of my brain, Sing's words—*thank you for trusting me*—reverberated again and again, but Alex's accusations overwhelmed the call. How could Sing have lied to me? Every word Alex spoke made sense. And the reality of betrayal tore my heart in half.

"Yet," Alex continued, "Phoenix swallowed the bait without care. We might wish to exonerate the lovesick lad, and we would have done so if he had merely helped a fellow Reaper learn the necessary skills. But when he shifted to conspiring with rebels to destroy the only means we have to set souls free from wandering without purpose in this world, he became guilty of treason. There can be only one punishment for such a crime."

"Death," Peter said, as if scripted. "And Shanghai as well. They conspired together. They're both guilty."

As the guard pressed the rifle barrel into my back, I cringed. Alex had set the trap, and we were the mice.

Alex smiled, obviously pleased with herself. "It would be such a waste to kill two powerful Reapers. I have an idea that not only will avoid wasting one valuable soul-collector, it will also provide our entertainment for the evening." Her Owl eyes slowly scanned us, obviously milking the pause for dramatic effect. "Phoenix and Shanghai will fight to the death. The one who kills the other will prove his or her loyalty, and we will grant mercy to the winner as a reward."

Shanghai's grip on my hand tightened. Her face grew red and taut. My blood boiled, and strength rushed back into my muscles. A fight to the death? Alex couldn't really believe that we'd try to kill each other, could she? Or was she counting on the energy dosage and the threat of killing Cairo to force us to obey her insane demands?

Alex nodded at Peter. "Take him away. Where he is heading, we won't need a photo stick."

"Let's go." Peter pushed Kwame toward the vacuum tube.

Struggling to free himself, Kwame called out, "Phoenix! Trust Akua! I am her father, but there is much more to explain."

"Shut up, fool!" Peter kicked Kwame in the stomach, then hammered him to the ground with his fists.

I took a hard step forward, but the guard grabbed my arm and jerked me back. "Don't move, or you're dead," he growled.

I steeled myself and concentrated on shifting to ghost mode, my only hope to escape the guard and save Kwame. As I tried to generate the desire to transform, Peter jerked Kwame to his feet and wrapped his cloak around him. Within seconds, Peter whipped the cloak away, and a new shimmer rode along the fibers. Kwame was gone.

While Peter went through the process of returning Kwame to the sphere, I altered my desire to our need to escape. With Peter busy, this might be our only chance. Yet, my need to become a ghost seemed canceled by the need to help whoever sat in the chair. I couldn't do both. Shanghai, too, seemed torn as she shifted her gaze between the sphere and the cloaked victim. We were both powerless to act.

Soon, Peter emerged from the vacuum tube and reverted to his physical state. He sank to his knees and wagged his head slowly, obviously shaking off the effects of being in ghost mode for so long.

"You'll be fine in a few minutes, Peter." Alex dropped the tube on the ground and looked at Shanghai and me, a glimmer in her steely eyes. "Prepare to fight to the death."

Shanghai glared at Alex, shooting poisoned darts with her fiery eyes. "You'll never... *never* get me to try to kill Phoenix." She spat with her words. "And he would never try to kill—"

"Shhh." I gave her a nudge. "Keep cool. Don't give anything away."

Shanghai growled but said no more.

"An emotional eruption is exactly what I expected."

Alex laughed softly. "You will be amazed at how quickly passion can be turned on its head." She nodded at Peter. "Release their energy."

Peter rose and walked toward me, staggering at first before steadying his gait. He grabbed my arm and twisted it behind my back. The guard aimed his rifle at Shanghai and slid his finger around the trigger. Even though I might be able to defeat Peter in his weakened state, I couldn't risk Shanghai's life. Whatever they wanted to do to us, we had to let it happen.

Reaching around me, Peter pressed my valve, making the center protrude. Energy leaked out. Pain ripped into my heart. The ravenous beast clawed inside my stomach. I could barely breathe.

"You understand by now," Alex said, "that the Gatekeeper's energy is powerful, but the greater power rests in your desire for another dose. Deprivation is often the maximum persuasion."

After nearly a minute, Peter clicked my valve back in place and gave me a shove. "That should be enough."

While I doubled over and gasped for breath, Peter held Shanghai and pressed her valve. As energy escaped, her face turned pale. Her body quaked. When another minute passed, he closed off the flow and let her go. Shanghai dropped to her knees and dry heaved. A string of saliva stretched from her lips to the ground.

"They're ready." Peter pushed the guard's rifle down. "We don't need a gun to their heads anymore."

I reached for a new desire to shift to ghost mode. The need was there, but the energy well had dried up. We had to stay in the physical realm.

At the chair, the bound figure now sat quietly. Whether it was Cairo or Sing, we would probably find out soon. Alex likely planned to pound us with her ultimate hammer at the most painful moment.

CHAPTER TWENTY-ONE

S EVERAL OTHER GUARDS joined us and formed a
semicircle near the Gateway triangle, a partial fighting
ring roughly ten paces in diameter. They looked like a line
of uniformed vultures waiting for a kill.

I shifted my stare to the ground and imagined Sing
straddling the prisoners' living quarters' window, ready
to pounce on the guards stationed at the door. Now we
were the distraction that would enable her attack. We had
become the evening's entertainment. Maybe Alex had
planned this all along. Her reason for recruiting Shanghai
had finally become clear.

Alex walked into the ring, helped Shanghai to her feet,
and began unfastening her weapons belt. "The rules are
simple. You will battle with fists and feet until one of you
is dead. The winner, or perhaps survivor is a better term,
will immediately receive an infusion of energy to counter
the effects of deprivation." She tossed Shanghai's belt to
Peter, then took off mine and draped it over her arm. "My
advice is to attack early while you are still able."

Peter and Alex laid the two belts on the ground and
backed into the line of guards. "Everyone will maintain

silence," Alex said, "while I provide the necessary narration at the appropriate times."

Standing hunched over, I stared at Shanghai. Only three steps away, she stared back at me, her mouth agape. As she pressed both fists into her abdomen, tears flowed freely down her cheeks. Pain continued lashing at my heart and stomach. Ravenous hunger burned, as if I hadn't eaten anything in weeks.

I gave the prisoners' living quarters a stealthy glance. No moving shadows appeared, but Sing might have already pounced on the guards and gone back inside to retrieve Colm's family. I wouldn't be able to follow her progress.

Kwame's words pounded my brain with pain-filled blows. *Trust Akua! I am her father.* Yet, the persistent questions added to the blows. How could Sing not recognize her own father? Someone had to be lying.

I wagged my head. Torture throttled my brain. That's why I couldn't think straight. That's why this flurry of facts didn't line up. No matter what happened, I had to trust Sing. Forget Kwame. Forget Alex. Forget all the confusing noise in my head. Just carry out the plan.

At the chair, the bound figure wiggled under the cloak's blanketing shield. Muffled cries sounded from beneath the hood, a gagged victim's desperate efforts to sound an alarm or tell me who he or she was. And we did need to know. If Sing sat there in bonds, our attempts to distract the guards would turn into a theatre of fools.

"Your hesitation is understandable." Alex stepped in and spread an arm toward each of us. "Isn't it fascinating how pain alters determination? How bodily desire makes resolve crumble?"

I fixed my stare on her. Those ghostly gray eyes pierced my mind and pulled at my thoughts, like a hand slowly uprooting a plant while the fibers strained to stay in the soil. The Owl had stretched her talons, and the mouse couldn't even squeak out a protest.

"A few minutes ago, you two were certain that you would never fight each other, much less to the death." Alex turned her mesmerizing gaze on Shanghai. "How many times have you sworn the night before not to indulge your body, perhaps with sweets or maybe rest from training, only to find your resolve melting in the morning? Your mind underestimates future hunger. It is blind to the chains of its master."

She laughed softly. "And now the effect is multiplied. You have been exposed to unfiltered power from on high. You hunger for another taste of exotic energy, a fresh supply of ecstasy that effervesces in a brimming cup. You are only moments away from sating the fury that burns in your body, that makes you ache for relief, and the Gatekeeper will provide it to all who simply submit to the natural order of this world."

Shanghai panted. Her fists tightened. As her cheeks flushed bright red, she groaned. "Help me.... Help me.... It's ripping me apart."

Alex's tone sharpened. "Shanghai, only one person stands between you and freedom from pain." She jabbed a finger at me. "As long as Phoenix lives, you will never be rid of that monster within. If you don't attack and destroy Phoenix, he will destroy you. Look at his eyes. See the hunger? See the torture? He will unleash that fury on you unless you strike first. It's the only way you can survive!"

Still panting, Shanghai jerked her head to the side, breaking away from the stare.

I tried to see her eyes. She was fighting the influence, but would she win? Maybe she was losing the battle and didn't trust herself to hold back if she were to launch an assault. Either way, I had to get the game going. Sing needed us.

I reared back, ready to pounce, but before I could move another muscle, Shanghai leaped at me. With fists and cloak flying, she smacked me across the cheek and jaw. Then she leaped and thumped me in the chest with her heel.

The powerful blow sent me hurtling backwards. I fell to my bottom, turned a somersault, and jumped to my feet. I pushed my cloak out of the way and set my arms and legs in battle stance. The assault's contact points burned but no worse than the inferno in my stomach.

Gasps and clapping hands sounded all around, but the faces in the crowd blurred. I could see only Shanghai. Her fists again tight, she prowled in an arc, snarling like a wild beast. With gritting teeth and fiery eyes, she seemed possessed, maniacal.

I took in a deep breath. If Shanghai had given in to the torture, she could focus on killing me while I had to battle her and my inner beast at the same time. If she wasn't simply putting on an amazing acting performance, I was in big trouble.

Forcing a snarl of my own, I ran at her and feigned a right-handed swing. When she raised an arm to block it, I followed with a left into her stomach, a solid blow, but I pulled my punch.

She reeled back and quickly regained her balance.

Sneering, she called out, "What kind of punch was that? You hit like a girl!"

"Like a girl?" I unfastened my clasp, whipped off my cloak, and laid it next to our belts. Raw anger boiled into my throat. I swallowed it down. I couldn't let the beast win. But pulling punches obviously wasn't going to work. I had to give this fight everything I had. "I was just matching your weak blows," I said, attempting a mocking tone. "If you want to fight like a man, bring it on."

A chorus of "oohs" and whistles sailed into the ring. Shanghai heaved rapid breaths, her arms like steel rods. She threw off her cloak and let it sail. Peter caught it and laid it next to mine.

Her fists again tight, she flew at me with a whirlwind of punches and kicks. I blocked each one, then landed a crushing blow to her face.

She backpedaled, cupping her hand over her nose. I charged after her. As she retreated, blood dripped between her fingers. When I focused on the red flow, she dropped to her back, thrust both feet into my gut, and sent me flying.

Two guards caught me and helped me stand. When Shanghai leaped upright, the guards shoved me into the ring. I pedaled my legs, trying to regain balance, but my momentum sent me straight toward her. I lifted a blocking arm, but her bloody fist sneaked past and slammed into my chin, though not with enough force to stop my momentum.

I fell overtop her and swung her downward. As we fell, I drove a fist into her solar plexus. When we crashed to the ground, I hammered my fist deeper.

She let out a loud oomph. I rolled off, jumped up, and planted my foot on her throat, applying enough pressure to immobilize her but not enough to crush her windpipe.

Her limbs stiffened. Gurgles and wheezes spewed from her mouth and nose, mixing with more streaming blood. She stared at me, her eyes wild. She clawed at my pant legs, but in her weakened state, she couldn't dig into my skin.

Finally, she exhaled. Her eyes fluttered closed, and her head lolled to the side.

Gasping for breath, I glanced around. No flare in sight. But Sing hadn't had time to get the family to safety and return to help us. At best, she might have herded them outside the compound. I needed to give her more time, but how? I had already beaten Shanghai.

When I lifted my foot from Shanghai's throat, Alex stepped into the ring again. "An efficient though underwhelming performance, Phoenix. Although your use of body weight as a weapon proved to be a stellar move, I am surprised at Shanghai's lack of foresight. Given her reputation, I expected a more dazzling display of athletic prowess."

I took a cleansing breath and glared at her. "You drained us. We can barely move, much less put on any dazzling displays. If you think you can do better, then why don't you do something more than bark at us from the sidelines like a cowardly Chihuahua?"

"My pleasure." Alex swung a leg and kicked me across the cheek. I staggered backwards, but Alex lunged and grabbed my wrists to keep me from falling. While her steely eyes trained on me, energy drained from my limbs. The will to fight leaked out with it. Although my feet still touched the ground, they felt like nubs attached to rubber bands.

"Instead of letting you turn her body," Alex continued,

"Shanghai should have done this." She swept a leg into mine, knocked my feet out from under me, and slammed me to the ground, my face in the dirt.

While the guards laughed, I pushed up with both hands. Now with eye contact broken, the energy leak subsided. My biceps flexed. Maybe I could fight Alex and maybe not, but I couldn't risk losing more energy. We still had to escape.

Alex helped me to my feet, withdrew a dagger from my belt, and pushed the hilt into my hand. "Shanghai is inferior to you. Finish her off. Drive the blade into her heart, and I will supply what you need. The hunger will vanish. The pain will disappear."

Sweat dampening my clothes, I laid a hand on my stomach. The monster clawed at my gut. The ring of onlookers spun in a slow orbit, then snapped back into place. At any moment, I might collapse, ending all hope of survival.

Alex motioned for the guards to part. She walked to my pedestal and picked up the vacuum tube. Peter now held the tablet and tapped on the screen. The familiar hum began again. "I have what you need." Alex's words reverberated, as if bouncing in an echo chamber. "The energy is here, and it is yours for the taking. Just strike Shanghai in the heart. End her suffering and yours. You will be free to help us take every prisoner to the Gateway where they will never suffer again. You will be a respected Cardinal, and you can even request Singapore as a roommate. All suspicions against her will be forgotten. We will allow you to take her as your friend, your lover, or whatever you wish. You will never be lonely again. In fact, you will have the freedom to see your family. And, of course, I will keep my promise about cutting your Reaper time. In seven years you will be free."

I licked my parched lips. Everything was turning upside-down. What was Alex doing? Didn't she consider Sing to be part of the Resistance? Had Alex already found my family? Nothing made sense. I had to keep fighting the piercing effect of those Owl eyes.

Alex extended the tube, crooning in a hypnotic cadence. "All you have to do is remove Shanghai as a combatant, and every comfort will be yours. Remember, she tried to kill you. She is your enemy."

I let out a loud groan. Gasping again, I pointed at Shanghai with the dagger. "If I kill her…" My voice squeaked, but I couldn't help it. "Will you give her an honorable funeral?"

Alex smiled. "Of course we will, Phoenix." Her tone dripped with syrupy sweetness. "In fact, we will expunge her record of all wrongdoing. She will be honored as a fallen heroine, a Reaper divine."

I gripped the dagger's hilt so tightly my entire arm shook. Although I hoped to keep everyone distracted with the funeral request, the tremors weren't part of the act. Every particle of my body ached for the energy infusion, to be set free from this torture. But I couldn't accept the release. The price was too high. I could never kill a friend. We had to attempt an escape before we ran completely out of energy—flare or no flare.

I threw the dagger, making it stick in the ground. I squared my shoulders and glared again at Alex. "Forget it. I'll die before I cause Shanghai any more pain."

Instead of launching into a new tirade, Alex just laughed. "We'll see about that." She strode to the chair, stopped behind it, and withdrew her sonic gun. Clutching the top of the captive's hood, she raised her brow in mock concern. "It seems that you will have to decide which friend of yours will die."

Alex jerked the hood back. Long red hair flew in disarray, some sticking to the captive's sweaty pale forehead. A tight gag pushed her cheeks inward, disfiguring her face.

I took a step, nearly falling forward. The captive's name tumbled from my lips. "Misty?"

Misty's eyes shot open. She shouted into the gag, but only stifled cries leaked out.

Alex began untying the gag. "I apologize. How rude of me." When it loosened, she tossed it to the ground and pulled the cloak's left sleeve back. The material slid under the binding rope, bringing Misty's hand into view.

I stared at Misty's finger. Her pewter ring was still there. She had kept our promise. She had stayed true. And for some twisted reason, Alex wanted me to see it.

Alex set the sonic gun at the back of Misty's head. "Feel free to converse, but don't take another step closer."

"Misty!" I extended my arms, but they were way too short. "Are you hurt?"

A sob contorted her face. Tears flowed. As she shook, her lips formed the first part of my real name, but she sucked it back and cried out, "Phoenix! Oh, Phoenix, I missed you so much!"

"I missed you, too!" I tightened a fist and shook it at Alex. "Let her go! She's innocent! She hasn't done anything to deserve—"

"Oh, shut up, Phoenix. I know that." Alex pressed the barrel against Misty's head, bending her neck forward. "This is unveiled, unbridled brute force. If I can get you to kill Shanghai, you'll be mine forever, but I doubt that you yet know yourself the way I know you. You hand over slavish chains in a way you don't yet comprehend."

She nodded at the line of guards. "Four of you hold him. Don't underestimate his strength." Peter and three guards stalked toward me. I readied my fists and leaped at Alex. Peter grabbed my arm and jerked me backwards into the foursome's clutches. As I struggled to get free, he twisted my elbow with incredible strength. Pain rocketed to my brain, sending blinding flashes across my eyes.

"Stop it," Peter growled, "or I'll break your arm."

I swallowed through my dry throat. How could I save Misty when I couldn't even budge?

"Now, Phoenix…" Alex's smile thinned out. "Who will live and who will die?"

"No. Don't. Please." Tears blurred my vision. "Let's make another deal. Any deal. We can negotiate. Please, just don't kill Misty. She's got nothing to do with this. She's inno—"

"Stop begging!" Alex shouted. "You know what I want, and I won't negotiate. Either Misty or Shanghai will die. It's up to you. You have five seconds to decide."

"Five seconds?" My breaths came in gasps. "But I can't—"

"One!"

"Alex!" I fought to wrench my arms free, but my captors held them fast. "Listen. We can be reasonable. I'll reap the prisoners. I won't do anything to stop you from—"

"Two!" Alex yelled, "Don't think I won't kill her, Phoenix. I already killed Colm. I'll kill Misty with a flick of my finger! I won't bat an eye."

"But she's just—"

"Three!"

Misty closed her eyes and wept. "Oh, Phoenix. I love you. I love you so much."

"Alex!" I shouted at the top of my lungs. "Listen to me!"

"Four!" Alex pressed harder, forcing Misty's chin against her heaving chest. "This is your last chance, Phoenix. Say you'll kill Shanghai right now or Misty is dead!"

"No!" I lunged, but the powerful clutches jerked me back. "You can't! You won't!"

"Wrong answer." Alex slid her finger into the trigger. "Her next destination is the abyss."

A scream pierced the air. A dagger flew by and sliced into Alex's forearm, knocking her gun hand back. Shanghai charged in the dagger's path, stumbling out of control. Peter let go of me, dove at Shanghai, and grabbed her ankle, sending her into a headfirst slide. When she stopped, she twisted back, and the two wrestled, punching and clawing.

Still holding the gun, Alex pulled the dagger from her arm and tossed it to the ground in front of me. Blood oozed from her wound. Without a hint of emotion, she switched the gun to her other hand, set the barrel against Misty's skull, and pulled the trigger.

The gun popped. Misty jerked. Her eyes rolled upward, then closed. She slumped in the chair, motionless.

Alex shook her head. "Such a waste."

"No!" I screamed. "You couldn't! You didn't!"

New pops sounded. Smoke erupted everywhere. With Peter no longer holding me, I snatched my arms free, clubbed the rifle bearer to the ground, and ran at Alex, scooping up the dagger on the way. I slashed the blade across her cheek, punched her in the eye, and shoved her with my foot. She flew backwards and struck her head on a pedestal, then lay there dazed.

I cut away Misty's bonds and spotted Shanghai and Peter. Shanghai's spent capsules still smoked near her hip. Peter held her down and raised a fist. I slung the dagger at him. The blade plunged into his thigh. Clawing at the hilt, he rolled off Shanghai and writhed in agony.

A yellow flare arced across the sky, fizzling as it descended.

I dug into my pocket and threw the capsules where I thought the other guards might be standing. More smoke erupted. Amidst shouts of confusion, I lifted Misty from the chair, hoisted her over my shoulder, and hobbled to Shanghai. She crawled on all fours and collected our cloaks and belts, her body barely visible in the haze. When she scooped up both sets, we broke through the wall of smoke and staggered toward the Hilton.

The searchlights followed us. Shouts flew from behind. Tromping feet drew closer. The Hilton lay only fifty steps ahead, though it warped and swayed from side to side. The lights illuminated a thin line dangling from the roof. "There's Sing's rope!"

"I see it!" As we picked up our pace, Shanghai put on her cloak and belt. "But you can't climb with Misty!"

"I have to try!"

We halted at the rope, wheezing. When I set Misty down to catch my breath, Shanghai fastened my belt in place and draped my cloak over my shoulders. "Listen! You have to… to leave her behind…. She's dead!"

"But her soul!"

"No time!" She fastened my clasp with a quick snap of

her hand. "We can't wait!" She leaped, grabbed the rope, and climbed hand over hand.

I looked back at the cloud of smoke. The guards had broken through and now closed in, seconds away.

Crouching low, I kissed Misty's cheek and whispered, "I'll be back for you." I thrust my arms into the cloak's sleeves, clutched the rope with two tight fists, and climbed behind Shanghai. Every inch felt like a mile, every pull like a knife blade ripping my muscles.

When Shanghai made it to the roof, she reached down. A shot rang out, then another. I grabbed her wrist. She hoisted me to the roof, and we tumbled over each other and lay facing the sky. Searchlights swept through thin smoke until they landed on us.

Sing appeared out of nowhere, still wearing a head scarf. She grabbed my arm and Shanghai's, and jerked us to our feet. "Let's go!" Sing hissed.

Shanghai and I stumbled along behind Sing, the search-lights tracking our every step. My cheeks burned. Blood dripped from my chin, but I couldn't give in to the pain. Somehow I had to survive to return for Misty.

I glanced at Shanghai. Her legs quivered. Her shoulders sagged. Although her eyes stayed open, they kept rolling upward as she battled to stay conscious and move forward.

When we reached the back edge of the roof, Sing ducked under the lights and pointed at the ground where streetlamps illuminated the backdoor area. Two guards lay motionless in front of the door. "I'll jump first," Sing said, "then you'll jump and use their bodies as a cushion."

"Are they unconscious?" I asked.

"Dead."

"How did you—"

"No questions!" Sing grabbed our collars and tugged us closer. "Just jump! The other guards are on their way!"

Sing leaped over the side, crashed onto a guard's stomach, and bounced to the ground.

She looked up at us and waved frantically. "Now!"

"Let's go," I said to Shanghai. "Aim for the closer guard. I'll land on the other one." We steadied ourselves at the edge of the roof and jumped.

CHAPTER TWENTY-TWO

SHANGHAI AND I landed feet first on the guards'
bodies and leaped to solid ground. When we righted
ourselves, Sing waved from between two cars parked at
the street. "This way!"

We chased after her, staggering and stumbling.
Shanghai favored one side while both of my legs cramped,
making us fall farther behind with every passing second.

After veering onto an angled side street, we turned
into an alley. When we caught up with Sing, she leaped
vertically, grabbed a fire-escape ladder, and pulled it down
to our level. As she scrambled toward the roof, Shanghai
followed, her shoes clanging on the metal rungs one slow
clump at a time.

I slogged behind them. My heart felt like lead, my feet
like concrete blocks. I urged my heavy legs upward, step
by painful step. It seemed that thoughts of Misty dragged
me back. I had to rescue her soul from those monsters.

Finally, I made it to the roof. Sing and Shanghai helped
me climb over the parapet, and we lumbered stiff-legged to
the other side of the building. Once we were out of view of
the street, Shanghai and I flopped to our backs, coughing
and wheezing.

Sing pushed the center of her valve, lay on top of

Shanghai, and embraced her. As I propped myself on an elbow and watched, the scene swayed like a pendulum. Sing locked her valve with Shanghai's, then, closing her eyes, Sing tightened her facial muscles. Shanghai gasped. After a few seconds, her eyes fluttered open, and her breathing settled.

"Phoenix's turn," Sing said, her tone calm and professional as she unlocked their valves. "Just rest for a while."

"Gladly." Shanghai pushed up to a sitting position. "Thanks for the infusion."

"You're quite welcome." As Sing crawled my way, I lowered my head to the roof again. The building spun. Sing's face appeared, the only stable image in the world. She lay on top of me chest-to-chest, locked our valves, and pressed her cheek against mine. "Don't worry, Phoenix. You'll feel better in a minute." She hummed the words, calm and soothing, like the whisper of a breeze. "Colm's family are all safe. No one will find them."

"Are you…" I could barely move my lips. "Are you okay with doing this valve thing?"

"Shhh. You're delirious." A tingling sensation flowed into my valve, fresh and soothing. "I don't have much left, but I'll give you all I can. And believe me when I say this." Her lips brushed my ear as she whispered, "I would give my life for you. Without hesitation."

I heaved in a breath, lifting Sing's body. The energy flow surged through my limbs and into my head, clearing my thoughts. The world stopped spinning. Everything in my vision clarified, sharp and in focus.

After a few seconds, I breathed a quiet, "I think I'm okay now."

"Good." Sing unlocked our valves, rose to her feet, and extended a hand.

I grasped her wrist and rode her pull to a standing position. Sing snatched off her head scarf and shook out her curls. Now wearing knee-length shorts with her ragged shirt, she didn't look much like a Reaper. "That escape was easier than I expected."

"You call that easy?" I sat down and leaned my back against the parapet. As I tried to settle my heart, Shanghai and Sing joined me, one at each side. A haze-covered moon and the glow of the lamps at street level provided enough light to see the rooftop and each other. "Give me a minute," I said, "And we'll talk."

While we rested in silence, the sounds of late evening wafted by. A radio played the news somewhere, and a dog barked, but no sirens sounded. Shouts from the direction of the prison ebbed and died away. Maybe the guards decided against pursuit. Since we weren't prisoners and since it would be nearly impossible to catch us in the dark, why waste the time and effort?

After taking a cleansing breath, I wrapped my cloak around myself and imagined Misty in my arms. Moments ago, I gazed into her beautiful eyes, heard once again her lilting voice, smelled her savory scent as I carried her body. All for the last time.

Like a dam bursting, sobs erupted from my gut. Spasms shook my body, and I rocked back and forth. "I'm so sorry, Misty! I'm so, so sorry!"

Sing stroked my shoulder, making quiet shushing sounds.

"It's not your fault, Phoenix." Shanghai pushed her fingers through my hair. "Alex is the murderer, not you."

"Alex gave Phoenix a choice," Shanghai said as she turned to Sing, "and he chose to spare me."

Sing nodded. "I get the picture. The ultimate ultimatum. Alex is the devil in a leather jacket."

When my spasms eased, I slid the pewter ring from my finger and painted a picture of Misty in my mind, recalling a time when she showed me one of her treasures. She wore a floor-length white gown, covered with lace and silk from top to bottom—her mother's bridal gown. Even while little, she kept it in a hope chest and waited for her turn to walk down the aisle. By the time she reached her thirteenth birthday, she had latched her matrimonial hopes on me.

But now it would never happen.

Swallowing back another sob, I slid the ring on and whispered, "Misty, I'll come back for you. Somehow I'll find your soul and get you safely to the Gateway."

Sing looked silently up at the sky, her eyes watery. "And I'll do everything I can to help you. I swear it."

Shanghai continued rubbing my shoulder. "Do you know what Alex meant by *the abyss*?"

I shook my head. "She mentioned it once before but didn't tell me what it is. Probably an idle threat."

"Don't be so sure," Sing said. "Rumors among my people say they have a place to torture souls."

"Rumors. The Jungle is filled with them." I blew out a sigh. "Maybe Alex is lying. Maybe she's been lying about more than I could imagine before."

Shanghai slid her hand into mine. "What do you mean?"

"The whole bit about testing to see if the energy would influence me. She kept goading me to kill you, but now I wonder…"

"Wonder what?"

"Well, like Sing said, the escape was easier than it might've been. Alex was knocked for a loop, but she wasn't unconscious. She could've ordered the other guards to storm out that back exit and chase us."

"So she wanted us to get away." Shanghai tilted her head. "But why?"

"It's a setup. The whole entertainment thing wasn't designed to test the energy's power. It was designed to prove my ability to counter it. Her words said to kill you, but her eyes said something else. She *wanted* me to conquer it."

"But killing Misty doesn't fit in," Shanghai said.

"That part I haven't figured out, but no matter what the purpose, Alex will use the abyss threat to get me back to the camp." I looked at Shanghai, then at Sing. As I clenched a fist, I raised my voice. "Well, Alex is going to get her wish. I *am* going back. I'll reap Misty's soul. And I'm going to rescue every single one of those prisoners. After that, I'll figure out how to get past the Gateway and see what's on the other side. One way or another, we're going to bring down the Council and put an end to their tyranny."

Shanghai pumped her fist. "Now that's swagger!"

A new tear crept down Sing's cheek as she whispered, "I'll keep hoping."

"While we're waiting for things to settle at the prison..." I leaned back and nestled between Sing and Shanghai, then wrapped an arm around them and drew them closer. They seemed happy to snuggle.

I gave Sing a quick summary of what happened while she was breaking the family out of the camp, including our staged battle to the death and Alex's constant enticement to take the energy from the depot tube, though I left out the part about Kwame… for the time being.

When I finished, I turned toward Sing. "So, where are the Fitzpatricks?"

"They're safe with my people," Sing said as she leaned her head against my shoulder. "The hardest part was relocking the door after I got them out. At least the prisoners I left behind were smart enough not to bang on it, but some of the women were crying. It broke my heart."

"I can imagine."

"And I have bad news. I heard Cairo's a prisoner in the camp now. I didn't see him or else I would've asked him to help me. He's in danger because Alex plans to terminate fifty prisoners each day until they're all dead and reaped."

"Fifty!" An image of Cairo playing his cello flashed to mind, then dozens of faces in the camp's living quarters. We had to get them all out, and we needed lots of help. "So do you have your people involved?"

Sing nodded. "The Eagle took Colm's family in. She's working on a new plan."

"Okay. That's good. But what's your role in the Eagle's plans? I get the feeling that there's a much bigger picture."

"I can't tell you. I'll spill everything soon, but I can't yet. Not until it's all over."

"Some of it already spilled," I said. "Peter captured Kwame and reaped him. Just before he went into the tube, he said he's your father."

"What?" Sing pulled away and looked at me. "My father? What are you talking about?"

"No joke. He said to 'trust Akua' and that there was a lot more to explain. But he didn't get a chance to say anything else before he got sucked into the vacuum."

Two deep lines dug into Sing's brow. "That makes no sense at all. My father died right after I went to Reaper training."

I gave her a light shrug. "Apparently Kwame's been dead for quite a while, so it's still possible. He was a level-three ghost all along, and I didn't even know it. But if he were your father, you'd have recognized him, right?"

Sing scowled. "Phoenix, of course I would know my own father."

"Then why would he say that? Can a ghost be disguised somehow? You said his voice was the same."

"That's true," Sing said with a faraway look in her eyes. "He did sound a lot like my father."

"And he had the same name, the same nationality." I picked up a chunk of gravel from the roof and tossed it. "Too many coincidences."

Sing held out her hand. "May I see your watch?"

"Sure." I withdrew it and handed it to her. "I think it's a little past eight."

"That's not what I'm interested in." Sing pulled out her flashlight and focused the beam on the cover's engraving. "Very strange."

I pointed at the watch. "It says, 'From A.' Is that supposed to be Akua?"

She shook her head as if casting off a daze. "This is all just too bizarre."

"Well, maybe—"

"Let's forget about it." She gave me the watch and slid her flashlight away, her gaze fixed on the roof. "It won't do any good to speculate."

"I guess not." I put the watch back into my pocket. "But there's more to tell. Alex said your mother has traveled beyond the point of no return, that she won't be coming back."

Sing jerked her head up. "What?"

"Alex knows you sent Tokyo to the Gateway, so she checked her status." I lowered my voice. "Your mother's gone."

Sing stared at me. Tears filled her eyes. After a few seconds, she whispered, "No."

"No?"

Her hands trembling, she raised her voice. "No! Alex is lying! My mother is too powerful! She's been preparing for this for—"

"Hey..." I stroked Sing's arm. "Don't get so worked up. Like you said, Alex is probably lying. She'd do anything to keep us from learning the Gateway's secrets."

"And now you know one of my secrets." Sing sniffed and brushed away tears. "I told you my mother was there, but I didn't tell you that I took her when you and I went to the depot. I couldn't risk Alex snooping around the Gateway network looking for her."

I continued rubbing her arm. "It's okay. I understand."

"So we'll just assume Alex is lying and stay the course." Sing shifted to her knees and looked toward the prison. The medallion slipped out again and spun at the end of its chain. "You're right. We have to go back and rescue all the prisoners."

Shanghai grabbed the edge of her cloak and used it to brush a dark spot on her shirt just below her ribs. "This will be the mother of all prison breakouts. Us versus an experienced Cardinal, an Owl, and armed guards. And they'll probably double security again before we return.

But we can do it." She pinched her shirt where she had been brushing. "Is this blood?"

I unhooked my flashlight, flicked it on, and aimed it at the spot. I dabbed it with my finger and shone the beam on the tip. "It's blood. And it's fresh."

"I thought I felt something." Shanghai lifted the hem of her shirt, exposing her skin up to her ribs. A raw gash marred the side of her muscular abdomen, and blood trickled into her pants.

"Bullet wound." I twirled my finger. "Turn a bit."

Shanghai twisted, revealing her back. No other marks appeared.

"It must have just grazed you."

"Does it hurt?" Sing asked.

"It stings quite a bit." Shanghai lowered her shirt. "A lot less than being punched by Phoenix. That one jab really packed a wallop. No one's ever bloodied my nose before."

"Sorry about that." I shone the light on her face. Although a red smear covered her upper lip, her nose had stopped bleeding. "Was your fighting all an act?"

"Sort of. I felt the fury, so I let it loose as far as I dared, sort of like a tiger straining against a leash. After you decked me, I faked passing out, so I heard everything." A new tear sparkled in her eye. "Thank you for sparing my life."

As I gazed at her, Misty's face flashed to mind, her horrified expression as the sonic gun went off. I barely managed a whisper. "You'd have done the same for me." I cleared my throat, turned off the flashlight, and clipped it to my belt. I had to change the subject or risk another breakdown. "Okay, what's the first step in our plan?"

Sing settled into my one-armed embrace, her head

again on my shoulder. "The Eagle heard that Erin's coming back shortly after dawn for the first executions."

"Dawn." Shanghai scooted close on my other side. "That doesn't give us much time."

"We got a new infusion of energy," I said. "Maybe we can shift to ghost mode and sneak into the camp that way."

Shanghai shook her head. "I've been trying. Maybe it's because we got a different kind of energy, or maybe what Sing gave us wasn't enough, but I couldn't transform."

"I'll give it a shot." I stared at my ring and concentrated on Misty's soul and my need to rescue her, but exhaustion overwhelmed the desire. Like Shanghai said, something was missing.

"No luck?" she asked.

"Nothing. We'd better get some advice." I slid an arm free, connected my clasp to my valve, and nodded at Shanghai. "Plug in, and we'll hear what Colm and Crandyke have to say."

She locked in her clasp. "Ready."

"Crandyke," I said into my cloak, "we need your advice. Do you—"

"You'd better believe you need my advice."

"Why? What's the matter?"

"Tori's been filling me in on what's going on in the corrections camp."

"Okay. That's good.... I hope."

"You hope? Of course it's good. Had I known that children were enslaved there, I would've been more helpful. But no, you didn't tell me about that. You keep counting on coercing me by holding me hostage instead of just appealing to my compassion for children."

"I didn't know you had compassion for children. You said you didn't have any loved ones."

"Shows how much you know. I had a wife and daughter who both died in the flu epidemic a few years back, and my parents died when I was little. I grew up in a foster care center with lots of kids. When the government closed all the centers down, I lost contact with most of my friends, but I never lost the memories. Some of those friendships kept me going when I was young."

"Sorry, Crandyke, I had no idea."

"Maybe you could have asked. You seem to fawn over the children, which I highly commend, but you don't care about old coots like me. I'm just another bug in your rug."

"Okay. You win. I should've been nicer to you." I let out a sigh. "Just tell me if you have any ideas. We're hoping to break back into the prison to rescue everyone."

"Well, let's see. What day of the week is it?"

"Wednesday.... Well, it'll be Thursday in a few hours. The electricity's still on in a lot of the buildings, so it's probably not quite nine in the evening."

"The camp gets supplies Thursday morning," Crandyke said. "A van comes from the warehouse. You know, food, office odds and ends, cleaning implements, that kind of thing. If you could hijack the van, you could drive right through an open gate."

"How early does it show up?"

"Before dawn. It brings coffee, so they make sure it's there for the morning shift in case they've run out. Caffeine addiction is epidemic among prison guards, as you might expect."

"Among Reapers, too." I pictured a group of guards gathered around a coffee pot, all of them eagerly guzzling.

"Could we spike their coffee with something to knock them out?"

"Exactly my thought. A strong depressant could do it. At that time of day, they might not notice that the coffee's more bitter than usual."

"Then we need a drug supplier. I'd have to mingle into the shroud, but there's no guarantee I'll find the right drug, and I don't have anything to barter with."

Shanghai whispered, "And we don't have that kind of time."

I nodded. Her sensitive Reaper's ears had tuned in quite well.

"Simple," Crandyke said. "I have a friend who's a doctor, and he owes me a favor. We were in the foster home together, and I didn't rat on him when he nailed the nanny's shoes to the ceiling. Anyway, his name is Dr. Rubenstein. If you tell Ruby that Crabapple sent you, he'll give you what you need."

"They called you Crabapple in the foster home?"

"Yes. Is that a problem?"

"No. It's... uh... fitting, I guess."

"We all thought so."

"So now we need a hijacking plan," I said. "Do you know the delivery drivers?"

"Not personally. I just approved the requisitions. I probably saw a name or two, but I don't remember them."

Shanghai touched my hand. "Colm's been listening. He has an idea."

I shifted toward her and trained my ears on her cloak. "Go ahead, Colm."

"First, I want to thank you." Colm's voice came through weak and jittery. "You risked your lives to rescue my wife, my daughters, and Colleen, and I am the most grateful man in the world... though I suppose I'm not really in the world anymore."

"You're welcome, Colm. I'd do it again in a heartbeat. I'm just sorry we couldn't save you as well."

Sing nodded. "Have no fear. Our allies put your loved ones in good hands. Fiona, Colleen, and your daughters will soon be on their way to a safe house, and they will be well cared for."

"Again, I am grateful." Colm's voice caught for a moment, forcing a pause. "Regarding your need to commandeer a delivery van, I once worked a carpentry job at an eatery near the corrections camp. I learned that it is a favorite early morning haunt for drivers who are about to go on their delivery routes. You could check to see if the supply driver is there and borrow his van while he is eating."

"And if he's not there?" I asked.

"Then I suppose you'll have to hide out near the camp and hijack the van. I apologize, but I don't have all the answers."

"No worries, Colm. Just give us the name of the restaurant. We'll take it from there."

"It's called Eggs & Stuff. They serve mostly breakfast."

I nodded. "Eggs & Stuff. I know the place. What time do they open?"

"At four, I believe."

"We'll be there a few minutes early." I focused on my own cloak. "Crandyke, what does the delivery van look like?"

"It's a full-sized van. White. The lettering says

'Mayfield Transport.' They contracted with us to do local deliveries."

"Any windows?"

"Only in the driver's compartment. One on each side. And the windshield, of course."

"Perfect. We can hide in the back. We just need a driver the gate guards won't recognize. They know all three of us."

"Fiona can drive it," Colm said. "She practically grew up on a farm tractor. She can drive anything."

I looked at Sing. "What do you think? Can you get her to help before she goes to the safe house?"

Sing blinked. "Fiona?"

"Right. Colm just said she can drive the delivery van."

Sing looked toward the edge of the roof. "If I'm going to catch her, I'd better go now."

"Alone? With your energy depleted? Between now and midnight is prime bandit time."

"Don't worry about me and those snakes. I'm like a mongoose." Sing rose to her feet and refastened her belt. "I'll ask the Eagle to bring Fiona to the restaurant."

"Good. Eggs & Stuff. A few minutes before four."

"And where should I meet you after I talk to the Eagle?" Sing asked.

"Back here, I suppose. We can sleep for a while until we go to the restaurant. It'll be too dangerous to hang around at street level."

"See you then." Sing jogged to the ladder, swung onto it, and disappeared below the roof line.

Now alone with Shanghai, I spoke again into my cloak. "Crandyke. Back to the doctor. Do you think he would treat Shanghai's gunshot wound?"

Crandyke's voice spiked. "She has a gunshot wound, and you're sitting around chatting about breakfast?"

"Well... yeah. We don't think it looks bad enough to—"

"Don't be an idiot, Phoenix. You can't see infection."

"I know, but we thought—"

"No buts. Get up and get moving. I'll guide you to the doctor's home, and Tori and I will come up with a plan to get that drug into their coffee, maybe disguise the taste somehow." He let out a huff. "At least someone around here has some sense. If it takes a dead seven-year-old girl and an equally dead paper-pushing clerk to save the prisoners, then so be it."

"Whatever you say, Crandyke." I stood and helped Shanghai to her feet. Keeping our heads low, we scurried along a series of connected rooftops. After traveling about a block, we reached the end of set of buildings. There we descended a ladder that dropped us toward an alley next to a dumpster brimming with broken furniture, including a legless table, mattress stuffing, and a beat-up sofa.

Once we arrived at street level, we jogged through the city to a middle-income section, Crandyke guiding us along the way. Compared to the rundown houses in my district, this area of detached homes and grass lawns seemed like a haven of riches, though not unexpected since a physician's practice couldn't survive in my neighborhood.

After finding the doctor's residence and convincing him that "Crabapple" had sent us, he stitched Shanghai's side and applied an antibiotic cream. The office visit also gave us the chance to use the toilet and wash our faces, hands, and arms. A mirror provided a view of my beat-up face—a bruise on my chin, a cut over an eyebrow, and scrapes on my forehead. By the time I finished cleaning up, gallons of red-tinged water had swirled down the drain.

Once we obtained the liquid drug in two vials, we walked out of the doctor's suburban neighborhood and back into the business district. As we marched, I slid out my watch and checked the time—a little after midnight. "If we hustle back to that roof, we can get maybe three hours of sleep. Sing's probably waiting for us."

Shanghai yawned. "Sleep won't come easy. That roof isn't exactly comfortable, but at least it's out of sight."

"I saw a sofa in a dumpster. The cushions should help."

We retraced our steps to the alley, careful to watch for bandits and prison guards. While climbing the ladder, we hauled the sofa cushions to the roof and dragged them toward the spot where we had rested earlier. As we drew near, Sing rose from behind the parapet, now dressed in typical Reaper garb, likely provided by the Eagle, though she still had no cloak. "You made it!" she whispered. "I was wondering if you got ambushed."

"No problems." I set a cushion at her feet. "Did you contact the Eagle about Fiona?"

"Yes. They'll both be at the restaurant." Sing helped us set the other cushions side by side, and we settled onto our makeshift beds—a bit musty, but far better than gravel and tar.

"Okay, Crandyke," I said into my cloak. "We're all gathered again. Did you and Tori come up with any ideas?"

"Logistics mostly." Crandyke's voice was strong and lively, loud enough for Sing and Shanghai to hear. "Tori said the guards all drink from a pair of community coffee pots located in the watchtower, so we'll have to spike both of them."

I nodded. "We also have a pot in a dining room in the Hilton, so we'll have to spike that one for Alex and Peter." I withdrew one of the vials and looked at the hazy moon through its transparent contents. "Based on what the doctor told me about how potent the drug is, I'll dump half a vial in each of the guards' pots and a full vial in the Hilton's. We have to be sure to knock Alex and Peter out."

"Good plan," Sing said, "but it's not as easy as it sounds. Even if we get inside, we have to scatter like invisible ghosts before Fiona drives away. It might take a while for them to drink the stuff and even longer for it to knock them out."

"You'll need the cover of darkness," Crandyke said. "Tori told me she went to both searchlights. She couldn't figure out how they work, but she saw power cords. Even if they're locked in place, you can cut them. You might get a jolt, but the guards won't be able to turn them back on."

"Good thinking," I said. "It'll still be before dawn, so that'll help."

Sing pressed a thumb against her chest. "Killing the lights will be my job. You two will have to dodge the guards until I can cut the power. We'll have to work out the details on the fly."

Shanghai stretched her arms and yawned. "We'd better get some sleep or *we* won't have any power."

I felt the watch in my pocket. It had no alarm mechanism. "I don't have a way to make sure we get up in time."

"Stay plugged in," Crandyke said, "And I'll wake you up in three hours. I'll count the seconds if I have to. Tori can help."

"Thanks, Crandyke."

While Sing and Shanghai curled on their cushions, I

laid my head and shoulders on mine, my feet propped on the roof's parapet. A cool breeze wafted over the warm rooftop, caressing my cheeks with shifting temperatures that soothed my tired body. Sleep would come soon. I could feel it.

A few stars shone through the haze, a rare sight in the city. Ever since the meltdown, no one in Chicago bothered to gaze at the heavens. The specter of what couldn't be seen… or reached… brought to earth the choking reality of our condition. We were trapped, human waste unable to escape from a tawdry shell, this dumpster called life.

And I was a waste-disposal unit, destined to haul forsaken souls to a shadowy door that opened to the unknown—the Gateway, that unexplained beyond-reproach expectation of release from this festering cavity.

A horn blared far away. A woman shouted, something about burning her hand on a candle, likely a cry of pain echoed within many a wall in the windy city. With electricity cut-off hour now past, the lights-out routine had been repeated a million times from row house to row house, from shanty to shanty. The Jungle natives did what they could to survive.

In my mind, a thousand matches touched a thousand candlewicks, giving light to an equal number of darkened chambers. A man carried a silver taper to a bedroom and checked on three sleeping children crowded on a bed. The wavering light fell across the contented faces, giving the man reason to sigh with relief.

A woman probed a pantry with the light of a stubby red candle, hoping to find something to prepare for the next day's meals. Her hands trembling, she grasped a can of beans, then a bag of rice, a thin smile on her face—one more day her children would go to bed without the pangs of hunger.

And in the glow of a flickering unity candle, two inches high and blackened by decades of anniversary celebrations, an old man kissed a frail old woman, slid into bed with her, and blew out the flame.

The scene faded to gray, then to black. All was silent. The city waited anxiously for dawn. They waited for someone to rise up and prove that their hopes and prayers weren't for naught. They needed a courageous warrior who would open the gate and show them the other side of eternity.

"Hope," I whispered. "It's all they have. Who'll keep it alive?"

"What?" Sing touched my elbow. "Phoenix, did you say something?"

"Just talking to myself." I settled deeper into my cushion. I had to do more than just talk about hope. I had to make it visible. Somehow Shanghai, Sing, and I would open the ultimate Gateway and see the wonders on the other side—stand together with our hands clasped and witness what has been hidden from everyone for so many years. And then we would return and tell the world about it.

CHAPTER TWENTY-THREE

"WAKE UP, PHOENIX. It's time to be a hero."

I opened my eyes and stared at the blackness. The scant array of stars had disappeared, and mist filled the air. A rumble of thunder coursed across the heavens. Where was I? Why did everything hurt so much? And who called from my cloak?

A new voice spoke up, quieter, childlike. "Phoenix, it's Tori. You have to get up. You have to rescue Misty's soul."

"Misty's soul?" Memories roared to mind—pain, so much pain and hopelessness. When Misty's terrified face appeared, a mental dagger shredded my heart. "She's... she's dead."

Crandyke's voice returned, soft and soothing. "I know what it feels like, Phoenix. When my wife and daughter died, I died with them... inside, I mean. The pain eases over time, but it never goes away. You just have to pick yourself up and do what you have to do. And what you have to do is get up and rescue people who can't rescue themselves. They're all counting on you. Like I said, it's time to be a hero."

The image of the camp prisoners blended into the memories, forlorn faces in a sea of misery. I nodded. "You're right, Crandyke. Thanks for the reminder."

"My first name is Albert."

I rubbed my eyes. "What?"

"Albert.... That's my first name."

"Okay... uh... Albert. Thanks again."

"But you can keep calling me Crandyke since you're used to it. I just thought you'd like to know."

"Sure. I'm glad to know." I drew a mental image of Crandyke... Albert... standing upright instead of lying dead on the sidewalk. Before last night, he had been just another soul, another bug in my rug as he had said. Now he had become a counselor, a guide, a friend. "I'll give you an update soon."

I rose to my knees. Sing and Shanghai slept on, both curled toward me with lips pursed as they breathed heavily. I compressed Sing's shoulder. "It's time to poison the coffee."

Bleary-eyed, she sat up and stretched her arms. "I could use some coffee, minus the poison."

"I think they serve unpoisoned coffee at Eggs & Stuff." I gave Shanghai's arm a gentle shake. "Ready to go to prison?"

"Been there, done that." She grasped my hand and pulled to a sitting position, rubbing her nose as she grimaced. "I dreamed you were punching me. It still hurts."

"Sorry. I probably thought you were Alex."

After we climbed to our feet and checked our weapons belts and the drug vials, we walked over the connected buildings toward the fire escape, then down to the street and through the sleeping city. With every step, I felt lighter, freer, as if I were walking through the Gateway and discovering the greatest secret in the world, though eventually thoughts of Misty dragged me back to reality. Still, the need to rescue her kept my feet moving swiftly.

When we arrived at the restaurant, we climbed another fire escape to the roof of a two-story building across the street. We stooped behind a parapet and watched the front window where "Eggs & Stuff" stretched across the glass in block letters, illuminated by a solitary streetlamp below us. Inside, the proprietors were likely brewing coffee and cooking breakfast on a gas-powered stove, but the typical breakfast aromas stayed out of smelling range.

Spits of rain dropped from the dark sky, enough to paint the pavement with a sheen that reflected the lamp's glow. Three vehicles—a modern four-door sedan and two old pickup trucks—sat in metered spaces, one on our side of the street and two in front of the restaurant. Darkness hid any passengers from view.

"No sign of the Eagle or Fiona," Sing said, "but they wouldn't make themselves obvious."

Soon, the loud rattle of an engine approached. A white van drove up and parked next to the streetlamp, parallel to the curb. Seconds later, the headlights darkened, and the engine died. Everything fell silent.

I leaned over the parapet. Only the top of the van was in view. "Anyone catch the words on the side? I can't see them from here."

"I saw *Transport*," Sing said. "The rest was a blur."

"That's got to be it."

After another minute, candlelight flickered inside the restaurant, drifting from the back toward the front. A man dressed in tattered jeans and a khaki shirt got out of one of the pickups and waited in front of the window. A woman unlocked the door and let him enter.

The van door opened, and a huge, muscular man stepped out. As he walked toward the restaurant, he tucked a long knife into a belt sheath and fastened a snap over it. Clean shaven and hair closely cropped, he looked like a pumped-up Marine.

Shanghai let out a low whistle. "He's practically a mountain. Getting the keys from him won't be easy."

"You're telling me." I stretched my fingers on each hand, still sore. "It might take all three of us."

The sedan's door opened. A woman stepped out from the driver's side and looked around. A veil covered her hair and face, revealing only her eyes.

"That's her," Sing said. "The Eagle."

I picked up a piece of gravel and threw it at the street next to her. When it clicked on the pavement, she looked up. I stood and waved. She nodded, walked around the car, and let Fiona out from the passenger's side.

"Let's go." Treading lightly, we hustled down the fire escape and across the street. When we arrived, I hugged Fiona and kissed her cheek. "I'm so sorry," I whispered. "I wish I could have done more to save Colm."

Tears sparkling, she patted my hand. "Don't fret, Phoenix." Her Irish-flavored voice sounded musical in the deadness of early morning. "We live in dangerous times. I am grateful for the years we had together."

When I stepped back, Shanghai wrapped her cloak around Fiona. "Colm asked me to do this. He is inside these fibers, and he hopes this embrace will last until he sees you beyond the Gateway."

Fiona bit her fist, then quickly pulled it down. She grasped an edge of the cloak and kissed it, closing her eyes as she inhaled through her nose.

While we waited, four men and a woman filed into the restaurant. More candles flickered to life, and each opening of the door sent a wave of chatter into the street.

Finally, Fiona released the cloak and looked at the van. "Is that our vehicle?"

I nodded. "I'm supposed to jump the driver and get the keys, but he looks like a tough customer."

"Of course he's tough. He's Irish. I could tell." Fiona gestured with her head. "Come on. I'll talk to him."

"Wait just a minute." I turned toward the Eagle and searched her eyes. "Listen, I don't know who you are, but I guess I have to trust you. Anyway, have you heard about Alex killing Misty or what she did with her?"

The Eagle nodded. "I heard." Her voice sounded gravelly, maybe intentionally so. "If I had to guess, Alex probably instructed Peter to reap Misty and put her soul in the depot's transfer sphere. I assume she will stay there until the camp prisoners are reaped. All the souls will be transferred to the actual Gateway at that time."

"Alex mentioned that she would take Misty to the abyss," I said. "She mentioned that place to me once before but didn't explain it."

"Ah!" The Eagle lowered her gaze. "And I heard Kwame is in the sphere as well. Alex would use such leverage, at least to gain an advantage."

"Well…" I cocked my head to try to see her eyes again. "What is the abyss?"

She refocused on me. "According to one of our spies, the Gatekeeper has a… well, I suppose you could call it a pool that tortures souls. He considers it the ultimate capital punishment, reserved for those who commit high treason. The pool is rightfully called the abyss. They say if you could hear the cries of anguish from a soul who's thrown in there, you'd understand."

My heart pounded. "When would Alex do it?"

"Since she plans to reap camp prisoners today, she would need a different collection sphere for them. I assume Erin will bring a new one this morning and take the filled one to the abyss sometime today."

"Do you think she would really send Misty to the abyss?"

"Impossible to know. Alex has a mean streak, and Erin is unpredictable. I wouldn't put it past either of them."

I nodded, my lips tight. "Then let's get this done."

"I agree." The Eagle walked back to her car and stood at the open door. "I'll wait to hear how you fare in the restaurant before I leave, but please hurry."

"Sure thing." I opened the restaurant door and ushered Fiona, Sing, and Shanghai inside. The chatter hushed. The customers stared, some sitting in booths and some at tables. No one breathed a word. Even the flames on the dozen or so candles scattered here and there seemed to stand at attention as if waiting for someone to break the silence.

Fiona walked straight to a booth where the van driver sat peering over the top of a menu. She pushed the menu down and looked him in the eye. "Will you help a grieving widow rescue some innocent folks before they meet the same fate as my dear husband?"

"I will." He slid out from his seat and rose to a towering height, his Irish brogue deep and lyrical. "Where is the scoundrel who would hurt your folks?"

Fiona's accent thickened to match his. "Are you delivering supplies to the corrections camp this morning?"

"I am."

"Well, they'll be executing everyone there shortly after dawn, even mums and their wee babes." Tears streamed down her cheeks. "It'll be a terrible carnage."

"There, there, now." The man picked up a napkin and extended it to her. "What is your name, good lady?"

She took the napkin and dabbed her cheeks. "I am Fiona, and my husband was Colm."

"Ah! And I am Liam." He picked up another napkin. "What can I do to help you?"

"Well, Liam..." Fiona's voice shifted to a furtive tone. "I need you to drive my friends into the camp.... Secretly."

Liam gave us a doubtful stare. "Reapers?"

"Of course they're Reapers. Who better to rescue lost souls than a Reaper?"

"Lost souls? You mean..." He leaned close to her. "Taibhsean?"

"No, not ghosts." She batted him away. "People. Family people who need help from good folks like us. Reapers hide in darkness like the shadows themselves. They leap from roof to roof and fly down from above like the holy angels. No one can rescue better than they can. All they need is a way to get past the front gate."

Liam shook his head doubtfully. "I want to help you, but..." He scanned the other restaurant patrons. "I have my own family to think about."

"What he's saying..." An old man chewing an unlit cigar hopped down from a barstool. No taller than Sing, he slid the cigar from his mouth and pointed it at Liam. "If word gets out that he helped resisters, he and his family will be the next camp rats. Extermination's flowing like storm water through the sewers. No one wants to be next. We have to protect our wives, our children."

Sing walked up to the man and spread an arm around his back. "If you really want to protect your loved ones, then you'll help us. The Council preys on your fears, but they're the ones who should cower. If everyone stands together, we'll be a force they can't possibly overcome."

"Maybe so." The man stuck the cigar back into his mouth. "But no one wants to stand up first. The first rat out of the hole gets his head chopped off."

I raised a hand and nodded at Sing and Shanghai in turn. "We three Reapers are already standing up. We'll take the first blows. Just help us save the camp dwellers—the fathers, the mothers, the children. That's all we ask. Spare them a little bit of the same love you show to your families. By helping us, you'll help them end their suffering."

Silence descended again. Candles wavered. A tear trickled down one woman's cheek. The cigar-chewing man sniffed and looked away.

Finally, Liam cleared his throat. "Well, since you put it that way…" He gave us a firm nod. "I'm your driver."

Applause broke out from the other customers. An old man wearing thick glasses shook my hand. A youngish pockmarked woman patted me on the back, then did the same to Shanghai and Sing. The cigar man hugged Sing, leaving a fleck of tobacco on her cheek.

We left the restaurant to the sound of excited chatter. Since we no longer needed Fiona as a driver, we sent her away with the Eagle. Liam guided Shanghai, Sing, and me into the van's rear compartment between shelves lining the side panels. Sing and Shanghai sat together against one shelf, while I sat opposite them, all three of us with our knees pulled close to our chests.

I flicked on my flashlight and ran the beam along the shelves, revealing plastic bins filled with stacks of office supplies from clipboards to staplers, some arranged neatly and some in haphazard array.

The engine started, once again rattling, and the van pulled into the street. Liam whistled a sharp note. "Keep your heads low. The lights'll be bright when we get to the gate."

"Will do." I followed the scent of coffee to a shelf near my head. Foil bags the size of large pumpkins filled the space, one with a torn corner, providing the rich aroma. "How many bags of coffee do you deliver there, Liam?"

"I haven't looked at today's order, but usually just one." He leaned his head back. "Unless they've got visitors staying in their dorm. Then two. But why anyone would want to visit overnight is a mystery to me. They say it's haunted. Spirits running around like vermin."

"I've heard that, too." I heaved a coffee bag from the shelf and set it in my lap.

Sing touched a corner of the bag. "So this is a week's supply. You can't pour the drug in there. It'll be too diluted."

"Then we'll have to brew the coffee ourselves, or at least get it started, and we'll put the drug directly into the pots." I shifted the bag to the side and handed a drug vial to Shanghai. "You can take care of the coffee in the Hilton, while Sing climbs to the roof. Then I'll spike the watchtower coffee. We'll meet in the prisoners' living quarters and hide until we think they're knocked out. Got it?"

I aimed my flashlight at Sing and Shanghai. They both

nodded but with doubtful expressions. I couldn't blame them. This journey felt like fishing for sharks with ourselves as the bait, especially since Alex expected our return. It would take a miracle for us to get out alive.

CHAPTER TWENTY-FOUR

I PUT THE FLASHLIGHT away and rested my head against the van's shelf. Lights streamed by. Cars whizzed past. A few honked, prompting Liam to honk in reply and shout something in a foreign language, probably Gaelic, but I couldn't translate. I knew a few Gaelic words but not those.

The city was waking up, and if everything went according to plan, Chicago would never learn how three stowaways led two hundred prisoners out of the infamous corrections camp right under the guards' snoring noses. And if we could penetrate the Gateway, maybe everyone's lives would change forever.

Thoughts of the Gateway resurrected Alex's mention of the abyss. I painted a mental picture—a swirling whirlpool of darkness with shimmering faces spinning around and around, all with eyes and mouths locked open in abject terror. Apparently the Gateway deniers weren't crazy after all. Maybe something sinister really did lurk in the Gatekeeper's domain.

When the van slowed, I shook the image away. Light poured in through the windshield. We all hunkered low. Shanghai covered herself and Sing with her cloak, and I ducked under mine.

The hum of Liam's opening window drifted by. Paper rattled. A guard's voice followed. "What do you have?"

"Printer supplies today," Liam said, "And coffee, as usual. Your order calls for two bags. Do you have visitors?"

"Yeah. Go to the dorm with the printer stuff and one bag of coffee. While you're dropping off coffee here on the way out, we'll have to search your van. Tight security today. We're expecting escape attempts."

"No problem." Liam chuckled. "Clean up the trash back there while you're at it."

"Now he wants us to play janitor." Something clicked. "Sign here."

After a few seconds, the van moved forward, its engine again making a racket. The lights dimmed. I peeked out from under my cloak. In the wash of searchlights, the Hilton drew closer.

"Everyone getting out here?" Liam asked.

"All but me," I said.

"Didn't you hear him say they're going to search my van? They'll find you."

"I'm counting on a sudden blackout. If you'll take your time going back to the gate, we should be okay."

"I will." Liam stopped the van in front of the Hilton's door. After getting out, he swung open the rear gate, using his massive body to block the light as he picked up a pair of printer toner cartridges. "When I give the word," he whispered, "make a run for it."

Shanghai and I lowered our cloaks. I lifted the coffee bag to her. As a searchlight beam angled away, Liam whispered, "Now!"

With the coffee in tow, Shanghai got up and hurried

past Liam. Sing followed in a blur. The rear gate slammed shut, leaving me alone in darkness.

Liam's head appeared at the driver's open window. "I will help your friends with the coffee, but I can't delay too much. Stay hidden."

I tried to match his Irish accent. "I will."

He smiled and tossed the key fob to me. "In case of emergency."

"Thank you." After stowing the fob in my tunic pocket, I retrieved a second bag of coffee and waited, imagining Liam leading Shanghai to the coffee maker. My mind shifted to Sing's likely progress as she set up a climbing line. In my mental scenario, she made it halfway up before a searchlight aimed its stabbing beam at her. Imaginary gunshots rang out, and she fell like a rag doll to the ground.

I shook the nightmare away, but anxiety pounded my brain. What were we thinking? Of course they would see her. I had to create a distraction.

I retrieved the fob and studied the buttons. In the dimness, a red one stood out—an alarm. I depressed it. The van's horn blared, repeating again and again. The searchlights swept to the van and trained on it. I threw my cloak over my head and peeked out from underneath.

Seconds later, Liam threw open the driver's door. "Whisht!"

I pressed the alarm button again, silencing the horn, but the searchlights stayed locked on the van.

"What do you think you're doing?" Liam hissed.

"Giving Sing a chance to get to the roof." I tossed the fob back to him.

"I think maybe you're a brick shy of a load." He sat heavily in the seat and thrust the key into the ignition.

"But you're probably right. I saw her climbing. She's a fast little runt, but if I could see her, it wouldn't have taken the guards long to spot her."

He started the engine and wheeled the van toward the front gate. "Your other friend is doctoring the coffee. No one's around, so she should be fine."

"Thanks, Liam."

As he drove slowly, the searchlights followed, keeping the inside of the van bright and forcing me to stay under-cover. Every few seconds, I peeked at the searchlight on the abandoned building. It had to turn off soon, or else this whole mission would be blown out of the water.

Liam whispered, "I'll stall as long as I can, but you'd better think about improvising somehow."

"If I can create a distraction," I said, "will you take care of the coffee?"

"Sure."

"I'll put the vial under the bag. Pour all of it into the pot."

"I will." Liam looked at me through the rearview mir-ror, his expression grave. "After I leave, I'll stay close to the camp for a while in case you need help."

"Thanks. That'll be great."

He stopped the van next to the watchtower, lowered the window, and leaned out. "Sorry about the horn. The button's a bit touchy."

"Yeah," a guard said. "So are we. Big day here. We're all kind of jumpy."

"Really? What's up?"

"I can't tell you. Sorry." The guard's voice drifted to the side of the van. "Is the back locked?"

"No. I'll get out and open it for—"

"No problem. I got it."

I readied my fist. I could take one guard out easily, but after that? No clue.

The door opened. The guard aimed a flashlight inside. I lunged, grabbed his arms, and hauled him in. With a quick punch to the jaw, I knocked him out cold.

The surrounding light dimmed. One searchlight down. Sing had done her job. The watchtower searchlight swept toward the darkened one, leaving the van in shadows. Guards shouted, some near, some far. Pounding footsteps followed. Sing wouldn't have time to get to the remaining light. I had to go for it myself.

After waiting a few more seconds for the immediate area to quiet, I jumped out. Ducking low, I ran to the watchtower and climbed up the narrow ladder attached to the side, making sure my feet pressed silently on each rung.

When I reached the bowl-shaped top, I crept over a metal railing and sneaked toward a female guard. She stood behind the light, her eyes following the beam as it scanned the roof near the other searchlight.

A radio in her hand buzzed, then a male voice crackled. "Is the light secure?"

She held the radio close to her mouth and pressed a button. "So far. It's as quiet as a cemetery up here."

"Probably just a malfunction on the other one, then. You might as well come down."

She attached the radio to her belt, muttering, "They're scared of their own shadows."

I threw my arm around her neck and squeezed, simultaneously cutting off her air and blood supply. She thrashed for a moment before drooping limply in my arms. I had to work fast. Sleeper holds rarely knocked anyone out for more than a couple of minutes.

After laying her on the watchtower roof, I jerked out my flashlight and aimed it at a tangle of cables. Just as Tori had reported, a thick power cord ran from an outlet embedded in the roof up to the light's housing.

"Proctor," the man in the radio said. "Want some coffee? The delivery man is brewing it himself. Says it's a special Irish blend."

I grabbed the power cord and pulled, but the plug wouldn't budge.

"Proctor?" the man said. "What's the word?"

I withdrew a dagger from my belt and set it against the cord. I held my breath, bracing for a shock.

The radio crackled again. "Proctor's not answering."

"I'll check it out," a woman replied.

Gritting my teeth, I sliced through the cord. Sparks flew everywhere. The jolt knocked me backwards, making me stagger to regain my balance. The searchlight blinked off. Now in darkness except for a minimal glow from distant streetlamps, I pushed the dagger back to my belt and crouched next to Proctor. After snatching her radio, I climbed over the railing and slid down the ladder.

When I neared the bottom, my feet slammed into something that gave way. A loud grunt sounded, then a thud. I grabbed my flashlight and flicked it on. A female guard lay on the ground, groaning.

I dropped to my knees, straddled her body, and slapped my hand over her mouth. As she struggled, I shone the light in her eyes. *Theresa!*

"Give me a sign," I hissed. "I'm going to uncover your mouth, and your first words had better prove that you're on my side. Otherwise, I'm going to have to knock you out. Got it?"

Her brow lifting high, she nodded vigorously.

I slowly peeled my hand back. She whispered, "I'm working for the Raven."

"That'll do." I jumped to my feet and hoisted Theresa to hers. "Sorry about the rough treatment, but I have to work fast."

"I'm fine." She smoothed out her dampened uniform. "It's okay."

I nodded at a radio clipped to her belt. "Give me cover."

Theresa grabbed her radio and pushed the talk button. "This is Andrews. I haven't figured out what's wrong with the light, but…" She glanced at me before continuing. "I'm guessing it must be something in the circuit for both of them to go down."

"Are you okay?" came the reply. "You sound shaky."

"I fell from the ladder. Not far, though. I'm all right."

"Well, that's good, but Eddings isn't responding from the other light station, so everyone is hustling to the rooftops."

"All clear here. I'll join them."

The van door closed. Liam was ready to go. I touched Theresa's shoulder. "Tell him you checked the delivery van, that the other guard went to the searchlight."

She nodded and pressed the button again. "By the way, the van is clean. I checked it out for Scott. He went to the other light."

"Thanks. I'll send it through."

The headlights flashed on, and the engine clattered to life. Liam drove away, apparently with an unconscious guard still inside.

I grasped Theresa's wrist. "Whatever you do, don't drink the coffee. We spiked it. Understand?"

She nodded. "I'll go to the Hilton and pour a cup for Alex and Peter."

"Thanks. Just don't be too obvious." While Theresa hurried toward the Hilton, I turned Proctor's radio down and, keeping it close to my ear, hustled through the darkness toward the prisoners' quarters. A wavering light in the distance guided my way, a single guard at the door holding a flashlight. The other guard had probably responded to a call for help from the searchlight roof.

Chatter buzzed through the radio's speaker, excited voices bouncing back and forth.

"The searchlight's been smashed."

"Did you see who did it?"

"I saw a shadow breeze by. I've never seen anyone who's that fast."

"Got to be a ghost."

"Don't be stupid. Ghosts can't smash a searchlight."

"I'll call Alex, anyway. A Reaper can help no matter who did it."

I firmed my lips. Perfect. Now I had an excuse to be in the yard. If the guard at the door happened to be listening in, this would be easy.

As I neared the quarters, I pulled my hood up and shaded my face. "Hey! I heard you're having some ghost trouble."

The guard's flashlight beam fell across my chest, illuminating my tunic and cloak. "Peter?"

"Right. Phoenix and Shanghai are gone. I guess you heard about them."

He nodded. "You got here fast. I heard they're just about to call for Reaper help."

I showed him the radio. "Alex has been monitoring. She sent me out a while ago."

The guard, a medium-sized guy wearing a rain slicker, looked up at the roof. "Do you really think a rogue ghost is doing all this?"

"Most likely. Who else could get up to those places?" I pointed at the door. "I saw one go inside just a second ago. Can you let me in?"

"An invisible one, huh?" He inserted a key into the lock and opened the door. "You Reapers sure are handy sometimes."

"Thanks." I turned my flashlight on and gestured for him to enter. "Escort, please? I can't handle two hundred nervous prisoners."

"Here's your escort." He shoved me through the entry. I stumbled forward to get my balance and spun back. The door slammed. I leaped to it and tried to turn the knob. Locked. I thrust my shoulder against the door. It rattled but held firm.

I stepped back and listened to the radio. Dead silence. I dropped it to the concrete floor. What a fool! That guard played me like a dollar-store banjo. Alex knew I'd come here and clued him in. But what did that mean for Sing and Shanghai?

Whispers crept up behind me, frightened and indistinct. I turned slowly. In the darkness, glowing eyes drifted closer as if floating on water. "Ghosts," I whispered.

One of the pairs of eyes drew within arm's reach. "Phoenix?"

I swung the flashlight that way. The beam passed

through the body of a male figure. His dark face, shaven head, and cloaked frame gave away his identity. "Cairo?"

He nodded, making his glowing eyes bob. "What's going on? How did I get in this place?"

I cringed. The poor kid! And his mother! Her words flowed back to my mind. *And since two Reapers showed up, well I guess that means Noah's gonna have blessings overflowing!*

I shook my head. I couldn't dwell on it. Yet, since he was already level two or higher, his accelerated entrenchment likely due to his being a Reaper, he could help our cause. "Listen. I'll tell you all I know soon. But bottom line is that you're a ghost now. I need you to go through this door and find—"

A light knock sounded. "Phoenix?"

"Shanghai?" I spun back. "Is Sing with you?"

"No. I thought she'd be with you."

"She's not." I took a breath. "Listen. This room is empty except for ghosts. The guards aren't asleep. They know we're in the camp."

"I guessed that. I had to knock a guard out to get to you. But that doesn't mean they know about the coffee. They might still drink it."

"True, but we can't wait to find out." I set a hand on the door. "The guard you knocked out. Did he have any keys?"

"Not that I noticed. I can look."

"No time for that." I turned to Cairo. "Want to help?"

His eyes widened. "Sure. Anything."

I pointed at the door. "Just walk right through and help the Reaper on the other side. Her name is Shanghai."

He visibly swallowed. "Okay. If you say so."

"I say so." I turned back to the door. "Shanghai, you said you memorized the camp layout on the tablet, right?"

"Right. There's not much to it."

"I'm sending a ghost to help you look for Sing and the prisoners. He can sneak around in places you can't. I'll let him tell you his story. While you're searching, I'll figure out how to escape from here. Then I'll go to the tower and try to open the front gate. If you can spring everyone, they can make a dash for it."

"Got it. Send him through."

I waved an arm at Cairo. "Go!"

With his hands out in front, he walked through the door. As soon as he disappeared, I aimed the flashlight at the room's upper reaches and locked its beam on an open window—Sing's escape hatch.

I detached my spool, pulled out some line, and threw the weight. The line wound neatly around a beam and held fast.

As more ghosts drifted toward me, I focused on the closest few—mostly men who looked at me with confused expressions. It would take too long to explain the situation.

"Sorry, guys. I have to go." I slid my flashlight away, climbed up, and eased my body through the window. After reeling in my line and reattaching the spool, I jumped and sailed to the ground.

The moment I gained my balance, I ran toward the tower, the breaking dawn providing light. No sirens sounded. Maybe the drug was working and the guards were out cold. With no radio chatter, it was impossible to tell.

Light rain pelted my cloak, prompting me to raise my hood. The sparse turf had softened, now somewhat slick. Since dawn had arrived, the streetlamps had darkened, and clouds shielded the area from the rising sun, giving me cover as I skulked across the yard toward the watchtower. At the top of the tower, no one stood in the searchlight perch. If Proctor had awakened, she wasn't in sight at the moment.

When I arrived, I stood close to the wall next to the ladder. The prisoners' quarters and the Hilton lay in view. I scanned the yard and the rooftops. No sign of Sing. A light flashed in the windows over my head. More lights came to life in surrounding buildings, including the Hilton. Electricity cut-off hours had ended.

Keeping my back to the wall, I edged around the tower to the entry door. As silently as possible, I turned the knob. Unlocked.

I stared at the door. Strange. Why would they leave it unlocked? I pulled it slowly open. The watchtower was a perfect place for an ambush, but I had to follow through. Too many lives depended on me.

CHAPTER TWENTY-FIVE

O PENING THE TOWER door revealed a concrete stairway leading almost straight up to an open area, separated from the stairs by a railing. A guard lay sprawled across the top three steps, a dark mug gripped loosely in his fingers. Coffee dripped from the cup's edge and trickled down the stairwell. No sounds emanated from above.

I withdrew a dagger and crept upward, one tip-toed step after the other. When my eyes rose even with the upper floor, I stopped and peeked into a circular room. A second guard sat in a wheeled chair, his upper body slumped over a desk. He blocked a monitor, one of more than a dozen attached to the wall above the desk and below a series of observation windows that encircled the room.

I hurried the rest of the way up and leaped over the guard at the top of the stairs. I ran across the concrete floor to the slumped guard, wheeled him away from the desk, and scanned the controls.

Switches and dials were embedded in the wall under the monitors, probably a way to manipulate the cameras. A pair of binoculars rested on the desk next to a three-foot-long control board, but with so many switches and dials, how could I figure out which one controlled the gate? Trial and error might trip an alarm and give me away.

I walked slowly around the room, looking through the surrounding windows at the prison yard and buildings. In the dim glow of the rising sun, the yard lay motionless. The entire facility looked like an abandoned town, forgotten for a century.

A pair of objects moved on the Hilton's rooftop. I scooped up the binoculars and used them to focus on two figures—Shanghai and Cairo, skulking low as they eased toward the back edge of the roof. Shanghai pointed at something in the direction of the parking area outside the camp. She then leaned close to Cairo as if speaking covertly. Seconds later, Cairo climbed down the front of the building, still inside the camp, while Shanghai disappeared on the opposite side.

I lowered the binoculars and set them on the desk. Whatever Shanghai was up to, I could trust her.

I studied the array of monitors. The screens displayed various rooms and corridors in the prison facility, including one that provided a view of the Hilton's dining area, but they showed no signs of activity.

A radio on the closest guard's belt crackled. "Phoenix? I see you in there."

I looked out the window again. Alex and Peter stood at the Hilton's door, Alex with a radio to her lips. Sing stood between them, her head low.

I spun the guard's chair and snatched the radio from his belt. Pressing the talk button, I kept my eye on Alex and forced a calm tone. "Just thought I'd get a better look at the sunrise."

Her soft laugh sputtered through the speaker. "I have to give you credit for ingenuity. I didn't expect the drugged coffee, but I was able to avoid it."

"How?"

"Let's just say that it's very difficult to keep secrets from an Owl."

I looked again through the binoculars and focused on Sing. Blood dripped from her nose. Apparently Peter had beaten her up. I shifted to Alex. No sign of last night's facial wound. How could that be? The mysteries surrounding this Owl grew deeper all the time.

"Where are the prisoners?" I asked.

"It seems that you are in the dark about many things." Alex let out a melodic hum. "You'll find out soon."

A horn honked. I put the binoculars down and looked out the front window. The Gatekeeper's limo waited at the main entry.

Alex's voice crackled again. "Phoenix, would you please open the gate? You'll find the switch on the control board—upper-left corner next to a small LED that should be blinking red."

I sidled over to the board and touched a toggle switch next to a flashing bulb. With Sing in Alex's grasp, what choice did I have? I flipped the switch. Outside, the gate dragged slowly across the entry road from left to right.

A scan of the room revealed three rifles leaning against a corner. I could try to shoot Alex from here, but the risk was too high.

Alex and Peter marched toward the portable depot, Alex carrying some kind of dark material tucked under her arm, maybe a folded garment. Peter, limping heavily, cradled a silver box, similar to the one Erin used to transport the collections sphere. His cloak flowed in the breeze, shimmering. Might Misty's soul be in its fibers? Or had he deposited her in the sphere already?

Sing walked in front of them, her hands and feet unbound. Every few steps, Alex gave her a shove from behind, sending her stumbling until she could recover her balance.

The radio crackled once more. "Come and join us, Phoenix. I'm sure Singapore would be glad of your company." Alex laid the garment on one of the pedestals, pushed Sing down to her knees in front of the primary one, and spoke again into her radio. "Of course you could stay there and get a better view of Singapore's execution."

I lifted the radio to my lips. "So you want me to come down so you can kill me, too?"

"Of course not. I have need of you. And there is still a way you can keep me from killing her."

I met her stare. Even from fifty paces away, her Owl gaze seemed to penetrate my mind. Again, I had no choice. I had to rescue Sing and Misty. "I'll be there in a minute."

At ground level, the limo passed by and parked close to the tower. A door in the abandoned building under the far searchlight flew open. Armed guards ushered a line of prisoners through—men, women, and children—most with bowed heads and shoulders, though a few walked upright.

I spied Theresa among the ten or so guards. As one of Sing's "people," she could be our way out of this mess. And Shanghai and Cairo lurked somewhere. Maybe they could provide some help as well.

"Phoenix, kindly close the gate before you come."

I hovered my finger over the switch. Leaving the gate open might provide the best chance of escape. "No can do," I said into the radio as I hustled down the stairs. "I'm already on my way."

I walked into the prison yard. The limo sat just a few

steps from the tower. A rear door opened. Erin emerged with her shoulder bag in place and a glowing sphere in her palms, uncovered in spite of the drizzle.

She smiled. "Have you come to escort me, Phoenix?"

"In a manner of speaking." I joined her and walked toward Alex and the pedestals, glancing around for Cairo, but he was nowhere in sight. Erin hummed a soft tune, apparently without a worry in the world. Yet, she had come to trade an empty sphere for one she would take to the abyss, where she would cast innocent souls like Kwame and the foreman and maybe Misty into a whirlpool of eternal torment. Such contempt for life made her as evil as Alex.

When we arrived at the depot, Erin walked past Alex, set the sphere in the main pedestal's depression, and withdrew a tablet from her bag. Standing with an arm shielding the tablet's screen, she nodded. "I am ready."

I glanced at the limo's open door. Only the chauffeur remained inside. Melchizedek hadn't come. Apparently he was satisfied with the camp's operation and didn't need to oversee another reaping.

Peter set the silver box at Erin's feet. "You know where to take this one," he said.

"I do." Erin flashed a sinister smile. "I hear another soul might be added to it before the morning is over."

"Perhaps." Peter fanned his cloak. "It's time to reap."

I spread out my arms. "I'm here, Alex. What do you want with me?"

Alex clipped the radio to her belt. "I want to perform a modified version of our earlier experiments. You might call it round three in our series of tests, and I need you as a test subject. You are more important to me than is a rogue Reaper like Singapore."

"Why? What's so important about me?"

"One moment please." She gave Peter a shove. "Make yourself useful."

After rolling his eyes briefly, Peter limped toward the prisoners.

I gave them both a stealthy scan. Something between these two had changed. Why the sudden lack of respect?

"What's so important about you?" Alex turned her gaze back on me, her irises again displaying a metallic luster. "Let's just say that your special talents are required for an assignment no one else has been able to accomplish. Don't bother asking about the details."

I nodded at Sing. "Let her go. Then I'm yours."

Alex reached into her jacket, withdrew a sonic gun, and pressed it against the back of Sing's head. "But Phoenix, she's part of the experiment, and you will decide whether or not she is set free."

As she paused for dramatic effect, I glared at her. She wanted me to ask how I would decide, but I wouldn't give her the satisfaction.

The guards called out commands and lined the prisoners in rows, then forced them to their knees in execution position. A few of the men struggled, but a smack of a gun butt to their heads squashed any hope of rebellion. Gasps erupted here and there, and a few children cried, but most of the prisoners stayed quiet.

Peter stood next to a male prisoner closest to the pedestals. "I'm ready."

As if summoned by his words, the sky darkened. Thunder rumbled. The spitting droplets increased to a steady drizzle, more stinging than usual, a reminder that our plans had fallen apart. Innocent prisoners might die in mere moments.

I shifted my stare back to Alex. Her plans were growing clearer. She again hoped to conquer my mind with some sort of coercion that involved threatening someone with death, Sing this time. I had to prepare myself for anything. I had overcome the energy's influence before, so I could do it again, but how could I overcome Alex and ten guards with rifles? Even with Theresa's help, it seemed impossible.

Alex nodded at the central pedestal. "You get the place of honor."

I looked at the disk. Alex probably wanted to empty my cloak to make room for souls, thinking I would eventually acquiesce to reaping the camp prisoners. Since the new sphere lay in the depression, the souls in my cloak would be safe from the abyss.

Heaving a resigned sigh, I shuffled toward the pedestal. As I walked past Sing, she gazed at me with sad eyes. Despair flowed between us. We both knew that the next few minutes would result in torture... or worse.

As I lifted a leg to mount the pedestal, Alex called out, "First drop your belt."

I unfastened my belt and let it fall to my feet, raising a squishing sound from the damp turf. Still behind Sing, Alex reached over and dragged the belt to her side. "Erin, you know what to do."

When I stepped up to the pedestal and straddled the glowing sphere, Erin connected my clasp to the tube. The familiar hum returned. Once the vacuum took hold, she stepped down and tapped the tablet screen. "Beginning suction."

I flexed my muscles. The pain of departing souls would soon come, but a new infusion of energy would bring relief and with it the ability to enter ghost mode. That might be my only hope to save everyone. "Good-bye, Tori," I whispered into the fibers. "Good-bye… Albert."

Energy flowed from my body, through my clasp, and into the tube, but no pain followed, no extraction of souls, only fatigue… weakness. My arms wilted and flopped at my sides. My legs buckled. As I dropped to my knees, a moan escaped my lips, but I quickly stifled it.

"That's good, Erin," Alex said. "He's weak enough for the final test."

CHAPTER TWENTY-SIX

E RIN SLID A finger across the tablet's screen. "He is probably well under two percent right now, lower than Mexico City's level before he died. As you guessed, Alex, this method is far more efficient than forcing a valve leak." She pushed the tablet into her bag. "Phoenix, you are free to detach."

As the hum died away, I reached for the connector, my arms shaking. My fingers slipped across the wet tube, but a second try unfastened it. Breathing shallow gasps, I reinserted my cloak's clasp. The void burned within. Spasms rocked my abdomen—pulses of pure torture. I could barely breathe.

"While we wait for Phoenix to stabilize," Alex said, "I think it's time to begin revealing all we recently learned about Singapore." She grabbed Sing's hair and jerked her head back, stretching her bruised face and forcing her eyes wide open. Blood streamed from her nose and dripped from her chin, past her dangling medallion, and down her chest. "This seductress is a pawn of the rebels, though she has no idea how they have used her."

Sing coughed loudly and clutched her chest, tucking her medallion away with a pinky finger, a stealthy move no one else likely noticed. "That's not true. I do know."

Her voice sounded rough, almost unrecognizable. "Tokyo and my father have been planning... planning for me to infiltrate the Gateway... ever since I was born. I am not a pawn."

I cringed. Why was Sing giving away information? For my benefit? Revealing her importance would get her killed for sure.

"Is that so?" Alex twisted Sing's hair. "Then tell me, why did your own father hide from you as a ghost?"

Grimacing, Sing firmed her lips and said nothing.

"You see," Alex continued, now staring straight at me, "the little liar has no explanation. She *is* a pawn, and the realization has rendered her speechless."

My heart pounded so hard it seemed ready to explode. A scream begged to escape my throat, but I swallowed it down. I had to concentrate on Alex and Sing. Of course there was an explanation for Kwame's claim to be Sing's father. He was trying to throw Alex off the trail, but I couldn't blurt that out. Giving Alex more information was the last thing I wanted to do.

"Although Singapore seems to have lost *her* voice," Alex continued, "*we* have much more to say." She released Sing's hair, stepped to one of the other pedestals, and scooped up the garment she had been carrying earlier. She shook it, making it unfold into the shape of a cloak. "A fine cloak Erin recovered in the shroud. One of our perimeter guards reported seeing Singapore give her cloak to a hooded woman. While Singapore stood calmly, that woman punched her in the face. We think her purpose was to fake an attack so she could explain the loss of her cloak, though we have not yet deduced the reason for the charade. We did, however, learn something important during that interchange."

I tried to catch Sing's gaze, but she averted her eyes. She wouldn't have done what Alex said. She was too trustworthy, too loyal to deceive me like that.

Alex raised a finger. "Before we reveal what else we learned, let's begin the next step in our experiment." She extended the sonic gun. "Take my place, press the gun against Singapore's head, and pull the trigger. I want you to kill her."

I took a deep breath, trying to settle my runaway heart. "If you're…" My own voice sounded worse than Sing's. I cleared my throat and continued, though pain throttled my words. "If you're threatening to… to shoot me if I… if I don't kill Sing… that won't work. I'd rather die than… than hurt her."

Alex let out a condescending laugh. "I know that, Phoenix. I'm not stupid." She called to the guards. "Execute one of the prisoners!"

Theresa withdrew a sonic gun, walked behind the closest kneeling man, and shot him in the back of the head. As the man toppled to the ground, a woman screamed but quickly silenced herself. Murmurs rose among the other prisoners, blending with the background cries of children. Peter wrapped his cloak around the man and began the reaping process.

I gulped. How could Theresa do that? Wasn't she on our side?

Alex laughed again. "Surprised, Phoenix?"

I clenched my teeth. She knew the answer.

"You see," she continued, "when the woman took the cloak, unaware that anyone was listening, she referred to

Singapore as 'the Raven' loudly enough for Theresa to hear. Theresa used that name to get away from you so she could tell us about the drugged coffee. Unfortunately, she couldn't get back in time to warn the tower guards, but that was a small matter."

I seethed. Yet another guard played me for a fool. But how could I have known?

Alex called to the guards. "One of you close the front gate."

While a male guard ran toward the tower, I rolled my aching fingers into a fist. "Cowards! You use innocent—"

"Shut up, Phoenix!" Alex extended the gun toward me again. "Put this against Sing's head right now, or I'll order another execution in two seconds!"

I crawled from the pedestal and allowed her to put the gun in my hand. As I curled my fingers around the handle, half my brain shouted, *Shoot Alex!* but the other half screamed, *No! Then everyone will die!*

I knelt behind Sing and pressed the barrel against the back of her head. As my heart raced, I whispered between gasps for breath. "Don't worry... I won't... kill you.... Just buying time... to think."

"I'm not worried, Phoenix." Sing coughed again. Blood dribbled from her mouth, joining the stream from her nose. "I trust you. I hope you'll keep trusting me."

The gate dragged across the entry road. When it clanked shut, my heart sank. Another escape option had been dashed.

Alex paced in front of Sing and me, Sing's cloak in hand. "As I was saying, we haven't yet deduced the reason Singapore faked the loss of her cloak. Since she is Tokyo's daughter, we believe she is able to withdraw souls without it. She is very powerful, and the Gatekeeper thinks her power will continue to grow, which is why he ordered her execution. Yet, I decided to keep her alive for a while longer." She stopped pacing and stared at me. "Why do you think that is, Phoenix?"

I glanced at the prisoners. Their murmurs grew louder. Something was definitely going on. Maybe they were planning an escape in spite of the closed gate. They would die either way, so why not?

When I refocused on Alex, I took a deep breath to quell the inner boil and spoke in a slow cadence. "I am not interested in answering the venom of a devilish witch."

"Witch?" Alex crouched in front of us and lowered her voice to a hissing whisper. "Only hours ago you hesitated for five seconds, and it cost you Misty's life. Now I will provide you with a revelation." Her eyes glinted once again—lustrous and penetrating. "You will learn that everything you have trusted in since this ordeal began has been a lie. Then I will give you the opportunity to renounce your loyalty to this liar, the one who has put you in danger time and time again in order to pursue a mad obsession. When you kill her, all will be forgiven, and I will release the rest of the prisoners unharmed. Otherwise, they will all die. You will buy Sing's pardon with their blood."

My hands shook. Spears stabbed my stomach. "But why am I so important? You could kill her yourself."

Her whisper lowered even further. "I know you have a special talent, Phoenix. The Gatekeeper knows it as well. He also ordered your execution, but I need you alive." She coughed to cover her next words. "To conquer him."

I felt my mouth drop open. Conquer him? What new deception was this?

Alex draped the cloak over Sing's shoulders. "Here is your mother's cloak, Singapore."

Sing trembled but stayed quiet, her stare fixed on a pool—a pink-tinged slurry of blood and dirt that grew slowly in the light rainfall.

"She lied to you, Phoenix." Alex rose and pointed at her. "That sniveling wretch is no friend of yours. The Resistance arranged to have her live next to you so she could begin a systematic seduction by romancing you while you were in a lonely, vulnerable state. She used her feminine wiles to capture your heart so you would help deliver her mother to the Gateway. But that wasn't enough for this vamp. She enticed you to bring her here so she could enter the Gateway herself, all because of an insane conspiracy theory that denies the reality of the Gateway's benevolence. If not for Singapore's wild obsessions, Colm would be alive. Misty would be alive. And now two hundred men, women, and children kneel in terror, wanting to know if your selfish, spellbound loyalty to this deceiver will cost them their lives."

I looked at the prisoners. They shivered in the drizzle, some weeping, all frightened—waiting for someone to make a courageous decision. As the void continued gnawing at my gut, my arms wilted. My trigger finger cramped. Would one little squeeze really set those suffering prisoners free?

Alex stabbed a finger at Sing. "Kill her, Phoenix! Be done with this wanton wench. My guard at the prisoners' residence building deceived you. Theresa deceived you. You are obviously too easily led by the nose. And now letting Sing live will serve only to prove your starry-eyed naïveté once again, and your unprecedented gullibility will mean the deaths of many children who just want a chance to leave this hellhole and go home in peace!"

Sing cried out, her words punctuated by gurgling gasps. "Do what... you think is right... I asked you to... to trust me... but either way you decide... I'll still love you.... I will always love you."

"More lies!" Alex shouted. "She has proven you can't believe a word she says. Kill her now and be done with it."

My entire body quaked. "I... I can't."

Alex waved a hand at the prisoners. Theresa walked behind a woman and shot her with the sonic gun. The telltale pop jolted my brain. She twitched on the ground for a moment, then lay motionless. Like a vulture, Peter descended on her body and covered her with his cloak.

A little girl screamed, "Mommy!" Two men leaped to their feet, but when a guard grabbed the girl and set a gun to her head, the men dropped to their knees again.

My arm shook harder. I could barely keep the gun in place. A barrage of images blazed in my mind—Sing and Kwame and Alex and Shanghai—all spinning in a wild vortex. Finally, Mex's image blended into the turmoil. With desperate pulls, he struggled to free himself from the life-sucking vacuum, the death penalty so callously executed by the will of one of the Council's minions, a sentence delivered because of evidence planted on him, planted by a son and his mother who had conspired to bring about this end at this moment. If I killed Sing, they would have their victory. If I killed Sing, Alex would win. If I killed Sing, my heart would shrivel up and die.

"You've run out of time, Phoenix." Alex's tone was cold and cruel. "Kill her now, or a child is next. You know I won't hesitate."

Again I glanced at the prisoners. Still kneeling, still shivering, still waiting for a decision that might rise above my cowardly stalling.

A rattling engine drew near. Alex turned toward the sound while I shifted my focus to Sing. Could it be Liam? Maybe... just maybe we had a chance.

I leaned closer to Sing and whispered, "Get ready to run. We're going to make a break for it. They can't stop all of us."

"In your condition?" Sing pushed something into my free hand. "I'm not running.... Search your watch.... The medallion is the key... Follow me... to the Gateway." She reached around, grabbed my gun hand, and pulled the trigger. The gun popped. Her head jerked. Her body fell limp, and she dropped face first into the muddy grass.

I tried to shout, but the words caught in my throat. Just as I reached for Sing, a van crashed through the gate, sending it flying. A swarm of male prisoners leaped up and barreled into Peter and the guards. Men and women scooped up children and stampeded toward the exit. Water and mud splashed. Shots rang out. Prisoners shrieked and groaned.

At the shattered opening, Liam leaped out of his van and yelled, "Get the little ones in!" He threw open a side door and ran into the streaming mob, grabbing children right and left.

I flopped to my seat next to Sing. My limbs felt like jelly. I couldn't help the prisoners even if I tried. My dear friend lay in the mud... dead. I had failed.

Alex raised a hand and shouted, "Let them go! All of them!"

The rifles silenced. Splashing footsteps continued,

though they slowly eased as the prisoners realized that they had been set free. At the entrance, Liam deposited children into his van and herded others beyond the gate, a worried expression on his face as he looked at me.

The entire scene became a blur. I didn't bother to keep watching. Liam would figure out how to get them all to safety.

I stealthily opened my hand. A photo stick lay in my palm. It had to be Sing's. I stuffed it into my pocket and grabbed her wrist. No pulse. No movement.

Erin lifted the sphere at the pedestal and pushed it into her shoulder bag. "Why did you let them go?" she asked Alex. "News will spread about this camp and your planned reaping."

"Let them talk. They don't know what we really planned here." Alex picked up the silver box and handed it to Erin. "As we discussed, these souls go into the abyss."

Erin nodded. "Have Peter put Singapore into my car. He can reap her on the way, and I'll throw her soul into the abyss with the others."

"Good. The worst thing that could happen would be for the daughter of Tokyo to return from the Gateway."

"Understood."

Alex gave Peter a shove. "Do as she says."

Scowling, Peter scooped up Sing's limp body, pulling her away from my weakened hand. As he carried her to the limo, I followed their progress, counting each slogging step. Although every nerve in my brain shouted for me to give chase, my muscles wouldn't respond. Alex had obviously drained my energy for this very reason. I couldn't grant Sing's last request. She would go to the abyss instead of the Gateway. And where was Misty? In Peter's cloak or in the abyss-bound sphere? It wouldn't do any good to ask a liar like Alex.

When Erin and Peter climbed into the limo, a cloaked figure with glowing eyes sneaked around the watchtower and ran to the trunk. He raised a finger to his lips, then dove through the trunk's lid and disappeared.

My mind shouted *Cairo!* but I kept silent. What could he do to help? Maybe nothing. Maybe everything.

"Well, Phoenix…" Alex reached down and grabbed my forearm. "Can you get up?"

I flexed my leg muscles. "Maybe."

She hoisted me to my feet and wrapped my weapons belt around my waist. Now that she stood within inches, her skin looked more youthful than ever, again no sign of a wound. "I'm sure killing your friend must have stabbed your heart. Even her betrayal couldn't soften the blow."

I blinked at her through the rain. Her voice had taken on a tone of genuine sympathy. It sounded so strange. With the van crashing into the gate, maybe she was distracted and didn't see that Sing had actually killed herself.

Alex fastened my belt in place. "I'm sure Shanghai will show up soon. When she does, you're both free to go."

"But… " I touched my spool and a dagger. I was now fully equipped. "Why did you go to all this trouble just to get me to kill Sing?"

"Phoenix?" Liam shouted from the van. "Are you coming?"

Alex waved. "He's staying. Take the wounded to DEO headquarters. Tell them I said to provide care for everyone."

Liam flashed a skeptical look, but when I gave him a nod, he nodded in return. "I will."

His van rattled to the outside street, followed by the limo and its smooth purr. Behind the two vehicles, dozens of former prisoners walked away quietly, staying close together as they faded into the shadows of the surrounding buildings.

Alex focused on me. "You ask why all the trouble? It's quite simple, Phoenix, and since we're alone, and since you're under my control, I can tell you."

"Under your control?" I brushed rainwater from my eyes. "What do you mean?"

"Remember our conversation in your apartment? I told you there was another issue or two, and now you're learning what I meant." She showed me her left hand. She wore Misty's pewter band on her ring finger. "Misty controlled you, but she is dead. And now that you killed Singapore and thereby destroyed your... shall we say... principles, you are mine."

"But how could..." Dizziness flooded my brain. I couldn't think of another word to say.

Alex laid a hand on my shoulder, steadying me. "I will explain much more later, Phoenix. For now, I will tell you that I know all about Maxwell, your grandfather. You inherited his power... and his weakness." She picked up the sonic gun and slid it behind her jacket. "Meet me at your apartment. While we're there, I will tell you about your new condo and see to it that you get an energy charge. I'm looking forward to telling you how you will take over for Peter."

I looked into her metallic eyes. The power in her vision was never stronger. "Take over for him?"

She set a fist on her hip. "Peter was supposed to

do what I need you to do, but he failed. After he reaps Singapore, Erin will kill him."

"But… but he's your son."

"*Was* my son. You're my son now." She reached into her jacket pocket and withdrew a thin chain and medallion. She draped the chain over my head and guided the medallion down until it rested on my chest where it glowed like a phosphorescent coin. From her jacket she withdrew a vial filled with red liquid, flipped the cap off, and poured a drop onto her fingertip. "Erin provided me with this supply of your blood." She smeared the drop over the surface of the medallion on both sides, smothering its glimmer. "Now I can track you when I send you to do my bidding. I will explain more when you come to your apartment."

She recapped the vial and glanced at the camp's entrance. "I'd better go. I will see you soon." As she walked toward the Hilton, her shoes squished in the mud. "Don't worry about the dead bodies. I'll send someone to pick them up."

I scanned the jail yard. The two executed prisoners lay in the mud, two more broken shells, two more deaths, two more tragedies. Yet, a couple of hundred had escaped. The guards might have wounded a few more, but they managed to get out. At least we had succeeded in some measure. But at what cost? Misty. Sing. Colm. The losses felt like a tourniquet around my heart, squeezing my life away.

Another squishing sound approached from the direction of the gate. I looked that way. Shanghai limped toward me, grimacing with each step as she leaned on her staff. "Phoenix! What happened? I just talked to Liam. He said Sing is dead!"

"She… I… I mean, Alex tried to get me to… to shoot

her, but…" My voice fractured into pieces. I couldn't say another word.

Shanghai wrapped her arms around me and whispered, "It's okay, Phoenix. Take your time."

Her body was warm, though wet. I returned the embrace with weak, jittery arms and swallowed to loosen my throat. "I held… the gun. I wasn't going to… to shoot. I saw Liam… coming, so I thought we had a… a chance, but Sing reached around… and pulled the trigger."

"I see. Another Alex ultimatum."

I nodded. "Alex said she'd let them go… if I killed Sing."

"So Sing traded her life to help the prisoners escape." Shanghai pulled back and looked me in the eyes. Tears tracked down her cheeks. "She must have known you'd try to fight your way out, that you would die trying, so…" She bit her lip hard. "So she saved your life, too."

"She did. That's just like her. She…" My throat caught again. "I… I can't…"

"Oh, Phoenix." Shanghai embraced me again. As we wept together, light spasms rocked our bodies.

Seconds passed—heavy, painful seconds. How many? I couldn't tell. Grief ravaged my mind. But I couldn't let the torture strangle my resolve. I had to move forward, figure out the puzzle, rescue Misty's and Sing's souls.

As Shanghai cried on, she hugged me more and more tightly. With her hand still clutching the staff, the wood pressed against my back. "So… " I cleared my throat. "How'd you get your staff?"

She drew back and held the staff in front of me. "It was really strange." She brushed away tears. "I found it in Liam's van when I ran to him for help. He had no idea how it got there."

I exhaled heavily and brushed away my own tears. "So you're the one who brought Liam here."

"I heard his van idling close by. He seemed like our only hope."

I glanced at the broken gate lying on the wet driveway. "Where were you when he crashed into the camp?"

"Over there." She gestured with her head toward the street's parking area. "Fighting a guard who was trying to shoot the van's tires. He was a tough customer."

"Then you saved most of the prisoners." I curled my aching hands into fists. "I couldn't save Misty. Or Sing. Or Colm. Just when they needed me most, I failed. I couldn't lift a finger to help any of them."

Shanghai gripped my arm. "You didn't fail, Phoenix. You're the bravest person I've ever met. For three years you've risked your life to help the desperate people of this city, and you sacrificed everything you love to save those innocent prisoners. In my book, you're a hero."

Her words felt like a warm blanket, comforting in spite of new pain cramping my legs. "You are, too, Shanghai. You're amazing."

She smiled. "Thank you for saying so."

My knees buckled, but Shanghai held me up and pushed the staff into my hand. "You look like you need this more than I do."

I gripped the middle and leaned on it. The cramping eased. "That helps a lot. Thanks."

"And let me give you something else."

"What?"

"Everything I have to give." She depressed her valve,

making the center of the clasped hands protrude. Her smile quivering, she pushed close and connected her valve with mine. As we embraced again, now chest to chest, she hummed, "I can't imagine how much you must be hurting, but I'll do everything I can to ease your pain."

Energy flowed into my valve—warm and refreshing. It seemed that Shanghai's love flowed with it, the combination strengthening my heart along with my muscles. Every passing second brought relief, vigor, and hope. With Sing's photo stick in my possession and Albert's soul still available to provide me with information, maybe we could get to the Gateway and the abyss. Maybe we could stop Erin and learn the mysteries beyond the veil. "You're already easing my pain, Shanghai. It feels wonderful."

"I'm afraid I can't give you much." She detached our valves but stayed close. Her lips drew within an inch of mine, as soft and inviting as ever. "But I can give you my love."

I slid back. "I... I can't."

Tears sparkled in her eyes. Her fingers ran along my hand until they found my pewter ring. "Too soon?"

"Yeah..." I nodded and looked down. "Too soon."

"I understand." She kept her hold on my hand. "So what's next?"

"Back to my apartment. I'll tell you on the way." With help from the staff, I walked toward the broken gate while she limped at my side, an arm curled around mine. "I'm going to need all your brainpower to figure out how to rescue Sing and Misty from the abyss, but it'll help that a spy stowed away in the limo."

"Cairo?"

I smiled in spite of the crushing grief. "You're as smart as they come."

When we exited the camp, we stood side by side and gazed at the sun rising behind the Chicago skyline. Though veiled by the usual meltdown haze, it seemed brighter somehow, as if it were trying to break through the mysterious fog that cast a shroud over the entire world.

Shanghai leaned her head against my shoulder. "So how are we going to do this? Do you have any clues?"

"Just something Sing gave me." I withdrew the photo stick and watch from my pocket and laid them in my palm. "It's her photo stick, and she said to follow her to the Gateway, to search my watch, and the medallion is the key. I'm guessing she means the medallion she was wearing, but it went with her body."

"I saw her medallion. Any clue what it is?"

I lifted the one Alex gave me. As my mind cleared further, a connection clicked. How could I have missed something so obvious? Images flashed—every time the medallion slipped from Sing's tunic and into sight. She wanted me to see it, but she couldn't tell me why. Otherwise I would have put a stop to her suicidal plans.

I whispered, "She said to follow her to the Gateway. Her medallion is a tracking device, and Alex has a way to locate it."

"Sing's been wearing it for a while," Shanghai said. "She must have been planning this all along."

I swallowed. The truth was so hard to believe, it seemed unwilling to come out. "Sing wanted to die," I said. "It was her only ticket to the Gateway."

"It's all... all so surreal." Shanghai took the watch and studied it. "Sing blazed the trail. Now we have to follow it. We'll see what's on the photo stick and try to find the Eagle."

I tightened my grip on the staff. "Maybe the Eagle will find us."

"You mean the staff? Do you think the Eagle left it for us?"

I nodded. "Maybe to let us know she's ready to help."

"But how could she get it? I left it with Mex's body."

"Who knows? I'm just guessing." As I pushed the photo stick back into my pocket, Bartholomew's words echoed in my mind. *If one of you chooses to die, I can send your soul to the Gateway. There you will be able to transfer your friend back to this side, and he can be restored to his body.*

I let out a sigh. Erin wouldn't bother to preserve Sing's body, so there was no hope to revive her, even if I wanted to.

"Is something else wrong?" Shanghai asked.

"Just that we need to hurry. Alex will be at my apartment with more energy for me, and she'll show me how the tracking device works."

"I'm all for that." Shanghai pushed the watch into my pocket. "But you're nearly out of gas. We'll need transportation."

I extended my thumb. "Let's see if hitchhiking will work for a change."

"Maybe someone will risk it. Your apartment's not far."

"After that, we'll get to the bottom of all the Gatekeeper's secrets."

"As long as we're together." Shanghai regripped my hand. "For Sing?"

"For Sing." I took in a deep breath. "Let's find out what's beyond the Gateway."

Made in the USA
Las Vegas, NV
09 December 2024

13735587R00229